Praise for
THE MARBLE INDEX

The KGB and British intelligence, Russian and English politicians and scholars (some historical, others fictional), famous British traitors Philby and Burgess, the cultures and atmospheres of Moscow and Cambridge, family intimacies and intrigues: all of these commingle in Thomas's highly suspenseful thriller, which critically hinges on the poet Wordsworth and the scientist Sir Isaac Newton. Wonderful reading.

–**Jo Ann Kiser**, author of *Sunday People, A Young Woman from the Provinces*, and *The Guitar Player and Other Songs of Exile*

Taut, cerebral, and full of Cold War shadows. A spy novel with both bite and heart, as thoughtful as it is suspenseful.

–**Charnjit Gill**, author of *Pray Tell*

In The Marble Index, author Howard Thomas creates a world of intrigue and suspense in mid-1970s Moscow and Cambridge, England. Trust me, you will find this cleverly written cold war thriller difficult to put down.

–**Jane Iwan**, author of *Refugee of the Heart and Black Hills Atonement*

At the height of the Cold War, love and intrigue collide in Howard Thomas's The Marble Index. Shifting between the cloistered halls of Cambridge University and the shadowed streets of Moscow, the novel follows two unlikely anti-Soviet protagonists whose destinies intertwine against a backdrop of espionage, betrayal, and intellectual pursuit. Fast-paced yet layered with historical and philosophical depth, The Marble Index is a gripping tale of secrets, loyalties, and the fragile line between truth and illusion.

–**Gary Demack**, author of *The Broken Fife*

HOWARD THOMAS

THE MARBLE INDEX

**A
SPY
THRILLER**

atmosphere press

© 2025 Howard Thomas

Published by Atmosphere Press

Cover design by Matthew Fielder

No part of this book may be reproduced without permission from the author except in brief quotations and in reviews. This is a work of fiction, and any resemblance to real places, persons, or events is entirely coincidental.

Unless author permission is expressly granted, any use of this publication to "train" artificial intelligence (AI) technologies to generate text is prohibited.

Atmospherepress.com

I dedicate this book to
my wife, Lu Shuo, and
my two sons, Jason and Jeremy.

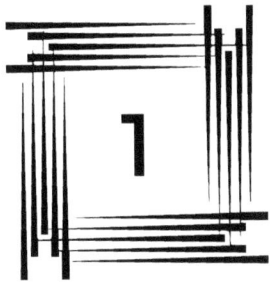

1

Alexei Kunayev awaited his turn with trepidation. It was the biannual evaluation session of Komsomol, the Soviet Communist Youth Organisation. He knew in his heart of hearts that he really had no grounds for unease. The outward level of his 'socialist consciousness' was so high that it was beyond reproach. But as he listened to the Secretary of the Organisation read out aloud the report of one of his peers, he began to have second thoughts.

Comrade Secretary was remonstrating from the podium with an unfortunate youth by the name of Viktor Burstein. One of the stukachi had informed on him for listening to the BBC World Service and claimed to have seen a copy of Aleksandr Solzhenitsyn's 'One Day in the Life of Ivan Denisovich' in his room, though the book itself was not produced in evidence.

Alexei pondered to himself the fickle nature of the Soviet regime. In 1962, when the novel had first been published, it had carried the blessing and authorisation of President Khrushchev as the first sanctioned literary revelation of life in the concentration camps. Artists and writers interpreted its publication as heralding a new intellectual freedom. Now, instead, the KGB and the Central Committee under Leonid Brezhnev's premiership had increasingly stepped up their repression of artists and dissident writers during this Cold War era of 1975.

Of course, Burstein's real crime in the eyes of the state was to be Jewish. Jews were automatically excluded from real political power, although their relative commercial prosperity was tolerated. They also had a stronghold on the arts and music. The Moscow Conservatory was predominantly Jewish. Jews were not allowed to make mistakes, however.

Comrade Secretary denounced Burstein for his sympathetic, Western tendencies and invited the Komsomol body to vote on his fate. Dutifully, everyone raised their hands to indicate that the transgressor should be excluded from Komsomol membership and his scholarship at the Conservatory withdrawn. That would mean this talented young musician would now have to take up employment as a minor public servant – that is if he were lucky. Others in recent years had not been so fortunate. Nikolai Bogach had received three years' imprisonment for attempting to establish the 'Organisation for the Struggle of Social Justice'. Anna Kekilova, a poet, had been forcibly taken to a psychiatric hospital for sending a letter to the Annual Congress renouncing her Soviet citizenship. Surprisingly, she was judged sane but ordered to remain in the hospital until she signed the statement that she wrote her petition while in a nervous condition. Andrei Mikheyev, a graduate physics student, had spent eight years in a concentration camp for trying to leave the Soviet Union and seek political asylum abroad.

In the circumstances, one could say that Viktor Burstein had got off lightly. He was probably not even guilty of the crimes of which he was accused. The Komsomol was merely a stepping-stone for stukachi to work their way up from the lower classes into influential positions in the Party's hierarchy. It was a habit first learned in elementary schools, where pupils were encouraged to spy on their fellows and inform the class leader of any minor misdemeanour of conduct or attitude. There were indeed only two ways of earning advancement through the schooling process. One was to be a brilliant student; the other was to be an informant or stukach. Every stukach even had to fulfil a quota, like a traffic warden giving parking tickets. Viktor Burstein was merely another statistic on the quota.

The bout of coughing and shuffling of feet subsided as Comrade Secretary laid down the dossier on Viktor Burstein and picked up the next one for scrutiny. A frisson of trepidation rang round the stark, echoing elegance of the neoclassical hall as the gathering of some several hundred young Komsomol members wondered who was next.

The Secretary uttered the words, "Alexei Nikolaevich Kunayev."

Alexei swallowed nervously, and the palms of his hands began to sweat. He knew that he had presented the image of a diligent and dutiful student over the reporting period, although his private thoughts were another matter altogether. As a high flyer, he was there to be shot down. His father, Boris Grigoriyevich Kunayev, had worked undercover as a KGB colonel at the United Nations in New York as Director of the External Relations Unit of the UN Information Department. He had returned to Moscow two years ago to take up his appointment at the First Department of the First Chief Directorate of the KGB, responsible for foreign operations in Canada and the United States. Consequently, he was held in some esteem by his peers, but envy and jealousy were strong driving forces to the ambitious stukachi, and no one was immune to criticism.

The Secretary cleared his throat and began to read from the dossier. "Alexei Nikolaevich Kunayev is an exemplary student..."

Alexei sank down in his chair with embarrassment. As he

did so, he caught the eye of a head turned in his direction. The girl was partially obscured by one of the Greco-Roman columns supporting the auditorium. She turned back to face the front almost immediately, and Alexei was left to contemplate the back of her head. She looked distantly familiar, although the fleeting glimpse of her features was insufficient to place her in his past.

Comrade Secretary's words drifted in and out of his absent mind. "... maintained a high level of socialist consciousness... academic brilliance... destined for high office in the diplomatic service."

Alexei was more interested in the girl. 'Fuck the Komsomol,' he thought. It was all the fault of that Pavlik Morozov. The story went that in the village of Gerasimova in 1932, Pavlik's father gave refuge to some fleeing kulak farmers who opposed the collectivisation of their lands by the state. The fourteen-year-old Pavlik, recognising his duty to Soviet society, informed on his father, who was subsequently shot. Enraged peasants thereupon lynched the young boy. Today, the Soviet Union maintains the house where the son betrayed the father as a communist shrine. In 1965, a statue was erected in Pavlik's honour. The Palace of Culture of the Red Pioneers in Moscow was named after him, and Komsomol taught Soviet youth that the life and deeds of Pavlik Morozov represented an ideal to which every worthy citizen should aspire.

'What a motherfucker,' thought Alexei to himself. Much as he detested his own father, the idea of turning him in to the authorities was abhorrent to him. The name was coming to him. Her dark hair was longer now. She was much fuller in the face. Five years had matured her considerably. She was Dina Russakov. They had attended high school together. Recently, he had heard on the grapevine that her father had been interned in the medical wing of Lubyanka Prison, notorious as the capital's extermination centre during Joseph Stalin's reign. It was rumoured that from 1934 to 1938, ten million people were slaughtered by the security directorate in the Great Purge. Among them was the cream of the revolutionary intelligentsia, the armed forces and even leaders of the intelligence service. Its mere name struck fear into the hearts of all Soviet citizens. And Dina's father was presently incarcerated there.

Comrade Secretary was reaching the end of his report. Alexei assumed it must have been relatively uncritical, as he concluded, "Shining example to all Komsomol members."

There followed a polite round of applause tempered with jealousy that someone had passed the ordeal so lightly.

"Fuck Pavlik Morozov," uttered Alexei under his breath whilst breathing a sigh of relief.

They made their way to Leningrad Railway Station on Komsomolskaya Square, only half seeming to be walking together in case a stukach decided to follow them from the Communist Youth building. Alexei walked past the main entrance, turned right and right again by the International Post Office and dodged into the goods entrance. When he reached the station buffet, Dina was already sitting at a table with two coffees. She continued to stir hers as Alexei slid into the high-backed wooden booth opposite her. Public places were often the most private places to talk.

"I'm sorry to hear about your father," began Alexei. "What is his crime?"

Dina looked up at him fiercely. "He committed no crime."

Dina lowered her voice. "He called his latest composition, a symphonic poem, 'Freedom for Czechoslovakia'."

"And for that, he's been imprisoned in Lubyanka," Alexei shook his head.

"Why should you be so surprised?" replied Dina. "And not only that, he has lost his post of professor of symphonic composition at the Conservatory. His name has been removed from the membership of the Union of Composers, and a ban has been imposed on the performance of all his works."

"But everyone knows that he is the most original Soviet composer today," protested Alexei. "The Union must surely lodge a protest."

Dina laughed forlornly. "They would rather look after their own livelihoods and play the official line of such as our eminent comrade Tikhon Khrennikov, the Soviet functionary composer."

"If he changed the name of the piece, would they release him?" asked Alexei.

Dina nodded. "They want him to call it the October Revolution."

"Then why doesn't he?"

"You don't know my father," Dina announced proudly. "Besides, why should a man who has been awarded the Lenin Prize for his services to Soviet music not keep his artistic integrity. Hasn't he earned at least that?"

Alexei nodded in agreement. "But what are they doing to your father in that hellhole? Are you allowed to see him?"

"Yes, but he is no longer my father. The psychiatrists have declared him insane and put him on some kind of depressant drug. It seems to have affected his memory. He doesn't always recognise me." Her words faltered. She stared straight ahead, and tears began to flow down her cheeks.

For the first time, Alexei realised how beautiful Dina had become. It was, however, unwise to show so much emotion in public. He leant over the table and offered her his handkerchief.

"Yes, andaksin," said Alexei.

"What?" asked Dina in a distant, tearful voice.

"Andaksin, the drug they're probably giving your father. It

causes hallucinations and loss of memory."

"How come you know so much about it?" she asked.

"My father..." Alexei began.

"Ah, yes," Dina countered loudly through a bitter-sweet smile, "your father, the KGB colonel."

"Keep your voice down," protested Alexei, as heads were turned in their direction. He did not like to correct her that his father was now a major-general. "I am not proud of my father's achievements," Alexei continued in a whisper. "I know how he came to occupy his present position of influence. On the backs of others."

"But you are following in his footsteps," she protested.

"Only for the moment," replied Alexei mysteriously.

"What do you mean?" she asked.

"I can say no more," he said, cupping her hands in his.

"Can I trust you?" she asked, as he was about to pose the same question. "Our meeting was not merely an accident."

"It seems there are things we both need to confide in one another. My parents are away at the family dacha on Pirogovo Reservoir. We can take my car back to our apartment."

They got up from their table, separated like strangers who had engaged in a casual conversation, and left by different exits. Just in case.

As they left, a young man sitting at a corner table scribbled a few notes on the corner of his newspaper.

The Kunayev apartment was situated on the Moskva River. It belonged to a block built in the Stalin era. The entrance hall gave into a living room opulently furnished by Russian standards. There were items of furniture made in the Eastern European Bloc – Czechoslovakia and Bulgaria, but most were American in design. The technology – television, radio, cassette recorder and high-fi were all Japanese.

Dina ran her hand over the smoked black glass top of the stereo system. "Fine example of Soviet workmanship, I see," she said, her voice heavy with irony.

Alexei did not rise to the bait. "Take off your coat," he said. "Would you like to listen to some music?"

"Do you have any Beatles? Let it be?"

"I certainly don't have Tamara Miansarova and Edita Piekha," joked Alexei.

Dina screwed up her face at the thought of those dreadful patriotic songs sung up by the acceptable public face of modern Soviet music.

"I can do better than that," said Alexei. "How about The Eagles or Billy Joel?"

"Billy Joel," said Dina. "I've never heard of him."

Alexei drew out a copy of the LP 'Turnstiles' and lowered the stylus onto the last track of side one. "This is my favourite," he declared proudly. "New York State of Mind."

"You've lived in America, haven't you?" she said, as the piano introduction oozed from the stereo speakers.

"Yes, when my father worked at the United Nations. We had an apartment on the Lower East Side of Manhattan."

"Is it as glamorous as those photographs of the skyline with the Statue of Liberty make out, or is it full of crime, degradation, and poverty as the Party would have us believe?"

"It is both," replied Alexei.

"I should like to see for myself," said Dina in a distant voice, devoid of any real longing, as if it were a forlorn hope.

"You make it sound as if you were thinking of defecting," said Alexei.

"Is that a question or a statement?" countered Dina.

"You asked me in the station before that if you could trust me," said Alexei, reassuringly placing his arm around her shoulders as he moved closer to her on the settee.

"And can I?"

"What do I have to do to prove it to you?"

"You could sleep with me."

"You know that KGB agents are trained to make love to people they do not even like. And even if they come to like and love them, they can still turn them over to the authorities to be tortured and exiled."

"Are you telling me you are homosexual?" asked Dina.

"Words, all words," replied Alexei. "If we are finished with the didactic exercises, why don't you let me take you into the bedroom and make love to you. Perhaps we could speak to one another more clearly in the morning."

2

The first weekend riverboat chugged downstream from the pier in front of the Kiev Station, past the Lenin Hills on the right overlooking the campus of the Moscow State University and skirting Gorky Park. The Moskva River was grey and sluggish as it begrudgingly forked off into the Drainage Canal developed to prevent the disastrous Spring floods in the centre of Moscow. Re-joining the Moskva some four kilometres further downstream, it created an artificial island. This was where many new building developments had been erected alongside the old, along the length of the embankment.

The Kunayev apartment was situated on the third floor, looking East across the Moskva River. Dina drew back the curtains, and to the North could just make out above the mist the top of Moscow's first skyscraper a thirty-three-storey block of flats built on the embankment in 1952. To the South lay the cathedral and tiered bell-tower of the New Monastery of the Saviour. Although further away than the tower block, it was considerably more visible, as if the fact that it had been established in the fifteenth century lent it a greater luminosity. It was formerly housed in the Kremlin. The golden dome of the bell tower shone out, as if declaring its presence to the world.

Originally intended as a burial place for the Romanov family, it had been closed to the public for many years under the pretext of restoration work.

Dina was wearing a red silk dressing-gown as Alexei padded naked out of the bedroom, running his hands through his collar-length black hair.

"Why don't you put some clothes on?" she said.

"Why, who's going to see me? Do you think my body might offend the neighbours?"

She turned back to the window. "I was looking at the Novospassky Monastery."

"Do you see anyone with binoculars waving back? If you want me to come away from the window, why don't you say so? I thought we were going to say what we meant in the morning."

"You mean that what we said and did last night was ambiguous."

Alexei smiled and knotted a blue cotton towel around his waist.

"There's a coffee for you on the table," Dina pointed with her left hand. "Is your apartment clean?" she asked.

Alexei nodded. "My father has it debugged every month for listening devices. It's clean."

"Good." She adopted a more businesslike attitude. "Come and sit down with me on the couch and tell me about your work at the Bauman Institute."

"How did you know I'm at the Bauman Institute?" Alexei was taken aback.

"Didn't I tell you yesterday that our meeting was not entirely a coincidence?"

"You mean that all this was planned?" said Alexei with a broad sweep of his hand, which also encompassed the bedroom.

"Not quite everything," she replied demurely, being careful not to bruise the male ego. "I work in the Central Index."

"You mean the KGB files?"

Dina nodded. "I'm a computer systems analyst. We have personal files on everyone. And I mean everyone. I just called up your personal file from data storage. Would you like to see a print-out?"

Alexei didn't know what to say.

"Don't worry, it's all good," she reassured him. "Actually, I lied. I don't have a hard copy of the file. That would have been too dangerous. Every print-out has to be authorised and recorded. But I have clearance to access the files as part of my work and read the details on a visual display unit."

"What exactly is your job?" asked Alexei warily.

"Normally, I'm responsible for the update of the United Nations personnel file, which still includes your father and, hence, you. Right now, I'm involved in a special assignment. We call it 'sweeping the archives'. Before the evolution of the computer, the index consisted of millions of cards housed in steel-doored rooms on eight floors of a building over on Machovaya Ulitza and Prospekt Kalinina. Ever since 1962, we've been converting the data to computer files on disc and microfilm. You can imagine it's a mammoth job that will never really be completed. In our new headquarters on the Moscow Ring Road, we hold all the active files that are in everyday use. But there's a lot of defunct material – we call them the 'dead files' – still over on Machovaya. Every so often, the Director of the Data Centre orders a sweep of the remaining card archives in case there's anything vitally important lurking in the vaults gathering dust."

"Do you ever turn anything up?" Asked Alexei.

"No," replied Dina. "It's a thankless task everyone tries to avoid. That is, until now."

"You mean you've found something important?" said Alexei, leaning forward with interest.

Dina nodded. "I think so. It dates back to the nineteen-thirties. In 1926, Vyacheslav Menzhinsky, who was Dzerzhinsky's deputy at the OGPU, became his successor as head of state security. When Menzhinsky died in 1934, he was replaced by Genrikh Yagoda."

"I remember my father talking about him," interrupted Alexei. "He was a trained pharmacist who pioneered research into scientific methods of extermination. He was the first to conduct human experiments in the cells below Lubyanka. Sorry, I shouldn't have mentioned that," he faltered, remembering the plight of Dina's father in the self-same prison.

She continued unabashed. "That's right. Yagoda was purged under Stalin's reign, and he admitted using poison to kill Maxim Gorky and also the man whom he succeeded at the OGPU, Vyacheslav Menzhinsky. In fact, Yagoda only lasted two years. Then the OGPU became a directorate of the NKVD, which also incorporated at that time most sections of the Comintern and the Communist International."

"This is a very interesting history lesson," said Alexei, "but tell me what all this has to do with what you found in the archives and my work at the Bauman Institute."

"Don't worry, I'm coming to that. All this is relevant." Dina was warming to her task. "Stalin was building up to the time of the Great Terror, with show trials, exterminations, and concentration camps. In 1936, Nikolai Yezkov, Secretary of the Central Committee, took charge of the NKVD."

"They called him the bloody dwarf, didn't they?" said Alexei.

"Yes, he was less than five feet tall, but he made up for his small stature with large acts of execution. Stalin realised the genocide was getting out of hand, and so he had Yezkov shot, ironically in the cell next to the one where Yagoda was killed. Then the fifteen-year reign of Beria began."

"I still don't see..." began Alexei.

"The point is this," Dina slapped her hands together emphatically. "Between the years 1934 and 1938, there were four effective heads of the State Security Services. They all hated each other, even murdering each other to gain office, so the NKVD was anything but efficiently run. There was internal turmoil, even though this was a period of great success for our infiltration abroad. The West, particularly Britain, romanticised about our revolution."

"You mean Philby, Burgess, and Maclean. The Cambridge connection and all that."

"Precisely," said Dina triumphantly. "The files for this particular period are very poorly maintained. Not that it matters much anymore. The so-called fourth man, Anthony Blunt, was unearthed and given immunity in 1964, and there never was a fifth man, in spite of the fears of Britain's Secret Intelligence Service. The usefulness of these ageing intellectuals is all played out. The fact that their files are somewhat sketchy does not cause much concern to my superiors. However, while sweeping the cards for 1934, I came across an unindexed entry. At the time, Guy Burgess was in his postgraduate year and paid a visit to Moscow. His talent spotter, Anthony Blunt, was on a sabbatical from Trinity College, Cambridge. Ostensibly, he spent the time studying architecture in Rome. But according to the lead card in the file, they rendezvoused secretly in Moscow and compiled a list of recruits from the glittering youth of Cambridge to the Soviet cause."

"I thought you just said there wasn't a fifth man," interrupted Alexei.

"That's right. With Blunt as the spymaster and the other three burrowing away in the confidences of the British diplomatic services and MI6, that was the total extent of the active infiltration. But apparently, there was a passive list of moles who were to remain under deep cover."

"And these are the names on this file," marvelled Alexei. "That is a bombshell. And you mean they are still in place, presumably now in positions of trust in the upper echelons of

British society?"

"The lead file card gives that impression," agreed Dina.

"The discovery of these names will bring you great credit," said Alexei.

"They would," replied Dina, with the emphasis on the second word. "But the only trouble is, there are no names. The file is missing."

Alexei was by now thoroughly engrossed in the story, his analytical brain working overtime. "How can you be sure there ever was a file?"

Dina shrugged her shoulders.

Alexei speculated further. "And even if there were, where is it now? Did Burgess and Blunt take it back with them to Cambridge, or did it get lost among the millions of other cards during the period of upheaval you described? Or maybe Burgess concocted the whole thing himself. He was renowned as a practical joker to the Soviet authorities. What do your superiors make of it?"

"I haven't told them," replied Dina.

"You haven't told them," said Alexei incredulously. "But if they found out, you would be in deep trouble."

"If, as we surmise, they are ignorant of the existence of the file, how can I be castigated for withholding something which to all intents and purposes never was. Besides, if I go to them and tell them I have found a single card, they may suspect me of concealing or withholding the rest of the file."

Alexei nodded in agreement as the full implications sank in. "What do you plan to do next?" he asked, sliding his right hand over her knee and caressing the inside of her thigh.

"Find the file," she murmured with pleasure. "I've asked to remain on for a further tour of duty at Machovaya Ulitza. If it's in the archives, I'll find it."

"But why such sudden fervour to aid the State Security Services?" asked Alexei. "After all, they're the people responsible for putting your father in Lubyanka."

"Precisely," replied Dina. "If I find the file, I can use it as a lever to bargain for my father's release. It's a fair trade. It could maybe even buy our passage to the West."

"That's a dangerous game to play, Dina – a game that could get both you and him killed. After all, is the list of names valuable? It was over forty years ago. The men concerned will be of retirement age, even if they do or did hold positions of trust in government, business, and civil service. It is too late to activate them as spies."

"The mere revelation of their existence would be enough to cast doubt on all the British intelligence and counter-intelligence work since the war," replied Dina. "It would embarrass the government and cause political and social unrest. The already uneasy relations between the American CIA and the British Secret Intelligence Service would be further strained. I think the list of names would be sufficiently damaging to warrant it as a considerable Soviet triumph."

"You have to find them first," said Alexei. "Realistically, your chances are slim."

"I could double my chances with your help." Alexei raised his eyebrows as Dina continued. "You yourself speculated that Blunt and Burgess may have taken the list back with them to Cambridge. That is where your work at the Bauman Institute comes in. You will shortly be assigned to a scholarship at the Cavendish Laboratories in Cambridge to pursue your studies in radio astronomy. That is what I read in your personal data file. Am I not correct?"

"You seem to know everything," agreed Alexei. "But even if I agreed to help you, where would I begin to look? And what is there in it for me? Are you not afraid that I will turn you over to the KGB?"

"In the station buffet, you intimated that you were contemplating deviating from the career pattern laid out for you by your father. You detest all he stands for. Am I not correct in suspecting that you plan to defect once safely in Britain?"

Alexei chewed his finger ends, uncertain whether to confide totally in Dina.

Before he could speak, she continued. "Your silence tells me everything I need to know. I think you will help me. As for what there is in it for you, I think I have something you want."

"And what's that?"

She took his hand and pressed it further up between her thighs. "One thing more. Something that might help you. The name of the file is the Marble Index."

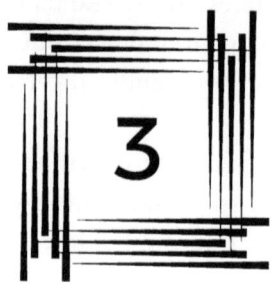

3

"Tell me, Father, were you an idealist when you were young?" Alexei asked his father over Sunday dinner.

Boris Grigoriyevich Kunayev put down his knife and fork and stared across the table at his son. "You imply that I am not one now."

Alexei's mother looked on with a weary expression of resignation, as if expecting another argument to break out. All the incipient signs were there. "Not over the dinner table, please," she implored.

"Mother, why do you always play the role of the United Nations peacekeeping force?" said Alexei.

"Because you know that I hate to take sides."

"No, Irena, let him have his say. There is such a thing as free speech."

Alexei laughed out loud.

Indignantly, his father continued, "Have you not read the constitution of the Union of Soviet Socialist Republics? One of its tenets is freedom of speech for all its citizens, both in public and in private. Article forty-nine specifically forbids repression of criticism."

"Comrade Andropov of the KGB would not exactly see

eye to eye with you on that point, Father. I distinctly remember that in one of his three Lenin Day Memorial Speeches, he emphasised the fact that criticism which could be construed as anti-Soviet could lead to internment."

"That is an entirely different matter," replied Boris Kunayev defiantly.

"What other kind of criticism is there then?" asked Alexei.

His mother motioned with her eyes for Alexei to finish his meal, but he was in no mood for familial appeasement.

"I am surprised at your attitude, Alexei. Did they not teach you in the Komsomol about socialist consciousness? And look at this." He leaned over to the armchair and picked up a newspaper. With his index finger, he jabbed demonstrably at a leading article on the front page.

"This is a eulogy in the Komsomolskaya Pravda about one of the most promising students whose record and career prospects within the party machinery are held up as an example. Do you not know his name?"

Alexei shrugged his shoulders.

Boris Kunayev continued. "His name is Alexei Nikolaevich Kunayev. Is this really the same person who challenges every Marxist-Leninist belief at my dinner table?"

"You have your public face and your private face, too, Father. You know this society is based on hypocrisy. We belong to a privileged class in a supposedly worker-state. We live in a luxury apartment equipped with foreign furniture. We shop in special shops patronised only by members of the Central Committee, where luxury goods are available. We have a country dacha on Pirogovo Reservoir, and people show us respect because you are a Major-General in the KGB, and they are afraid of you."

"And is that so bad?" asked Kunayev senior in his defence.

"No, it is wonderful," replied Alexei, "but is it communism?"

"Don't blame your father," interjected his mother. "He had

no choice. I remember when I first met him at the Caucasian mountain spa of Kyslovodsk. He was so excited, waiting for the results of the Selection Board of the Soviet Services HQ. He thought he was going to move into a job with the Party Executive. What he didn't know was that the Marx-Engels School at Gorky was really an establishment run by the Recruiting Division of the Moscow Secret Service Headquarters."

"You don't really expect me to believe that my own father was so naive."

Boris Kunayev was about to jump to his own defence, but for once he sensed that the argument would be more palatable coming from Alexei's mother.

"Every student believed that he was attending the Marx-Engels Institute. Even when they were transferred to the Lenin Technical School, students were led to believe they were receiving schooling for a future Party career."

"And all the time, they were being trained as future spies," said Alexei incredulously.

Irena Kunayev nodded her head.

"But why didn't you opt out when you discovered the truth?" asked Alexei.

Boris Kunayev laughed at the naivety of the question. "You really do have a lot to learn about the Soviet system. What do you think would have happened to me if I had refused to conform to the career laid out for me? I should now be fitting exhaust systems to cars in the Moskva factory or serving behind the tie counter in GUM."

"But you would still have had your integrity," replied Alexei vehemently. "And how did you manage to reach the top at such a relatively young age? Through a bloody purge of your elders."

Irena Kunayev sprang to her husband's defence. "You cannot blame your father for the deaths caused by Stalin's Great Terror. He was only a student at the time. It was only because a whole generation of Soviet leaders was wiped out that his promotion within the Komsomol and the Party was so rapid. Look at Brezhnev, Andropov, and Kirilenko. They just happened to be there at the right time."

"Hmm," said Alexei sceptically.

"And I expect you to make the most of your current opportunities," added Boris Kunayev. "Look at Andropov's son, Igor. He is of your generation. He is already a senior researcher at the Institute of the United States. And by all accounts, he has certainly not inherited the intellect of his father. With your talent, you should go right to the top. To the Politburo, even."

"You're only thinking of the reflected glory for yourself," said Alexei bitterly. "Just because you can't even make it onto the Central Committee…"

"That's not true," interjected his mother. "Why, he's been proposed as a candidate member several times. It's only the Brezhnev mafia that's kept him off."

"And if you don't look to your own laurels, it will be the Andropov mafia that keeps you out of high office, Alexei," added his father.

"Igor Andropov doesn't worry me," replied Alexei defiantly. "Everyone knows that it's sheer nepotism that's got him where he is today. He tows the party line and keeps his nose clean. That's the most you can say in his favour."

"When you get back from your secondment to the Cavendish Laboratories in Cambridge, I expect you to take up your place at the Moscow State Institute of International Relations," said Boris Kunayev. "You'll really be a high-flyer then."

Alexei glowered at his father as if the distinction was of little consequence to him.

Kunayev continued, "Igor Andropov only gained a place at the Institute of the United States because its Director, Georgi Arbatov, was a friend of his father. I could have done the same for you, but no, you insisted on winning your place on merit.

Do you realise that there is only a yearly intake of sixty students at the IIR, with forty applicants for every place? And at least half of those sixty are reserved for children or relations of Central Committee members, regardless of their entrance examination results."

"So much for the system of meritocracy," jibed Alexei. "I don't know that I wish to belong to such a falsely selected elite."

"Just what do you want?" asked his mother. "What has brought on this sudden mood?"

"Maybe it's because I met Dina Russakov at the Komsomol meeting on Friday. She told me about her father's internment in Lubyanka. For my mother country to put one of its leading composers and conductors in prison, there must be something seriously wrong with its ethics."

"You know that he committed a crime against the state," said Kunayev.

"What sort of a crime is it to name a piece of music after a Soviet satellite country?"

"It's what is implicit in the title that constitutes the crime," replied his father. "The anti-Soviet implication is that the USSR is acting in a repressive manner over another country's sovereignty."

"But it's true, isn't it? Russian tanks did roll into Prague in 1968, and Czechoslovakia has been under the Soviet thumb ever since. It did happen, didn't it?"

Kunayev faltered. "Well..."

"Didn't it?" said Alexei, more emphatically this time.

His father did not reply.

"You see what I mean," said Alexei, celebrating his victory with little relish, but rather with an air of desperate resignation.

"I hope you're not going to see her again," said Kunayev to break the silence.

"Who?" asked Alexei.

"Dina Russakov. It wouldn't be good for you to be seen with her in the circumstances."

"Your cynicism never ceases to amaze me, Father," said Alexei, keeping his temper remarkably under control.

"Besides, the family is Jewish, isn't it?"

"As a matter of fact, it's not. Not that it would make any difference to me, at least."

"Even so, I don't want you to see her again. It wouldn't look good."

"What would you say if I told you that Dina and I screwed in your bed all day Friday? What would you say if I told you she was pregnant and that you were going to be the grandfather of a bastard? What would..."

"That's enough, Alexei. Enough!" screamed his mother. "I won't have such talk. Go to your room. When you've had time to reflect on your behaviour, I expect you to apologise to your father."

Alexei got up from the dinner table without meeting the eyes of Boris Kunayev, strode in a purposely controlled manner to his bedroom door, opened and closed it softly behind him, and threw open a pocket map of Cambridge on his bed.

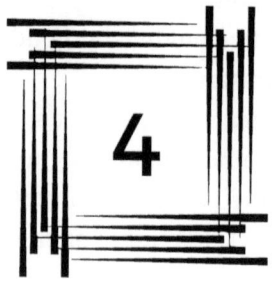

4

Alexei Kunayev stared out of the window as the landscape flashed by on the last leg of his journey to Cambridge. The train had left London's King's Cross nearly an hour ago. People sitting around him seemed mesmerised by the hypnotic rattle of the bogies over the tracks and the rolling motion of the carriage, like children being lulled to sleep in a giant cradle by a locomotive lullaby.

Opposite him sat a woman in her late twenties. She was reading a paperback book, which Alexei took to be a romantic novel, judging by the cover. From time to time, she turned the pages more rapidly as her pulse quickened and she became engrossed in what Alexei took to be the love scenes. He could sense her own arousal through the words on the printed page. Whenever she became aware of his studying gaze, she would look up at him, red with embarrassment and self-righteous anger in her eyes that he had dared to penetrate her private thoughts. After staring him down, she turned the page and creased it down firmly with her wet thumb, her eyes racing ever onwards, her fingers caressing line after line, her mouth devouring the author's passion.

Alexei focused his eyes on that area between the glass of the carriage window and the foreground, where everything was blurred and green. This was a comfortable place belonging to no one and yet everybody. He was not violating anyone's physical or mental territoriality – a difficult accomplishment in a crowded, enclosed space such as a railway carriage. However, to reach this psychological haven, he needed to stare directly through the reflection of the woman opposite in the window. The glazed-out-of-focus look in his eyes was designed to reassure her that, should she look up and glance at his reflection, she could not infer that he was watching her by stealth.

The quiet rustle of her tights rubbing against each other as her legs moved with excitement drew his attention to the fact that she was wearing a particularly short skirt. His eyes peered surreptitiously ever deeper into that dark area between her thighs, and his thoughts turned to Dina Russakov. His intellect couldn't come to grips with their relationship, if one could call it that. Had she sought him out, or had he hunted her down? Why had they made love so early – almost as soon as they had said hello? It was like a bond between them, as if they had shaken hands on a business deal. But it hadn't been simply casual sex. Both had needed it, wanted it at that given moment. He hadn't felt empty afterwards as he had done after screwing some other girls on their first encounter. They had been KGB groupies. If it could have been arranged, they would rather have slept with his father. Power was their aphrodisiac.

Dina was different. She wanted him for himself. Of course, through him, she hoped to secure the release of her father, but she also wanted him for himself. Alexei was convinced of that. Without a doubt, he wanted her. He felt his penis hardening inside his trousers as he longed to explore that dark area once again. A sudden jolt of the train threw him back into the present. The brakes were being applied as they pulled into the station.

Alexei looked up to be greeted by the accusing eyes of the

woman opposite. He guiltily remembered where his eyes had been transfixed, and his cheeks reddened. This time, it was her turn to stare him down triumphantly. Stubbornly, his penis refused to relax. The tell-tale hardening increased. He wished he had a newspaper with which to cover it. Alexei wanted to tell the stranger that it was not her sensuality that had caused his arousal. She was merely a sexual surrogate for someone sitting at a desk in the files of the Central Index in Moscow. That would deflate her feminine ego. Alexei decided against it. After all, it was too complicated a story to relate to a stranger. She wouldn't understand, let alone believe it. Besides, if she needed the escapism of a romantic novel to obtain her sexual pleasures, he was doing her a favour by apparently paying her a compliment.

Freight wagons were being shunted sluggishly into sidings as the train pulled into the station. Alexei began to rise to his feet. The book on the woman's lap lay open now. It was rather larger than he had at first imagined. After sitting opposite her for over an hour, Alexei suddenly realised that the woman was rather plain. Her hair was untidy and her make-up badly applied. Her eyes were still fixed on the place where he had been sitting. And she was smiling. There was a kind of vacant, opaque look in those eyes. He didn't recognise the language on the printed page of the book. It certainly wasn't English. After a long moment where the synapses in his brain shunted into place like a train hitting the buffers, the message was relayed. Braille. She was blind, or at least partially sighted. He had imagined everything. He wanted to apologise profusely, but then realised that, in her eyes, he had nothing to apologise for. Checking his thoughts again, he pondered whether, in fact, though blind, her other senses were enhanced and that she had felt everything that had happened between them since the train had left London.

She spoke for the first time. "Excuse me, is this Cambridge?

Have we arrived?"

"Yes, we have," he replied, deciding that this answer just about covered all the things he wanted to say to her. "Can I help you out?" he offered.

"No, that's alright," she said.

Not wanting to tax his brain further with the implications of this response, Alexei grabbed his bag and stepped out onto the platform. It was not quite what he had expected. Already disoriented by the confusing encounter on the train, he looked around him with amazement. Instead of a reflection of the Renaissance splendour of King's College Chapel as echoed in the words of William Wordsworth's 'immense and glorious work of fine intelligence', he found a shabby, run-down, parochial edifice, hardly befitting the freight yards of Murmansk, never mind the seat of English learning. All around, students back from the summer vacation, or freshers, arriving for their first term, talked with nervous excitement as they poured out through the ticket barrier.

Alexei joined the flow and was carried along in the rush. As the guard dispossessed him of his ticket, up ahead in the station forecourt, he could make out a line of black limousines like the Zils, Volgas, and Chaikas ranged in Dzerzhinsky Square for the disposal of members of the Central Committee and high-ranking officials of the KGB.

Suddenly, above the sea of heads was raised a placard which read 'Alexei Kunayev' in large capital letters. For a split second, he panicked. Jet-lagged from the Aeroflot flight and bemused by the idling of his thoughts on the subsequent train journey, he imagined the KGB were there waiting to pick him up. Yes, the black Volgas even carried the tell-tale KGB radio aerials. They must have homed in on his anti-Soviet thoughts, suspected his incipient plans for defection, captured Dina Russakov and tortured her into submission. Or maybe his father had given him away. Paranoia hardened in the arteries of his brain. He couldn't turn back. The surge of undergraduates carried him ever onwards. Some even pointed at the placard bearing his name and laughed. If only they knew the cruel fate in store for him.

Despite his resistance, the throng seemed to push him inevitably towards his captors. He could see the man now, wearing a long trench coat and black leather gloves. He must be the KGB Colonel in charge. Alexei thought it strange that a man of such rank should be so young, almost the same age as himself, early twenties. As Alexei approached, the man seemed to look straight through him. Surely, they would have been issued with photographs so that they could recognise him. They were now standing face to face. At first, the man continued to peer over the tops of people's heads, rotating the placard like a battle standard.

He suddenly became aware of Alexei's presence at his side. "Is it you?" he asked in perfect English, much to Alexei's surprise.

Why didn't he speak to him in their native Russian?

"Shall we take a ride?" He asked further. "Or would you rather walk?" The man opened the back door of the black Volga, inviting him to get inside. Sensing Alexei's resistance, he continued cheerfully, "OK then, let's walk. It's not far, and besides, it's such a lovely day."

Alexei was astounded at the subtlety of the mental intimidation methods. The man closed the car door, gave a dismissive nod to the driver, and took Alexei by the arm. Alexei couldn't see the Colonel's backup team. He surmised they must be well-camouflaged to provide their escort. He looked over his shoulder to study the face of the duty driver. He was smiling. And students were getting into the back of his car. Alexei was totally disoriented. As the doors closed, a sign became illuminated above the windscreen. It read CAMTAX. As Alexei racked his brains to work out what the initials stood for, the truth suddenly dawned on him. This was not a KGB Volga but an Austin Cambridge taxi. He was in England, not in Moscow. The state security services had no jurisdiction here. He felt foolish that he had allowed his imagination to run away with him. Travel and fatigue played tricks on the mind. Still, there was the question of his mystery companion. "Who are you?" he asked bluntly, as they walked down Station Road, past Great Eastern House.

"My name's Andrew Marriott," he replied. "I'm sorry, I should have given you a placard with my name on it. The college asked me to come and meet you. We have adjoining rooms at Trinity."

"And I thought you were from the KGB," said Alexei with some relief.

At this, his companion burst out laughing. "And I thought Russians weren't supposed to have a sense of humour."

Alexei wanted to reassure him that he had been in deadly earnest, but having to explain the background to his apprehensions would have led him into disclosing his innermost thoughts, and so far, he was not sure that he could trust this stranger. Alexei decided to turn the tables and question Marriott. "Are you a member of staff?" he asked.

"No, not yet," he replied. "I'm studying for my PHD, my doctorate, that is."

"Are you a scientist?" Alexei continued.

"No, my field is literature – Wordsworth and Coleridge. Wordsworth mainly. And you?"

"Radio astronomy. I'm on a sabbatical from my scientific institute in Moscow to attend the Cavendish Laboratories."

"Then you're coming to the wrong college, Alexei. Old Cavendish was a Peterhouse man."

Eager to display his knowledge, Alexei countered. "Yes, but the Cavendish professorship has invariably been held by a Trinity man – Clerk-Maxwell, J.J. Thomson, Rutherford, and so on. Not that I aspire to the professorship, you understand. Not yet."

"You're remarkably well-informed," marvelled Marriott. "If you're here on a spying mission, I think you're wasting your time. You seem to know it all already." The mention of spying touched a bare nerve in Alexei. Marriott sensed the cooling in his companion. "Just a joke, you understand. You needn't be so touchy here." He slapped Alexei on the back as they neared the centre of town. "No KGB reception committee, I promise."

By now, they had walked down Hills Road, turned left down Lensfield Road, and right onto Trumpington Street. Marriott pointed out the Fitzwilliam Museum and Peterhouse on the left. The disappointment Alexei had experienced at his first architectural encounter with Cambridge at the railway station had been replaced with a sense of wonderment. On opposite sides of Trumpington Street stood St Catherine's College and Corpus Christi College before they arrived at the neo-Gothic splendour of King's. Where King's Parade merged into Trinity Street stood the turreted Gatehouse, which gave onto the Great Court of Trinity College. Alexei looked up at the statue of Henry the Eighth, which appeared to be grasping a piece of wood in his hand. "What's that?" he asked.

"Just a chair leg," replied Marriott in a matter-of-fact way.

"A chair leg," echoed Alexei incredulously. "What on earth is Henry the Eighth doing holding a chair leg?"

"It's tradition," Marriott explained. "It should be a sceptre really, but what started as an undergraduate joke has become a tradition."

Alexei marvelled at the tolerance and eccentricity of the British. Just imagine a statue of Lenin or Marx being given the additional blandishment of a chair leg in Red Square, and the Politburo deciding to perpetuate a student prank as a serious Soviet tradition. It was unthinkable.

At the porters' lodge, Marriott introduced Alexei to the head porter, a certain Mr Crowther, who, although apparently a college servant, seemed to carry the mantle of great authority. In his training, Alexei had been taught about the ambiguous master-servant syndrome in British society.

"It's a pleasure to have you with us, sir," said Crowther. "You're on E4 Stairs in Great Court, first floor, next to Mr Marriott here. It's Sir Isaac Newton's old room. Here are the keys."

"Thank you, er, Mr Crowther," replied Alexei, already showing the head porter the degree of deference, which he was obviously accustomed to receiving.

Crowther turned away. The audience seemed to be at an end. Alexei and Marriott walked on through the Great Gate and turned right. Up ahead lay the Chapel and the Master's Lodge.

"This is the Great Court," said Marriott. "It's the largest court in both Oxford and Cambridge."

"You sound like a Texan boasting of the biggest and best," replied Alexei.

"Funny you should say that," said Marriott as they mounted the winding stone steps to the first floor, "I thought I caught a trace of American in your accent."

Alexei was about to divulge the fact that it was his father's undercover work at the UN that had taken him to America, but thought better of it, at least for the moment. "Our English tutors in Moscow were American," he improvised. "I suppose some of their drawl must have rubbed off on us students."

"Ah," said Marriott, apparently satisfied with the explanation.

At the top of the first flight of stairs, two doors stood next to one another in one corner. "Your trunk came last week," said Marriott. "We put it in your room under lock and key for safety."

"I'm honoured to be occupying Newton's old room," said Alexei.

"The college thought it would be a nice gesture," replied Marriott, "to uphold the scientific traditions of the rooms. More recently, it was occupied by Edgar Douglas Adrian. He studied medicine as an undergraduate and eventually returned as a lecturer and finally as Master of the college. He began in rooms in E1 before moving up one flight to E4."

"Yes, I've heard of him," added Alexei. "He was President of your Royal Society and won the Nobel Prize and also the Order of Merit. His speciality was research into the physiology of the brain and nervous system."

"You really are remarkably well-informed," marvelled Marriott as he drew back the outer heavy oaken door to reveal the more conventional one beneath.

"Why two doors?" asked Alexei as he turned the key in the lock.

"That's in case you don't want any unwelcome visitors," explained Marriott. "If you close the outer door, it means you don't want to be disturbed, and anyone attempting to disturb you is liable to be fined by the college. It's called 'Oak Up'. Hence the oak door."

"I suppose this is another one of your curious traditions," replied Alexei.

"That's right," conceded Marriott good-humouredly. "It comes in handy if you're studying for your finals, but even more so if you're smoking pot or having sex in your room and you don't want the senior tutor to find out. Having a woman in your room, or for that matter a man," he gave Alexei a searching stare, "is frowned on by the college establishment. You can get yourself sent down if you're found out. If you have 'oak up', only the senior tutor, accompanied by the chaplain, is allowed to break through it if they suspect you are up to something. By the time they get the search party organised, you can dispose of the evidence, or your partner can have her or his clothes back on and be involved in a deep game of chess or mah-jong."

"It sounds like quite a game," exclaimed Alexei. "So that's what you English get up to behind closed doors. I've read 'Washington Behind Closed Doors' by Woodward and Bernstein, but Cambridge behind closed doors seems much more interesting."

"Listen, I'll leave you to get organised for half an hour. I'll give you a knock then. The senior tutor has arranged a sherry party before dinner. It's high table, by the way, so wear a collar and tie. I'll lend you a gown."

"Thank you," said Alexei.

Marriott stopped at his own door and turned back, "Oh, and no 'oak up' in the meantime, eh?" He smiled.

"No, of course not," replied Alexei, rather more seriously than was necessary. He turned and closed the door behind him. His metal trunk stood in the centre of the room, covered with stickers announcing his destination in both Russian and English. No doubt it had been opened and his belongings turned over by the Soviet customs authorities, although there was no sign of a forced entry. He reached into his wallet and took out the keys. Snapping back the catches, he lifted the lid. Everything looked far too neat. He had packed in an untidy manner deliberately. The trunk had definitely been opened. Still, it was no more than he had expected. Besides, there was nothing incriminating to be found.

It felt remarkably warm for October. The central heating radiators were unbearably hot to the touch. Alexei flung open the leaded window which gave onto Great Court. To the right, he could just make out the corner of the sixteenth-century Chapel and Clock Tower. In the centre of the court stood the beautiful canopied fountain, whose water supply rose from a pipeline laid by the Franciscans in the early thirteen hundreds from springs over a mile away across the river.

'So,' thought Alexei to himself, 'these were the rooms and this was the view that had inspired Sir Isaac Newton to write his 'Principia Mathematica'.

In the morning, he vowed to visit the college's Angel Court, where an apple tree grew directly descended from Newton's tree at Woolsthorpe Manor, which first set him thinking about the notion of gravitational theory. Alexei was overwhelmed by the sense of history. His own research into radio astronomy, although in modern terms far in advance of Newton's achievements, did not carry the same historical significance. He was merely one in a long line of postgraduates from universities and scientific institutes all around the world to come to Cambridge and the Cavendish Laboratories as research students. He was, however, following in distinguished footsteps, as one of the first overseas graduates was Ernest Rutherford from New Zealand, who later became a Cavendish Professor.

Having unpacked his trunk and disposed of his clothes and belongings in the cavernous wardrobe and drawers, he changed into a sober suit made in Finland, which his father had bought for him at the shop reserved for KGB personnel.

There came a knock at the door as he was adjusting the Windsor knot in his silk tie. "Time to face the welcoming committee," exclaimed Marriott mischievously, as he popped his head around the door. "Here's your gown," he offered, extending the formal black robe. "Sorry about the soup stains."

Alexei was beginning to get in tune with the English sense of humour, which appeared intent on undermining and deflating authority and tradition. "If I get hungry, I can always suck it," he quipped.

Marriott sensed that he was entering into the spirit of things, contrary to the dour impression he had received on their first encounter at the railway station.

They made their way down the stairs, across Great Court

and into Nevile's Court. Alexei followed Marriott through a low portal, under which he had to duck his head, and came to an abrupt halt before a door bearing a brass plaque announcing 'Dr Fischer'. Marriott gave a short, sharp rap and entered before waiting for a reply.

The rooms were illuminated by soft red lighting from several table lamps, which gave an intimate atmosphere. The quarters were more opulently furnished than Alexei's room and had a permanent, lived-in quality. Marriott strode straight up to a rather portly man in his early forties with a mop of curly brown hair. He looked like an overdressed cherub with a ruddy face, soft mouth, and dancing eyes. He was rather too effeminate for Alexei's liking – the type of man who made him feel uncomfortable.

"Dr Fischer, may I present Alexei Kunayev," announced Marriott.

Fischer turned from an animated conversation he was having with a rather large-boned lady and extended his hand in welcome. Alexei shook it with as much warmth as he could muster, as the hand was sweating and oozed a sickly-sweet smell. Alexei wanted to wipe his hand immediately after contact. Instead, he uncomfortably hid it in the folds of his gown like an incriminating piece of evidence.

"May I call you Alex?" said Dr Fischer.

Alexei preferred the full version of his name. Even his mother called him Alexei. However, he didn't feel comfortable about contradicting the pouting senior tutor. "Please do," he replied.

"My name is Gerald Fischer. You can call me Gerry."

Alexei nodded as Fischer called for a college servant with a tray of glasses. "Sherry," he said. "I'm sure you'd prefer a vodka or schnaps, but you'll acquire the taste for this in time."

Actually, Alexei couldn't stand the taste of vodka but didn't bother to disillusion his companion. "Cheers," he said, raising his glass.

"What's your line?" asked Fischer. "Astro-physics, isn't it?" he offered.

"Radio astronomy," corrected Alexei.

"Quite," said Fischer, as if the two meant the same thing to him. "My forte is philosophy," he declared, as if this were a much more important subject for study. "Wittgenstein, to be precise. Of course, he was an old boy of the college."

"There are many famous graduates of Trinity," added Alexei, "philosophers, politicians, scientists."

"I'm pleased to see that you place scientists last on your list," interjected Fischer. "All that useful, practical stuff is such a bore."

Alexei did not rise to the bait of an argument on the relative merits of philosophy and science. He said merely, "I believe that Wittgenstein was the son of a leading Austrian steelmaker. His early schooling was in mathematical and rational sciences, and in the first decade of this century, he engaged in aeronautical research in England, where he was instrumental in developing the aeroplane engine. Only later, by way of diversion, did he turn to philosophy." He left Fischer rambling on about Tractatus Logico-Philosophicus and Philosophical Investigations.

"Nice one, Alex," Marriott whispered as he drew Alexei diplomatically away to his next encounter. Standing alone in a corner of the room, staring out defiantly at the gathering, was an athletic man of just over six feet with sandy hair, which glowed red in the reflection from the coal fire. "Dr McCabe," announced Marriott, determined to break the barrier of hostility.

Begrudgingly at first, the alien averted his penetrating gaze from the back of Dr Fischer to make eye contact with Andrew Marriott. "Yes," he uttered in a manner that would have intimidated most people.

Marriott, however, seemed familiar with the game and persevered with his introduction. "This is our research student from behind the Iron Curtain. Alexei Kunayev."

"Kunayev," said McCabe, as if swilling an unfamiliar wine around on his palate. "Any relation to Dinmukhamed Kunayev?"

"No," replied Alexei rather hesitantly, not wishing to incriminate himself by association, even though he did not recognise the name. The Christian name did not sound Russian. Its origin lay somewhere in Central Asia. "I'm from Moscow. You may have heard of my father, Boris Grigoriyevich Kunayev." There was a pause. "He's a diplomat," Alexei added as an afterthought.

McCabe smiled as if he understood the implications of this euphemism. There was a longer pause. Marriott decided to interrupt the apparently meaningful silence. "Dr McCabe is my English tutor. Wordsworth, Coleridge, and Southey."

"And Shelley," interjected McCabe.

"And Shelley," agreed Marriott.

"Wordsworth was a Trinity man," continued McCabe. "Coleridge went to Jesus. Wordsworth was the older man."

Alexei noticed that McCabe laid emphasis on the word 'older' as if there were some kind of sexual connotation. He seemed to be reading innuendo into everything, or perhaps this was simply the ambiguity of the English language.

"How old are you, Alexei?" he asked.

"Twenty-three," he replied.

"Marriott here is twenty-five. The same age difference as Coleridge and Wordsworth."

Alexei did not understand the tack of the conversation.

McCabe ploughed an inevitable furrow. "Of course, they were all radicals, one might even say Communists." He shot a quick glance at Alexei. "Coleridge got into trouble with the Master of his college for writing his drama 'The Fall Of

Robespierre' at the time of the French Revolution. Southey preferred dressing up in women's clothes."

Alexei decided he was not going to fit in if this were typical of the conversation in senior common rooms. What kind of response was this man attempting to elicit? If he were seeking to make the foreigner feel ill at ease, he was certainly succeeding in that, Alexei decided. He would not, however, give him the satisfaction of evoking hostility. Alexei remembered his father's cool response when interviewed by the American broadcasting corporations about his covert role at the United Nations in New York. "It must be the effect of the daffodils," he declared, echoing Boris Kunayev's words – it must be the effect of the Big Apple.

McCabe roared with laughter, causing everyone else at the sherry party to wheel round. Having satisfied themselves with the identity of the person responsible for the outburst of merriment, they at once turned back to their own company.

Changing tack altogether, Marriott said, "Dr McCabe is very fond of Russian music."

"You are a fan of the Famous Five, then," posed Alexei.

"Only of their founding father, Glinka," replied McCabe. "I can't stand all that trashy Tchaikovsky and Rimsky-Korsakov. Give me Mikhail Ivanovich Glinka, the Father of Russian music, every time." McCabe was now in full flow. "He was, of course, a true European in musical terms. He studied composition in Berlin, blending folk themes of Russian song with the great traditions of European music."

"I prefer Shostakovich," declared Alexei. "He's more avant-garde, non-conformist."

"That hardly rings true of a man who wrote his Second Symphony to celebrate the tenth anniversary of the October Revolution," countered McCabe.

"What about The Nose?" asked Alexei defiantly.

"Only a Communist could write an avant-garde opera

called The Nose," said McCabe contemptuously. "No, he's a party man through and through. Just like you, no doubt."

Alexei couldn't decide whether this was intended as an insult or a compliment, or maybe even just a statement of fact. Was McCabe a true-blue Tory or an intellectual pinko, defending his moderation in the face of a real red Communist? Maybe the whole act was mere bluster to disguise his real beliefs.

"I suppose Fischer has been filling your head with stories about Trinity old boys," resumed McCabe, assuming a much more civilised tone.

"Only Wittgenstein," Marriott offered.

McCabe scoffed. "Typical. I don't suppose he mentioned Burgess, Philby, or Blunt. You won't find those names in the college prospectus. No glowing testimony to their notoriety."

Alexei blushed at the mention of the celebrated moles, who had betrayed Britain to the Soviet Union. For no good reason, he blurted out, "Donald Maclean often used to come to dinner at our apartment. He was a friend of my father." He could have bitten his tongue off. After carefully guarding his responses all day until he was more sure of the trustworthiness of his new companions, in one moment of weakness, he had released a piece of valuable information into the wrong hands.

McCabe sensed the gaffe. It showed in the triumphant expression on his face, although he did not remark on it.

People were moving towards the door as the dinner bell sounded. "At such moments as these," he said, "I would have to agree with the famous remark of James the First on his visit to Cambridge –were he to choose, he would pray at King's, dine at Trinity, and study and sleep at Jesus."

Alexei recalled the earlier conversation about Wordsworth and Coleridge.

5

As Dina Russakov made her way to work on Monday morning, she was glad that she did not have to go to the main KGB headquarters at Dzerzhinsky Square. That building also contained Lubyanka Prison, where her father was incarcerated. It would have been too painful a reminder if she had had to work under the same roof.

Some of her work colleagues had been rather surprised that she had not been suspended, in view of the secret nature of her work. With her father discredited, she herself represented a security risk by association. However, her superiors had not even hinted at this possibility.

The anonymous new KGB building stood on the Moscow Ring Road, where the Sadovaya was intersected by Prospekt Kalinina (formerly known as Vozdvizhenka Ulitza). Like many streets in Moscow, the name had been changed to replace the old religious or Imperial connections with new ones honouring revolutionary or military heroes. In this case, the man who gave his name was Mikhail Kalinin, a former Soviet head of state.

As usual, Dina emerged from the Arbatskaya metro station at around seven-forty. Rather than travel directly to the Smolenskaya Station on the ring road itself, she preferred to get off one stop earlier and walk along the most modern section of Prospekt Kalinina. This new development was undertaken in the late sixties to accommodate the volume of motor traffic moving to and from the Kiev Station and the West. It cut a swathe straight through one of the quainter, more rundown areas of Moscow.

Off the wide avenue, a number of old streets still remained. Dina could not bring herself to look right up Suvorovsky Boulevard to the Tchaikovsky Conservatory, where her father once worked. Instead, she stared straight ahead across the Novy Arbat.

The twenty-minute walk took her past galleries of shops and cafes, among which were the Novoarbatskiy supermarket and the Podarki gift shop. Eating houses included the Valday, the Pechora, and the Angara, together with the Arbat restaurant. The latter housed up to two thousand diners and was among the largest in Moscow. Many KGB staff preferred to eat there rather than in the staff canteen. For this very reason, Dina tended to avoid this establishment and preferred to lunch at the Metelitsa ice-cream parlour, which also sold warm snacks.

She didn't have any close friends at the Registry and Archive Department, of which she was a member. The stukach system instigated in the High Schools was perpetuated within the ranks of the Komitet Gosudarstvennoy Bezopasnosti. Any idle talk over the dinner table was likely to find its way back to her superiors. Rather than having to be constantly on guard, she preferred the relaxation of walking the last lap to work alone and dining alone. Besides, she currently had plenty to occupy her mind.

The illuminated globe advertising the Soviet state airline, Aeroflot, which surmounted The Arbat, served as a reminder of Alexei's recent flight to the West. She was counting on his research in Cambridge to discover the whereabouts of The

Marble Index, assuming that her own efforts in the files of The Central Index proved fruitless.

A further plan to secure the release of her father was also being nurtured during these contemplative morning walks. They involved her ultimate superior, Mikhail Andreyevich Suslov, Chief Ideologue and number two in the Party Secretariat after Brezhnev. She knew his son, Misha, a junior researcher in The First Chief Directorate of the KGB, of which ironically Alexei's father was the Head. Suslov was an old man like every other member of the Politburo. Separated from his wife and family, isolated politically, he was a vulnerable yet still powerful member of the Central Committee of the Communist Party. Ultimately, he had the final say on whether Vladimir Russakov remained in prison, was transferred to a psychiatric institution, or even released and totally rehabilitated to resume his former position at the Conservatory and place in society. Dina saw in the vulnerability of the ageing Chief Ideologue another means of applying pressure on the system. The means, however, for the time being remained vague.

She stopped at number 26 Prospekt Kalinina, to stare through the window of Moscow's largest bookshop – Dom Knigi. Without thinking, she went up to the first floor, where the foreign language books were housed. In the English section, she took volumes of poetry down from the shelves and caressed the covers. She only had a smattering of the English language – a distant legacy of her High School days. The unfamiliar alphabet gave her sudden comfort. They reminded her of Alexei now in Cambridge. Flicking over the pages of largely incomprehensible print gave her strength and a sense of optimism.

Her hands ran over the bindings of books of poetry filed in alphabetical order – Scott, Shelley, Southey, Wordsworth. One of the last books on the bottom shelf was the collected works of William Wordsworth. It was a purely random choice. Apart from many short poems, it contained one lengthy piece, the title of which she did not understand. As the crisp new pages fluttered by, she thought she caught sight of the word Cambridge, or was it Coleridge? Retracing her steps, she couldn't rediscover its location. Perhaps she had imagined it.

Suddenly, she looked at her watch. It was nearly a quarter past eight. She was late. Quickly, she replaced the book on the shelf, dashed down the stairs, and out into the cold morning sunlight. Turning right, she fled up the avenue past the Melodiya record shop and the Octyabr cinema decorated with revolutionary mosaics. She arrived at the intersection of the Sadovaya Ring Road breathless and yet elated. There seemed to be no obvious reason for her high spirits, yet she entered the KGB building with a renewed sense of optimism. The guard on the door in a full military uniform gave her a reprimanding look as he examined her security pass with its distinctive diagonal red stripe. He scrutinised the photograph as if he didn't recognise the physical likeness before him. Dina stood there with her hand out for what seemed an abnormally long time. Eventually, the tableau was broken as he slapped the laminated card back into her open palm and gave her a perfunctory gesture to proceed with his hand.

Dina took the stairs up to the first floor and pushed open the double doors, which gave onto a long passage, brightly lit and spotlessly clean. Red doors on the left bore the words 'systems analysis'. Green doors on the right bore the word 'programming'. As she passed a glass-panelled door, it opened to reveal the rush of the air-conditioning system required in the disc and tape store to keep the contents clean of dust and at a constant temperature.

"Hello, Dina," said a tall, thin, young man with sunken cheeks, wearing a white coat and his identity card tagged to his lapel. "Boychenko's looking for you."

"Let him look," said Dina with newfound confidence.

The young technician was alarmed at her response. "You know what comrade supervisor is like about punctuality. I told him you had a query on the update run of the UN personnel file with one of the programmers. I don't think he believed me, though."

Dina warmed to his concern for her. "It was nice of you to try and cover for me, but don't risk putting yourself in jeopardy, Nikolai. You know that I'm persona non grata at the moment, what with my father and everything. Still, I appreciate it." She reached up and placed her right hand gently on his cheek as a gesture of gratitude.

Nikolai Koroteyev glowed with pride.

Dina thought to herself that maybe she did have a friend in the Computer Centre after all. "I'd better be going before Comrade Boychenko catches up with me," she concluded breezily. "See you later, Nicki, and thanks again."

The rush of the air-conditioning returned to a distant roar as Nikolai Koroteyev closed the disc and tape storeroom door behind him.

No sooner had Dina re-emerged from the ladies' cloakroom and reached for the door handle to the systems analysts' office than it opened abruptly before her. There stood her boss, Konstantin Boychenko, a large man with bushy eyebrows and thick jowls. He spent too many lengthy lunchtimes at the Arbat and Praga restaurants and took too little exercise. But there was nothing wrong with his sharp, analytical brain when it came to computer science.

"Why were you not in your office at eight o'clock?" he demanded.

Dina thought it was worth a try. "I had to consult one of the programmers about the data vet in the update run. It was urgent."

"Which programmer?" He pursued his line of questioning.

Dina thought quickly. The first name that came into her

mind emerged. "Comrade Anatoly Dobrynin."

"Hm," he grunted.

She knew that although he was a meticulous man by nature, he would not check on this, as he did not see eye to eye with the chief programmer, Jerry Semichastny, and would not approach him or his staff unless he absolutely had to. The need to corroborate her story came low on his list of priorities in that regard.

"And everything is now in hand" he said.

"Yes," she replied, "Everything is well in hand."

Whether he was satisfied or not, this brought their conversation to a close, as he turned on his heels and headed for his office.

Alexei's main base of work was the new Observatory, some five miles southwest of Cambridge at Lord's Bridge. However, on his first day of term, he was due to report to the Director of the Cavendish Laboratories, Professor Sir James Harcourt, at the new site on Madingley Road.

The Director was a man of only average height, but his straight back and imposing bearing lent him the impression of being a good deal taller. His handshake was firm, and his welcome seemed genuinely friendly. Alexei took an immediate liking to the man as they sat down on opposite sides of the desk in his office in the Bragg Building. Alexei did not have the feeling of an encounter with a supposed superior. The professor sat on a similar-sized straight-backed chair. There was no sign of the large swivel or leather-studded chair, designed to assert the authority of those who were unsure of their status and needed such material trappings. Here was a man at the top of his profession, respected by his peers, who could afford the luxury of modesty and humility.

Indeed, anyone would feel humble in this office, on whose walls hung the portraits of many past distinguished professors associated with the Cavendish. Over Harcourt's left shoulder on a pedestal stood a marble bust of the man whose name was commemorated in the Laboratory – Henry Cavendish.

Alexei drank in the historical background as Harcourt opened a folder in front of him, which Alexei took to be his curriculum vitae. The professor's bifocals hung low down on his nose as his eyes pored over the notes. Alexei detected a note of neglect in the Director's appearance. His shirt cuffs were frayed, and his tie, bearing a coat-of-arms, looked old and well-worn. His blond hair was swept straight back and tucked behind his ears. As he leaned forward, strands of hair kept falling down over his eyes, and he had to keep constantly replacing the errant wisps in their proper place. His face was very pink and looked like that of an ageing choirboy. There were no bags under his eyes. Alexei thought that this was the face of a man without excesses, who had dedicated his life unstintingly to his work, for which he had been rewarded with the Nobel prize for physics in 1972.

Harcourt slipped the spectacles off his nose and looked up. "Well, Mr Kunayev, firstly, I should like to say how pleased we are to have you here in our establishment."

"Thank you, sir," replied Alexei.

"As you may know, it has been a tradition of this university to accept research students from foreign countries from as far back as 1895. The Cavendish has acted as a second home to students of chemistry, biology, radiography, my own discipline of physics of the pure and nuclear kind, and, more recently, of your discipline of astronomy and radio astronomy. All are welcome. The research programme in radio astronomy, begun at the Cavendish in 1946, has expanded so rapidly that we have had to expand to several other sites in and around Cambridge. You, no doubt, will spend the majority of your time at the Mullard Radio Astronomy Observatory. Martin Harvey, the Director of the Observatory, has already been briefed on your arrival. I see from your file that you are a student at the Higher Technical Academy."

"That's right," confirmed Alexei. "It's also more commonly known as the Bauman Institute. It's probably the largest of Moscow's institutions of higher education, with over ten thousand students."

Harcourt nodded knowingly. "I understand that in its early days in the nineteen hundreds, when it was known as the Imperial Moscow Technical Academy, it was a centre of revolutionary activity. Indeed, it took its name from a murdered student, N.E. Bauman, in a clash between the Bolsheviks and the imperial forces."

"I believe so," agreed Alexei, who was actually unsure of the origin, but was prepared to take the professor's word for it.

Harcourt continued, "Please convey my regards to your Director Kuznetzov on your return."

"I will," said Alexei, impressed that the man should be so widely travelled in the scientific world. He wondered whether Harcourt had travelled to Moscow, or whether he and Kuznetzov had met at some international conference. Not wishing to become involved in a conversation about Moscow, which might lead him up some embarrassing avenues, he diverted the line back to the work of the Observatory. "I understand that your early work involved the tracking of satellites."

"Quite so," replied Harcourt with a wry smile. "At the time, there was no such thing as the British space programme. We were forced to content ourselves with leading the world in radar observation of hmm," he paused, "Soviet satellites."

The two men smiled at the nicety of the irony.

"And now, twenty years later, you invite me here, a Russian, to observe you, observing us observing you."

"Oh, I think our work has progressed a great deal since

then," said Harcourt. "Nowadays, scientific exchange is based on mutual trust. The days of Lev Landau and Pyotr Kapitsa are in the dark and distant past."

The names meant nothing to Alexei. Politely, he asked, "Who were these men – Landau and Kapitsa?"

"It is of no consequence," Harcourt shrugged his shoulders. "Let's talk about your own work. I'm sure that's far more interesting."

With a nagging doubt still in his mind over the mysterious men mentioned by the professor, Alexei responded, "Well, basically, I'm following in the footsteps of my compatriot, the Russian astronomer Schlovsky, who first put forward the corona theory of the Milky Way. It was measurements taken here at the Lord's Bridge Observatory which later confirmed his theory."

"I'm afraid this is all a little beyond my scope," said Harcourt, rising from his seat. "I'm sure that Martin Harvey, Director of the Observatory, will prove a far better listener."

This dismissal confirmed Alexei's suspicion that the professor had simply wanted to change subjects quickly after having touched on Landau and Kapitsa, rather than out of a genuine interest in his own speciality. Alexei also rose to his feet.

Harcourt came around the side of his desk and took Alexei by the elbow. "Before you leave this morning, allow me to give you a brief tour of the Laboratory."

"Fine," Alexei agreed, as the two men left the Director's office and walked down the resonant marble hallway.

Harcourt came to a halt below a painting halfway up a flight of stairs. "Up there," he declared, "you see the portrait of this foundation's patron – William Cavendish, the Seventh Duke of Devonshire."

"I thought the founder's name was Henry Cavendish," interrupted Alexei, surprised that Harcourt could make such an elementary mistake.

"No," the Professor corrected, "Henry Cavendish was the Peterhouse student who lent his name to the Laboratory. William Cavendish, the patron, was Chancellor of the University some a hundred and twenty years later."

Alexei thought that this was typical British eccentricity. A man called Cavendish founded an institution and named it after another man who was also called Cavendish.

The pair moved on to the accompaniment of Harcourt's running commentary. "The need for teaching experimental physics at Cambridge was first recognised in a report of a syndicate in 1869. It recommended the appointment of a professor and the provision of lecture rooms, laboratories, and equipment. James Clerk Maxwell was the first to occupy the Chair." Harcourt and Alexei arrived outside the entrance to the museum. The professor continued, "In here, you'll find many of the pieces of equipment Maxwell used for his research. And this is the man himself." Harcourt pointed at a marble bust.

Alexei read the inscription 'dp/dt' where the name of the sculpted subject should have been. "What does this mean?" he asked.

"Oh, that's just one of Maxwell's little jokes. It's a differential coefficient. In the second law of thermodynamics, dp/dt=JCM. It's a pun on Maxwell's initials." Harcourt looked at his watch. "You must excuse me. I have work to attend to. Please feel free to browse around the museum. Martin Harvey doesn't expect you at the Observatory till this afternoon. Any time you have a problem or query, do not hesitate to come and see me." He extended his hand, and the two men shook hands.

Alexei did have a query he wanted to put to the Director, but this was not the opportune time to raise it. *Who were Landau and Kapitsa?* The answer would have to wait till later.

Alexei returned to college for lunch with the names of Landau and Kapitsa gnawing at his curiosity. He was also intrigued to discover the identity of Dinmukhamed Kunayev, the man bearing his surname mentioned by Dr McCabe. The English tutor seemed to have more than a passing knowledge of the Soviet Union, as evidenced by his love of Glinka. He also held a controversial view of English Romantic poets, describing them as radicals and even communists.

As Alexei was leaving the refectory hall to cross Great Court, he bumped into Andrew Marriott. "Care for a coffee?" he asked.

"Fine," agreed Alexei.

"I'm on my way to Dr McCabe's. I'm sure he wouldn't mind me bringing you along."

Alexei hesitated an instant, but then fell into step with his companion as they crossed the nineteenth-century New Court. Outside the English tutor's room, they stopped and listened. The strains of a piano concerto filtered through the door.

"Glinka?" queried Marriott, turning to Alexei.

"Sounds more like Rimsky-Korsakov to me," countered Alexei, as Marriott knocked boldly.

Immediately, the music stopped, and after a few seconds, the door opened. McCabe did not seem too pleased by the interruption. "Yes?" he demanded peremptorily.

"You invited me to coffee, remember?" said Marriott.

McCabe's demeanour softened slightly.

"I brought Alexei along for the ride."

McCabe looked from one to the other, then said begrudgingly, "Come in."

The room was very sparsely furnished. The walls were bare apart from one small pastoral English watercolour. It was the room of a man who did not wish to betray his personality through his material possessions. There was, however, a rack containing a very impressive collection of mainly classical records, with Glinka well in evidence, together with the French folk-protest singer, Georges Brassens. In the corner of the room by the window looking out onto New Court, Alexei saw that the music centre was still turned on. As McCabe went into the kitchen to see to the coffee, Alexei approached the music centre and saw that the tape deck was running. Perhaps the tutor had been listening to a pre-recorded tape when they had interrupted him. On closer examination, however, Alexei saw that the function switch was set to radio and that the record and play buttons were both depressed. McCabe had been recording from the radio onto a blank tape. Indeed, he still was, but now with the external volume turned right down. McCabe re-emerged from the kitchen with a tray containing three mugs of coffee. "You're out of luck if you wanted sugar," he declared in Alexei's direction. "I never touch the stuff, and I don't keep it, especially for uninvited guests." McCabe's hostility was even more evident than on their first encounter.

"That's alright, I prefer it without," replied Alexei, thankful that this was indeed the truth.

"Hm," snorted McCabe, placing the coffees on a small table in the centre of the room.

"What was the music you were listening to?" asked Alexei.

"Oh, some Mozart piano concerto," replied McCabe with a dismissive gesture of his hand. "I sometimes think that BBC Radio Three is run by Germanophiles. If it isn't Mozart, it's Beethoven. Have you finished that essay on Wordsworth's Prelude?" he asked, turning to Marriott, apparently happy to change the subject.

"Here it is," replied Marriott, placing his work in a folder down on the coffee table.

"I'll read it this afternoon and go over it with you this evening," said McCabe.

"Fine," said the postgraduate.

"I've just spent my first morning at the Cavendish," said Alexei, leaning forward on the couch to pick up his cup of coffee. "Professor Harcourt is a brilliant man."

"Not bad for a naturalised foreigner," agreed McCabe, with scarcely hidden contempt.

"You mean he isn't English?" said Alexei.

"No," scoffed McCabe. "He's a Polish Jew who changed his name to disguise his past."

"I didn't know that," interjected Marriott.

"There are a lot of things you don't know," replied the English tutor emphatically.

"Whilst on the contrary, you seem remarkably well informed about everyone," Alexei cut in.

"It's my curious and analytical brain at work. Nothing is ever quite what it seems. The study of literature has taught me that. If you peel away the surface, you never know what you'll find. Poetry is, after all, mere words. It is the way they are put together in the context of the poet's life that gives them substance and meaning."

"But don't you agree, Dr McCabe, that a poem is entitled to its own integrity, without being ascribed some biographical, moral, or allegorical significance?" argued Marriott.

"Wouldn't you say that Wordsworth's Prelude is a highly biographical work on his early life in the Lake District and as a student in Cambridge? It is necessary to understand his background in order to understand the poem."

"Well, yes, but that's different," protested Marriott.

"Ah, I see," said McCabe, feeling that this self-incriminating admission had won him the argument. "You are inferring, Mr Marriott, that a piece of poetry can be divorced from its creator and treated as a separate entity with a life of its own. Surely, the whole art of the poet is to speak to each and every one of us through his poems – to create personal resonances, to which each of us can relate from his own experiences. The

Albatross in The Rime of the Ancient Mariner can be seen to represent Coleridge's guilt."

"What had Coleridge to be guilty about?" asked Alexei.

"His sexual perversions, his infatuation with Southey, his radical politics. Take your pick."

Alexei felt that this was the time to spring the surprise question on McCabe, when he was at his most eloquent; his most dominant, his most outgoing. For reasons as yet unclear, he seemed to be the one person most informed of the underbelly of Cambridge life.

"Why should Professor Harcourt feel guilty at the mention of Lev Landau and Piotr Kapitsa?" he asked bluntly.

McCabe stopped dead in his tracks. "I'll say this for you, Mr Kunayev, you certainly know how to kill a conversation." He gathered up his thoughts. "You could call Landau and Kapitsa Harcourt's own personal albatross. I'm surprised you haven't at least heard of Piotr Kapitsa." He scrutinised Alexei's face in search of an expression betraying former knowledge but found none. "Have you at least heard of Meyer Trilisser?" McCabe prompted further.

Alexei nodded. "He was a Party archivist who created the Soviet Index, which keeps dossiers on all potential enemies of the state."

"True," McCabe agreed, "but earlier than that in the nineteen-twenties he was responsible for setting up the foreign department of the Cheka."

"Wasn't that the forerunner of the KGB?" interjected Marriott, intent on not being left out of the conversation.

"Yes," said McCabe wearily at this declaration of the obvious. "Can I continue?"

Marriott was suitably deterred from further interruption, as his tutor went on, "Trilisser's brief was to establish close links with foreign communist parties with the objective of developing industrial and scientific espionage in the Western world. He decided that if Russia were to obtain the West's technological secrets, it must employ dedicated Russian scientists rather than trust defecting scientists from the target countries. Trilisser chose Piotr Kapitsa, the son of a Czarist general – one whose background represented everything the Bolsheviks rejected and detested. What better choice for an agent than one who could be looked upon as a refugee from Communism? And so, Piotr Kapitsa was awarded an industrial research scholarship, enabling him to come to Britain from Leningrad in 1921 and study here at Cambridge University."

"Fascinating," said Alexei, as the implications began to dawn on him.

McCabe continued. "Kapitsa's arrival marked the beginning of what was to become a steady infiltration of Cambridge University by Soviet government agents such as Lev Landau, Alan Nunn May, Guy Burgess, Donald Maclean, and Kim Philby – some of whom you may have heard about."

Alexei nodded as he remembered his earlier slip of the tongue about Maclean. "Yes, I can see that, but how is that directly a source of embarrassment for Professor Harcourt?"

"No one in Cambridge ever dreamt that one day Kapitsa's knowledge would put Russia ahead in the scientific stakes. He was such a promising student that he came to the attention of Lord Rutherford, the man who split the atom. At the time, he was Director of the Cavendish Laboratories and made Kapitsa his assistant."

"So that is where the story ties in with Professor Harcourt, the current Director of the Cavendish. I can see how it could be embarrassing to him and the institution. I only hope he doesn't see me as his latter-day Kapitsa."

"Well, are you?" asked McCabe. "Is that why you're really here?"

"Of course not," interjected Marriott, jumping to the defence of his friend.

Alexei was amused at the sight of two Englishmen fighting over his integrity. "Is that the end of the story?" he asked, without answering the pertinent question.

"Not quite," responded Dr McCabe. "Kapitsa was given a rare honour for a foreigner at Cambridge. He was elected Fellow of the Royal Society. Not only that, at a cost of fifteen thousand pounds, the Royal Society built for him the Mond Laboratory to carry on his research into the development of the atom. Then, in 1934, Kapitsa went to Moscow on holiday, but he never returned."

"You would have thought that would have deterred the university authorities from offering scholarships to foreign students in potentially sensitive subjects in the future," said Marriott. "And yet here we are forty years later, and nothing has changed."

"It says something for the enlightenment of your university," marvelled Alexei.

"Some would call it political naivety," opined McCabe. "On his return to Moscow, Kapitsa was appointed Director of the Academy of Sciences and pursued the research, the groundwork for which had been provided courtesy of the Cavendish. In spite of his defection, the university authorities even tried to induce Kapitsa to return to Cambridge to conclude his work. Such was the goodwill that they even sold the Russians the equipment Kapitsa had been working on just before he left. And they loaned him two Cambridge assistants for three years, as they were familiar with his research."

"Unbelievable," declared Alexei.

"So, as you can see, there is no need for the Soviet Union to indulge in industrial or scientific espionage where England is concerned. We are only too pleased to share our knowledge with our so-called enemies," McCabe concluded. He finished off his coffee and turned to face Alexei squarely in the face. "You can forget whatever briefing you were given by the

Director of your Institute and by the KGB before your departure from Moscow."

"You seem to be making a lot of assumptions about my reasons for being here," said Alexei on the defensive.

"Well, why are you here, then?" challenged McCabe.

Alexei was tempted to make known his considerations about defection and his search on behalf of Dina Russakov for the Marble Index, but decided that discretion was called for on this occasion. Dr McCabe was far too well-informed for his liking. Alexei suspected him of being either a recruiter for the British Secret Intelligence Service or a spymaster acting for the Soviet Union, who preyed on idealistic undergraduates. Until he knew which side of the fence he was on, the English tutor had to be treated with the utmost caution. He could be a dangerous man to have as an ally as well as an enemy.

In order to bring this clash diplomatically to a close, Marriott rose to his feet and said, "Isn't it time we were going? If you want to get to the Observatory in time, Alexei, you'd better start making tracks."

McCabe's question remained unanswered as the two students headed for the door.

"I'll see you this evening, Marriott, to discuss Wordsworth's Prelude. And Alexei, I hope we can continue our conversation also," said the tutor, who was now in a highly charged state.

Neither Alexei nor Marriott said another word until they were well on their way back across New Court. "Sorry about that," said Marriott.

"On the contrary," replied Alexei, "that's the most interesting cup of coffee I've ever had."

"He certainly takes a bit of getting used to, but he really knows his stuff," said his companion.

"That reminds me," said Alexei, stopping in his tracks, "there was something I meant to ask him."

"Can't it wait?" said Marriott.

"No, I'll go back and ask him now," insisted Alexei.

Marriott shook his head. "It's your party, old chap. Listen, after my tutorial tonight, why don't I show you round the Cambridge watering-holes?"

"Watering-holes?" queried Alexei, unfamiliar with the expression.

"Pubs," replied Marriott.

"Ah, yes. Good idea," he said, wheeling round and heading back in the direction of the English tutor's rooms. The identity of the Dinmukhamed Kunayev McCabe had mentioned at the sherry party, was still preying on his curiosity. Who was this Russian, who bore the same family name?

Alexei was about to knock on the tutor's door when he noticed that the outer oak door was also shut. He recalled Marriott's explanation of 'oak up' and its significance.

He was about to turn away when he heard the distant strains of a piano concerto coming from inside the rooms. It sounded very much like the same piece he had heard when they had arrived for coffee. Now it was unmistakable. Alexei recognised a familiar passage of Rimsky-Korsakov's piano concerto in C sharp minor. He rubbed his forehead. McCabe had insisted that he didn't like the Russian romantic composers like Tchaikovsky and Rimsky-Korsakov. And yet, here he was recording one of these pieces from the radio and presumably now playing it back at his leisure. What was even more intriguing was the fact that he was doing it behind the privacy of securely closed doors. The oak was up.

Alexei decided that this bore further investigation as he made his way quietly down the staircase with its marble balustrade.

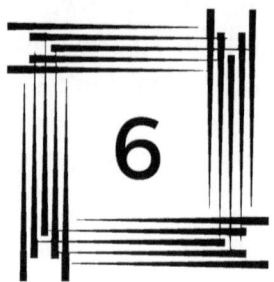

6

Alexei had just finished writing up his diary after dinner when there was a knock on his door.

It was Andrew Marriott. "Ready for our pub crawl?" he asked. "I could certainly do with a drink to steady my nerves after my tutorial with McCabe. He tore my essay on Wordsworth's Prelude to shreds. I think he must be in a really foul mood."

"Is he ever in a good mood?" asked Alexei. "He seems to be permanently on the offensive."

"That's only with people he doesn't know," replied Marriott, standing with his back to the fireplace, legs astride. "When he really gets to know you, he can be really quite endearingly offensive."

They both laughed at the expense of the absent English tutor.

"What was he like when you went back to see him this lunchtime?" asked Marriott.

"I didn't get to see him," replied Alexei. "He had 'oak up' on his door."

Marriott frowned. "I wonder what he was up to."

"He was listening to that music we heard when we arrived for coffee."

"What's so important about that that he can't be disturbed?"

"I don't know, but I'm pretty sure it was Rimsky-Korsakov, and he said he couldn't stand that composer."

"Maybe that's McCabe being typically perverse," said Marriott dismissively.

"There's more to him than meets the eye," said Alexei. "He knows more about people than Moscow's Central Index File. I bet he has dossiers on everyone. Look at Professor Harcourt and Piotr Kapitsa. No doubt he's compiling one on us right now. Where does he get all this Russian background information from?"

"The only thing I can think of is his chess connection. He's not exactly a grandmaster, but I understand his rating is well over 200. He plays against Russian emigres and graduates from Eastern Bloc countries. There's one woman in particular, I believe. She's supposed to be a Russian countess or something. She comes up from London or he goes down there for the odd weekend. Nobody knows much about their relationship. He just says he's off to a chess congress. That's all we ever get out of him. Oh, and of course, he's very close to Martin Harvey."

"You mean the Director of the Observatory?" said Alexei.

"That's right," replied Marriott.

"What's the connection with him?" asked Alexei.

"Chess again. Harvey translates Russian chess books into English."

"He never mentioned to me that he spoke Russian," said Alexei.

"He probably didn't want you to show him up. It's a different story translating chess books with all that specialised vocabulary and great big dictionaries to help you, and holding a fluent conversation with a genuine Russian. Are you going to keep me here talking all night or are we going to sink a few pints? Or should I say, in your case, paint the town red??"

Alexei looked vacant.

"Oh, come on!" said Marriott, grabbing Alexei's jacket from behind the door and throwing it at him. As they ran down the echoing staircase and across Great Court, the head porter was emerging from his lodge.

"I hope you two gentlemen will be returning to college in a sober state tonight," he said.

"Don't worry, Mr Crowther," replied Marriott as soberly as he could. "Two halves at the Cambridge Arms and an early night for us."

Crowther shook his head and walked away across the Court. He'd heard it all before.

"I've got a surprise for you," said Marriott as they turned left and walked up Trinity Street into St John's Street.

"What's that?" asked Alexei.

"You'll see when we get there," replied Marriott. "First of all, I'll give you a conducted tour of Cambridge pubs which no longer exist."

"There's two," said Alexei, pointing across Bridge Street at the Baron of Beef and The Mitre, which stood side by side.

"You wouldn't like them," said Marriott dismissively. "They're full of students. Here on the left, we have the Red Lion Inn."

Alexei looked down a deserted yard full of derelict buildings.

Marriott continued his guided tour. "This was one of the haunts of the famous highwayman and robber, Dick Turpin." Before Alexei had time to react, his companion had dragged him across the road and was looking up at an old house with grotesque masks above the windows, bearing the number four Bridge Street. "And this was the Hoop Inn. In the nineteenth century, this was the headquarters of the Whig Party. The Eagle in Bene't Street was that of the Tories. Politicians used to meet in pubs. Smoke-filled rooms and all that."

"Now it's my turn to get thirsty," interjected Alexei.

"I'm just working you up to it," replied Marriott. "Here is my final literary taster. The Hoop Inn is immortalised by William Wordsworth in his Prelude." Marriott cleared his throat and began to quote from memory:

"Onward we drove beneath the Castle; caught,
While crossing Magdalene Bridge, a glimpse of Cam,
And at the Hoop alighted, famous Inn."

They crossed the Chesterton Road traffic lights past Castle Hill on the right. Without warning, Marriott stopped dead in his tracks and opened the door of a pub, which nestled snugly on the corner of a side street.

"And what's the history of this place?" asked Alexei.

"Don't worry, I'm not going to bore you anymore. I thought the name of this pub might be of interest to you."

Alexei turned around and craned his neck to look at the painted sign above the door. It bore the portrait of a peri-wigged academic with the words Sir Isaac Newton. Alexei smiled. "Highly appropriate," he agreed. "I don't suppose the old man will be actually serving up the drinks?"

"You'll need him to pay for the round, though," said Marriott, with a mischievous look on his face.

Alexei thought for a moment. "I give in," he said eventually. "What's that supposed to mean?"

"Whose portrait is on the back of a pound note?" asked Marriott delightedly.

It began to dawn on Alexei. He felt in his wallet and pulled out a pound note. Staring out at him from the reverse side was the picture of Sir Isaac Newton. "It's my round first, I suppose," he said.

"Seeing as how you've already got your money out, how

can I refuse?" Marriott opened the pub door and followed Alexei into the snug.

The pumps on the bar bore the logo – Greene King. "Two pints of bitter," said Marriott to the attentive landlord. "My friend here's paying." He went and sat down at a table in the corner next to an open coal fire. The copper-topped table with its heavy wrought-iron legs was warm to the touch, and its shiny surface glowed red in the reflection of the dancing flames.

Alexei placed the two brimming straight pint glasses down and edged in alongside his companion on the bench wall-seat. "What shall we drink to?" he asked.

"How about international understanding?" offered Marriott, tongue in cheek.

"That sounds a bit dry," replied Alexei. "To love," he toasted.

"Why not go all the way?" added Marriott. "To sex."

"I'll drink to that," agreed Alexei.

They both took a long draught. Marriott wiped his lips and said, "And that's about as close as you'll get to sex in Cambridge. I suppose you Muscovites have nothing better to do in those long Winter evenings when it's twenty degrees below and all your plumbing's frozen solid. Here in Cambridge, sex is as hard to find as a page of the Daily Telegraph without a printing error."

"Am I to take it that you mean very rare?" quizzed Alexei, unfamiliar with the typographical 'inexactitudes' of the daily newspaper.

Marriott nodded earnestly. "Women are outnumbered ten to one. You don't need to be an Isaac Newton," he waved his hand around the pub bearing the famous scientist's name, "to realise what that means. Mind you, there is an above-average number of the other, so that's some compensation."

"The other what?" queried Alexei.

"You know – gays, queers."

Alexei still looked bemused, whilst other people in the small saloon bar were turning their heads in their direction.

Marriott mouthed 'homosexuals' as if he were talking to someone hard of hearing.

"Oh," said Alexei.

"It's all those gay, arty types you find in a place like Cambridge. You're not gay, are you?"

"No, I'm not gay," replied Alexei, latching onto the expression.

"Have you got a girlfriend in Moscow, then?" Marriott pursued his line of questioning.

Alexei hesitated. "Yes," he said finally.

"You don't sound too sure."

Alexei was aware that his companion could mistake his hesitation for a cover-up of his preferred sexual tastes. "Her name's Dina," he said emphatically. The disclosure of her name couldn't do any harm. "How about you?"

"I'm engaged," replied Marriott, "to a girl back home. Her name's Sarah. I suppose we'll get married eventually."

"Where's home?" asked Alexei.

"Cockermouth," replied Marriott. "It's in Cumbria. In the North West. The Lake District. It's where Wordsworth was born."

"Is that why you are doing your doctorate on his poetry?"

"I suppose so. I'm almost following in his footsteps. I even went to school in Hawkshead like him."

"But you didn't go to the same college," interjected Alexei. "I thought that Dr McCabe said that Wordsworth was a student at St John's. What are you doing at Trinity?"

"The plain fact is that I applied there, but they wouldn't have me, so I had to settle for next door, so to speak. In fact, you can see Trinity from Wordsworth's old room. I'll show you on the way back tonight. What about you and Dina?" he asked, turning the line of questioning back on his companion. "Will you get married and live happily ever after?"

Alexei was still unsure how much to divulge to this relative stranger, who was pretending to the status of a friend. "How about another pint?" he replied, draining his glass quickly.

Marriott's was still half-full. "Steady on, the night is young. Besides, it's my round."

"Typical English sense of fair play," laughed Alexei. "Every man must pay his round in turn. If I pay for two, then I have a psychological and moral advantage over you. Is that it?"

Marriott shook his head. "You Russians are too damn clever for us poor Englishmen. Just to prove it, I'll let you buy me another pint." He too drained his pint and offered the empty glass to Alexei. The froth glowed red in the fire's reflection as it slid down the side of the glasses. Alexei felt comfortable and secure as he approached the bar to order another round. The effect of the alcohol was already beginning to work. Having given the correct change, he made his way back to the table with the refilled glasses.

"So, tell me," said Marriott, renewing the conversation. "What do you hope to get out of your year in Cambridge?"

"I suppose that I'll just carry on with my research and report back to my professor on my findings when I get back to Moscow."

"Does that mean you intend to be an academic all your life?"

"Certainly not. When I've finished at the Bauman Institute, I shall take my place at the Moscow State Institute of International Relations." Alexei winced inwardly as this was the career plan mapped out by his father and not his preferred vocation. "I shall eventually join the diplomatic service, serving my country in one of the many foreign embassies or even at the United Nations like my fa..." Alexei checked himself, "at the United Nations," he stated with finality, hoping that

Marriott had not heard the rest of the sentence.

Apparently, he had not. Indeed, he did not seem to be paying all that much attention to his companion's answer, as he drained the last dregs of his second pint. He caught Alexei's reproachful gaze. "Sorry, old chap. I was listening, honestly. How about a change of scenery? Drink up." He made encouraging motions with his hand.

Alexei responded and finished off his pint. "Are you taking me to another one of Wordsworth's pubs?" he asked.

"No, this one really exists," replied Marriott. "And I don't think our William would have been seen dead there."

They replaced their glasses on the bar and re-emerged into Castle Street. It had fallen dark since they had first arrived. Everything seemed to be closing in on Alexei. He was unused to the strong English beer, which was flat and lukewarm, yet deceptively potent. He liked the feeling of being far away from the inhibitions of Moscow. He could think more clearly now, removed from familiar company and surroundings. Yet his present situation was also fraught with unfamiliar dangers. He was safe insofar as no one knew anything about him, except what he himself wanted to tell them. At the same time, he was equally vulnerable to his newfound acquaintances – Marriott, Dr McCabe, Professor Harcourt, Dr Fischer, and Martin Harvey. Question marks hung over all of them. None of them seemed to be exactly what they purported to be.

Alexei tried to dismiss this as another case of the paranoia that had overcome him at the railway station at the sight of what he took to be the black KGB Volga limousines. Indeed, as they crossed Chesterton Road traffic lights, a Camtax taxi was indicating to turn right into Northampton Street. Alexei sucked in the cold Cambridge air through his teeth and wondered what Dina was doing at that very moment. The traffic lights turned green, and the taillights of the taxi disappeared together with Alexei's thoughts of Moscow.

Having crossed Magdalene Bridge and passed the old Round Church, Marriott guided them right down Green Street and up the steps of the Green Dolphin Hotel. They turned left opposite the reception and entered the lounge bar, which was open to non-residents. The atmosphere was intimate and subdued with an undercurrent of piped music. Groups of people huddled conspiratorially in the separate, high-backed booths. The calm was spasmodically broken by a high-pitched cry of disbelief in an upper-class voice. As Alexei approached the bar, he noticed that every other sentence was punctuated with the word 'darling'. He also noticed that the clientele was predominantly male and began to feel uncomfortable. "Why have you brought me here?" he asked.

"I could say to make you feel at home," replied Marriott mischievously, but seeing Alexei's discomfort, added, "No, really, it's just to show you how the other half of Cambridge lives. You don't mind, do you?"

"No, of course not," he replied with little conviction.

"I mean, I'm sure there are such places in Moscow. You can't tell me there are no such things as homosexuals in the Soviet Union."

"There are, but it is against the law." The cause of Alexei's embarrassment stemmed from an incident in his adolescence. His latent, ambiguous sexuality had been exploited by an older boy, who had tried to seduce him, but without success. Although he was now a normal heterosexual, the incident caused him to feel guilt-ridden in the presence of homosexuals. His hostility, in hindsight, to the gay youth was transferred to any homosexual he came across. He was aware of the faces turning in their direction as Marriott ordered the drinks. He wished that they weren't two men together. People would think that they were lovers, he and Marriott. Alexei longed for the company of women.

Thankfully, he accepted the pint of beer as Marriott guided

them away from the exposure of the bar to the safe haven of a cubicle. "Doesn't it worry you what they're thinking about us?" asked Alexei. "And what would your friends think if they saw you in here?"

"Oh, they'd think it was quite a laugh," replied Marriott. "We sometimes come in for a bit of fun. Like I said, I'm sure Wordsworth wouldn't have been seen dead here. On the other hand, it would have suited Coleridge down to the ground. In his Biographia, he claims to have led a life of gross sexual irregularity in Cambridge. And that was before he met Southey. What have you got against gays anyway?"

Alexei improvised a perfectly plausible answer. "It's a sign of weakness. It's the most common means of blackmailing someone into becoming a spy. It's the favourite KGB ploy – entrapping a politician, businessman, or diplomat and then using the evidence of his sexual perversion as a tool of blackmail."

"You seem to know a lot about it," said Marriott.

"All Soviet citizens are warned about it before they travel abroad. It's standard procedure," replied Alexei in an offhand manner. Just as he was convinced that he had cleared his hurdle satisfactorily, the doors opened, and another male couple entered the lounge. One was a very pretty young man with blond hair. He looked tanned and healthy and wore pale green trousers and a short-sleeved denim shirt. The other man was much older and shorter. They looked an incongruous pair.

As Alexei idly viewed their arrival, he suddenly realised that he knew the older man and began to blush uncontrollably. He leaned forward over the table towards Marriott, who had his back to the door. "It's Dr Fischer," he hissed through his teeth.

Marriott turned around to see before Alexei could warn him not to. Fischer and his companion were coming over. Alexei tried desperately to keep his reddening face under control.

Dr Fischer seemed to squirm with delight as he arrived at their booth and noticed Alexei's embarrassment. "So, then Alex, I see you've already sought out our favourite meeting place."

Alexei didn't know where to put himself. He wanted to run out into the street, but Fischer's man-friend was barring his exit.

"This is Kurt," Dr Fischer introduced the stranger. "He's German. Alex is Russian," he explained.

Kurt leaned down over Alexei, who noticed the gold medallion hanging around the German's neck.

"You must come to some of our little social gatherings. If I'd known you were... if I'd known, well, you know," said Fischer with a wicked wink in his eye. He was obviously enjoying every moment of the charade. "No doubt we'll be bumping into each other again. Come on, darling," he addressed Kurt. The two men drifted away and joined another group of obviously old acquaintances.

Marriott could restrain himself no longer. He spluttered into his beer, spraying it all over Alexei. "Sorry," he said, "but you should see your face."

"Can we go now?" he asked in an over-controlled voice.

"I think we'd better. You never know who you're going to meet."

With ill-concealed haste, Alexei dragged the still sniggering Marriott through the doors and out into the street.

"I think that's one game all between you and Fischer," said Marriott.

"What do you mean?" asked Alexei, regaining his composure.

"I think our senior tutor has just got his own back for that stroke you pulled on him at the sherry party about Wittgenstein. He doesn't like being belittled intellectually."

"Hmm," said Alexei indignantly.

"I think this calls for a little light relief," said Marriott. "As promised earlier, I'll show you Wordsworth's old room. From the outside, anyway."

Having got over his embarrassment, Alexei felt much better and entered into the mischievous spirit of his companion. "Just so long as we don't meet Coleridge and Southey along the way. Kurt and Fischer were enough for one night."

"No, I promise," pledged Marriott solemnly.

Having reached the end of Green Street, they crossed St John's Street and walked down a narrow alley between the two colleges of Trinity and St John's.

"This is Kitchen Lane," Marriott explained as he came to a halt. Pointing up at a large first-floor window on the right-hand side, he declared, "That was William Wordsworth's old room. If it were daylight, you could see the inscription in that stained glass. It was lying awake at night on his bed in that room, gazing through this window towards Trinity that he wrote the lines in The Prelude –

> "And from my pillow, looking forth by light
> Of moon or favouring stars, I could behold
> The antechapel where the statue stood
> Of Newton with his prism and silent face,
> The marble index of a mind forever
> Voyaging through strange seas of thought alone."

Marriott moved off. It was only when he had gone several steps that he realised Alexei was still standing transfixed, looking up at the stained glass window. "I know that poetry is a moving experience, but not particularly when I recite it. Come on. We have other pubs to visit before the night is through."

"The marble index," mouthed Alexei. "The marble index," with a tone of utter disbelief.

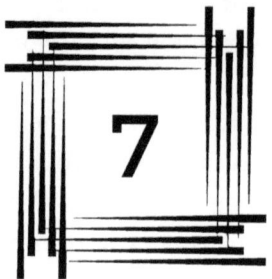

7

On Monday evening, Dina made the long and tedious journey back to the family apartment on the metro. On the return trip, she entered the Smolenskaya station opposite the new KGB headquarters and settled down in her seat for the half an hour it took to reach Izmaylovskaya.

The doors closed, and the announcement came over the speakers: "Caution, the doors are closing. The next stop will be Arbatskaya."

Stations flew by, and the carriages became more and more tightly packed as they passed through the Square of the Revolution in rush hour. Up above on ground level, a granite statue of Karl Marx stood between the Moskva and Metropole Hotels. Dina liked to project in her imagination the sights on the Moscow streets. Anything was more desirable than taking in the drab surroundings of the metro trains. There was not even any graffiti to liven up the subterranean boredom. Writing slogans on public transport was antisocial and could even be construed as political subversion.

She was tempted to scrawl the title of her father's symphonic poem, 'Freedom for Czechoslovakia', on the back of the next seat. Instead, she breathed on the window and wrote the initials VMR and ANK with her index finger. They represented the two most important people in her life – her father, Vladimir Maksimovich Russakov, and Alexei Nikolaevich Kunayev.

As she became aware of people around her staring at the window, she hastily rubbed it off with the back of her glove. All that remained was a dirty smear on the carriage window, but it had been her brief personal statement of revolt, however small.

It was ironic that the next station was Dzerzhinskaya. Up above on ground level stood Dzerzhinsky Square, named after Feliks Dzerzhinsky, founder of the secret police, then known as the Cheka. Until 1926, it had been known as Lubyanka Square, when it housed the Ministry of the Interior and the infamous prison of the same name. The head office of Dina's workplace, the KGB, stood on the perimeter of the square, and her father was confined in the bowels of the same building. Both he and Dina were presently underground at the same location, though their situations were entirely different.

Tears welled up in her eyes as she felt the physical closeness. As an only child and also as a girl, she had always felt a great affinity with her father. Since her mother had died of cancer two years earlier, the bond between them had become even more secure. Not only did she admire and respect him as a person and a musician, but she also loved him for what he was – her father. She couldn't imagine any other man in her life; that is, until Alexei had come along. True, she was manipulating him to her own ends, but in him, she saw the reflection of her father as a young man, strong and full of principle. She wondered whether she could have them both or would have to sacrifice one to achieve the salvation of the other. It was not a choice she wanted to have to make.

The lights flickered as the brakes were applied and the loudspeakers announced "Kurskaya. Transfer to the Circle Line." Passengers changing lines to travel North to Leningrad

Station or South of the river to Paveletsky Station got out of their seats and headed for the doors. The number of commuters was thinning out. The Kursk Station was the largest in Moscow and, following reconstruction work in 1972, it was also the capital's most modern terminus.

The inevitable monotonous voice announced, "Caution, the doors are closing. The next stop will be Baumanskaya." The name of every station seemed to strike at her very heart. Dina had travelled this line for several years and heard the names of the outgoing and oncoming stations as just so many landmarks on the Moscow metro plan. Now they all seemed to hold a special significance.

Alongside the Lefortovsky Palace, housing the historical archives of the Ministry of War, stood the Bauman Institute or Higher Technical Academy, where Alexei was a student. Dina closed her eyes but couldn't blot out the aching pain. She yearned to be entwined in his arms once again.

The air in the metro was stale and lifeless. The people were emotionally dead, intellectually stunted, ideologically repressed. She was determined not to be like them. She had to escape, whatever the cost. Could it be achieved with the preservation of both Alexei and her father, or would it cost one of them their liberty indefinitely or even their life?

The loudspeaker announced first "Elektrozavodskaya" and then "Semyonovskaya". Dina kept her eyes firmly shut until the disembodied voice declared, "The next stop will be 'Izmaylovskaya". This was where she got off. Emerging into the waning daylight, Dina looked across the MI7 Motor Route to the green expanse of Izmaylovsky Park. She turned left and headed in the direction of the old Royal Estate, where the five green domes of the Cathedral of the Intercession could be seen above the dark trees on the skyline. Turning left again, she skirted the Estate towards the Izmaylovo Sports Palace.

The housing complex overlooking the recreation centre

was built in the early seventies. Many prominent people in the world of politics, journalism and the performing arts had apartments there. However, they all represented the official party line in their respective disciplines. Non-conformist views or activities soon brought reprisals from the other residents who had the power to vote members out of their homes by decree of the local Party Committee. No doubt the question of Dina's continued residency would arise on the agenda of the next meeting, in view of the discredit of Vladimir Russakov.

Dina opened the door into the cold apartment. The central heating system was always breaking down. She speculated that perhaps it had been turned off deliberately to make her life as uncomfortable as possible. It would take more than a low room temperature to dull the fire in her soul.

She turned on the light. There were several letters on the mat. She picked them up and placed them on the bureau. Then she went over to the window to draw the curtains. In contrast to the Kunayev apartment, this was very sparsely furnished. Her father was not a man inclined to material possessions. The one concession was an upright piano in the corner of the lounge. She ran her fingers over the polished wooden top. A thin layer of dust was disturbed. The decaying notes of Vladimir Maksimovich Russakov's first piano concerto hung in the air.

Dina shivered inside her coat. The cold and the sorrow chilled her to the very bone. She went into the kitchen and made a cup of coffee. Caressing the cup of liquid in her hands, it gave her a sense of warmth and company. She returned to the lounge, took off her coat, and sat down at her father's bureau. She took out the address and telephone book and a pad of writing paper. Dina wrote down a list of individuals and institutions whose help she could enlist in securing the release of her father. The Union of Composers, the Soviet Society of Psychiatrists and Neurologists, the Procurator-General, the Minister of Health, the Academy of Medical Sciences, the Central Committee of the Communist Party, the Union of Writers, the editor of the liberal monthly magazine Novy Mir, and Georgi Sloboda, the family doctor and friend. Some of them would invariably tow the party line, but that was no reason for her not to make her petition to them.

She added a final name to the list in bold print – Mikhail Suslov, the Chief Ideologue of the Communist Party. He was responsible for the Ministry of Culture and for censorship. Although it may not have been his say-so that had put her father in a psychiatric prison hospital, it was certainly his signature that could secure Vladimir Russakov's release. Dina had never seen him in the flesh, but he had appeared on Brezhnev's right hand on many state occasions on television. She knew his face. She resolved to get to know the man behind the face.

Her mind wandered back to that night when they had come to seize her father. She leaned back in the chair and stared blankly ahead at the wall.

It had been three o'clock in the morning. Both she and her father were fast asleep. There was a loud banging at the door, loud enough to wake up the whole neighbourhood. The arrest party consisted of four officers of the militia and two doctors. One of the doctors who identified himself as forensic scientist Boris Vladimirovich Shostakovich of the Serbsky Institute declared that he was concerned about Russakov's dissident way of thinking, and asked him to accompany them voluntarily to undergo psychiatric tests.

Vladimir Russakov asked the police officer in charge if he had a warrant from the Procurator-General to enter the apartment and carry out the arrest. The officer replied that they did not intend to arrest him and that they were only there to accompany the doctors. Russakov protested that the inviolability of a Soviet citizen's home was protected by the constitution of the USSR. He knew in his heart of hearts, however, that if he protested too much or resisted the doctor's overtures, the militia would be forced to arrest him.

Dina, meanwhile, was becoming hysterical. Russakov tried to calm her down for fear that they would take her, too.

"What do they want, Papa?" she cried. "Why do you want to arrest my father?" she shouted angrily. "You have no right. Do you know who this is? This is Vladimir Maksimovich Russakov the greatest living Soviet composer and conductor. How dare you enter our home uninvited? Leave, now. I order you to leave. Now."

Russakov remained calm. He realised that any display of emotional behaviour would give the militia the excuse they were looking for to forcibly detain him and his daughter. "What exactly is my dissident way of thinking?" he asked the doctor, unsure in his own mind what crime he was supposed to have committed.

"If you come along with us, we can discuss this at greater length at the clinic," the doctor replied hazily.

"I am entitled to an explanation," said Russakov firmly.

"We have reason to believe that you are suffering from paranoid schizophrenia. You have shown delusions of self-importance and slandered the Soviet State."

"In what way?" Russakov pursued his questioning.

After some reflection, Dr Shostakovich replied, "Your new orchestral work. You have called it Freedom for Czechoslovakia."

Vladimir Russakov understood at once. There had been two notable events in recent years to give enlightenment to his case. In 1969, Major General Grigorenko, who had a distinguished military career and was a holder of the Order of Lenin, had urged the withdrawal of troops from Czechoslovakia. KGB Colonel Dr Luntz of the Serbsky Institute diagnosed Grigorenko as suffering from paranoid schizophrenia, and he was subsequently interned in a psychiatric ward for indefinite treatment. Then there was the case of Ivan Yakhimovich, a charismatic workers' leader on a collective farm in Latvia, who protested at the trial of young intellectuals and wrote a letter to Mikhail Suslov outlining his complaints. He also condemned the invasion of Czechoslovakia. For his pains, he was arrested by the KGB and committed to a psychiatric hospital in Riga.

Thus, Vladimir Russakov was well aware of the precedents set in such cases. In the ensuing five years, political and intellectual dissidents had banded together to contest the laws that made defamation of the Soviet state and social system and anti-patriotic slander in verbal, printed, or any other form a criminal offence. Soviet authorities had got around this problem by simply ignoring the law and using psychiatry as a weapon.

"Am I to take it that I am being arrested under Article 70 or Article 190-I for anti-Soviet agitation and propaganda?" Russakov asked.

The police officer in charge replied, "As I said before, we have not come to arrest you. We have come to ask you to accompany the comrade doctor to undergo tests for your own good."

"And if I refuse?" said Russakov. "May I point out that Article 49 of the Constitution forbids repression for criticism of the state?"

Shostakovich interjected, "But it is an entirely different matter when individuals such as yourself transform criticism into anti-Soviet and anti-social activity. You are clearly ill and in need of medical help."

"You seem to have reached your diagnosis very quickly, doctor," said Russakov, "without even the necessity of an examination."

"I've heard enough," said the police officer impatiently.

"Let us get on with the job at hand. Comrade Russakov, I request you to come along peacefully and of your own free will, otherwise..." he faltered.

Dina understood the implications and grabbed her father around the neck with her arms. "No, you shall not take him. You shall not. I won't let you!"

"It's alright, Dina," said her father calmly.

Dr Shostakovich obviously wanted to bring the discussion to a conclusion. "By the powers invested in me under the regulations on the emergency hospitalisation of mentally ill persons who are a public danger, I formally request that you, Comrade Vladimir Maksimovich Russakov, accompany me to Lubyanka psychiatric hospital. If you refuse or resist, I shall lawfully engage the assistance of members of the militia to expedite your cooperation."

Russakov realised that a forcible arrest would look worse for him once his case came before a commission. It would only provide more ammunition for the prosecution's case. He turned to Dina and held her firmly by the shoulders. Leaning forward, he kissed her on the forehead and said, "Do not worry, Dina. I shall be free again before you know it. Contact Dr Sloboda to make representations at the commission. He will secure the services of a psychiatrist for my defence and solicit testimonials from my colleagues as to my mental state. Both you and they know that I am not mad and speak only the truth."

Dina wiped away the tears from her eyes and reluctantly allowed her father to disengage her arms from around his neck. She reciprocated his smile bravely as the militia took her father through the door.

Dr Shostakovich was the last to leave. He closed the door without looking back.

Dina turned away from the bureau to face the door, as if half-expecting her father to walk through it at any moment. Her hands rested on the small pile of correspondence she had found on the doormat. Idly, she leafed through them. Her eyes alighted on an official-looking letter bearing a government seal. As she had only been allowed one visit to the prison psychiatric hospital, Dina suspected it might contain news of her father.

Eagerly, she ripped open the envelope and read the contents. From – Professor G.V. Morozov, Director, The Serbsky Institute of Forensic Psychiatry, Kropotkinskaya Ulitsa, Moscow – I am writing to inform you of the transfer of your father, Vladimir Maksimovich Russakov, from Lubyanka prison psychiatric hospital to the Serbsky Institute of Forensic Psychiatry. I can report that your father is in good physical health, but that his mental state continues to give the authorities grounds for concern. He will remain here until further notice to undergo renewed tests and a special examination. The commission into his case will convene on Tuesday, the fifth of October, at nine am at the Serbsky Institute. The commission will comprise resident forensic psychiatrist B.V. Shostakovich, professor D. Luntz head of the special examination department, professor A.A. Portnov – director of the Institute of Psychiatry of the Academy of Medical Sciences, and professor V.M. Morozov – head of the department of psychiatry in the Institute for Advanced Medical Training. As the subject's closest relative, you are entitled to a representation of two recognised medical or psychiatric specialists on the commission. Their names must be forwarded at least twenty-four hours before the commission is timed to sit. We await your further instructions in this matter. Yours sincerely, G.V. Morozov.

Dina crumpled the letter up in dismay. The commission was due to take place the following morning. How could she find the time to prepare the case for the defence, solicit testimonials, and enlist medical support at such short notice? Besides, the twenty-four-hour deadline was long since passed. She looked at the date on the letter. It read Wednesday, the twenty-second of September, only a few days after her father had first been detained. The envelope was also franked 22.9.75. 'How could it be possible?' Dina wondered to herself. The letter had only arrived since she had been away at work that very morning. It must be a deliberate ploy to give her no time to gather her defences. They had kept her in the dark for nearly a fortnight, and then they had sprung this on her.

Dina was in despair. She began to sob and rocked backwards and forwards in the chair. "No, no, no," she cried to herself, pressing her fingers into her eyes so hard that they began to burn. Just as suddenly as she had descended to the depths of despair, her spirits rose again. Sitting upright in the chair, she thumped the bureau top with her fist and shouted, "No, I won't give in so easily. That is just what you want, isn't it?" she inveighed against the absent faces of authority ranged against her. "Papa, I won't let you down. I will do exactly what you told me. The Russakov family is made of sterner stuff. You won't break me or my father as easily as that." She shook her fist defiantly.

She picked up the letter and the list of names and addresses and telephone numbers she had written down and set off to visit her closest ally – their family doctor, Georgi Sloboda, who lived at the other end of the apartment block. Down two flights of stairs and across an external walkway, she ran rather than walked. It was a cold evening, but she had not bothered to put on a coat. Outside apartment number 14A, she stopped and knocked loudly at the door.

After a few seconds, it opened to reveal the benign, bespectacled face of Dr Georgi Sloboda. He was wearing a sloppy cardigan and baggy brown corduroy trousers, in contrast to his normal smart working suit. His avuncular appearance disguised a hard-headed medical brain, renowned in the field of neurology, and respected for his forthright opinions. Although he was no relation, Dina had called him uncle from being a little girl, and the name had stuck.

"Uncle Georgi," she cried and flung herself into his arms.

"What's the matter, Dina?" he asked. "Why, you're freezing. Come into the warm right away."

Unlike the Russakov apartment, that of the Slobodas was cosy and warm. The remains of dinner were still evident on the dining-room table, which Larissa Sloboda was busy clearing away as soon as she heard Dina's arrival. Even in front of close family friends, she was immensely house-proud.

"I'm sorry to disturb your evening meal," said Dina, feeling the pangs of guilt at imposing her problems on them at that hour.

"Don't be silly, Dina," said Larissa, "you know you're welcome any time. Now tell us what the matter is. Is it news of your father?"

Ding slumped down on the settee and thrust the letter from the Serbsky Institute into Georgi Sloboda's hand whilst Larissa poured them all good stiff measures of vodka and placed them on the coffee table.

"Why, this is scandalous!" exclaimed Sloboda, having quickly perused the letter. "And you say you only received it this morning?"

Dina nodded.

Georgi Sloboda was clearly outraged. He stomped off in the direction of the phone. Having consulted the medical directory, he rang the home telephone number of Dr Morozov, Director of the Serbsky Institute. He let it ring for a considerable time before it was answered. "Morozov," he stated with barely concealed hostility, "this is Dr Georgi Sloboda, Secretary of the Moscow branch of the Soviet Society of Neurologists and member of the permanent committee of the Academy of

Medical Sciences. I have in my hands a letter concerning the commission of enquiry into comrade Vladimir Maksimovich Russakov. No doubt you can guess the reason for my calling."

Faint mutterings could be heard at the other end of the line. "Be quiet, man," said Sloboda. "Now listen to me. You know as well as I do that what you have done falls well outside the provisions of the regulations of the 1961 Act. Minister of Health, Comrade Petrovsky, is a very good personal friend of mine. I am sure he would be only too pleased to hear of someone flouting the rules laid down by the Ministry and the AMS. You know as well as I do that he is a stickler for the rules. If the terms of the regulations are not adhered to, the findings of the commission of enquiry are invalid, and I can legally have their recommendations set aside and declared void. As a result, comrade Russakov could be released without further investigation." He let the implications of this statement sink in at the other end of the line. There was a silence whilst Morozov was obviously thinking.

Sloboda continued, "I therefore insist that you put back the date and time of the commission to allow for proper medical and psychiatric representations on our behalf. If you do not accede to our demands, I shall have no option but to set in train my formal complaint to the Minister."

There were further distant mutterings on the line. Dina craned forward in her seat, eager to pick up the thread of the conversation.

Sloboda was nodding. "Yes, yes, yes, that is understood. I shall be there in person."

"Well?" asked Dina apprehensively.

"Well," replied Sloboda, "he refused to put back the commission any later than tomorrow morning with the excuse that it was the only time when the other members could be present. But he waived the twenty-four-hour rule, and we shall be allowed to attend with full representation."

"What about your threat to go to Minister Petrovsky?" asked Dina. "Couldn't we pursue that?"

"I wish we could," replied Sloboda, "but it was all a bluff. I rather think Comrade Minister would take the side of the Institute on this matter. However, we have gained some concessions. At least we can be present to record the conduct of the commission of enquiry, and put your father's case. Now we have little time and many things to do. There is no time to waste. Tell me everything you know, Dina." He sat down on the settee next to her, and the correspondence, papers, lists of telephone numbers, names and addresses were laid out on the coffee table in front of them. He raised his glass of vodka, knocked it back in one swift draught, smacked his lips, and began to prepare his notes.

8

Alexei hardly slept a wink that night. He lay awake on his bed, exactly as Marriott had described, Wordsworth gazing out of his open bedroom window from St John's towards Trinity. Alexei was in a sense reciprocating this vision, only his room faced inwards on the college across Great Court.

For the first time, he speculated on the meaning of the Marble Index. When Dina had told him about her discovery of its existence, he had assumed that it represented some kind of code name coined by the fecund imagination of Guy Burgess or Anthony Blunt. In his mind, it was merely a list of names, an alphabetical index like the Central Index of the KGB itself.

Now he saw it in a fresh light. Whilst its very existence and location were still open to considerable doubt, this second allusion to it in the poetry of William Wordsworth made its significance even more intriguing. Maybe it wasn't just a code name, maybe it was actually a clue to its very whereabouts. The only trouble was as yet, Alexei did not know what was in Wordsworth's mind when he had first used the expression, not to mention when Burgess and Blunt had re-coined it.

He couldn't wait until morning when the college library would open, and he could pick out the poet's collected works.

Presumably, it would be annotated to clarify any obscure allusions. Of course, he could have asked either Marriott or even McCabe, who were both experts on Wordsworth, to enlighten him, but he still had this faint feeling of paranoia in their presence, or more likely, it was just symptomatic of his own guilt complex. At this thought, Alexei recalled the conversation in McCabe's room on the nature of poetry. The tutor had maintained that the Albatross in The Rime of the Ancient Mariner represented Coleridge's guilt, just as Pyotr Kapitsa was a personification of Harcourt's guilt.

Just what was the marble index in Wordsworth's mind, and did it correspond exactly to what was in the mind of Burgess and Blunt? Or did it, on the other hand, mean something entirely different? Alexei would have to work this out on his own. Whatever the case, it was a remarkable discovery. He longed to contact Dina and tell her all about it, but communication would be difficult, if not impossible. He couldn't write openly to her as all mail into the Soviet Union was opened and censored, particularly in her case, as her father was the subject of an enquiry. He would have to find another way.

Once again, Alexei recalled the words of Dr McCabe. He had described Wordsworth's Prelude as a highly biographical work. The art of the poet was to create personal resonances to which each of us can relate from his own experiences. In other words, whilst in his own mind, Wordsworth had been clear as to what he was referring to in 'the marble index', anyone reading the passage without referring to the glossary could conceivably relate it to some other totally different concept or experience in their own lives. Alexei hoped beyond hope that Burgess and Blunt were fully aware of the significance of the expression and had lifted it intact with its exact attendant meaning, rather than endowing it with their own personal significance.

Alexei watched the luminous hands on his bedside clock

crawl around through the early hours of the morning. He could hear the clock on the college chapel strike every quarter, the sound echoing and decaying away to nothing around Great Court. Gradually, the wan morning light crept over the River Cam, and a pale glow highlighted the grey outline of the sixteenth-century Hall and Nevile's Court. Alexei raised himself up on his elbows and looked out of the window. He was still fully clothed from the night before. He suddenly felt a fuzziness in his brain, which he remembered must have been brought on by the imbibing of numerous local beers. He began to wonder if his drunken imagination had been playing tricks on him. In fact, his mind was a complete blank after the time they had walked down Kitchen Lane between St John's College and Trinity. He didn't remember returning to his room at all.

With a supreme effort of recollection through the mists of sleeplessness and alcoholic haze, he convinced himself finally that Marriott had uttered the words 'the marble index'. The rest of the quotation was lost on him, although he seemed to remember that the name of Newton was in there somewhere. Only this was probably his mind transposing his preoccupation with Sir Isaac Newton's theories, or the pub of the same name, or the fact that he was occupying the distinguished scientist's old rooms. Alexei began to regret that he had not had the benefit of a good night's sleep. He recalled his words to Dina on that first night they had slept together: "Perhaps we can speak to one another more plainly in the morning" – as if by some trick of magic, the morning brought a fresh start, a clean slate, uncluttered by everything that had taken place the night before. It had not been true then, and was certainly not the case now.

Alexei rubbed the sleep from his eyes, got up from his bed, and splashed cold water over his face from the sink. After all, there was no such thing as the absolute truth. Everything was tainted with subjectivity. He couldn't wait any longer. It was still only twenty past seven, and the library didn't open till nine. He put on his coat and, still shivering from the night's exposure, he stumbled down the stairs, across Great Court into New Court. He edged his way round the perimeter of the quadrangle as if afraid to be seen out in the open centre, or not wanting his footsteps to be heard on the crunching gravel.

Eventually, he arrived outside the library entrance. There was no sign of life. Tentatively, he tried the door handle, and surprisingly, it gave. Either it had not been locked from the night before, or one of the porters had opened it up early to save time later. Like many other aspects of Cambridge college life, the locking and unlocking of doors and gates had a certain mystical quality.

Alexei slipped inside. The library itself was on the first floor. He crept stealthily up the steps. Halfway up the stairs stood a bust of J.J. Thomson, familiar to Alexei as a past Director of the Cavendish Laboratories. In this instance, however, he was commemorated as a distinguished Master of the college. The statue's white, unseeing eyes seemed to follow Alexei on his continued journey to the top of the stairs. He even looked back, sensing that someone was following him.

The theme of guilt still haunted his inner thoughts as he pushed open the door to the Wren Library itself. The early morning quiet lent the place an eerie quality. Libraries possessed an intensive, compulsive quietude, but this was normally induced by the concentration of studious minds. On this occasion, the library was completely empty. It stretched away a hundred and fifty feet in a narrowing perspective to the South window by Cipriani, which depicted Sir Isaac Newton being presented to George the Third. It was a baroque masterpiece with panelling and decorative carving in limewood by Grinling Gibbons. Displayed in covered glass cases on either side of the centre aisle were original manuscripts, the oldest of which was an eighth-century Epistle of St Paul, said to have been written by the Venerable Bede.

Alexei wandered down the centre aisle past the seventeenth-and eighteenth-century busts of Trinity men such as Whewell, Barrow, Bacon, and Newton. In fact, there were several busts of Sir Isaac Newton, who was perhaps the most famous fellow of the college. The display of antiquities and historical manuscripts would, under normal circumstances, have proved fascinating to Alexei. However, on this occasion, all that he was interested in was the poetry of William Wordsworth, be it in the poet's own hand or in a twentieth-century edition.

Next to a display case bearing Wittgenstein's original notebooks stood stack upon stack of volumes of poetry with particular emphasis on collections by Byron and Tennyson, who were both famous members of Trinity. Alexei ran his fingers along the books on the bottom shelves, where he would have expected to find the works of William Wordsworth. There were none there. He couldn't believe it. How could there be such a glaring omission? It seemed there was a conspiracy against him.

He looked up to see the statue of Lord Byron brooding over him as if in disapproval. Alexei reasoned that perhaps it was because Wordsworth was a member of St John's College and not Trinity that his works were not included in the library, but this seemed totally unreasonable. Then it struck him. Andrew Marriott was doing his thesis on William Wordsworth, and Dr McCabe was a specialist in the English Romantic poets. Between them, they had probably borrowed all the available works. It looked, after all, as if he would have to consult one of them as to the significance of the quoted passage. Alexei felt a deep annoyance. It was still important to him to preserve his independence of action. He didn't feel ready to rely on the good offices of his new acquaintances.

He stood there motionless like the other busts and statues, contemplating his next course of action. He heard the chapel clock striking eight o'clock. The college would be stirring into life. Retracing his steps, he ran down the stairs and, giving a final backwards glance at the bust of J.J.Thomson, he closed the outer library door behind him.

As Georgi Sloboda drove Dina across Moscow early on Tuesday morning to the commission of enquiry at the Serbsky Institute, there existed a quiet calm between them. Sloboda had used all his considerable professional skills to instil a sense of assurance and optimism into his companion.

He had affirmed that any trace of hysteria or emotional outburst on their part would play straight into the hands of the prosecution. They must remain level-headed and rational at all times.

As the pale blue Zils drew to a halt at some traffic lights, Sloboda turned to his right and said, "You understand, Dina, that this is a politically motivated case?"

Dina nodded.

"The phrase used in Director Morozov's letter, 'special examination', tells us that. You may have noticed that he made no mention of psychiatric diagnosis."

"Is that why they moved him from Lubyanka to the Serbsky Institute?" asked Dina.

"Correct," replied Dr Sloboda. "As this was not a criminal case covered by Article Seventy of the 1960 Criminal Code, which is punishable by deprivation of freedom from six months to seven years, they have resorted to the pretext of abnormality of behaviour, which covers a multitude of sins. It's an unusual case, really, as it revolves around the title of a musical work. It is not an article in a dissident publication, or a political tract expressing so-called slanderous remarks about Soviet ethics or politics. It is therefore not Samizdat as such. So, they could never make the vital allegation of 'intent' to undermine the Soviet state stick. It would never hold up in court." Sloboda put the car in gear and pulled off again into the traffic.

"Do you think it will be easier to secure my father's release from the Serbsky Institute?" asked Dina.

"Well, if there were any integrity or autonomy in the Soviet Society of Psychiatrists and Neurologists, I could give you an emphatic yes to that question. Unfortunately, the organisation is manipulated by the KGB, and psychiatry as a whole is dominated by the school of Snezhnevsky, the current Chief Psychiatrist of the Ministry of Health. It is his controversial theories on schizophrenia that hold sway, and his complicity that allows the Ministry of Internal Affairs and the Ministry of Justice to treat dissent as a form of psychological abnormality. How was your father when you saw him last?"

"It was only a few days after he was first detained," recalled Dina. "He seemed subdued and incoherent. He told me he had been having hallucinations. His memory seemed a little hazy, and he was afraid of what would become of him." She swallowed hard to maintain her composure.

"Hm," said Sloboda. "It sounds like they've been administering some kind of depressant drug."

Dina remembered Alexei's words. "A friend of mine thought it might be *andaksin*," she said.

"It's possible," replied Sloboda. "Who was this friend?"

"Oh, just a friend," she replied, "just a friend."

"Hm," pondered Sloboda. "It's designed to induce the onset of mild paranoia, so that when he comes before the commission, he will exhibit all the signs that the psychiatrists have attributed to him. The drugs *aminazin* and *sulfazin* are most commonly used to treat political dissidents. They induce shock and depression; symptoms that a mental patient would be expected to evidence."

Dina shot a worried look across at her companion.

Sloboda smiled and patted her on the knee. "Do not worry, Dina. I'm only preparing you for the worst. I should be deluding us both if I told you that I expected Vladimir Maksimovich to be his normal, healthy self. Better fear the worst and be pleasantly surprised is my philosophy."

Dina reciprocated his reassuring smile.

By now, they were crossing Borovitskaya Ploshchad and travelling West down Volkhonka Ulitza. Past the Tolstoy Museum on the left and the Pushkin Museum on the right, they were now on Kropotkinskaya Ulitza. This was one of the most remarkable streets in the old quarter of Moscow, where almost every house and building was of some historic or architectural significance.

Just before the junction with Kropotkinsky Pereulok, Sloboda slowed the car down and pulled into the right-hand side of the road. Opposite stood a daunting pair of high steel gates flanked by two armed sentries. Behind stood an old stone building resembling an ambassadorial residence, such as those of Denmark and Finland just around the corner.

"Well, that's it," said Sloboda, "the Serbsky Institute." As they both looked across the road, a tall man in the uniform of a KGB Colonel was being saluted by the guards as they allowed him onto the premises.

"Who's that?" asked Dina. "Do you recognise him?"

"Unfortunately, I do," replied Sloboda. "That's Dr Daniel Luntz, head of the special examination department of the Serbsky Institute."

"But he's a KGB officer," protested Dina. "And he's one of the four men on the commission of enquiry. I remember his name from Director Morozov's letter. Surely that can't be right."

"I did warn you that the Institute was merely a tool in the hands of the KGB. Colonel Luntz comes to work in his military uniform and then miraculously transforms into Dr Luntz."

"Then we have no chance," said Dina, choking back the tears.

"Of course, we have," said Sloboda firmly. "Luntz is not a medical specialist. The only two words he knows are 'paranoid' and 'schizophrenia'. His only tactics are those of fear and intimidation. If we show him that we can stand up to him and break down his case with rational argument, we can beat him. We can. But I need your help. So, pull yourself together, Dina. Make your father proud of you." He leaned over and gave her a warm embrace.

Pulling the steering wheel sharply to the left, the Zils crossed the traffic and came face to face with the steel gates of the Serbsky Institute.

At nine o'clock prompt, Dina Russakov and Dr Georgi Sloboda were ushered into the committee room of the Serbsky Institute, where Vladimir Maksimovich Russakov was due to face the commission of enquiry. A large oval table was prepared with around a dozen place settings, consisting of blank note pads and pens, glass tumblers and jugs of iced water. A male secretary sat in one corner to take shorthand notes and minutes of the meeting. A small Japanese pocket tape machine rested on his lap.

The four members of the commission were already seated at their places on the far side of the table. Only the Chairman, Boris Vladimirovich Shostakovich, acknowledged the arrival of Dina and Dr Sloboda. He peered over the edge of his reading glasses and indicated for the usher to show them to their appointed seats directly opposite. The atmosphere was glacial, not to say hostile. Sloboda seemed unruffled by the cool reception. He took a drink of water, cleared his throat, and took a very upright position in his chair.

"Gentlemen," said Shostakovich finally, "shall we begin. Dr Sloboda, Miss Russakov, may I introduce the members of the commission in this case?" He gestured to his left, "Professor Portnov, Director of the Institute of Psychiatry of the Academy of Medical Sciences; Professor Morozov, Head of the Department of Psychiatry in the Institute for Advanced Medical Training." Turning to his right, he concluded, "and my colleague Professor Luntz, Head of the Special Examination Department at the Serbsky Institute."

Immediately, Dr Sloboda stood up and declared, "I wish to protest the composition of this commission."

In a calm, over-controlled voice, Chairman Shostakovich replied, "To which member in particular do you object?"

Sloboda pointed directly at Shostakovich himself. "To you, comrade. Are you not a forensic psychiatrist, and does not your experience only encompass criminal cases?"

"It is true that I am a specialist in the branch of forensic psychiatry," replied Shostakovich.

"As this is not a criminal case, and comrade Russakov has not been brought before a court, I maintain your ineligibility to serve on this commission."

"My capacity on this commission," replied Shostakovich, "is that of Chairman. I am wearing the hat of the Academy of Medical Sciences, not the hat of forensic psychiatry."

"That is highly convenient," said Sloboda scornfully. "You realise that, according to the regulations, relations or representatives of the subject have the right to challenge the composition of the commission."

Shostakovich smiled and turned to the official notary. "Your protest is duly noted. Now, may we proceed?"

The male secretary obligingly made notes on the verbal exchange. The first skirmish appeared to be over.

Sloboda sat down and leaned back in his chair. After a brief pause, he again rose to his feet. Shostakovich gave him a questioning look. The other members of the commission were beginning to become impatient.

"Yes, doctor?" said the Chairman.

"As I intimated on the telephone last night, I wish to have the commission deferred to a later date."

"I see no reason..." interjected Dr Luntz, whose impatience had finally got the better of him.

"There is every reason," said Sloboda emphatically. "We haven't been given sufficient time to enlist our own expert psychiatric witness, nor to solicit the written testimony of friends and work colleagues of comrade Russakov as to his mental state, both of which are essential to our defence."

"This is merely a preliminary commission," replied Shostakovich. "The main commission is scheduled for a later date. You may bring full representations to bear then."

"Hm," snorted Sloboda, sceptically and again sat down. Before he had the chance to lodge any further protests, Shostakovich hailed the usher. "Bring in comrade Russakov."

Flanked by two armed officers in KGB uniform, Russakov entered the committee room. His movements were uncoordinated, and he required assistance to walk. His face was drawn and unshaven. His empty, expressionless gaze looked straight ahead. He didn't seem to notice the presence of his daughter, Dina, and Dr Sloboda. There was no emotional acknowledgement. Nothing.

Sloboda felt Dina's whole body trembling by his side at the sight of her father in such a state. He clasped her hand under the table and whispered in her ear, "Remember what I told you, Dina. Let me do all the talking, and don't give them the satisfaction of seeing you break down." She nodded in assent.

Vladimir Russakov was led to the head of the table. One of the guards drew back the solitary chair, whilst the other guard put his hand on the patient's shoulder, coercing him to sit down. When he was in place, the two officers withdrew to stand one on either side of the window overlooking Kropotkinskaya Ulitsa.

Sloboda rose to his feet.

"I must protest. This man has obviously been subjected to the forcible treatment of chemical drugs. From his lack of muscular control, I would surmise that comrade Russakov has undergone treatment with aminazin. How can he be expected to defend himself before the commission if he is not in full command of his mental and physical faculties?"

Dr Luntz pounced on this. "So, then you admit that comrade Russakov is deranged?"

"Only through your inhuman treatment," retorted Sloboda.

"Gentlemen," interjected Chairman Shostakovich, "this and other issues will receive full discussion during the course of the commission of enquiry. Now, may we begin?"

Dr Sloboda and Dr Luntz exchanged hostile stares across the table as Shostakovich continued, "Comrade Vladimir Maksimovich Russakov was detained on Monday, the twentieth of September, under the regulations on the emergency hospitalisation of mentally ill persons who are a public danger. Notably under sections 3b, and I quote 'irregular behaviour accompanied by psychological disorder (hallucinations, delusions, a syndrome of psychological automatism, a syndrome of disordered consciousness, pathological impulsiveness) if accompanied by acute affective tension and a stirring towards its active expression'. And 3d, 'a hypochondriac delusional condition, causing an irregular, aggressive attitude in the patient towards individuals, organisations and institutions'. After his committal, comrade Russakov was subjected to compulsory treatment under the supervision of Dr Daniel Luntz of the Special Examination Department of the Serbsky Institute. Professors Portnov and Morozov have confirmed Dr Luntz's diagnosis."

Dr Sloboda interrupted Chairman Shostakovich, "Would

you mind telling this commission exactly how comrade Russakov manifested this so-called psychological disorder, and exactly which individuals, organisations, and institutions he has threatened and how?"

"With pleasure," replied Shostakovich. He opened the file in front of him and took out several pieces of typed paper. "I have here notarised statements from comrade Russakov's colleagues at the Tchaikovsky Conservatory attesting to his deviant behaviour. For example, on the third of September, he was verbally abusive and physically aggressive towards Assistant Director Polyakov of the Conservatory when asked about his latest composition, a symphonic poem entitled, I believe, Freedom for Czechoslovakia. On the ninth of September, at a meeting of the Soviet Union of Composers, comrade Russakov was publicly critical of the works of Tikhon Khrennikov for their patriotic Soviet themes. Of course, everyone knows that Khrennikov is the premier Soviet composer."

Dina couldn't resist a contemptuous snort. She knew that her father occupied that position. This temporary diversion caused Vladimir Russakov to look at his daughter for the first time. There was a glimmer of recognition, the spark of emotional response. Immediately, one of the guards stepped forward and laid his hand on the prisoner's shoulder. Russakov's gaze immediately frosted over. He was an automaton once again.

Dr Sloboda was not at all surprised by these contrived pieces of corroborative evidence. These people had obviously been subjected to pressure from the Director of the Conservatory and from the local Communist Party Committee, which oversaw the Union of Composers. There was no such thing as a free trade union in Soviet society.

Shostakovich pressed on, "And then there is the question of the composition itself – 'Freedom for Czechoslovakia'. This represents a direct slander on the foreign policy of the Soviet

Union with regard to our allies in the Eastern Bloc."

"If it were a slander," countered Sloboda, "why has comrade Russakov not been committed before a criminal court?"

"We have our reasons," replied Shostakovich obscurely.

"And I know very well what those reasons are," retorted Sloboda.

"You know very well that you would not win. And so, you resort to the use of psychiatry for punitive purposes at the behest of the KGB.

"You are a disgrace to your profession, all of you. When the World Psychiatric Association hears of this, you will be struck off the International Register."

Shostakovich responded calmly. "Dr Sloboda, I shall pretend that I did not hear those remarks." He turned to the official notary. "Strike the doctor's utterances from the official record."

Sloboda realised he had pushed his criticism to the limits and returned to a state of composure.

"The solution is very simple, doctor," said Dr Luntz with blinding frankness. "If you can persuade your patient to change the title of his work to 'October Revolution', he will be discharged from our care forthwith."

"There, we have it," replied Sloboda triumphantly, "the real issue... forget all talk of psychiatric analysis and paranoid schizophrenia, the real issue is one of propaganda." He turned in the direction of Russakov and asked him directly. "Are you willing, Vladimir Maksimovich, to meet their request, to change the title of your symphony?"

Russakov gave him a blank look as if questioning the doctor's own sanity. "Symphony, what symphony?" The syllables stumbled off his tongue.

Dina was barely able to control her distress. Sloboda echoed her emotions. "I refuse to allow this commission of enquiry to continue until comrade Russakov is brought before us in a rational state of mind."

Dr Luntz replied, "It is for the very reason that comrade Russakov is not in a rational state of mind that he finds himself in psychiatric care in the first place."

"You know precisely what I mean," retorted Sloboda, "untainted by your mind-destroying drugs, that is what I mean by rational."

Luntz replied, "So long as comrade Russakov manifests the symptoms for which he was originally interned, his course of treatment will continue under my supervision."

Dr Sloboda knew that he could not win this argument.

Chairman Shostakovich brought the meeting to a conclusion. "Under Section 8 of the regulations, this commission will reconvene in one month's time, on the fifth of November. Dr Sloboda, Miss Russakov, you may have access to your patient during regular visiting hours. If there is any improvement in comrade Russakov's mental state in the meantime..."

"In other words, if he changes his mind," interjected Luntz.

Shostakovich frowned at his companion. "I repeat, if there is any improvement in comrade Russakov's mental state in the meantime, he may be released on his own recognisance."

The committee rose as one. The two guards took Russakov securely in their grasp and led him swiftly away. Dina and Dr Sloboda were left alone, save for the usher, who appeared unmoved by the events of the past hour.

As Dina and Dr Sloboda got back into the Zils, which was parked around the side of the Serbsky Institute, the stress of the experience finally began to tell. "They're never going to set him free," sobbed Dina.

"Of course, they are," Sloboda consoled her. "I guarantee that. Pressure from outside the Soviet Union is growing. I am told by a reliable source that the press in Western Europe and the United States has mounted a campaign to free Vladimir Maksimovich."

"What can they do?" replied Dina desolately.

Sloboda ushered her into the front passenger seat of his car before going around and sliding into the driver's side. "You heard me mention the World Psychiatric Association," he said, "well, I happen to know that comrade Snezhnevsky, the Chief Psychiatrist of the Ministry of Health and Secretary of the AMS, is about to attend an international congress in Vienna. He won't want this affair hanging over his head, or he will have to face some rather uncomfortable questions from his international colleagues. I'm sure that he will be bringing pressure to bear on the Serbsky commission to bring the enquiry to an equitable conclusion, and that means one that will cause him the least embarrassment."

"But it doesn't necessarily mean that they will free my father," said Dina. "They could simply make encouraging noises about his imminent release until the international congress was over, and then, well, you know."

"Yes, I know exactly what you mean, Dina," said Sloboda as he turned the key in the ignition. "They can be damned devious when they have to be, but so can I." He engaged gear and accelerated hard. The Zils slewed round on the gravel forecourt and, wheels spinning, shot out through the gates into the mid-morning traffic.

Realising they were travelling East, Dina said, "Where are we going?"

"I'm taking you home," he replied.

"No, I must get back to work," she insisted.

"What, after that ordeal?" protested Sloboda. "It is my medical opinion that you should take the rest of the day off to recuperate."

"No, I have things to do," she insisted once again.

From experience and from the tone of Dina's voice, Sloboda knew it was pointless trying to dissuade her. She was about as stubborn and hard-headed as he was. He immediately performed a U-turn and headed West in the direction of Zubovskaya Ploschad. Here they joined Smolensky Boulevard, which formed part of the Moscow Ring Road. After a couple of miles, they reached the Intersection with Prospekt Kalinina.

During the car journey, Dina had time to reflect. She knew that the battle lines were drawn. It would take a tremendous struggle to have Vladimir Maksimovich liberated. She would have to use all her mental and physical resources in the battle. She steeled herself for this task. She had a strong ally in Dr Sloboda and a distant ally in Alexei. Having spent the last twenty-four hours brooding over the commission, the question of her search for the marble index had temporarily been suspended. This had now to be reinitiated.

Despite his misgivings, Dr Sloboda could sense the hardening of Dina's resolve. She would come through the experience. There were no frailties in her mental make-up, just as there weren't any in that of her father. He only hoped that he could get to Vladimir Russakov in time before the chemical drug treatment had done irrevocable damage. He pulled the Zils into the side of the road outside the KGB building. "Are you sure you'll be alright?" he asked.

Dina pursed her lips and forced a smile. "I'll see you tonight," she replied, "and don't worry about me. Tell Larissa I can't wait to sample her beef stroganoff. See, I haven't lost my appetite."

Sloboda laughed and was extremely impressed with Dina's resilience. "I'll break open a bottle of Mukuzani if you like."

"That would be lovely," she replied, getting out of the car. She ran up the steps without looking back, but could hear the Zils accelerating away as Dr Sloboda put his foot to the floor. He always drove as if he were in a desperate hurry. So was Dina, but in a different sense.

The guard checked her pass. He didn't query the fact that she was nearly three hours late for work. It was not his place, though his disapproval was self-evident. She raced up the stairs to the first floor, opened the double doors, past the tape store and pushed open the red door on the left marked 'systems analysis'. She threw her coat over the back of her chair rather than leave it in the cloakroom and sat down at her desk.

Eyes were raised in her direction, but they were lowered again almost immediately. It was not so much that she was unpopular at work, but rather that her colleagues were frightened to be seen associating with her for fear of reprisals on them and their families.

Dina had barely had time to open her desk drawers and take out the print-out of the UN personnel file update run when she felt a shadow fall across her back. She knew who it was without looking around. Boychenko's steely voice said softly, "Miss Russakov, this is the second time this week that I have had cause to speak to you on the question of punctuality. Would you care to account for your whereabouts for the past three hours? I should first of all warn you that I have spent most of this morning in programming with comrade Semichastny, and Anatoly Dobrynin was in my line of sight, so that avenue of escape is now closed to you."

Although no one's head was turned in their direction, it was evident that all attention was focused on the imminent storm that was about to break. Boychenko was renowned for his short fuse of a temper. Everyone looked forward to his outbursts, as long as they themselves were not the butt of his venom. It helped to relieve the monotony of the work.

Dina remained calm. "I had a written dispensation from Chairman Andropov to attend the commission of enquiry into my father's case. A duplicate memo was sent to your office. I left it with your secretary, and the staff branch was also informed."

"Yes, of course," said Boychenko, the wind taken completely out of his sails. "Of course, I knew about that, you foolish girl," although obviously he didn't. Either his secretary had failed to bring it to his attention, or he himself had overlooked it in his in-tray.

Boychenko tried his best to extricate himself. "That doesn't mean you can sit around all morning, or what's left of it, twiddling your thumbs. The work has still got to be done. I expect you think your comrades here," he gestured extravagantly around the office, "should cover for you and work twice as hard in your absence. We expect everyone to pull their weight. And that includes you, comrade Russakov. Is that understood?" When he knew he was in the wrong, Boychenko wouldn't admit it. He tended to resort to ridicule and sarcasm. His overweening manner was brought to bear in belittling his staff, particularly the female members, who were often reduced to tears.

Dina, however, was made of sterner stuff. She also knew that he held a secret longing for her. The fact that she wouldn't entertain his amorous advances meant that his scorn was twice as acerbic. Still, it was also a hold she held over him. "I should like to talk to you on another matter," said Dina. "Would you care to continue our conversation out here, or would you rather we step into your office?"

As the subject of Dina's question was unknown to him, and as he felt he had been sufficiently humiliated already for one morning, he replied brusquely, "Yes, step into my office." The decided advantage of home territory appealed strongly to him.

Dina followed Boychenko down to the far end of the systems analysts' office – an open-plan affair in which members of the executive staff supervised clerical grades in the submission of trial programs, vetted amendments, and checked print-outs against master copies. The verbal exchange had not gone unnoticed. Much as Dina was a person whose company was strictly to be avoided, they could not help but admire her for standing up to comrade supervisor.

Boychenko opened his office door and entered, leaving Dina to follow and close the door behind her. He strode around his desk and sank down into a large leather swivel chair. He leaned forward menacingly over his desk and indicated for Dina to sit down opposite him. His natural height advantage, together with the additional height of his chair, meant that Boychenko towered over Dina; this was a typical psychological management ploy. He raised his eyebrows and waited for her to speak. Unabashed, she spoke up confidently. "As you are now aware," she stressed, playing on the embarrassment of Boychenko's former ignorance, "my father is the subject of a commission of enquiry and has been detained for psychiatric tests at the Serbsky Institute."

Boychenko nodded.

It distressed Dina to talk about it, but her resolve was strengthened by a desire not to give her supervisor the satisfaction of seeing her anxiety. "Not that this will in any way affect my work, you understand," she continued, "but I should like to put in a request to serve another tour of duty on sweeping the archives over on Prospekt Marksa."

Boychenko looked rather puzzled at her sudden interest in the redundant card indexes. "Would you care to explain why?" he asked.

"Certainly," she replied. "I feel that my presence here is inhibiting my work comrades and affecting their efficiency." This was indeed true. The other systems analysts had been constantly on edge for the past two weeks. Amongst other things, they feared that they would be called on by the commission of enquiry to give evidence against Dina Russakov and so to discredit the whole family. The local Party Committee could instruct them to fabricate stories about her disloyalty, lack of commitment, and general anti-social behaviour. As yet, it had not happened. If she were out of their sight, she would also be out of their minds.

"Your sensitivity towards your work colleagues is indeed touching," said Boychenko contemptuously. He suspected an ulterior motive but couldn't put his finger on it. He leaned back in his chair, and his face broke into a broad smile. "Of course, you could make life much easier for them and for yourself if you consented to come out to dinner with me."

Dina had been expecting this. He always resorted to emotional blackmail to try and put forward his sexual advances. Other girls in the office had succumbed under the pressure, but it hadn't made their lives any easier. Once he had slept with them, Boychenko had cast them off and made their lives even more of a misery. To Boychenko, Dina represented the ultimate, unattainable woman and was thus his greatest challenge. To date, she had rejected his advances out of hand, but things were different now.

In order to attain the ultimate goal of the release of her father, she was willing to resort to any extremes, which formerly would have been unthinkable. "I'll send a car round to pick you up. It's Izmaylovsky Park apartments, isn't it?" he asked.

"That's right. 37C. I'll look forward to it." As Dina got up from her chair, she turned back and added almost as an afterthought. "Oh, and the other matter, my secondment to the archives."

"It's as good as done. I'll have it sanctioned by the staff branch immediately. And take the rest of the morning off, Dina. I'm sure the experience of the commission must have been an ordeal for you. You can report to Prospekt Marks this afternoon."

It was as simple as that. Dina felt a surge of power that she could manipulate men so easily. But at what cost? The time for redemption would come later. As she came out of Boychenko's office, the low rumble of gossip decayed into a stony silence. When they saw her put on her coat and head for the door, the mutterings began again. Dina smiled inwardly as she speculated on their interpretation of her encounter with Boychenko. No doubt they thought she had been suspended and sent home under threat of appearing before the Personnel Director to be censured for her poor work attendance and insubordinate attitude. She wanted to tell them that she had wound Boychenko around her little finger, but her personal satisfaction would have to suffice.

She gave them not a second glance and breezed down the stairs and out of the main entrance past the amazed armed guard in uniform. It was still only eleven o'clock as she entered the Smolenskaya metro station and travelled the two short stops to Kalininskaya. Instead of turning left and crossing the road from the exit to bring her to the archive building on Prospekt Marksa, Dina went around the corner to the new building of the Lenin Library.

The original site was used for the archives of the Czarist Foreign Ministry, and before that, as the palace of Natalya Naryshkina, the mother of Peter the Great. The new library made no attempt to blend in with the classical architecture of the original, and its facade was in fact a replica of a rejected design for the Dniepr Hydroelectric Power Station.

Dina knew exactly what she was looking for as she entered one of the twenty reading rooms. Out of the fifteen million books, she was only interested in a handful – those written by and concerning Mikhail Andreyevich Suslov, Chief Ideologue and Second Secretary of the Communist Party of the Soviet Union. He headed the departments of propaganda, culture, science, and education, and as such was the second most influential person in the Politburo after General Secretary Brezhnev. More importantly, he had the ultimate say in the fate of her father, Vladimir Maksimovich Russakov. It would be his signature and not that of Dr Shostakovich or Dr Luntz of the Serbsky Institute, which would ensure rehabilitation and freedom.

Along one wall of all the reading rooms were stacked in alphabetical order the collected works of Politburo members, past and present. They included their articles and drafts of speeches made at public occasions, such as the Lenin Day Memorial. Dina knew as well as anyone that all the material had been carefully selected, vetted, and edited. For example, in speeches made before 1953, all praise of Stalin was removed, whilst all mention of Khrushchev was deleted from the dates 1953 to 1964. Comrade L.I. Brezhnev's ran to seven volumes, whilst Mikhail Suslov's ran to a more modest two.

Dina took down the tomes from the shelf and retired with them to a reading cubicle. In the front of the first volume was a potted biography of the subject, outlining his life and achievements. She read as follows:

> 'Mikhail Andreyevich Suslov was born in 1902. After a glorious career in the Komsomol, he became a full member of the Communist Party of the Soviet Union at the age of nineteen. His early interest in ideology, for which he was to show such an outstanding aptitude later in life, was already being put to good use as an instructor at Moscow State University and the Stalin Academy of Industry. From there, he graduated into executive positions in the Communist Party Central Control Commission in Moscow.'

Dina noticed that there was no mention here of his involvement in the Stalinist purges in the Urals and the Ukraine. These episodes had been conveniently omitted.

Prior to the Second World War, comrade Suslov was Party First Secretary in the city of Rostov-on-Don, Deputy to the Supreme Soviet, and a member of the Central Auditing Commission of the All-Union Communist Party. In 1941, he became a full member of the Party's Central Committee. During the war, comrade Suslov served on the Military Council of the North Caucasian Front and as Chief of Staff of the Stavropol partisan forces. After the war, in 1946, he became a member of the Central Committee's Organisation Bureau (Orgburo). Next, he rose to the position of Secretary of the Central Committee, and in 1949–50, he was editor of the Party's key publication, the daily newspaper, Pravda. It was from this intellectual foundation that comrade Suslov came to be regarded as the Party's leading authority on ideology and orthodox Marxism. In consolidation of this position, comrade Suslov was appointed Head of the Soviet delegation and Chairman of the Communist Information Bureau (Cominform).

Dina noticed further that no mention was made here of his instrumental part in implementing Stalin's ideas, and his brief fall from favour in 1953. In fact, in most people's minds, Suslov was still closely associated with Stalinism. She read on.

'Comrade Suslov's ideological strength was put to the test in 1956 when he was called to the Soviet Embassy in Budapest to fight off the insidious liberalisation of Marxist Communism.'

Dina again found herself reading between the lines. It had been the Russian troops that had suppressed the Hungarian uprising and not Suslov's powerful ideological arguments. As a prominent member of the Central Committee, he resisted the liberalisation policies of First Secretary Khrushchev and was instrumental in the appointment of Leonid I. Brezhnev to the post. Dina knew that he and Brezhnev had vied for top office and that he had lost out thanks to the power of the Brezhnev mafia behind the scenes. From this point on, he had to settle for the number two position in the Secretariat of the Politburo. Dina skipped a few pages to bring her right up to date.

'In March of 1975, comrade Suslov was appointed Chief Ideologue, a position which also carries control of the Ministry of Culture, the Academy of Sciences, the Komsomol and education system, the Union of Writers, Composers, Artists and Journalists, censorship, Tass, and the Novosty Press.' The list of responsibilities seemed endless. It went on and on. At the bottom, there was a brief personal resume. Comrade Suslov is married and has one son. The family lives on Kutuzovsky Prospekt. Ever since the age of thirty-seven, comrade Suslov has suffered from maturity-onset diabetes. It is a manifestation of the man's fortitude and dedication that he has contributed so much to his country despite this disability. Dina snapped the book shut. The germ of an idea was taking shape in her mind.

9

Alexei returned from the Mullard Observatory at lunchtime. He had given the Director, Martin Harvey, the excuse that he wished to consult some reference works at the Library on the Madingley Road Site of the Cavendish Laboratories. It was a perfectly plausible pretext, and Harvey had raised no objections. The fact that the various departments of the Cavendish were scattered in and around Cambridge eminently suited Alexei's purposes. It gave him flexibility of movement and time to pursue affairs even more important than his own academic studies.

He just had to find the significance of the marble index in Wordsworth's Prelude. It was preying on his mind. At number twenty, Trinity Street stood Heffers, the university bookshop. The college library may have been stripped bare of Wordsworth's works, but surely the premier bookshop in Cambridge would have a healthy stock. Stopping just inside the main doors, Alexei consulted the store guide. English literature was situated on the first floor. Swiftly, he made his way up the open-plan stairs two at a time, brushing past an alarmed shop assistant with an armful of books on the way.

The atmosphere was similar to that of a public library. People appeared to be using it as a reference library rather than as a commercial bookseller. They would browse all day without buying anything. The fact that Alexei was in such a hurry to reach the shelves of English poetry signalled the fact that he was a potential buyer and not a lingering browser. He ran his finger along the spines of the books ranked in alphabetical order. Shakespeare was never-ending. Shakespeare, Shakespeare, and yet more Shakespeare. The S's seemed to go on forever. He seemed to be running out of shelves.

At last, he reached the W's. He seized the first volume of Wordsworth with such alacrity that the whole metal shelving structure shook. A girl assistant with owlish glasses looked up from her desk to see what the disturbance was. Alexei's smile made her rapidly lower her eyes again.

He returned to his quest. Volume One of the Everyman's Library edition of Wordsworth's poems. He perused the contents page, which listed an interminable number of odes, pastoral poems, and so on. Volume two was the same. With desperation, he grabbed the third and final volume. With great relief, his eyes alighted on The Prelude, comprising some fourteen different sections, or books as they were called. Book Three of The Prelude was entitled Residence at Cambridge. Book Six was entitled Cambridge and the Alps. He turned first to Book Three and began to read.

> *"It was a dreary morning when the wheels*
> *Rolled over a wide plain o'erhung with clouds,*
> *And nothing cheered our way till first we saw*
> *The long-roofed chapel of King's College lift*
> *Turrets and pinnacles in answering files,*
> *Extending high above a dusky grove."*

The words seemed to echo and reflect Alexei's own first impression of Cambridge. Following the disappointment of the railway station, it was not until he saw the facade of

King's College that he became fully aware of the architectural treasure-house of Cambridge. He read on and came across the passage Andrew Marriott had quoted to him about the Hoop Inn, a public house which once stood in Bridge Street and was a meeting place for political cliques. This was all very interesting, but not what he was looking for.

'The Evangelist St John, my patron, was.' In other words, he was a member of St. John's College.

> "Three Gothic courts are his, and in the first
> Was my abiding place, a nook obscure,
> Right underneath, the college kitchens made
> A humming sound, less tuneable than bees,
> But hardly less industrious; with shrill notes
> Of sharp command and scolding intermixed."

Alexei recalled his trip with Marriott to Kitchen Lane between St John's and Trinity to see the outside of Wordsworth's old rooms. It was certainly in a far from salubrious spot.

> "Near me hung Trinity's loquacious clock,
> Who never let the quarters, night or day,
> Slip by him unproclaimed, and told the hours
> Twice over with a male and female voice.
> Her pealing organ was my neighbour too."

This reminded Alexei of the sleepless night he had just spent lying awake on his bed, listening to the Trinity Chapel clock strike every quarter until dawn, when he had run down to the Wren Library. He felt a distant sympathy with Wordsworth's juvenile recollections as an undergraduate. He continued to read.

> "And from my pillow, looking forth by light"

Alexei felt a frisson of excitement. This was it; the passage he had been searching for. He looked up from the page guiltily, as if half expecting a stukach or a KGB agent to be peering over his shoulder. The nearest person to him was the girl assistant in the owlish spectacles, and her mind was otherwise occupied in cataloguing an influx of new books. Alexei relaxed. He read on slowly now, savouring every word, as if the whole mystery of the marble index was about to be unfurled to him. In his heart of hearts, though, he knew that the quest was only just beginning.

> "And from my pillow, looking forth by light
> Of moon or favouring stars, I could behold
> The antechapel where the statue stood
> Of Newton with his prism and silent face,
> The marble index of a mind for ever
> Voyaging through strange seas of Thought alone."

His recollection had been correct. The name of Newton was in there, and the marble index seemed to be referring directly to him. How could a person be a marble index? Was it some kind of scientific term? Alexei read the passage again. The antechapel presumably referred to the antechapel of Trinity College Chapel, which Wordsworth could see from the window of his room in St John's. There must be a statue of Sir Isaac Newton in the college antechapel.

Then it struck him. The marble must refer to the statue itself. A marble statue of Newton. But what about the index? Could it refer to the eminent scientist's mind? It said 'the marble index of a mind'. Index inferred the storage of information in a rational, alphabetical form. Was the information stored in the real mind of Newton or in the abstract structure of the statue itself?

Infuriatingly, there was no glossary, no asterisk indicating that the reader refer to an explanation by the editor. It was left to the interpretation in the reader's mind. At least one thing was definite. Wordsworth was envisaging in his words a marble statue of Sir Isaac Newton, which stood in the antechapel of Trinity College. That was Alexei's next obvious port of call.

He closed the book, put it under his arm, and approached the girl assistant. He took out a ten-pound note, placed it in front of her, and without waiting for change or a receipt, dashed out of the shop. Heffers was almost directly opposite Trinity. Past the porters' lodge and through Great Gate he ran. Turning right, he came face to face with the sixteenth-century chapel.

After stopping an instant to catch his breath, Alexei stepped momentously over the threshold. Straight ahead of him stood a marble statue. Alexei approached it tentatively, as if afraid of waking the silent monument. He examined the base, which was inscribed with Macaulay. He turned to his right and, with precipitate steps, approached the next statue. This was Tennyson. By now, he was becoming more and more agitated. Where was Sir Isaac Newton? To the right of the chapel entrance itself stood another marble statue. Alexei didn't dare look at the inscription. Despairingly, he saw that the base bore the name Whewell.

Instinctively, he looked back over his right shoulder. Straight ahead of him, across the floor and to the left of the antechapel entrance, stood an imposing figure in academic cap and gown. It was Newton. He was sure. He had walked right past it in his haste. With a sense of wonderment, Alexei crossed the antechapel and came to a halt below the smooth, white marble figure of Sir Isaac Newton. This was indeed the marble index of Wordsworth's Prelude. He felt like shouting out loud, proclaiming to the world that he had found the marble index.

He wished that Dina were there to share the joy of his discovery. He had fulfilled her obligation. Her father would go free. They could be reunited. He could trade the marble index with the KGB for their freedom. He and Dina could defect together to the West. Then he had to check himself. What, in fact, did he know?

The marble index was a statue of Sir Isaac Newton, but how did it tie in with the supposed list of names in the archives of the KGB Central Index? Was this indeed the marble index as envisaged by Burgess and Blunt? It was such an unusual expression that it just had to be the same. Alexei tried feverishly to convince himself of that. Burgess and Blunt were both literary men, and both were members of Trinity College. The allusion would be well known to them.

He studied the marble statue more closely. True to Wordsworth's lines, Newton held in his hand a glass prism, through which he had discovered the spectrum and the composition of white light. The colours of the rainbow had first been revealed to him and set down in his treatise on Opticks. His other hand was outstretched as if pointing towards infinity. His face was indeed silent, and Wordsworth had readily captured the great scientist's expression in his words 'voyaging through strange seas of thought alone'.

Alexei bent down and examined the base. It was inscribed 'Newton qui genus humanum ingenio superavit' and on the back of the statue it read 'posuit Robertus Smith ST Collegii Lujus S. Trinitas Magister – MDCCLV. L.F.Roubiliac.' The latter was presumably the name of the sculptor. It rang a bell with Alexei. Louis Francois Roubiliac. He seemed to know that name. Then it came to him. That morning in the Wren Library. The centre aisle was flanked with busts of Francis Bacon, Isaac Newton himself, and many others, all by the same sculptor, Roubiliac. In Trinity College, both in the antechapel and in the Wren Library, there was a veritable index of the works of

Louis-François Roubiliac. And Sir Isaac Newton appeared to be his favourite subject. There were two busts in the library and a full-size statue in the chapel. Alexei did not know if this fact was of any relevant significance to his investigation, but it struck him nevertheless as very interesting.

He circled around the statue, taking in every detail of the structure. His eyes were momentarily distracted to the far wall beyond Newton's empty gaze, which bore the large inscription in Latin 'pro muro erant nobis tam in nocte quam in die'. Below in alphabetical order were column after column of names. The Roman numerals MCMXXXIX–MCMXLV concluded the commemoration. Alexei surmised from the date that these were the names of the young men of the college who had been killed in action in the Second World War, and his thoughts turned to the millions of Russians who had died in the same conflict on the Eastern Front. Shaking his head in remembrance, his thoughts returned to the present task at hand. Once again, he looked up into the white, unseeing eyes of Sir Isaac Newton and wondered what secrets they held.

The tolling of the chapel bell roused Alexei from his reflections. It was one o'clock. Whilst he was in town during the day, Alexei decided to look over the site of the old Cavendish Laboratories. He was now familiar with the new Madingley Road complex and the Mullard Radio Astronomy Observatory, but the original Victorian buildings in the centre of Cambridge, dating from the 1870s, were as yet a mystery to him.

Besides, he had an ulterior motive. He recalled from his conversation with Dr McCabe that the special laboratory financed by the Royal Society to further the research of his countryman, Piotr Kapitsa, was situated on that site. Curiosity and a nagging sense that somehow Kapitsa was caught up in his quest for the marble index drove him on.

Emerging into Trinity Street, he turned left into King's Parade, then left up Bene't Street. The entrance to the New

Museums Site, as it was incongruously known, was from the pedestrianised Free School Lane. Past the Whipple Museum housing an exhibition on micro-spectroscopy, Alexei came to a halt beneath an archway through which he could see the uneasy mixture of dark Victorian edifices and sandy-coloured computer departments. Hanging in a glass frame under the arch was a faded ground plan of the site. Alexei ran his fingers over it. According to the plan, the Mond Laboratory was straight ahead through the archway. He walked on through and came face to face with a circular, sandy brick structure with curved glass surrounds like the visor of a motorcycle crash-helmet.

There was a plaque to the right of the front door. Alexei approached and read the inscription – Committee for Aerial Photography. Perhaps he had misread the plan. There was nobody about to ask, so he returned to the archway and consulted the plan once more. It was clearly marked The Mond Laboratory dead ahead across the courtyard. Mind you, the map was almost as aged and faded as some of the surrounding buildings.

He returned to the circular edifice. Indeed, inside, he could make out photographs hanging in the entrance. They were clearly taken from the air of the countryside and installations of a scientific nature.

Taking his courage in his hands, Alexei pushed open the door and went inside. A porter stood behind a reception desk. "Yes, sir, can I help you?" he enquired.

"Yes," replied Alexei, "I'm a research student at the Cavendish. I've just arrived and am feeling my way around."

The porter smiled understandingly.

Alexei continued, "I was looking for the Mond Laboratory. I understood this was it."

"I'm sorry, sir. As you can see, this is the Department of

Aerial Photography. I'm afraid I've never heard of the Mond Laboratory."

Alexei became rather suspicious at this reply. "Then perhaps you can explain to me why it says on the site plan under the archway that this building is called The Mond."

The porter continued to give him a blank look. Alexei persisted, "It was built in 1933 with finance from the Royal Society Ludwig Mond fund, and was designed specifically to further the research of Piotr Kapitsa into high magnetic fields and low temperature physics. You have heard of Piotr Kapitsa?"

The porter shrugged his shoulders. The conspiracy to cover up the fact that Piotr Kapitsa had ever existed and been an embarrassment to the Cavendish and its Directors, past and present, even went so far as to change the names of the buildings and instruct the staff to deny all knowledge of him.

The porter scratched his head and then replied, "Oh, you mean the Low Temperature Physics Group, sir? That's at the New Cavendish on the Madingley Road site. If you go up Magdalene Street and turn left along Northampton Street..." he began to give directions.

"Yes, I know where it is," replied Alexei rather brusquely.

The porter looked crestfallen.

"How long have you been working here?" asked Alexei.

"Just under a year, sir," replied the porter.

Alexei nodded pensively. Staff were changing all the time. It was perfectly feasible that this man genuinely knew nothing of the former use to which the Department for Aerial Photography had been put. It was also not uncommon to leave old maps up on walls. Perhaps it had been a legitimate move to relocate Kapitsa's research to a different site. But if the Mond Laboratory had been purpose-built for him and his research, it did strike him as strange that it had been moved.

The porter looked on in silence as Alexei turned away as if to leave. "I hope you find what you're looking for, sir," he said.

"So do I," replied Alexei. "So do I."

As he had made the pretext of wanting to use the Cavendish Library to enable him to get away from the Observatory, Alexei felt it best for him to at least put in an appearance there to corroborate his story. He was sure that Martin Harvey wouldn't bother to check up on him, but thoroughness was one of his chief traits. More and more, he was beginning to behave and think like a detective rather than a research scientist, although his analytical faculties were proving an asset in both disciplines.

As he walked over Magdalene Bridge and turned left into Northampton Street, he was tempted to call in for a lunchtime drink at the Sir Isaac Newton public house, which stood just a hundred yards further up Castle Street on the right, but he resisted the temptation. Instead, he crossed the roundabout and followed Madingley Road past St John's College athletics ground on the left and Churchill College on the right. Opposite the Solar Physics Observatory ran the long, winding approach road to the New Cavendish Laboratories site, which overlooked a vast expanse of open country, partly occupied by the University Rifle Range.

The varied nature of the research and the growing number of students and staff had long since meant that the New Museum's Site in the centre of Cambridge was inadequate. Hence, the New Cavendish, which was completed earlier that year at a cost of two million pounds. There were four main buildings. The first block was for research into solid state physics; the second block was for teaching; the third and fourth blocks were for astronomy.

Alexei entered the main building named after Sir Lawrence Bragg, a former Director and famous for his work in X-ray crystallography. The Bragg Building contained the Director's office, where Alexei had met Professor Harcourt on his first day, the Museum, the Library, and several departments of the branch of physics. Alexei decided first of all to check out the porter's story at the Department for Aerial Photography. On the first floor, as part of the open-plan Museum, stood exhibits of early apparatus, which had played a historic part in the research of the Laboratories – Wilson's Cloud Chamber, Bragg's X-ray spectrometer, Rutherford's Atomic Disintegration Chamber, and many more. Each exhibit stood outside the appropriate research department.

Alexei wandered past the departments of High Energy Physics and Solid State Physics until he came across what he was looking for – a door marked 'Low Temperature Physics', and below in much smaller print in brackets it read (formerly Mond Laboratory).

What he had been told was correct. There was, however, no mention of Piotr Kapitsa. His attention was then attracted to two exhibits of similar design on either side of the entrance to the department. He peered at the explanatory plaques. The one on the right read, Ashmead's Helium Liquefier built in 1949. The one on the left read, Kapitsa's Helium Liquefier built in 1934. So, the name of Piotr Kapitsa did live on, at least in equipment developed by and named after him in the field of low-temperature physics.

With his curiosity at least partly satisfied, Alexei retraced his steps towards the Library. Outside the small lecture theatre in room 133, his attention was drawn to a series of framed photographs of distinguished-looking individuals. On closer inspection, Alexei found them to be likenesses of all past Cavendish Professors from the first, Clerk-Maxwell 1871–79, through Lord Rayleigh 1879–1884, J.J. Thomson 1884–1919, Lord Rutherford 1919–1937, Sir Lawrence Bragg 1938–1953, Sir Neville Mott 1954–1957, and finally the current Director Sir James Harcourt 1971–1975.

Lord Rutherford's term of office covered the period when Piotr Kapitsa was a research student and, latterly, Assistant

Director of the Cavendish, until he returned to the Soviet Union in 1934. Alexei reflected on the significant contributions each of these eminent men had made in their respective fields of science. No wonder graduates from all over the world were attracted to the Cavendish to serve under such distinguished teachers.

Indeed, the number of Nobel Prize winners who had begun their research here was staggering. Alexei idled on in the direction of the Library until his attention was captured by a display cabinet on electron microscopy, next to which stood the microscope developed by Siemens and another used by Hirsch, Whelan, and Horne. As he turned away from this exhibit, he came face to face with another display of smaller group photographs, which complemented those of the past Directors farther along. These were labelled 'physics research students' and dated from the earliest of 1897 up until the present day.

There appeared to be several rows of students standing behind a seated front row, comprising the departmental professors and the Director himself, who sat in the very middle. Underneath, every group member was named according to his position in the ranks. Alexei speculated whether Kapitsa had been erased from the picture gallery of distinguished old fellows. He tried to recall the year when his countryman had first arrived in Cambridge as a research student. He seemed to remember that Dr McCabe had stated sometime in the early nineteen twenties.

He began, therefore, with the group photograph for 1920 and worked his way along. Kapitsa was nowhere to be seen. Neither did he appear in 1921. Alexei felt a shiver of excitement as, third time lucky, the name of P.Kapitsa was to be found on the extreme right of the back row in 1922. He looked very much like the new boy, an outsider in an ill-fitting suit, and wearing a distinctly ill-at-ease expression in the company of such distinguished scientists.

Alexei was intrigued by the permanent photographic records. In the middle of the front row sat J.J. Thomson, flanked on his left by Professor Sir Ernest Rutherford, and on his right by F.W. Aston. In 1919, J.J. Thomson had been made Master of Trinity College and found that he did not have the time to be Cavendish Professor as well. Alexei remembered the marble bust of J.J. Thomson, which he had seen on his early morning expedition halfway up the stairs in the Wren Library. When Thomson had retired and was succeeded by Rutherford, the Laboratory had been turned over almost entirely to nuclear physics.

In spite of this, Thomson seemed to maintain his place in the hierarchy. Well into the late nineteen-twenties, Thomson held onto the centre spot until finally giving best to Rutherford and sitting on his immediate right hand. More fascinating still was the progress of the minor players in this frozen black and white drama. Alexei concluded that the nearer the front row and the closer to the middle one was, the more important a position one held in the Cavendish hierarchy and in the esteem of its Director.

In 1923, Kapitsa moved from standing on the extreme right of the top row to the extreme left of the middle row. And in 1924, he was sitting on the extreme left of the front row. By 1926, there were now four rows, three standing and one sitting. Kapitsa was maintaining his position on the extreme left of the front row. Alexei also noticed that his whole demeanour had changed. From the shifty individual in the baggy clothes, he had become a smiling, relaxed figure in a smart, double-breasted suit. He was an establishment figure and no longer an outsider. No wonder Lord Rutherford had trusted him sufficiently to make him Assistant Director of the Cavendish.

In 1927, Kapitsa was seated second from the left on the

front row. In 1928, he was seated second from the right on the front row. Alexei considered that Kapitsa's ambitions were transparently clear and vividly illustrated by these group photographs. His object was to move closer to lord Rutherford, who by now occupied the central position, and so inveigle himself into the great man's confidences. These pictures certainly did appear to tell a story.

From 1929 onwards, Kapitsa was seated three from the left next to C.T.R.Wilson, then J.J.Thomson, and then Lord Rutherford; until in 1933 he occupied the seat three from the right, a similar number of places away from the Director himself. He was no longer described below as P.Kapitsa but now as Professor Kapitsa. He had now well and truly arrived.

Alexei looked eagerly for the next movement but was disappointed that in the 1934 photograph, Kapitsa had disappeared altogether. Then he recalled that the Mond Laboratory had been built in 1933 and that Dr McCabe had told him that in 1934, Kapitsa had returned to Moscow, supposedly on holiday, but had never returned. That must be the end of the line.

Alexei had a feeling of anti-climax. The series of group photographs seemed to be telling their own story, or perhaps Alexei had been reading into them what he had learned from the historical background. What had happened from 1934 onwards was literally a closed book.

1934. Alexei had a nagging feeling that this year was significant in some way, apart from the fact that it had marked the disappearance of Piotr Kapitsa from the Cavendish Laboratory. Suddenly it came to him – the Marble Index. Dina had told him that Burgess and Blunt had secretly rendezvoused in Moscow in 1934 to compile The Marble Index. Guy Burgess had refused the offer of a fellowship at Trinity College in order to visit the Soviet Union. And Anthony Blunt had visited the Russian capital during his sabbatical year as a don at Trinity when he was supposedly studying architecture in Rome.

Burgess, Blunt, and Kapitsa had found themselves in Moscow at the same time. Was this sheer coincidence, or had they known each other at Cambridge? Was Kapitsa somehow involved in the compilation of names on The Marble Index? Alexei speculated that he would certainly be in a prime position to judge other research students, both foreign and British, and even members of the professorial staff who could be sympathetic to the Soviet cause.

For the first time, Alexei envisaged the names on The Marble Index as being those of eminent scientists. Until that moment, he had associated the names of Burgess and Blunt with people in literary circles who might have found themselves in politics, diplomacy, and even the secret service later in life. Now his search for The Marble Index took on an entirely different complexion. The year 1934 could be highly significant indeed.

Alexei remained staring at the group photograph for 1934 as if half-expecting Piotr Kapitsa to suddenly appear at Lord Rutherford's right-hand side. He had enjoyed the uninterrupted quiet of this part of the Bragg Building and was so engrossed that he failed to hear footsteps coming up the central staircase. At the last instant, Alexei recognised the back of the figure and ducked quickly into the alcove beside the small lecture theatre in room 133. Turning to the right at the top of the stairs, the figure stopped outside the door immediately in front of him. Alexei had been in that room once before. It belonged to Professor Sir James Harcourt, Director of the Cavendish, and his visitor was none other than Martin Harvey, Director of the Mullard Radio Astronomy Observatory. Alexei wondered whether Harvey had come to discuss him with Harcourt as the door opened and the visitor stepped inside. He had no way of finding out. Instead, he slipped next door into the Library, where he was supposed to be, and tried, without much success, to focus his concentration on his research into radio astronomy. Hard as he tried, the year 1934 and The Marble Index refused to retreat to the back of his mind.

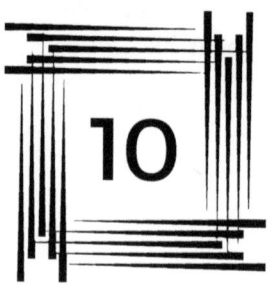

10

Dina mounted the steps of the KGB Archive Building on Prospekt Marksa. Inside the entrance, she was confronted by a guard who asked peremptorily, "Name?"

"Dina Russakov," she replied, showing him her security pass with its diagonal red stripe. "I've been seconded from KGB ADP to carry out a sweep of the archives."

The guard's face broke into a smile. Anyone seconded here must have been punished in some way. It was not a job for which people volunteered. He checked his staff list. "Ah, yes," he declared as he discovered the memo from Boychenko to Staff Branch, a copy of which had been forwarded to the appropriate department. "Which floor would you like to peruse?" he asked.

"1930s on the third floor," she replied.

"Ah," the guard said knowingly. "So you've been here before," implying that this was not the first time she had been in trouble.

"Yes, I've been here before," replied Dina defiantly, "and I shall be here again tomorrow. I don't recall seeing you here before, though. Is this your normal station?"

It was the guard's turn to feel embarrassed now. "No, I'm usually on patrol in Dzerzhinsky Square."

"I see," replied Dina, implying that he, in turn, must have committed some misdemeanour to end up on guard at the Archive Building. He became annoyed at the tables suddenly being turned on him. "My patrol had a full complement, and the captain asked for a volunteer to fill this post. Being of good socialist consciousness, I put myself forward."

"Of course," said Dina with mocking scepticism. Sensing that he was beginning to lose control of this battle of wits, the guard came around the side of his desk and produced the security keys, which unlocked the steel-doored elevator. There were no stairs. Each of the eight floors could only be reached by keying in from the ground floor into the locking system. Dina smiled sweetly at him as she entered the elevator.

"I've enjoyed our little conversation," she said. "I hope we can continue it tomorrow."

The guard scowled as the doors closed and the lift mechanism slid smoothly into action. Upon reaching the third floor, the doors reopened automatically, and Dina emerged into a strange, silent world. There was a stale, musty smell emanating from the millions of pieces of card and paper up to fifty years old, which were packed tightly into row upon row of dull grey filing cabinets. They stretched some two hundred yards away into the distance and rose to a height of twenty feet from the floor. This necessitated the use of sliding steps, which ran along well-oiled rails in order to gain access to the uppermost files.

The rows of cabinets were aligned in alphabetical order. Dina was used to working in an artificial atmosphere where the needs of the computer ensured that the temperature was constant and the air dust-free. On the contrary, the air in the archives was not designed to be healthy and life-supporting. It had a distinctly dead and decaying feel about it. From its beginning in the early nineteen twenties as the brainchild of Meyer Trilisser, a revolutionary Bolshevik Party archivist and subsequently Head of the IN, the Foreign Department of the Cheka, the Central Soviet Intelligence Index had become the most comprehensive and detailed of any Intelligence Library in the world.

Initially, it had been a collection of biographies and dossiers on a wide range of people, from politicians to members of the military forces, to businessmen and merchants. It had a dual role, not only to keep up-to-date dossiers on all potential enemies of the state, but also on people, especially abroad, who could, by blackmail or financial inducements, be coerced into serving the Soviet regime. In the subsequent fifty years, it had outgrown its original home and required a permanent staff of two hundred specialists to maintain it. The sheer volume of information stored on paper meant that it had become unmanageable, and, from 1962, all the data in active use had been transferred to computer disc and tape, and also to microfilm and microfiche. These records in everyday use by agents of the KGB were housed in the purpose-built centre on the Moscow Ring Road, where Dina was normally stationed.

The building on Prospekt Marksa was usually the reserve of historical researchers and archivists. From time to time, however, the Director of the Computer Data Centre would receive a directive from the Politburo to sweep the archives with the object of turning up some piece of vital intelligence which was lying neglected among the millions of entries. It was like looking for a needle in a haystack. Everyone knew this from the First Secretary of the Party down, but the practice still went on. Dina was thankful that it had, otherwise she would not have stumbled across The Marble Index, which could provide her with the ammunition to secure the release of her father, Vladimir Maksimovich Russakov.

The Central Index was, in fact, made up of many different indexes. There was the yearly index, the country index, the personal index (one for Soviet nationals and one for aliens), the Vecheka index, the OGPU index, the NKVD index, the MVD-MGB index, and the KGB index – all the latter being updated versions of Trilisser's original index. The whole thing was cross-referenced, people to people, people to places, people to events and so on. It was like an extinct prehistoric monster whose carcass now lay rotting. Boychenko often likened it to one of those deep-frozen mammoths that kept getting dug up in the frozen wastes of Siberia. Whatever analogy people drew about the Central Index, it was certainly an amazing encyclopaedia of information about the Soviet Union since the Revolution.

The year 1934, in which Dina was particularly interested, was a period of transition. It marked the death of the head of state security, the OGPU, Vyacheslav Rudolfich Menzhinsky, and his replacement by Genrikh Grigorevich Yagoda and the inception of the NKVD. In fact, as Dina had related to Alexei at his parents' apartment, Yagoda had even been responsible for his predecessor's death. Menzhinsky was, like Dzerzhinsky before him, a Pole. He was more interested in counterespionage than in spying abroad. However, and this was of particular significance for Dina, Menzhinsky did take the view that the only worthwhile intelligence to be gained abroad was in the field of science. This was in sharp contrast to his own aesthetic tastes, which preached the value of an artistic education. Indeed, he was even known to his countrymen as 'The Poet of the Cheka'. It was Dina's fascination with this bizarre character in the first place that had led her to fix upon the year 1934 in her initial sweep of the archives.

Ironically, it had been her father, Vladimir Maksimovich Russakov, who had drawn her attention to Menzhinsky through their shared obsession with the music of composer Mikhail Glinka. Russakov couldn't understand how a man of such good taste who filled his office in Kaljayev Place with icons, paintings, oriental works of art, and statues could also blithely sign death warrants. Dina pondered on this dichotomy as she walked slowly down the external aisle of the Index, looking up at the year markers.

When she reached 1934 with in brackets OGPU (Obedinennoe Gosudarstvennoe Politicheskoe Upravlenye), she turned left and proceeded halfway down into the heart of the metal maze. The letter M occupied several dozen ranks of files from floor to ceiling, and Menzhinsky himself monopolised almost one whole rank on his own. Dina grabbed hold of one of the sliding step ladders and brought it into line with Menzhinsky's files. The place where she had discovered the card divulging the existence of The Marble Index was seven from the top. She stepped onto the first rung of the ladder. The sound of heel meeting metal resonated around the Index like an echo in a deep natural canyon. Dina continued her ascent to a height of about fifteen feet. She had no head for heights, so she resisted the temptation to look down, particularly as the sliding structure was trembling under her movement.

Eventually, she reached the file she had been looking for. It was labelled V.R.Menzhinsky BI to CAS. This alphabetical section contained not only Cambridge but also Burgess and Blunt, which was highly convenient. Dina flicked through the cards as far as Cambridge. Under Cambridge University, it read 'intelligence officer in the field, Igor Khopliakin'. There was then a further sub-section headed pro-Soviet British nationals. Top of the list were J.D. Bernal and Maurice Dobb, who were titled 'principal case officers'.

In other words, Khopliakin was the central driving force from the Soviet Embassy in London, whilst Bernal and Dobb represented the recruiters in Cambridge itself. The method of communication was described as 'hidden code in correspondence chess game'. A section headed 'Soviet nationals in place' was headed by Lev Landau and Piotr Kapitsa.

Dina was unfamiliar with the names of Bernal and Dobb,

and Landau and Kapitsa, but decided to bear them in mind for future reference. Now, where had it been, The Marble Index? Dina had not dared to remove the card from the Central Index. If one of the random searches at the door had uncovered it in her possession, its existence and possible importance would have been given away. She had decided that it would be much safer left in its original place. After all, it had remained undetected for forty years. It was highly unlikely that anyone apart from Dina would rediscover it now.

Her fingers flicked over the yellowing pieces of card. She had to use her fingernails to separate them, for they clung together as if reluctant to divulge their secrets after all these years. They smelt of old money left in a wallet or the pages of a book on an antiquarian's shelf, neglected, and no longer of any use or interest to anyone, except to Dina, that was.

Begrudgingly, the cards separated. Quite often, there were copies of letters, photographs, newspaper cuttings, or documents to elaborate or reinforce a particular point being made on one of the index cards.

Dina worked her way back from Cambridge University to Guy Burgess's card, which was cross-referenced with Anthony Blunt and The Apostles, which Dina believed to be an elite secret society. There was a copy of a letter from Nikolai Bukharin, Chief of the Comintern, to Ossip Piatnitsky, Chief of the International Liaison Section, recommending Burgess's recruitment to the Soviet cause and his assignment to Samuel Borisovich Chan, the Resident Director of the Soviet Secret Intelligence Service in Britain.

This followed an approach from Guy Burgess himself directly to Bukharin in person in Moscow in 1934. The Bukharin letter was asterisked and also cross-referenced. It read 'see P.Kapitsa and L.B.Kamenev re Kharkov Institute consultancy'. Eventually, Dina would have to check all these cross-references. It was a source of amazement to her how all these characters and events were interrelated. It was truly a web of intrigue. She felt that she was now getting close. It had been under Burgess's heading that The Marble Index card had appeared. Before the Bukharin letter, there was a resume of Burgess's visit to Moscow in 1934 with a homosexual friend from Oxford called Derek Blaikie, who was also a Communist. Dina saw the heavy irony in the fact that a pair of homosexuals sympathetic to the Soviet regime should have visited the country at that time. In March 1934, homosexuality, after a period of sexual liberalisation following the Revolution, had once again become a criminal offence. Indeed, it was seen by the authorities as the product of a bourgeois society. No doubt the English intellectuals had conveniently overlooked this fact when throwing their support behind the Communist cause. Besides, she could well understand how these effete young Englishmen would have got on well with the likes of Menzhinsky. Lenin had called him a 'decadent neurotic'. He came from an upper-middle-class family, despised the stupidity of the proletariat, and held court in his office lying on a settee, wearing a Chinese silk dressing gown and painting his toenails and fingernails. If this represented life for the head of state security in the Soviet Union, it was no wonder that undergraduates from similar backgrounds in England, who led a cloistered existence in Cambridge and Oxford, were attracted by the lifestyle behind the dogma.

Dina's fingers pressed on. She prised apart the next cards and there it was – The Marble Index. It followed directly behind the card relating to Burgess's visit to Moscow in the Summer of 1934. From her vantage point, fifteen feet above the ground, Dina surveyed the rest of the files on that floor. There was no one else to be seen, and not a sound to be heard. With the subtlety of a surgeon performing a delicate operation, she withdrew the card and held it up to the light between her thumb and index finger. It read 'The Marble Index' as compiled by Guy Burgess and Anthony Blunt for the attention of Nikolai Bukharin. "In order to prove our good faith to be allowed membership of the Comintern, there follows a list of names of eminent scholars whom we have recruited from the ranks of Trinity College, Cambridge, to serve the cause of the Soviet Union now and in their future careers. These seven have pledged themselves in writing wholeheartedly to Marxist Communism."

Dina speculated on the motivation behind Burgess's appeal directly to Bukharin. He could just as easily have given the names to Samuel Cahan, the Resident Director of the Soviet Secret Intelligence Service in Britain, or even to Bernal or Dobb in Cambridge. By going over their heads, it was obviously an attempt to boost his own reputation in the eyes of the Comintern and so enhance his own career. Moreover, to this end, Burgess might even have invented the names or plucked them at random from the College register. On the other hand, they may have been genuinely recruited by Burgess, possibly from the ranks of the secret society known as The Apostles. Dina had no way of knowing. She just had to believe they were genuine; otherwise, her quest was in vain.

The burning question was, where was the list of names designated as The Marble Index now? Had it ever existed? Had it been removed by Burgess on his return to England or by Bukharin himself to be stored in a safer place? One corner of the card was slightly torn. From the jagged tracery, it looked as if another card had once been stapled to the back. Dina turned the card over. The centre was less faded, like the space where a painting had been hanging on a wall. At the corners of the space, the fibres of paper were sticky to the touch. Dina deduced that the smaller index card originally stapled to the lead card had subsequently been stuck with glue or adhesive tape to the back. It had since either been torn away or worked loose on its own to become detached.

In her own mind, Dina was convinced that this card had contained the names of The Marble Index. As she held the card up to the light, she noticed in one corner the faint remnants of a coloured drawing. It was in the shape of an arc and looked to have been done in children's coloured crayons. She wondered what it was supposed to represent. It was red at the top and violet at the bottom. Of course, she realised, it was a rainbow.

Strangely, it brought back to her the memory of that night when they had come to seize her father. After Dr Shostakovich and the militia had departed with Vladimir Maksimovich Russakov, Dina had sat crying by the open window all night.

As the dawn had broken over Izmaylovsky Park, there was a light shower of early morning rain. And as the first rays of sunlight rose above the five green domes of the Cathedral of the Intercession, producing a halo or corona effect, the light had been refracted through the water droplets to produce a magnificent rainbow. All the colours of the rainbow were clearly visible and discernible, from red through orange, yellow, green, blue, indigo, to violet. The tears rolled down Dina's cheeks then, as they did now, so vividly was the memory recalled. A tear fell from her face onto the card in her hand, landing on the faded crayon drawing. As the moisture saturated into the fabric of the card, the colours were brought vividly back to life, just as vividly as the memories in Dina's mind.

By mid-afternoon, Alexei had become thoroughly engrossed in his research at the Cavendish Library. As Professor Harcourt had intimated on their first encounter, the Cavendish had been responsible for pioneering work in the field of radar observation, not only in terms of man-made satellites but also naturally occurring radio sources. It was during experiments in 1967 by Bell and Hewish that pulsars were discovered. This followed earlier work by Ratcliffe, head of the radio-ionosphere group, into radio emissions from the sun itself. In terms of observation, early interferometers had been replaced by the first supersynthesis telescope at Lord's Bridge. Instead of two separate aerials, each of which received the same signals from the same source, being coupled to a receiver, the supersynthesis system had been developed, which produced greater resolution and sensitivity. This high resolving power was achieved by the technique of aperture synthesis using eight paraboloidal reflectors, the telescope itself operating under direct computer control.

Alexei had been given strict instructions by the Director of the Bauman Institute, Professor Kuznetzov, to make a special report on the development of aperture synthesis and the use of the Lord's Bridge telescope in obtaining detailed maps of radio sources such as quasars, radio galaxies, supernova remnants and hot hydrogen clouds. He was busy poring over a map of radio galaxy Cygnus A when there came a tap on his shoulder. Alexei was so deep in thought that he gave a sharp cry of surprise. Regaining his composure, he looked round to find the figure of Professor Sir James Harcourt, Director of the Cavendish. "There you are, Mr Kunayev. I was told I would find you here. Would you come with me, please?" he said.

Alexei remembered that before going into the Library, he had seen Martin Harvey entering the Director's office. So, they had been discussing him after all. Alexei could only speculate what was in store for him. Maybe it was simply that Harvey had been complaining that Alexei had absented himself from the Observatory under a false pretext. Maybe they had been putting him under observation and knew all about The Marble Index. Alexei didn't know what to think. Sheepishly, he followed several paces behind Harcourt as they made their way along the gallery of photographs and exhibits towards the top of the stairs, opposite which the Director had his office. Instead of turning right, Harcourt turned left and proceeded down the stairs into the entrance hall. Alexei was about to question where they were going when he was struck dumb by the sight that met him from the head of the stairs. Some two to three dozen of the research students and graduates, together with their professors, were congregating below.

As he followed Harcourt down the steps, every single head was turned in their direction. Although they were probably all looking at the Director, Alexei felt as if their gaze was actually fixed on him. He was overcome by the same paranoid sensation he had experienced at the railway station. Alexei felt as if he were about to be denounced as a Russian spy, his motives brought into question and made a public example, in case any of the other foreign graduates had the idea of using their research at the Cavendish as a cover for illicit activities. His thought processes became more and more irrational as he reached the foot of the stairs.

Professor Harcourt turned to him and said, "No doubt you have been admiring our photographic gallery in the Museum, Mr Kunayev."

Alexei's heart dropped. They knew all about his observations on Piotr Kapitsa and the possible connection with The Marble Index. His covert quest was well and truly blown. "Well, yes, I had noticed it," replied Alexei weakly.

"Good," said the Director briskly. "Right, come along, everybody. Outside please. We don't have much time." He and Martin Harvey began to shepherd the research students out through the front door of the Bragg Building, leaving Alexei rooted to the spot in the middle of the entrance hall. He couldn't understand why Harcourt did not now want the others to be present at his public denunciation. Harcourt turned to him and said, "You too, Mr Kunayev. The man is waiting."

This sounded terribly ominous. Who was the man? Maybe it was a representative of the British Secret Intelligence Services, or on the other hand, a delegate from the Soviet Embassy, come to claim immunity on his behalf. The spectre of the black KGB Zils limousines rose to the forefront of his mind as it had on his arrival at Cambridge railway station.

Alexei was suddenly transported to Dzerzhinsky Square in Moscow. Before he knew it, Martin Harvey was physically propelling him out into the courtyard in front of the Bragg Building. Alexei saw no sense in resistance. The game was up. There was a row of chairs set out, and the professors of the respective departments were taking their seats. It looked to Alexei like an inquisition. The middle seat was empty as Professor Sir James Harcourt instructed the research students to line up in three ranks behind the row of chairs. So, his peers were to be present after all. Alexei couldn't grasp why Harcourt should want to carry out his trial in public in the open air. Surely, he would just have called him into his office and told him that his abuse of the trust the Cavendish Laboratories had placed in him meant that he would have to leave. The stage was set. Alexei lingered on the edge of the stage management being arranged by Harcourt. The Director suddenly approached him. Alexei knew that the moment had arrived.

"Come along, Mr Kunayev. The man is waiting," reiterated Harcourt. "Just stand here."

Alexei did as he was told and found himself on the extreme right of the back row. He couldn't understand it. Now. He felt as if he were being lined up in an identity parade. Professor Harcourt disappeared momentarily. Alexei surmised that he had gone to fetch the man. A few seconds later, the Director re-emerged from the shadows with a companion bearing a tripod and a camera. The event was being recorded.

Alexei braced himself for the ordeal and waited for the call to bring him down to the front before his peers and the collected academics of the Cavendish. It was just like the bi-annual evaluation session of the Komsomol. The moment never came. Professor Harcourt took his seat in the centre of the Front row. The photographer set up his equipment. There was a momentary silence whilst everyone focused on the camera lens. There was a distant click, a sense of release of tension, and it was all over. People began to drift away as quickly as they had congregated.

Alexei was baffled by the whole affair. Then it struck him where he had been standing – on the extreme right of the back row, in the exact spot where Piotr Kapitsa had found himself in that first photograph in 1922. Alexei realised he had been posing for a group photograph of Cavendish research students, which would eventually find its way into the gallery of the Museum, along with all the others since 1897. It would be labelled 1975, and the name of every graduate would be recorded, including his own. What is more, he would start his career in exactly the same position in the ranks as his fellow countryman, Piotr Kapitza.

Alexei had allowed his imagination once again to run away with him. Everything since the time he had left the Library was the product of his paranoia. Only the coincidence of his position in the group photograph was real, and that irony was not lost on him.

At precisely eight o'clock, the black Chaika drew to a halt outside the Izmaylovsky Park apartments. Dina drew back the corner of the curtains in time to see Konstantin Boychenko getting out of his car. The burly figure moved with surprising speed towards the apartment block entrance, and Dina waited for the imminent knock on the door.

She had spent an embarrassing ten minutes trying to explain to Dr Sloboda and his wife why she had to cancel her dinner appointment with them. Dr Sloboda had been most surprised that she should prefer to go out on the town and live it up in view of her father's current plight. He expected her to be too distraught and inconsolable in the circumstances to be able to enjoy herself. On the other hand, Larissa Sloboda had seen it as a therapeutic exercise to take Dina's mind off her other problems. She had been most understanding and not at all put out that her specially prepared beef stroganoff would go to waste. Nevertheless, the cancelled dinner date had preyed on Dina's mind. She only had limited experience in using people to her own ends. It did not come easily, but she was learning.

She had made herself look attractive for Boychenko, but not too attractive. Sufficiently to make him feel flattered to be seen in her company. She wanted to keep him sweet in order to allow her freedom of movement at work. She had already engineered her secondment to the Archives, and a little impunctuality and absenteeism here and there in order to pursue her cause would also be overlooked if she kept on the right side of him.

She was only prepared to go so far, however. Dina was aware of what Boychenko desired ultimately from the relationship, and she was not prepared to give it to him. She intended instead to hold out the promise without delivering the goods. There was a knock at the door. Dina took one last look in the mirror before opening up.

The heavy figure of Boychenko with his bushy eyebrows and thick jowls filled the doorway. He was wearing an astrakhan coat underneath which Dina could make out a black tuxedo and bow tie. His six-foot-two-inch frame and overbearing expression made him a daunting figure. "Dina, my dear," he said, "you look lovely", taking her by the shoulders and kissing her on both cheeks.

Dina was rather taken aback by this sudden outburst of charm. It was so totally out of character. She understood now how women could become ensnared in his grasp. "Thank you, comrade Boychenko," she replied.

"Oh, Konstantin, call me Konstantin," he said, echoing his plea to her in his office.

"You, too, look very dashing, Konstantin," said Dina, reaching up and pretending to straighten his bow tie, playing on his male vanity. He offered her his arm. "Shall we go? I have a table for eight-thirty. They will keep it for me, of course, but you know what a stickler I am for punctuality."

"Then let's be on our way," said Dina briskly. They made their way down the three flights of stairs, and Boychenko opened the car door for Dina to slide into the front passenger seat of the luxurious Chaika. He brought the limousine to life, and in next to no time, the MI7 motor route had carried them to the heart of Moscow.

Intersecting the Sadovoye Koltso ring road, they journeyed on down Kirova Ulitsa, through Dzerzhinsky Square, along Prospekt Marksa past the KGB Archive Building. At the next crossroads, Boychenko turned right onto Gorkovo Ulitsa. Immediately on the left at number three stood the impressive twenty-two-storey Intourist Hotel, which had three magnificent restaurants of its own – the Intourist, the Zvyozdnoye Nebo, and the Valyutny Zal.

On the opposite side of the road at number six stood the Aragvi restaurant.

Boychenko pulled the Chaika into the forecourt and got out. He went around and opened the passenger side door for Dina, who alighted with the assistance of Boychenko's arm. There was a queue outside the restaurant waiting for admission by the shviytsar. These were people who either did not have a reservation or whose social status meant that they had to wait in line, even though they did have a booking.

Boychenko went straight up to the doorman. The shviytsar had obviously noticed the automobile and might even have discerned the KGB parking permit on the windscreen. In any event, he was suitably servile and unquestioningly opened the door to the restaurant. Dina could hear faint mutterings of protest from those in the queue as she swept through the entrance and deposited her cape at the cloakroom. Almost immediately, they were accosted by the smiling figure of the maître d'hôtel.

"Comrade Boychenko," gushed the administrator. "It is an honour for our humble establishment to serve you. It has been at least a month since you have graced us with your presence."

"Pressures of work, you know, Felix," replied Boychenko. The administrator touched the bridge of his nose knowingly with his finger. "Come," he beckoned, "I have reserved the best table for you and your beautiful companion." He surveyed Dina with obvious approval.

The administrator led them to a table in a quiet alcove on its own, surrounded by exotic plants and safely away from the gaze of prying eyes. "Here," he said proudly, drawing back the chair for Dina to sit down. In spite of the obnoxious company, Dina was getting a taste for this kind of life, although the servility and special treatment rankled with her conscience. "I will send an ofitsiant over immediately," said the administrator as he retired discreetly, smiling and bowing his head all the while.

Boychenko picked up the menus and handed one to Dina. "Whatever you like, my dear. Expense is no object."

Dina shuddered at the thought of how Boychenko would expect his extravagance and generosity to be repaid later. She would meet that obstacle when she came to it. For the moment, she was determined to take advantage of the situation. "What do you recommend?" she asked.

"The chicken tabaka is of course exquisite," he replied, "but I prefer to have chicken satsivi myself, followed by khachapuri for the main course."

Dina surveyed the menu. She pondered. "I think I'll have shashlik for openers and chicken tabaka with green beans in sour cream sauce."

"Fine," said Boychenko, approving of her choice.

The ofitsiant approached their table. "Are you ready to order?" he asked.

Boychenko gave him the details and added, "Oh and a bottle of Mukuzani to follow."

At this, Dina felt a pang of conscience, as this was the very wine Dr Sloboda had bought in especially for the dinner at their apartment.

"Now tell me, Dina," said Boychenko, leaning across the table and clasping her hand between his, "how are you bearing up to the ordeal of your father's internment?" His thick, bushy eyebrows were raised questioningly, and his voice had an apparently sympathetic tone. Dina knew that this was all part of Boychenko's grand design to get her into bed. Slowly but firmly, she withdrew her hand from between his and placed it on her breast. She accompanied the gesture with a heavy-hearted expression, which was specially induced for the benefit of her companion, although her genuine feelings ran much deeper.

"As well as can be expected under the circumstances," she replied. "The commission is to reconvene in one month's time. Until then, my father is to remain in the hands of the forensic psychiatrists of the Serbsky Institute."

"Those bastards," said Boychenko vehemently.

"And what's worse," continued Dina, "he's being subjected to treatment by depressant drugs such as aminazin."

"Bastards," repeated Boychenko, as if these expletives were a demonstration of his moral support.

"At least he's better off there than in Lubyanka Prison psychiatric hospital," said Dina.

"I didn't know he'd been in Lubyanka," exclaimed Boychenko. "He's certainly lucky to have been moved from there. How did you manage to achieve that concession?"

"Basically," said Dina, "it was because he could not be tried for an offence under the criminal code. It was termed a crime against the state, and as such, he could only be detained in a normal psychiatric hospital, if one can call the Serbsky normal."

"Does that mean you have access to him?" asked Boychenko with a studied look of concern on his face.

"Yes," replied Dina. "I am entitled to visit him on Tuesdays, Thursdays, and Sundays. I was going to ask you about that." Her eyes moistened with tears, and she allowed her hand to stray once again down onto the table.

Correctly reading the body language signs, Boychenko again cradled her small white hand in his, which this time she allowed him to caress. His eyes wandered over her face, reading her every emotion and looking deeply into her green eyes.

She sobbed, "I was wondering..." She sobbed again.

"Yes?" he coaxed.

"I was wondering whether you would allow me time off work to visit him."

"But of course," said Boychenko. "It is permissible on compassionate grounds. There's no need to trouble yourself. It is the least I can do."

"Oh, thank you," said Dina with exaggerated gratitude. "I don't know how I can ever thank you."

"I'm sure we can think of something," replied Boychenko ambiguously, although the meaning was transparently clear to Dina. At this moment, the afitsiant reappeared with the bottle of wine. He uncorked it and poured a small amount into Boychenko's glass. He rolled the liquid around, caressed the glass, smelt the bouquet, and finally took a sip, which he rolled extravagantly around on his palate. He looked straight into Dina's eyes and, wetting his lips with his tongue, said, "Perfection, sheer perfection."

Dina averted her eyes so as not to be drawn in by his ravenous gaze. She was saved from further sexual harassment by the return of the afitsiant with the entrees. The sight of food was certain to take Boychenko's mind off Dina's body at least temporarily. Although he was renowned for his sexual appetite, the Director of the computer centre was even more famous for his love of good food. With the manners of a ravenous pig, Boychenko polished off his chicken satsivi in next to no time, whilst Dina picked tentatively at her shashlik.

The administrator had obviously warned the afitsiant about Boychenko's eating habits as the main course appeared at their table almost immediately. Dina pondered that her companion had very little time for lingering over the culinary delights. For him, eating was an instant experience, a fleeting moment of pleasure before rapidly moving onto the next course. She wondered morbidly if he treated sexual experience in the same way and hoped she was never in a position to find out. The girls in the office, who had enjoyed, if that were the right word, his sexual favours, never talked about what it had been like. They were far too frightened of him to openly discuss their experiences.

The afitsiant removed Boychenko's empty plate and placed the khachapuri cheese pie down in front of him. This disappeared with a similar alacrity to the first course. Dina could only sit and wonder as she daintily cut up her pressed fried chicken tabaka. The meal served to establish a period of comfortable silence. Whilst Boychenko was eating, he was in no mood for making small talk. This enabled Dina to relax and accustom herself to Boychenko's company. She felt strangely secure as her host wielded a great deal of influence and power, generated not only by his status within the state security services but also by his personal presence and dynamic magnetism. Power in itself was an aphrodisiac to many women. The fact that a man could command respect through his position in society made him appealing, even though he may not in himself be very good-looking.

Dina looked across at Boychenko and wondered what really motivated the man. Presumably, his parents were still alive and he had strong family connections, though she could never recall him talking about them. To them, he would probably be their loyal, dutiful, and loving son, Konstantin, the apple of his mother's eye, not the brutal masochist he appeared to his staff. [Sadist]

Dina thought it was strange how each person could project so many different faces to the world, every one of which was real and yet none presented the whole picture. She began to think that maybe Konstantin Boychenko wasn't such a bear after all. Dina looked up from her chicken tabak and caught her dinner companion gazing lustfully at her. This proved a salutary lesson and served to remind her what his expectations for the evening were. She shuddered at the thought and tried to project Alexei's image into Boychenko's place, to enable her to endure his company all the better.

He leaned over and refilled her glass with the Mukuzani. "You were deep in thought," he said.

She improvised her reply. "I was just thinking how considerate you had been. It is only when there is a crisis in your life that you learn who your real friends are."

"It's the least I can do for one of my best members of staff," he replied. "When this is all over and your father has been released, as I am sure he will be, you will be most welcome back at the data centre. It was a shrewd move of yours to lie low in the Archive Building for a while. It not only takes the pressure off you but also off your work colleagues. And I have a further suggestion to ease the pressure even more."

"What is that?" asked Dina.

"It must be difficult for you living alone in your father's apartment, surrounded by hostile neighbours. Not only that, living in the suburbs means that you have to engage in tiresome travelling on the metro back and forth to work."

Dina nodded in agreement, not realising what was coming next. Boychenko continued. "Now it just so happens I have a second small apartment on Kutuzovsky Prospekt in the heart of the city, which I use when I've been working late at the office and need to stay overnight. It's not often that I'm there, as I much prefer to return to my beach house in Strogino."

Dina's heart sank as she realised the proposition that was about to follow.

"Well," said Boychenko, "what would you say to taking over this apartment until you've got your personal problems sorted out? You can treat the place as your own. I'll give you the only key," which he conveniently produced from his jacket pocket and placed down on the table.

"It's very kind of you, but I couldn't," replied Dina, knowing full well that it was going to be very difficult to refuse Boychenko's offer. In spite of his remarks, the implication was clearly that he was offering her the opportunity to become his mistress. He picked up the key in one hand and, with the other, firmly grasped Dina's wrist. She knew that physical resistance was futile. He placed the key in her open hand and gradually released his grip. "There," he said, "that wasn't so difficult after all, was it?" He continued to look straight into Dina's unflinching gaze.

Now was the time for her to call on all her reserves of strength of will and put the key down on his side of the table. Boychenko's words, 'a small apartment on Kutuzovsky Prospekt', echoed around her head. Somehow, the address seemed significant. Then she recalled her visit to the Lenin Library that afternoon. Her research into the background of Second Secretary and Chief Ideologue Mikhail Suslov had revealed that he was separated from his wife and family and lived on Kutuzovsky Prospekt. This was indeed fortuitous as Dina's long-range plans for her father's release hinged on obtaining the sanction of Suslov himself. The opportunity to be near him could not be missed.

Slowly, she curled her fingers around the key. Boychenko's delight was undisguised. Dina allowed herself the luxury of a smile that she could make such a fool out of him over her motives. Of course, he interpreted the smile as a sign of her agreeable assent. She marvelled at the vanity of the man, who expected her to fall prey to his advances as easily as that. Still, she trembled at the prospect of the price he would expect her to pay.

"Shall we go there now?" he asked, eager to consummate their deal at the earliest opportunity.

"Not tonight," she said, producing a small capsule from her handbag. "Our family general practitioner, Dr Sloboda, has prescribed me these pills to enable me to sleep. I must take one now so that I shall be ready to go straight to bed as soon as I get back to my apartment."

Boychenko didn't press her. With remarkable self-control for him, he said, "Of course, whatever is best for your health." He was obviously pleased with the evening's handiwork and was satisfied that he had at least got her to accede to his demands to take the apartment. She was too great a conquest in his eyes to push her too far in one go and risk jeopardising his whole grand design. She was the ultimate sexual prize and worth biding his time over.

Dina breathed a sigh of relief. The pressure was momentarily released. The problem of keeping Boychenko at bay and yet still holding out the prospect of her sexual favours presented as great a challenge as securing the release of her father. Until that moment, Dina had one seemingly insurmountable problem. Now she had two. In a strange sense, they could actually cancel one another out if her designs on Mikhail Suslov came to fruition.

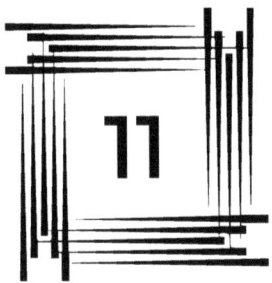

11

Alexei was lying on his bed, waiting for dinner time, still reflecting on the ordeal of the afternoon's group photographic session at the Cavendish, when there came a knock at his door. Before he had time to decide whether to remain silent or invite his visitor in, the door burst open and the breathless figure of Andrew Marriott appeared. "Come in," said Alexei rather ironically.

"Sorry," said Marriott, snatching at his breath, "but we don't have much time."

"Much time for what?" asked Alexei.

"How do you fancy a bit of detective work?" replied Marriott with a counter question. "I know you're curious about Dr McCabe and what he gets up to. Well, now's your opportunity to find out."

Alexei just lay there on the bed.

"Well, you are interested, aren't you?" pressed Marriott.

"Yes, I suppose I am," conceded Alexei, thinking about the tutor's specialised knowledge of the history of the Soviet state security agencies, his love of Russian music, his mention of the mysterious Dinmukhamed Kunayev – the man who bore the same surname as him, and his unequalled knowledge of the personalities and affairs of Cambridge life such as the real background of Professor Sir James Harcourt. All these aspects added up to a man who was not quite what he appeared to be.

"Just what are you proposing to do?" asked Alexei.

"Follow him to London," replied Marriott.

"What?" exclaimed Alexei.

"Where's your sense of adventure?" said Marriott. "Look, remember me telling you about his supposed trips to the capital to visit a Russian countess and play in chess congresses?"

Alexei nodded. "Well, I overheard him telling Dr Fischer at lunchtime that he had to go down to London unexpectedly this evening, so now's our opportunity to find out whether he's telling the truth."

"You mean follow him?" asked Alexei incredulously.

It was Marriott's turn to nod eagerly.

"What if he sees us?" asked Alexei.

"He won't. Not if we're careful."

Alexei was highly sceptical, although the idea did appeal to him. What was even more intriguing was Andrew Marriott's motives in all this. Out of the blue, he was inviting Alexei on a spying mission on his own tutor. Alexei chewed it over, then suddenly flashed out a totally unexpected question in Marriott's direction.

"Just tell me one thing," he posed, "have you taken any books on Wordsworth out of the Wren Library?"

Marriott was taken aback by the seeming irrelevance of the question. "What the hell has that got to do with anything?"

"Just answer the question," said Alexei calmly.

"As a matter of fact, no. No, I haven't. But I don't see what that's got to do with whether you'll agree to come with me to London and follow McCabe?"

"More than you'll ever know," replied Alexei, seemingly satisfied that Marriott was not a party to the alleged conspiracy to conceal the origin of the Marble Index from him. For if Marriott were not responsible, then by process of elimination in Alexei's mind, it must be Dr McCabe who was hoarding the entire works of William Wordsworth from the Wren Library for whatever motives, logical or irrational.

Marriott stood there at the foot of the bed whilst Alexei continued to ponder. "Does that mean that you're coming or not?" he asked, starting to get frustrated. "The train leaves in less than twenty minutes."

"Then we'd better hurry up or else we'll miss it," said Alexei, jumping off the bed and startling his companion with his response.

"You know, sometimes I just can't make you out," said Marriott, shaking his head as Alexei flung on his jacket and headed for the door.

"What makes you think we won't be spotted?" asked Alexei as they hastened up Trumpington Street and turned left into Bateman Street.

Passing the University Botanic Garden on the right, Marriott replied, "The 17.24 to King's Cross is the train everyone takes when they're going up to London for the evening or weekend. Dr McCabe won't see us in the crowd.

"And even if he does, we can just say that we're off to Covent Garden Opera or the South Bank for a concert. It's a perfectly plausible explanation, so there's no need for us to even try and avoid him, although obviously we'll try and keep out of sight."

For the time being at least, Alexei's mind was put at ease. He wasn't used to doing things on the spur of the moment, but the idea of an adventure began to appeal to him more and more, especially as freedom of movement was very tightly controlled in and around Moscow.

It was just turning twenty-two minutes past five as they raced across the station forecourt past the rank of black Camtax taxis. Marriott had been right. The southbound platform on the opposite side of the rails to the ticket office was packed with commuters and students. Marriott paid for two return tickets whilst Alexei scanned the sea of faces from the anonymity of the shadows.

"Can you see him?" asked Marriott, joining his companion.

"No," whispered Alexei in return, "but then there are so many people over there, I could easily miss him. Are you sure he'll be on this train? He might have gone down earlier."

"I'm sure," replied Marriott.

"How can you be?" asked Alexei.

"I've followed him before," said Marriott and then continued, "but only as far as the station. I've never gone all the way down to London."

People on the opposite platform began to ease forward in anticipation of the train's arrival.

"Here it comes!" exclaimed Marriott. "Wait until it's pulled into the station, then leg it over the footbridge as fast as you can. That should ensure we're not seen."

As the sound of the bogeys on the tracks became audible, Alexei suddenly jerked his companion back into the shadows and pointed across to the southbound platform. "There he is," he hissed through his teeth.

They both saw Dr McCabe rising from a covered shelter where he had obviously been sitting reading his newspaper. He appeared to look straight at them, but his gaze was distant and vacant. The brakes brought the 17.24 to King's Cross to a squealing halt. Marriott dragged Alexei by the arm as they crossed the barrier and ran towards the footbridge. By this time, they were meeting people coming the other way who had just got off, and their progress was impeded. The stationmaster was just waving his flag as they jumped aboard the first carriage, and the train was set in motion.

"Well, we made it," said Alexei.

"But not with much to spare," replied Marriott, wiping his brow. Cautiously, he looked back the length of the carriage to see if he could catch sight of Dr McCabe. "I can't see him," he concluded. "Hopefully, he's at the back of the train. That's where the empty seats will be, if there are any. I think we'd better stay here if you don't mind standing."

"How long is the journey?" asked Alexei, forgetting that he had made the trip in reverse on his arrival in Cambridge.

"About eighty minutes," replied Marriott.

Alexei made himself comfortable for the trip by jamming himself in the corner next to the toilets. He could just see through the sliding door towards the people sitting on the outer seats of the far side. Marriott had already given him the all clear as far as McCabe was concerned, so he was able to idly scrutinise the faces of passengers as they fell into that trance-like state induced on train journeys. Suddenly, he pulled back in horror as a familiar face confronted him.

"What is it? Is it McCabe?" asked Marriott frantically.

"No, no," replied Alexei in a state of shock.

"Just act natural," exclaimed Marriott, sure that it must be McCabe. "If you try and hide, he's bound to suspect we're spying on him."

"It's not McCabe, I tell you," insisted Alexei.

"Then who is it?" pressed Marriott.

"No one, no one at all," asserted Alexei. "No one you know, anyway." Marriott took a sneaking look at the faces of the passengers, the length of the carriage, but recognised no one. A thought suddenly occurred to him. "It's not someone who's following you, is it?"

"No, of course not," replied Alexei, indignant at the very thought.

"Are you hiding something from me, Alexei?" asked Marriott.

"For the last time, no, I tell you," exclaimed Alexei, giving even more of an impression that he was disturbed, and so fulfilling Marriott's suspicions.

Sensing that he wasn't going to get a straight answer, Marriott turned away and looked out of the side window as the freight sidings slipped by. Alexei remained crouching in his corner haven whilst he counted to one hundred, at the end of which he chanced another look down the centre aisle of the carriage. It was her, alright. He would have recognised her anywhere. It was the girl who had sat opposite him on his train journey from London to Cambridge the previous weekend.

The sight of her brought the whole experience flooding back with all its attendant guilt over her supposed blindness, the latent sexuality of the situation, both real and imagined, and the transposition of Dina for her. She was still reading a book. Alexei wondered whether it was another romantic novel or even the same book as last time. Even from this distance, he could discern her fingers flitting lightly over the braille characters and her mouth echoing the words on the page.

He recalled Marriott's questions – Are you hiding something from me? And is someone following you? In his own mind, Alexei was unsure whether the real answers to these questions were negative or positive. It certainly was a coincidence that he should encounter the same girl who had given him his emotional baptism into Cambridge life.

He longed to know whether she was totally blind or only partially sighted. Perhaps she was acting as Dr McCabe's lookout. If he were involved in subversive activities, what better backup than an accomplice who would scarcely arouse suspicion? Alexei checked himself for contemplating such absurd thoughts. The paranoia engendered by the stukach system in the Soviet Union and perpetuated in the Komsomol youth organisation was being illogically transposed to British society. This woman, whoever she was, was certainly no danger to him and could not possibly be involved with Dr McCabe.

The only lingering doubt remaining in his mind was the

coincidence of their second encounter on a train. He wondered who she really was and where she was going. This was an even more intriguing question than what Dr McCabe was up to. In fact, he would rather have followed her movements than the tutor's, such was his curiosity. For a blind person, she showed a great deal of independence.

He studied her features through the carriage door. It was like a two-way mirror. He could see her, but she could not see him. Alexei's self-confidence and composure began to return. Marriott was standing, looking out of the window on the other side of the carriage. From time to time, he would put his head out of the window and let the rush of wind blow over him as the intercity train reached speeds in excess of one hundred miles per hour.

He obviously found the experience exhilarating and was totally oblivious to Alexei's contemplations. The eighty-minute journey passed by very quickly until the noticeable slowing down as they reached the suburbs.

The express pulled into platform ten at King's Cross and St Pancras at six forty-five. Marriott looked at his watch and said, "We're a minute late. You just cannot rely on British Rail to be on time." Alexei was about to respond with a condemnation of the Soviet rail system when he realised that his companion was indulging in the favourite English pastime of irony and sarcasm.

"Are we going to get off first?" he asked.

"No," replied Marriott, "let's hang back until McCabe has got off, and then we can follow him. We know he's not in this carriage, so there's no danger of being seen. Just relax for the moment. I'll keep watch." He joined Alexei on his side of the carriage, which was nearest to the platform, pulled down the window, and chanced a look back the length of the train.

Doors were being flung open, and people were alighting. As they struggled with heavy pieces of luggage, railway porters rushed up with their trolleys offering assistance. The disembarkation had begun. People in the front carriage were taking suitcases and bags down from the racks, putting on their coats, and struggling up the aisle towards the door where Marriott and Alexei were stationed.

Whilst Marriott kept an eye out for Dr McCabe, Alexei was curious to find out how the blind girl would manage to get off the train. She had spurned his offer of assistance on their first encounter, so presumably she was perfectly capable of looking after herself despite her disability. She produced from her handbag one of those expanding white sticks comprising three interlocking sections, which she used to tap her way down the aisle towards the exit door. Instinctively, Alexei drew back the sliding door as she came towards him. Her eyes looked straight at him, although there was no sense of recognition, which convinced Alexei that she was totally blind. Instead, she smiled as if acknowledging his helpful gesture. As she reached the door, Alexei drew back to allow her to pass.

"Andrew!" He hailed his companion, who was still keeping watch by the window. Marriott turned around and, seeing the blind girl, opened the door to let her out. Alexei posed the same question as on their first encounter, "Can I help you out?"

This time she replied, "Yes, thank you." Alexei was rather surprised as he had expected her to turn him down.

"Oh," he exclaimed. The girl seemed to register his unease. He wondered whether she had recognised his voice. Blind people were supposed to have highly developed senses. He took her by the elbow and began to help her down the steps off the train.

"What are you doing?" exclaimed Marriott frantically. "Do you want McCabe to see you?"

By this time, Alexei had one foot on the step and the other on the platform. He had forgotten all about the danger of being seen by the tutor. He held the girl's outstretched hand, and the couple were frozen momentarily in a tableau. He looked into her opaque eyes. He was sure they had reacted at Marriott's mention of McCabe. Rapidly, he assisted her down the steps, pointed her in the direction of the ticket barrier, and leapt back up onto the train.

"Are you deliberately trying to blow our cover?" said Marriott. "If you want to advertise the fact that we're on the train, why don't you do a song and dance number on the platform. Maybe McCabe will see us then."

"Don't worry," Alexei reassured him. "I was only on the platform for a couple of seconds."

"That's all the time it takes," retorted Marriott with extreme annoyance. As they were still arguing, Alexei looked over Marriott's shoulder and suddenly whispered, "Get down."

As Marriott did not respond immediately, Alexei bodily dragged him to the floor. "Now what's the matter?" asked Marriott.

"It's McCabe," whispered Alexei, "he just passed by."

Tentatively, they both got to their knees and peered around the edge of the window to see Dr McCabe striding away towards the ticket barrier and the exit.

"Right, action stations," said Marriott, opening the carriage door and stepping out onto the platform.

They both followed at a safe distance as the tutor, carrying a small attaché case, reached into his pocket and produced his ticket for inspection at the barrier. He had just caught up with the blind girl, who was immediately in front of him in the queue. She seemed to be having trouble finding her ticket, and McCabe leaned forward as if to lend assistance. Eventually, they both passed through and then stood on the other side, exchanging a few words.

Neither Marriott nor Alexei could make out what it was about, but from a quiet conversation, the encounter became quite animated with McCabe gesticulating at her. Alexei began to wonder whether his initial premise had been correct. Perhaps the two did know one another after all. Perhaps she was telling him that two men were following him as she had overheard them mention his name. The girl seemed to be holding onto his sleeve, but eventually McCabe pulled himself away. Alexei thought that he saw McCabe take something from his pocket and press it into her hand, but from that distance, he couldn't be sure.

"What was that all about?" he asked. Marriott shrugged his shoulders as if it were of little consequence.

Alexei wondered if he was reading too much into it. Maybe McCabe had just been returning the girl's ticket to her, and she wanted to thank him for his assistance. After all, a blind person would instinctively hold onto the person they were talking to in order to gauge their distance and hold their attention.

In any event, the two had now separated. The girl was heading for the Euston Road exit whilst McCabe was heading for the steps leading down to the underground.

"Just stay well back," said Marriott. "Look casual and don't make any sudden movements that could attract attention."

In the concourse, McCabe bought a ticket from one of the automatic dispensers and went down the escalator, indicating Circle Line West. Alexei and Marriott bought tickets to the value of fifty pence, not knowing how far the tutor's eventual destination might be. As McCabe was nearing the bottom of the escalator, his pursuers were just beginning their descent.

As he turned left out of sight, they bounded down the steps two at a time on the outside so as not to lose him. As they stood at the bottom of the steps, they could hear the vibration of an approaching train and the accompanying rush of air in the tunnel. They looked at one another and raced on up the passage so as not to lose their quarry. Up ahead, they could see the blur of a train as it pulled into the station. The hydraulically operated doors were about to close as they found themselves on a virtually deserted platform.

"He must have got on," said Marriott, lunging forward and jamming his foot in the doors so that they automatically reopened.

Following Marriott's lead, Alexei jumped on board. The doors reclosed, and the underground train jerked into motion. In a matter of seconds, they had left the bright platform lights behind and were hurtling through the dark subterranean tunnels. Alexei and Marriott hung onto the straps as their bodies swayed from side to side. No sooner had the train reached peak velocity than it began to slow down again and make its next stop. Alexei read the mosaic inscription on the curved tunnel wall – Euston Square.

"Where's McCabe?" he asked. "Is he on the train?"

"I don't know," replied Marriott, "he could have given us the slip at King's Cross. We'll just have to wait and see. It's no good for us to walk the length of the train to find him. That would give the whole game away. Just keep your eyes peeled at every stop to see who gets out onto the platform."

"OK," nodded Alexei as the train picked up a fresh batch of passengers and continued on its way. They followed the same observation procedure at Great Portland Street, Baker Street, and Edgware Road. By the time they reached Paddington, Marriott was beginning to get despondent. "We must have lost him," he said, and began to relax his security measures so far as to step out onto the platform and wander about during each stop.

Still, they decided to carry on as the Circle Line would eventually, as its name implied, bring them back again in a loop to their starting point of King's Cross. Notting Hill Gate followed Bayswater. The next stop was High Street Kensington.

Once again, Marriott hopped out onto the platform,

throwing his earlier precautions to the wind. No sooner had his feet touched the platform than he leapt back onto the train as if he had been walking on hot coals. With a triumphant clenched fist, he addressed Alexei.

"Got him!"

Alexei followed his companion's line of sight and saw Dr McCabe making his way towards the exit. They both jumped off the train and pressed themselves against the inner subway wall, hidden from sight behind a chocolate dispensing machine. As the tutor's figure began to disappear up the steps towards the exit, Marriott and Alexei rushed forward in pursuit. They were some fifty yards behind as McCabe surrendered his ticket at the barrier. Hot on his heels, they emerged into the fresh air of Kensington High Street.

"There he goes," said Alexei, pointing excitedly at a disappearing figure striding south in the direction of Olympia. They were now well and truly entering into the spirit of the chase.

McCabe crossed the road and turned right up Holland Walk, which skirted the east side of Holland Park. The autumnal dusk provided good cover for the two pursuers, and they could easily slip behind the trees in the park, should the tutor happen to turn around. Past the Commonwealth Institute with its distinctive copper-sheathed roof, McCabe turned sharply left and headed off across the open expanse of green. He seemed to be making straight for an old disused bandstand, whose faded gold and green paintwork echoed the colour of the dead and decaying leaves which the wind had drifted into piles around its base. As Alexei and Marriott looked on from a discreet distance, McCabe mounted the steps of the bandstand. He took something from his coat pocket and, with his back turned to them, appeared involved in some activity.

"What the hell is he up to?" asked Marriott.

"Search me," replied Alexei as McCabe came down the

steps and headed off in the direction of the King George VI Memorial Hostel.

"Quick, let's take a look," said Marriott, rushing forward to examine McCabe's handiwork, but not at the expense of losing their quarry. "I think he concealed something," said Marriott, "but I couldn't see what it was. I wish we'd thought to bring a torch!" he added as an afterthought in annoyance at his lack of foresight, as his eyes peered through the twilight and his hands felt their way around the central column in search of whatever McCabe had left behind. Meanwhile, the tutor was disappearing into the distance.

Marriott looked over his shoulder and exclaimed, "It's no use. We'll have to leave it. Come on, or else we'll lose him."

Alexei was about to follow when, among all the spray-painted slogans and graffiti on the interior of the bandstand, he noticed an obviously recent addition. At eye level on the central column were three parallel chalk marks. He touched them with his finger. The chalk dust was dry and flaky. Could this have been McCabe's handiwork? And if so, what did it mean?

Alexei was about to shout after Marriott to come and take a look, but his companion was already halfway across the park in pursuit of the tutor. Alexei decided to keep his discovery to himself as he bounded down the steps and attempted to catch up with Marriott.

"Did you find anything?" he asked.

"No," lied Alexei convincingly. By this time, McCabe had reached the Belvedere Restaurant in the Holland Park grounds. Alexei and Marriott watched from the haven of the Flower Garden with its statues of the Neapolitan wrestlers. The restaurant was in darkness and its windows boarded up for the night to protect it from nocturnal vandalism. McCabe stopped and appeared to be surveying the lie of the land. They could see the whiteness of his breath in the chill evening air.

They listened for his movements whilst trying not to make a sound themselves. Both pursuers and quarry were still. Waiting.

As if finally satisfied that he was alone and unobserved, McCabe opened his attaché case and took out a white supermarket plastic bag wrapped up tightly. Like a tramp rummaging through rubbish, he then thrust his hand into the wire-mesh wastepaper basket clamped to the corner of the restaurant building. It appeared to be full of greaseproof bags, miniature bottles of lemonade, ice cream wrappers, cigarette packets and the remnants of people's picnic lunches. McCabe placed the plastic bag at the bottom of the pile of rubbish and covered it over again. He stood back as if to ensure the unobtrusiveness of his handiwork before making off in the direction of Abbotsbury Road.

Immediately, Marriott rushed forward. His sudden reaction caused the sleeping peacocks in the Flower Garden to be disturbed, and several let out a piercing, high-pitched cry. McCabe appeared to look back but was by now too far away to discern the cause of the commotion. Marriott spread himself flat out on the floor, flattening a flower bed in the process.

"Quick, let's take a look," he said as Alexei spread-eagled himself next to him. Together, they sprinted up to the side of the restaurant, whilst keeping one eye on the disappearing figure of McCabe.

"Watch him," instructed Marriott, nodding in the direction of the tutor. Meanwhile, he rummaged in the litter bin and retrieved the white plastic bag, which was tied up with a rubber band. Deftly, he undid the wrapping, placed his hand in the bag and brought out a small, unmarked cassette tape. He was about to put it in his coat pocket when Alexei stopped him in his tracks. "What do you think you're doing?"

"Confiscating the evidence," replied Marriott.

"Put it back," said Alexei.

"What?" exclaimed Marriott.

"Put it back," insisted Alexei.

"But how will we find out what's on the tape?" protested Marriott.

"Presumably, someone is due to pick up the tape. If they find out it's been removed, that will only arouse suspicion, and whatever McCabe is up to, he will probably become ultra-cautious or even suspend his activities altogether. This is obviously a regular drop-off and pick-up. If you're so curious, you can always follow him again. Now put it back."

Obviously torn between two minds, Marriott eventually gave in to Alexei's argument, repackaged the tape, and put it back underneath the pile of rubbish in the basket.

As they set off in pursuit of McCabe, Alexei said, "If there is a next time, remember to bring a portable cassette player so that you can listen to the tape on the spot and put it straight back."

"I've got to hand it to you," said Marriott, "you're a highly methodical person."

"It's my scientific training," replied Alexei. "You artistic types are too impulsive for your own good."

By this time, they had once again got McCabe in their sights and had left Holland Park altogether. McCabe emerged onto Holland Road opposite the Olympia exhibition centre. He crossed the junction of Hammersmith Road and Kensington High Street and headed down a small side street. Alexei and Marriott continued to follow at a discreet distance. As he turned the corner into Avonmore Road, Marriott tapped his companion on the shoulder and pointed up at the street sign. As Alexei read Addison Bridge Place, Marriott said, "You're not going to believe this, but Coleridge lived here at number seven in 1811–12."

The theme of the romantic poets, Coleridge and Wordsworth, seemed to be dogging Alexei wherever he went.

"I thought I recognised the name," confirmed Marriott.

"We can't seem to get away from Wordsworth and Coleridge," said Alexei, realising that the full implication and significance of The Prelude and The Marble Index were lost on his companion.

"Come on," said Marriott, "we don't want to lose him." McCabe turned right down Matheson Road, then left into Mornington Avenue.

"He obviously knows his way around," observed Alexei as the tutor finally came to a halt, looking up at one of the five-storey buildings. He went up the front steps and pressed one of the half dozen buttons corresponding to one of the flats on the block. He had obviously been expected, as within a matter of seconds, the door opened and a woman appeared on the doorstep:

She looked quite tall and slim. She was wearing a long Afghan coat, and her long black hair was tied back severely against her head.

"The countess?" queried Marriott. "Does she look Russian to you?"

"Now, how should I know?" replied Alexei. "Let's get a little closer to try and overhear them talking. We should have a better idea about her nationality and identity then."

Emboldened by their success, Alexei and Marriott closed the gap on their prey as the couple emerged onto West Cromwell Road. They crossed over and turned left into North End Road,

"Look," said Marriott, pointing at the illuminated circular red sign. "They're heading for the underground station."

At the last instant, McCabe and his companion turned into the entrance to a public house adjacent to the West Kensington underground station steps. The sign above the door read The Nashville. From inside came the harsh, echoing sound of a band performing live.

"Well, what do we do now?" asked Marriott. "If we follow them in, we're bound to be seen. If we wait outside, we'll never discover what they're up to."

"Stay there a minute," said Alexei, peering round the brown marble-tiled doorway of the old Fuller's public house. In front of him, there were two men blocking the entrance, one sitting at a table and the other, in a faded brown leather flying jacket, leaning against the table with one leg across the doorway. There was a tin of money and a roll of cloakroom tickets on the table. One of them saw Alexei and said, "It's a quid to get in, mate."

Alexei nodded and looked past them into the interior of the music lounge full of smoke and flashing lights. On a postage stamp-sized stage, a punk-type four-piece was bashing out some kind of frenetic, protest, anti-capitalist music. Up against the speakers at the right-hand side of the stage, McCabe was remonstrating with his companion. Alexei wondered how they could hear one another above all the noise. Then they moved into that quiet area behind the speakers despite the efforts of a roadie to keep them front of house.

Alexei motioned to Marriott. "Come on, it's safe to go in."

"Two quid," said the man at the door. He didn't move his leg out of the way until the money had changed hands.

Marriott followed Alexei cautiously into the music lounge. "Where are they?" he asked.

"At the top end behind the stage," replied Alexei. "They edged their way between the tables and the freakish spectators."

"I can't see them," said Marriott.

Alexei looked at the area where McCabe had been, but now he was nowhere in sight. He rushed up to the roadie and said. "Where are they? Have you seen them?"

"Who's that, mate?" came the reply.

"The couple who went backstage," insisted Alexei.

"Nobody's allowed backstage, mate." Alexei began to push his way past the roadie when the man grabbed hold of his arm. "Sorry, mate, you heard what I told you. Nobody's allowed backstage."

"I just want to..." began Alexei.

"Just nothing," came the reply more aggressively now.

Marriott saw that his companion was getting into trouble, so he came up to lend assistance.

"Is he with you?" asked the roadie, addressing Marriott, who nodded in agreement.

"They're back there, I tell you," insisted Alexei.

"There's nothing back there except the emergency fire exit," said the roadie dismissively.

"What?" said Marriott with dismay. "You mean you can get out back there?" fearing that McCabe had given them the slip.

"Yeah, but it's only used for loading and unloading the band's PA!" said the roadie.

Before he could conclude his explanation, Alexei and Marriott were retracing their steps through the crowd of punks towards the exit. As they rushed past, knocking the doorman's leg out of the way, he shouted after them. "What's the matter then? Didn't you like the show? There's no pass-out, you know. Once you're out, you're out. There's no getting back!"

With these words ringing in their ears, they turned left and ran past a side alley, up which they could see the illuminated fire exit, through which McCabe and his female companion had presumably slipped. Alexei was strangely reminded of the Kitchen Lane between Trinity College and St John's, onto which Wordsworth's old room in Cambridge looked out. Down the steps into the West Kensington tube station, they dashed and, without bothering to purchase a ticket, leapt over the barrier and ran down the steps.

Then they had a decision to make. One escalator was

marked District Line East, and the other District Line West.

"What do we do now?" asked Alexei. Marriott pondered a moment before replying. "You take East and I'll take West."

"That would seem appropriate for a citizen of the Soviet Union," quipped Alexei, trying to relieve the tension of the situation.

Forcing a smile, Marriott added, "I'll see you back at King's Cross at say nine o'clock. Meet me in the station bar."

Without wishing to waste further time, they went their separate ways. Alexei felt uncomfortable about trailing McCabe on his own, as it was basically Marriott's idea. If the tutor spotted him, he would have to carry the responsibility of the spying mission on his own. He hoped that McCabe and his lady friend had gone West.

This hope was soon dashed as he reached the eastbound platform and saw the couple standing on the edge waiting for the next train. It crossed his mind that he could easily abort the mission at this point, give up the chase, and return immediately to King's Cross. Marriott would be none the wiser.

After all, they had only assumed that McCabe had entered the underground station. He could just as easily be walking the streets of West Kensington at that very moment.

Alexei thought this would have been the easy way out if he wanted the quiet life. But he was becoming accustomed to the thrill of intrigue in his quest for The Marble Index, and if McCabe were involved in subversive activities, he wanted to know about it.

The escape through the fire exit in The Nashville was an obvious ploy to throw any potential pursuers off the scent. McCabe expected to be followed. His activities had all the hallmarks of a professional spy. As Alexei hung back in the shadows of the staircase, waiting for the train to arrive, he sifted the evidence over in his mind. The three chalk marks he had found on the bandstand in Holland Park were a signal for someone that a drop had been made. Alexei knew this from his father's work in New York. He ran several agents and would often pick up material from dead drops all over New York. Central Park was a favourite. This practice ensured that the agent and his master were never seen together. The use of a portable dead-drop in which written or indeed tape-recorded material was placed among discarded objects lying in plain sight without arousing any interest or suspicion, was favoured by KGB and GRU agents.

Before he could reflect further, the eastbound train pulled into the platform, and the couple got on. Alexei raced down the steps and, dodging among the shadows, managed to jump into the adjacent carriage. Immediately, he squatted down out of sight and prepared himself for a long journey. The next stop was Earl's Court. He chanced a look towards the next carriage and, to his surprise, saw McCabe and his friend alighting. Not only that, they were walking in his direction. He did not dare get off in front of them and so had to remain squatting out of sight. People had got off and others had got on. The doors were still open.

Alexei wondered how long the time delay was. Ten seconds. Twenty seconds.

McCabe was just passing his door as the hissing sound he feared began. The doors were closing. If he stuck out his foot to force them to reopen, McCabe was bound to see him. If he did nothing, the doors would close irrevocably, and he would be carried away to the next station, his quarry lost. In the event, he did nothing, paralysed by his own indecision.

The doors closed. McCabe and his female companion passed by. He had lost them.

Then, to Alexei's surprise, the doors reopened. Someone further down the train had obviously obstructed the doors, forcing them to reopen. Alexei saw his chance and leapt out onto the platform. He found himself only ten yards behind the couple with no cover in sight. He turned on his heels and began to walk in the opposite direction, in order to at least put some distance between them.

When he thought it was safe, he looked around. They were nowhere to be seen. Alexei retraced his steps and went through the opening marked District Line Southbound. He was getting used to living on his nerves.

Was this a case of McCabe travelling one stop and changing routes in an attempt to throw off any potential pursuers, or was he finally heading for his ultimate destination? Only time would tell.

Down another escalator and following the southbound signs, Alexei emerged onto another platform just in time to see a train pulling into the station. Its destination, illuminated on the front, read Wimbledon. Casually, he got on some two carriages further down from his quarry. Fortunately, they were so engrossed in one another's company that McCabe and his companion seemed oblivious to everyone else.

Alexei settled down to his accustomed squatting position. He wondered where Andrew Marriott was now. Presumably, he had realised pretty quickly that he was on the wrong trail and would already be on his way back to King's Cross. Alexei was still unsure what Marriott's motives were in all this. Why should he be so curious about McCabe's private life? It crossed his mind that Marriott wanted to use his findings to blackmail his tutor into giving him favourable marks for his thesis. After all, he was always complaining that McCabe had a low opinion of his work. This seemed too simplistic an explanation.

Meanwhile, the train hurtled on through West Brompton, Fulham Broadway, Parsons Green, and arrived at Putney Bridge. This was the last stop North of the Thames, and this was where McCabe and his lady friend got out. At the barrier, Alexei remembered that he had not purchased a ticket and so pressed a pound note into the inspector's hand. Before any argument could ensue, he rushed past, out into New Kings Road.

McCabe and the woman were already walking over Putney Bridge in the direction of the High Street. As he looked over at the River Thames, Alexei recalled that this was the starting point of the Oxford and Cambridge boat race, from Putney to Mortlake. On the far embankment, Alexei could see an impressive new multi-storeyed building with three enormous illuminated neon letters dwarfing the riverside. They read ICL, which meant nothing to him.

As McCabe reached the far bank, the couple turned left and entered the forecourt of the building. Waiting for them at the front entrance was a man carrying several large tapes under his arm.

As Alexei approached the front of the building, he read the inscription above the door – International Computers Limited, ICL House. Whatever they were up to, Alexei speculated, it was highly unlikely that they were on their way to a chess congress as McCabe had intimated back in Cambridge to Dr Fischer. After a brief greeting, the three moved on down Putney High Street. At the corner of Disraeli Road, they stopped and stood talking halfway up the steps to a grimy Victorian building. Alexei was able to close up as they had their backs to him, and he slipped into a shop doorway close by. He could now, for the first time, faintly make out the voices which carried on the chill night air. The woman was saying, "I think it's worked. The pressure should tell in the end."

The other two were nodding enthusiastically. Alexei thought the voice sounded too English to be English. It rang of the kind of English taught to foreigners in language schools and was known as received pronunciation. He was sure she was a foreigner, but there was no trace of Russian in her accent. He listened again, and what he heard made him gasp with surprise. The woman said, "What about Kunayev? Have you made contact?"

"It's all taken care of," McCabe replied.

They all seemed pleased with this response. The way the woman had pronounced the name, his name, Kunayev, convinced him she was Russian. For the first time, he felt frightened.

The three people disappeared up the steps. His heart was beating rapidly, and his hands were visibly shaking. Taking his courage in both hands, he approached the front of the building. A greenish brass plaque announced Eternit House. Radio Free Europe. This was the home of the radio station that broadcast Western propaganda to countries behind the Iron Curtain.

Alexei stepped back onto the road and almost fell under the wheels of a speeding black London taxi.

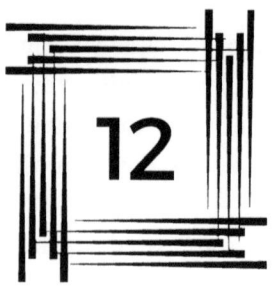

12

Dina walked through the gates of the Serbsky Institute on Kropotkinskaya Ulitza with great trepidation. Thursday was one of the regulation visiting times at the psychiatric hospital.

This would be the first time she had seen her father since the commission of enquiry. He had barely recognised her on that occasion, such was his subjection to depressant drugs. She had no Dr Sloboda to lean on for emotional support this time. She was totally on her own. The prospect of meeting the man who was once her father, indeed still was, underneath the drug-induced persona, frightened her. What could she say to reassure him? Would he even understand her?

One of the KGB guards pinned a visitor's badge on her coat and rang through from his post to reception in the main building to forewarn them of her arrival. As she walked up the long gravel driveway, she jangled two sets of keys in her coat pocket – one to the family apartment in Izmaylovsky Park and the other to Boychenko's apartment on Kutuzovsky Prospekt. The previous evening, she had returned to her father's flat without incident.

For once, Boychenko had been the perfect gentleman. He had seen Dina to her door without making any pretext for wishing to enter for a nightcap or any other such euphemism. She had been so impressed with his gentleness and tenderness that she had even rewarded him with a kiss on the cheek, much to her own surprise as well as to his delight, even at such a small token of affection. She had not, in fact, taken the sleeping pill prescribed to her by Dr Sloboda in case Boychenko was tempted to take advantage of her drowsy state. She need not have feared on that account, for the eventuality did not arise. As his black Chaika had disappeared into the night, Dina began to think that perhaps Boychenko's reputation was ill-informed and ill-founded.

She appreciated the dangers inherent in this supposition, as many other girls in the office had been lulled into exactly the same sense of false security.

And as a result, they had been mentally and emotionally scarred for life.

Dina was determined that the same would not happen to her. After all, it was she who was in control. It was she who was manipulating him, not the other way around. She was able to justify her actions to herself insofar as they formed a part of her overall scheme to free her father and escape with Alexei to the West.

For the time being, she banished all thoughts of Boychenko from her mind as she entered the front door to the Serbsky Institute. A nurse in a stiff white uniform noted her time of arrival in a register and then led her off to a wing where secure patients were being treated in individual rooms rather than on open wards.

Outside room 4E, she stopped, took out a bunch of keys and unlocked the door. She stepped back for Dina to pass by and said starkly, "You have half an hour. No more, no less." She looked at her watch and made a note of the time.

As Dina entered the room, she heard it click and the key being turned in the lock. The room was very white and bare. There were no windows, and a lone light bulb shone out starkly from the ceiling, protected by a wire mesh. There appeared to be no switches on the walls to turn the light on and off. Neither was there any source of heating in the room. Dina shivered as much out of a sense of horror as a reaction to the lowering of the temperature. The wall-to-wall whiteness made her screw up her eyes as her pupils contracted. It was like being snow-blind.

Across the white floor, lying on white sheets, clothed in a white smock, was her father, Vladimir Maksimovich Russakov. The pallor of his face matched the overall whiteness of the room. Her immediate reaction was to shrink back in horror. Steadying her nerve, she consoled herself by humming the opening few bars of her father's first piano concerto, which he himself had conducted so brilliantly in performance only the previous year at the Tchaikovsky Concert Hall with Svyatoslav Richter as the soloist. She continued to approach him step by furtive step, hoping that the melody line of his personal favourite composition would evince some flash of recognition, some spark of intelligence. Instead, he just lay there with vacant eyes, his head propped up under a bolster in a semi-sitting position.

Slowly, she lowered herself onto the edge of the bed and gently took both his hands in hers. They felt icy cold to the touch. He formerly had such a ruddy, glowing complexion. Now his face and body looked emaciated.

He had obviously lost a lot of weight. Underneath the white smock, he was naked. His hip bones protruded through the garment as if his whole body were crying out for help. Dina felt his brow and brushed aside the unkempt locks of his dark, matted hair.

How could they do such a thing to her father, a man who was so fiercely patriotic and had upheld the Communist values of the Soviet Union all his life? And this was the way he had been repaid. Her heart was filled with hatred and contempt for Dr Luntz and Dr Shostakovich, who abused and betrayed the good name of medicine and psychiatry and who practised their trade at the behest of the agencies of the KGB and the GRU. At least they had to live with their own consciences, which Dina would have found no easy thing in their position.

Clinically, she eliminated from her mind the drugs to which her father might have been subjected, as Dr Sloboda had explained the symptoms to her beforehand. Sulfazin raised the temperature to 104 degrees and made bodily movement painful. Reserpine caused extensive brain damage. Andaksin provoked hallucinations and loss of memory, whilst Aminazin produced extreme shock and depression. Dina examined her father's arm, which was riddled with injection marks and accompanied by a skin rash. She surmised the cause was Aminazin, as excessive injections of the drug brought about exhaustive collapse, severe skin reactions, and a lack of muscular control, as evidenced at the commission of enquiry. Another side effect of Aminazin was to attack the memory system, which could explain why Vladimir Maksimovich had not recognised her on their first encounter since his arrest. In his waking hours, her father would now exhibit all the signs of chronic schizophrenia, which would validate the forensic psychiatrists' opinion of his health. So long as treatment continued, Vladimir Maksimovich would appear at the next month's commission of enquiry looking for all the world the epitome of a mental patient. This was in spite of the fact that everyone present knew that the symptoms were drug-induced on the orders of the very doctors who were charged with treating the patient. It was a vicious circle to which Dina could see no way out.

If she were not careful, she too could end up in a mental institution. She had to be strong. She had allies in the persons of Dr Sloboda and Alexei Kunayev. She had an influential figure in Konstantin Boychenko, whom she could manipulate to her own ends. What she really needed was either the bargaining counter of The Marble Index or the signature of Mikhail Suslov, the Chief Ideologue and Second Secretary, on a release document. One was either misplaced among millions of other card files in the KGB Central Index or tucked away in some obscure Cambridge archive, whilst the other was as yet inaccessible at her social level. She was working on the second as her newly acquired apartment on Kutuzovsky Prospekt made her an instant neighbour of high-ranking party officials, including Leonid Brezhnev, Yuri Andropov, and Mikhail Suslov himself.

Her immediate thoughts returned to her father. Should she leave him to rest or try and rouse him from his collapsed state? Dina wondered whether she could bear to see him once again in that conscious, drugged condition.

Before she could reach a conclusion, the decision was made for her. Vladimir Maksimovich's eyelids fluttered and then opened. He stared straight ahead in his propped-up position, the length of the room. He seemed totally unaware of Dina sitting by his side on the edge of the bed.

Softly, she called out to him, "Papa." There was no response, so she called again, "Papa, it is Dina."

Vladimir Maksimovich blinked as if to clear not only his vision but also his faculties of memory and speech. Slowly, he opened his mouth and, with great effort, tried to articulate. But there was no sound.

She clasped his hands more tightly now between her own in an attempt to generate some reciprocal warmth and feeling. His eyes began to close again. Sensing that he was about to drift back into drugged semi-consciousness, Dina became more agitated and cried out, "No, no, Papa. Do not leave me again. I won't let you go."

The sudden raising of her voice caused the video camera

high up in the corner of the room to be activated. It audibly zoomed in on the father and daughter. The entire scene was being monitored and taped from a studio in the basement of the Institute. Dina began to shake her father by the shoulders to try and bring him to life. She was getting hysterical by now.

The door suddenly opened, and the nurse reappeared in the company of a male orderly. They stood an instant framed in the doorway as Dina rocked her father back and forth in her arms, laughing and crying and humming the melody of the beloved piano concerto.

"Your time is up," said the nurse harshly. "Visiting time is over."

"No," sobbed Dina as the orderly prised apart her embrace and physically lifted her off the bed. Her whole body was curled up as if in a foetal position.

"You realise I will have to make out a report on your behaviour," said the nurse with stiff formality. "You may have put your visiting rights in jeopardy." From behind the curtain of her hysteria, Dina rationalised that the nurse and the Director of the Institute belonged to a state of inhumanity far beyond that of her father, even in his drug-induced condition. And she felt sorry for them. Despite her animosity and hatred, she felt compassion, for they too were victims of the same system that had found her father guilty of a crime against the state and incarcerated him in a psychiatric institution. They, too, were victims. They were all victims.

Without looking back at her father, Dina allowed herself to be escorted from the secured room and down the corridor. She offered no resistance.

Meanwhile, in room 4E, Vladimir Maksinovich Russakov lay back on his pillow, closed his eyes, and began haltingly to hum the opening few bars of his piano concerto in

C sharp minor.

"I waited for you till eleven. Where did you get to?" said Marriott, bursting into Alexei's room without bothering to knock.

Alexei had been carefully rehearsing and re-rehearsing his lines on his way back to King's Cross and on the train journey up to Cambridge. Now the time for explanation had really come, and he was unsure what to say.

In view of his continued silence, Marriott ranted on, "Well, did you follow him? Did you lose him or what? Tell me."

Alexei had wondered whether to take the easy way out and simply pretend that he had not caught up with McCabe or that he had given him the slip, but he suspected that he would not be capable of carrying off the deception convincingly enough to fool Marriott. "I er..." he hesitated.

"Come on, spit it out," encouraged Marriott.

"I was late," said Alexei eventually.

"Well, I know that," said Marriott contemptuously. He had obviously been storing up his anger overnight.

"I didn't come back till the early hours of this morning," said Alexei.

"You mean you followed McCabe all night?" exclaimed Marriott.

"No, I wandered round the West End. I needed to think."

"But you still haven't told me about McCabe," insisted Marriott.

"OK, I followed him, alright!" said Alexei finally, with a certain amount of relief that he could at least tell that much of the truth.

Marriott remained silent now, encouraging Alexei to elaborate. "Well, where did he go? What did he do? Who did he meet?" coaxed Marriott in view of his companion's silence.

"Before I do," said Alexei, "just tell me one thing."

"What's that?" asked Marriott.

"Why did you suggest we follow him in the first place?"

"I told you before!" replied Marriott. "Curiosity. There's something not quite straight about him. Oh, he's a good tutor alright, and he knows his subject, but he's not quite what he seems. All that Russian background knowledge. It's not normal. Everything points to him being a spy or at least a recruiter."

"For the KGB, you mean?" prompted Alexei.

"I suppose so," replied Marriott.

"If that's the case," rationalised Alexei, "why is he so open about it? You'd think he'd keep quiet about his communist sympathies and affiliations rather than be so blatantly obvious about it."

Alexei looked Marriott straight in the eyes. "And what's more, if you're right, why are you divulging it to me, a Russian of all people? For all you know, I may be a Communist infiltrator working in collaboration with Dr McCabe."

Marriott's face dropped. "You're not, are you?"

"No, of course not," Alexei reassured him, having tested his reaction. "If anything, I'm on your side. No, I think McCabe could just as easily be a recruiter for the British secret intelligence services."

"You found something out, didn't you?" said Marriott, smiling now. "You followed him and you found something out."

"Well, yes, I did," admitted Alexei.

"Come on then. It's like trying to get blood out of a stone, to make you talk," said Marriott. "Tell me where he went."

Alexei took a deep breath and began: "Well, I managed to follow them on the underground as far as Putney. There, they got off and picked up a third person outside the offices of ICL. That's a big computer firm. Then all three of them went into the headquarters of Radio Free Europe. And that's where I left them."

Marriott was poised, leaning forward in his chair, waiting for Alexei to continue with his story, but nothing further was forthcoming. "And is that it?" he said.

Alexei shrugged his shoulders. "I didn't dare go inside or wait until they came out again in case they saw me. I thought I'd done enough. Besides, that tells us a lot. The business with the tapes means he's probably a broadcaster on Radio Free Europe. They broadcast programmes behind the Iron Curtain like the BBC World Service and the Voice of America. That would explain how he knows so much about the Soviet Union. If he doesn't broadcast himself, he could be a researcher."

"Hm," said Marriott, sounding far from convinced. "It still doesn't tell us which side he's on. What was on the tape that McCabe hid in the wastepaper basket in Holland Park? And who was supposed to pick it up?"

"You'll have to go back the next time and wait and see. We know where McCabe ends up, but we don't know who his contact is. I suppose he could be working for both sides, for the British overtly and the Communists covertly."

"I feel as if I know even less than when we started," said Marriott, cradling his head in his hands. "Did you manage to overhear any of their conversation?" he asked finally.

"No, I didn't," lied Alexei. "I was just too far away." He didn't intend to tell anyone that he had overheard his name being mentioned. Much as he trusted Marriott, this piece of information was too personal to be divulged.

Marriott shook his head. "Shame about that. Ah, well, I reckon we'll have to try again next week." He turned and began to leave. "See you at dinner!" came his parting shot.

"Yes, see you," replied Alexei, who thought that the conversation had come to rather an abrupt end. The door closed, and Alexei stared hard at the ceiling. Something in Marriott's reactions had not rung true. His responses looked equally as rehearsed as Alexei's own. It was as if they were both reading from a prepared script.

Why should Marriott confide in him his fears that McCabe was a Communist sympathiser who might even be recruiting and propagandising for the Soviet Union, when Alexei was a supposed Communist himself? And another thing, Marriott had not seemed surprised to learn that McCabe had entered the RIB building. It was as if he knew already.

Alexei remembered the time when he was in his early years at High School. His father had caught him listening to Radio Free Europe. Instead of being annoyed at the juvenile rebellion against socialist attitudes and the glorification of capitalist values, his father had just laughed and said, "Do you know that the RFE headquarters in Munich is almost entirely run by KGB infiltrators. You listen carefully to the propaganda, my son. You will find its subtle nuances are pro-Soviet and not anti." Alexei had listened, and his father was right. In spite of the words themselves, the message was decidedly pro-Moscow line. From that moment on, he never listened again.

Alexei heard the door to Marriott's room open and then close. It was not yet dinner time. He jumped to his feet, sensing that he knew already where Marriott was going. He heard the distant footsteps echoing down the stone steps. Marriott was already at the bottom. Alexei opened his door and, cat-like, ran downstairs into Great Court. He could see Marriott ahead of him striding out in the direction of New Court and fell in behind. As he disappeared through the staircase portal, Alexei gained ground quickly. The door immediately to the left on the ground floor was closing fast. Alexei had been in that room once before. It belonged to Dr McCabe.

The reason for Marriott's visit could have been perfectly innocent – a social call or a literary query. After all, they did have a tutor-postgraduate relationship. But coming so soon after Marriott's visit to Alexei's room for an update on McCabe's covert activities, it was too much of a coincidence.

This time, the outer 'oak up' door was not in place, and the inner lighter door had not been properly closed. Alexei pressed his ear against the gap. He could hear voices.

McCabe was saying, "How much did he tell you?"

"Almost everything," replied Marriott, "but not in much detail. He kept it short and to the point."

"Do you think he trusts you now?" asked McCabe.

There was no audible response, but Alexei could visualise Marriott nodding his head in assent. He pressed himself closer to the door. Everything had gone quiet. Alexei wondered if they had heard a noise. He didn't know whether to stay still or take cover.

Then he heard McCabe say, "Did you close the door properly?"

This caused Alexei to turn on his heels and hide behind one of the pillars in New Court quadrangle. Out of sight, he could hear the tutor's door open.

McCabe looked around the deserted entrance hall, gave a look of satisfaction and then disappeared back inside his room.

Alexei heard the door closing with great relief. He didn't dare return to his listening post for fear of being caught. Besides, he would not now be able to hear, and had, after all, heard enough already. It was obvious to him now that Dr McCabe and Andrew Marriott were involved in some form of conspiracy to ensnare him in some way. The one pretended to be his friend and the other his enemy, whilst both were on the same side. But which side? Alexei still did not know whether they were working for the British secret intelligence services with a mandate to test his reactions, and if favourable, to recruit him into MI6, or whether they were agents of the KGB or some other Communist country commissioned to ensure that he did not betray his socialist consciousness.

He no longer knew whom he should trust.

On the way back to his room across Nevile's Court, he passed the Wren Library. The head porter and his assistants were carrying large boxes up the stairs. The library was not normally open at that time. "Hello, Mr Crowther," said Alexei. "What are you doing?"

"Good day, Mr Kunayev," replied the head porter formally. "We're just returning these volumes to their proper place. They've been on loan to St John's College for an exhibition to celebrate one of their most distinguished former scholars."

"Who might that be?" asked Alexei out of a passing interest.

The reply, however, came as a shock. "William Wordsworth. His old rooms, which overlook Kitchen Lane, are normally used for private banqueting facilities, but they've been opened up to the general public for a short period. The Master of St John's asked the Wren librarian to provide him with all the Wordsworth first editions for use in a display stand. We were only too pleased to oblige, as we have a reciprocal arrangement with most colleges. However, I must say that we're pleased to have them back in our safekeeping." He patted the boxes affectionately as if they were his own cherished private collection.

So, this explained why Alexei had not been able to find any volumes of Wordsworth's poetry when he wanted to discover the origin of The Marble Index. Marriott had denied taking them out, which had led Alexei to assume that it was Dr McCabe who was hoarding them. In fact, neither had been responsible. Alexei wondered whether Crowther was a literary man himself or just had an acquisitive attitude towards the Wordsworth first editions.

"Tell me something, Mr Crowther," he said, "does The Marble Index mean anything to you?" Not really expecting the head porter to be aware of the literary allusion, he was rather surprised to hear the response.

"Why yes, sir, it's a quotation from Wordsworth's Prelude. It refers to the statue of Sir Isaac Newton in the college ante-chapel."

"Thank you, Mr Crowther," said Alexei.

"It's a pleasure, sir," said the head porter.

Alexei moved on in the direction of Great Court. He was strangely reassured by Crowther's answer. If a man in his menial position understood the allusion, surely men of the intellect of Guy Burgess and Anthony Blunt would have understood it and used it in full knowledge of its significance.

The secret of The Marble Index and its hidden list of names was definitely tied up with the marble statue of Sir Isaac Newton. Alexei was convinced of that. If only those vacant white eyes could see, and that resolute mouth speak. He returned to his room on E4 stairs, ironically, the former rooms of Sir Isaac Newton himself.

Having spent a couple of hours at the archive building on Prospekt Marksa, Dina returned at lunchtime to Boychenko's apartment on Kutuzovsky Prospekt. Many eminent people, including artists, writers, high-ranking party officials and diplomats, lived in the large pink brick apartment blocks.

Stretching West from Kalinin Bridge across the Moskva River, it ran along the route of the old main road to Smolensk, Minsk and Warsaw. It had been thoroughly modernised from 1957 onwards, when the old district of squalid izbas, or huts, had been torn down.

Dina emerged from the Kutuzovskaya metro station. On her right stood the enormous cylinder of glass and aluminium containing the famous Panorama of the Battle of Borodino. The building was opened in 1962 to mark the 150th anniversary of the battle, and behind it stood the little wooden house known as Kutuzov's Izba, where the field marshal commanding the armies defending Moscow in the 1812 campaign made the decision to abandon the capital to the French.

Dina continued to walk West in the direction of the Triumphal Arch, which was a monument erected to mark the eventual victory over Napoleon. She stood looking up at the Arch with its paired Corinthian columns, topped by a chariot drawn by six horses and driven by an allegorical winged figure of Glory. The Arch originally stood at the point where the road from St Petersburg entered Moscow, and during Imperial visits to the capital, the procession of the Czar passed through the Triumphal Arch on its way to the Kremlin. Like the Moscow Triumphal Arch in Leningrad, it was demolished as a relic of the past but was re-erected in the upsurge of patriotism after the Second World War. In terms of symbolism to the outside world, the Triumphal Arch and the Serbsky Institute represented both the best and the worst of the Soviet Union.

Dina turned around and began to walk back East in the direction of the centre of Moscow. She was just idly passing her time, contemplating her next course of action. Her target, Mikhail Suslov, lived somewhere along this beautiful avenue, but she did not know his exact address. At the junction with Bolshaya Dorogomilovskaya Ulitza, there was a row of public telephone booths. The directories were missing, so Dina placed a two-kopeck piece in the slot and dialled directory enquiries. It was a long shot, as Suslov was probably ex-directory anyway.

After a series of long buzzes, which showed that the number was ringing, she was connected to one of the operators. "Hello," she said, "can you tell me the telephone number and address of comrade Suslov, first names Mikhail Andreyevich. The address is Kutuzovsky Prospekt, but I don't know the number."

Dina waited; she realised that the operator would probably

know the name but hoped that her matter-of-fact enquiry would not evoke any suspicion of her motives. As the silence continued, she prepared herself to slam down the receiver in case the call was being traced. All trunk calls and foreign calls were monitored and recorded. In addition, any suspicious local call had to be referred to a supervisor to see if it merited investigation. There was a clicking on the line as the time rolled over one minute. Dina became more and more agitated.

Eventually came the response, "I'm sorry to keep you waiting, caller. What is your number, please? Maybe I can ring you back. Replace the receiver and wait there."

Immediately, Dina let go of the telephone as if it were red hot, and let it fall swinging on its flex. As the door closed behind her, she could still hear the distant crackling voice of the operator saying, "Hello, caller. Are you there, are you there?" It was obvious they knew the call was coming from a public telephone booth and not from a private number, and they were trying to trace the location by either keeping her on the line or setting up their equipment ready for the call-back.

If Dina had remained there, no doubt a black KGB Chaika would have drawn up outside the booth. She would have been bundled inside and taken away for questioning. Ordinary citizens who tried to contact high-ranking party officials for whatever motives, however innocent, were highly suspicious and had to be actively discouraged.

Dina continued to walk towards Kalinin Bridge and the centre of town, chancing a look over her shoulder at the telephone booth. As she did so, a black limousine pulled up alongside the booth, and two men got out. They collared a man who was just about to open the door and presumably investigate the receiver hanging loose from its cradle. As she had not replaced the receiver, they had been able to establish a trace. It was fortunate she had left when she did. Remaining calm, she continued to walk away without looking back.

Mikhail Suslov lived somewhere along Kutuzovsky Prospekt. She would just have to keep walking up and down the neighbourhood in the hope that eventually she would come across him. She could try asking in the local shops or the caretakers in the blocks of flats, but they could so easily be stukachi that this course of action was too risky to undertake.

Some residences bore commemorative plaques denoting famous former inhabitants. At number 22, the film director Alexander Dovzhenko had lived, whilst number 7 had been the home of A. T. Tvardovsky, the poet and editor of Novy Mir. At number 1, Kutuzovsky Prospekt stood the Ukraina Hotel, outside which appropriately enough was a statue of Taras Shevchenko, the Ukrainian national poet.

It was by now well past Dina's regular lunchtime, and she was a fair way away from her habitual haunt of the Metelitsa ice cream parlour on Prospekt Kalinina on the far side of the Moskva River. Instead, she decided to call in at one of the non-residential restaurants at the Ukraina Hotel. Despite its pseudo-classical exterior, this 29-storey hotel was only built in 1956, and the interior was relatively modern.

To the left of the main entrance was a buffet that sold snacks and cold drinks. Dina felt as if she could use an alcoholic drink both to settle her nerves after the experience with the telephone and prepare her for another long afternoon in the archives, so she went instead into the 3-lounge bar. Soft piped music and deep carpets had a relaxing influence in themselves. A couple of brandies would also help along the way. Sitting on barstools were what looked like out-of-town businessmen or foreign tourists.

The barman was pouring large measures of vodka, and he was obviously having trouble trying to refuse an offer to join in the round. Staff were forbidden by the hotel management to accept tips or free drinks.

"I am sorry, sir," said the barman in a heavy Russian accent as Dina approached the bar, "I cannot drink."

"Can't drink. A barman who can't drink. That is the darndest thing I ever heard," came the reply from a man in his mid-forties in a dark-blue pin-striped suit. Out of the corner of his eye, he spotted Dina and addressed her, "Say, honey, you'll let me buy you a drink, won't yer?"

Dina's high school English was able to interpret the gist of the American's question. Very softly, she replied, "No, thank you."

"Oh, go on," he persisted. "I hate to drink alone." He eyed her up and down appreciatively.

"No, really, thank you," she said with insufficient assertion to deter the advances of the drunken predatory American.

"I'm sure there's something I can get you," he continued, his voice heavy with sexual innuendo.

Then Dina had an idea. When the barman relievedly moved away to serve other customers, she drew the American to one side and said, "You can do something for me."

"What's that, honey? And what do I get in return?" He was obnoxiously drunk.

Dina put on her most seductive expression. "You have one hundred dollars?" she asked.

"For you, honey. Sure!" he replied, thinking to himself that Moscow whores were cheap at the price. He took out his wallet and pulled out a hundred-dollar bill.

Dina took a pen and a scrap of paper from her handbag and wrote in Russian, 'Give me the address of Second Secretary Mikhail Andreyevich Suslov, and this money is yours.' She then folded the piece of paper in two. Dina realised that local hotel staff would know the addresses of famous residents in the area. They probably ate in the restaurant and even drank in the bars.

The temptation of hard foreign currency, which was highly sought after on the black market and could also be spent in the Beryozka shops on foreign consumer goods not normally available to Soviet citizens, would be too much for any employee to resist. Of course, he would be suspicious as to why the American would want the address, but the money would overcome any doubts. And as for the American, he would think she was handing over the money to the barman for safekeeping or because he was her boyfriend or pimp.

Dina was banking that in his confused, alcoholic state, he would be prepared to believe anything. She stayed around the corner out of sight whilst the American went about his business. In a few seconds, he returned with a triumphant look on his face as if he had just clinched a multi-million dollar contract. He handed Dina the piece of paper. On it, the barman had scribbled 14/31 Kutuzovsky Prospekt. Dina beamed with delight, which the American took to be approval of the deal. She had presumably received instructions from her pimp.

Now Dina had to play out the rest of the charade. "What is your room number?" she asked.

"12104," he replied, swaying from side to side on the spot.

"You go up. I will follow," she said encouragingly. Dina wondered just how naive the man could be. The combination of alcohol, his own sense of vanity, and the deal struck was apparently sufficient to set him on his way. "Don't be long now!" He wagged his finger at her as he staggered into the foyer and pressed for the elevator.

Once he had disappeared from sight, Dina waited until the barman's back was turned before swiftly crossing the bar and running out of the main entrance into the street. She didn't want him to get a look at her in case he was asked to identify her at a later date. She was out. She had the address. It had worked like clockwork. Maybe her luck was about to change. She hurriedly put some distance between herself and the Ukraina Hotel, and before she knew it, she had arrived back at the junction with Bolshaya Dorogomilovskaya Ulitsa. With some alarm, Dina realised that she had returned to the location of the telephone booths from which she had attempted to call comrade Suslov. Maintaining an even pace, she walked straight past them. In fact, they were all deserted, and there was now no sign of the black KGB Chaika. She casually looked up at the number of the apartment blocks. In large black wrought iron, the figures read 31.

Ironically, Dina had attempted to contact Suslov by telephone from virtually in front of the very block in which he was a resident.

Taking her courage in both hands, she mounted the front steps. She wondered whether a caretaker would challenge her in the entrance hall, as visitors were often vetted in such sensitive areas, but the foyer was deserted. Maybe he was on his lunch break or was away on a commission for one of the residents. Whatever the reason for his absence, Dina breathed a sigh of relief, as this made her access that much easier.

Quickly, she raced up the steps to the first floor, pushed open the fire door, and peered down the brightly lit carpeted corridor. The cool rush of air that greeted her reminded her of the conditions of the tape and disc store at the KGB computer data centre where she worked. She associated in her mind air conditioning with the preservation of computer data and not the cossetting of individual people. She wondered whether Suslov would have a KGB or GRU guard to look after him. Knowing the way that the Politburo tended to neglect its former heroes and treat them so shabbily, Dina was hopeful that the ageing party executive was no longer deemed worthy of personal protection.

As she walked down the corridor, she reflected on how different things might have been. Indeed, earlier in the year, when it was rumoured that First Secretary Brezhnev had suffered a stroke and had briefly disappeared from active political life, Mikhail Suslov had been regenerated to share the

Party leadership with Andrei Kirilenko. But at the age of seventy-three, he was by now too old to command the post of General Secretary on a permanent basis. And when Brezhnev had recovered, he had simply slipped away again into the background once the expediency of the moment was over. No wonder he was an embittered old man to have been so used and abused by the Party he had served since his initiation into the Komsomol in 1918.

Halfway down the corridor on the right-hand side, Dina found herself outside room 14. It struck her that the barman at the Ukraina Hotel might have given the American a false address in return for the one hundred dollars.

Doubts began to bombard her from all sides. Even if Mikhail Suslov did answer the door, what was she going to say to him? Please release my father from the Serbsky Institute. Should she grovel on her knees and beg him, or offer him her body in return for her father's freedom? The whole strategy now seemed so far-fetched and impossible.

She walked on past the door marked 14. She then became angry with herself. She had come this far and was not about to give in now. Dina turned smartly on her heels, and before she knew what she was doing, she knocked loudly on the door. To her initial horror, the door sprang open on the impact of her fist and was accompanied by a voice from inside saying, "Come right in, it's open."

Doing as she was bidden, Dina entered the apartment and closed the door behind her. She found herself in a hallway.

The voice said again, "I'm down here in the lounge."

She followed the sound of the voice down the hall and emerged into a luxurious lounge. Standing with his back to her was a very tall, upright figure of a man. He was facing a large marble fireplace, on which he appeared to be arranging a group of oriental China ornaments.

Suddenly, he looked up into the mirror above the fireplace

and caught sight of Dina's reflection behind him. Immediately, he wheeled round.

Obviously, he had been expecting someone, although not her. The two confronted one another with a stare. Neither knew what to do or say next.

After a long pause, the stern features of Mikhail Suslov broke into a wide grin, and he burst out laughing. Dina recognised him from the photographs she had seen in Pravda and on posters at party rallies. He looked much older than in these flattering representations, but she was impressed with his stature and bearing. She imagined that as a young man, he had cut a tall and dashing figure.

"I take it you are not from Politizdat," said Suslov, clasping his hands behind his back.

"No," replied Dina rather nervously.

"I was expecting a publisher's representative at any moment, but I'm sure he is no way nearly as attractive as you."

Dina smiled, unsure what to say next. Strangely enough, Suslov did not seem at all perturbed or embarrassed by the situation. If, as Dina suspected, his lifestyle was lonely and isolated, maybe he would be only too glad of a little unexpected female company.

"Sit down," he said, gesturing to an armchair, and showing the lead by taking a seat himself in a high-backed wickerwork chair. "Would you care for some tea?" he asked as Dina struggled to open her side of the conversation.

Despite his initial surprise, Suslov was now acting as if he were used to entertaining strange ladies who wandered in off the streets. He picked up a samovar from a glass-topped table and poured out the boiling water into an ornate teapot. He then filled two teacups and handed one of them to Dina. She had just taken a first sip when there was a knock at the door.

Suslov made no move to go and answer it. "Did you close the door behind you?" he asked.

"Yes," replied Dina.

"Good," he said, continuing to sip his tea.

"Well, aren't you going to answer it?" she said, which was the greatest number of words she had uttered since entering the apartment.

"No," smiled Suslov. "After all, it is only that stuffy old representative from Politizdat who's come to discuss the publication of my latest series of speeches for the Politburo."

The knocking at the door continued. Suslov leaned back his head and closed his eyes as if he were listening to a particularly beautiful piece of music.

Dina wondered whether she should leave there and then, but her legs simply wouldn't respond to the messages from her brain. The knocking finally stopped, and Suslov opened his eyes.

"There," he said with satisfaction. "Now, where were we?" He cupped his hands and leaned forward in his chair. "Let me guess. You are an aspiring young actress who wants to break into films. At a screen test for Mosfilm, you were guaranteed a part provided you slept with the director. As Chairman of the Committee for Cinema, you wish me to intervene on your behalf to ensure that you get the part. You find me kind and considerate. You are so grateful that you offer to sleep with me instead. How does that strike you as a scenario?"

Dina was speechless.

Suslov continued, "Or how about this as an alternative? Your brother is the editor of an underground dissident publication. He is being pursued by the KGB. You appeal to me as Chief Ideologue of the Communist Party to permit the dissemination of your brother's propagandising without fear of internment. In return, you offer to regenerate my love life. Don't look so surprised. I've heard them all." He addressed Dina directly, causing her to squirm with embarrassment.

"Actually, it's my father," she blurted out.

"Ah," said Suslov, leaning back in his chair with a knowing air.

"He's been imprisoned in the Serbsky Institute and is being subjected to mind-destroying drugs." She broke down in tears at the memory of her father lying prostrate on that deathly pale bed.

"Bravo," said Suslov, clapping his hands as if applauding a performance.

"You are indeed an outstanding actress. If I didn't know better, I would say that those tears were real."

This apparent callousness made Dina break down even more, combined with a feeling of hurt and resentment towards Mikhail Suslov.

He continued, "You know as well as I do that your father is alive and well and probably living on a state pension in a dacha at Sochi on the Black Sea. Really, the KGB will have to learn to do better than this. They must think that I am an absolute fool. I always thought of Comrade Andropov as a clever man, but I'm beginning to have my doubts."

"What are you talking about?" screamed Dina. "You stupid, senile old man. Stop playing these games. I'm talking about saving my father's sanity and even his life, and all you can do is play some clever, intellectual party game."

"Come along now, young lady. You know as well as I do that you're a KGB swallow."

"A swallow," retorted Dina. "What on earth is a swallow?"

"It's no use playing the innocent with me," replied Suslov. "Your masters have tried every conceivable trick to compromise me sexually. I may be a vulnerable old man, but my wits are as sharp as they ever were, and it will take more than the appeal of an attractive young woman to dislodge me from my position in the Politburo. If Andropov wants the number two position, he'll have to wait until they carry me out in a gun carriage coffin through Red Square. I may have lost my political power. I may have lost my wife and family, but I still have my Party status of Second Secretary, and you'll never take that away from me as long as I live."

Dina didn't know how to respond. She and Suslov did not appear to be on the same wavelength, although he gave the impression of knowing what he was talking about.

Mikhail Suslov tuned into her genuine state of mental confusion without completely dropping his defensive guard. "Are you trying to tell me that you are not a swallow from the KGB stable sent to entrap me? This is not a setup, and you are not carrying a personal bugging device? There is no cameraman in the next apartment training his lens on us through a peephole in the wall of the bedroom?"

Dina shook her head slowly as the awareness of what he was saying began to dawn on her. A man in his position had constantly to be on his guard from the dirty tricks department of the KGB, who set out to discredit him and have him removed from office. The Chairman of the KGB, Yuri Andropov, was indeed his political opponent for top office in the Politburo together with Chernenko, Gorbachev, and Romanov. Suslov had mistaken her for a high-class prostitute or a swallow, as he called them, employed by the State Security Services to entrap and compromise him. "I do work for the KGB," she admitted, adding quickly, "but I'm a systems analyst in the computer data centre. My name is Dina Russakov. My father is Vladimir Maksimovich Russakov, the composer and orchestral conductor."

"Ah," he said, the name obviously registering. "Yes, I recall the case. Dissidence and psychological disorder, wasn't it, if my memory serves me correctly?"

"Those were the charges," replied Dina bitterly, "but he was innocent. He is innocent."

"That isn't what the commission of enquiry decided," said Suslov.

Dina looked around the room. It was obviously the residence of a man of learning. Apart from volumes of political works, there were also bookshelves containing Shakespeare, Goethe, Balzac, and many more classics in their original language. Beneath the display cabinets containing items of porcelain, silver, and jade, accumulated from visits by foreign delegations, there was a collection of classical records.

"You are a man of discrimination and good taste," said Dina.

Suslov raised his eyebrows, unsure how to take this compliment. He allowed her to continue.

"You appreciate fine music. Do you have a copy of Tchaikovsky's 1812 Overture in your collection?"

"But of course. I have the entire repertoire of all the major Soviet composers," replied Suslov.

"And what does the overture commemorate?" asked Dina.

"It was written to celebrate the National Exhibition of 1880."

"But what event or chain of events does it actually commemorate?" pressed Dina.

"The victorious Fatherland War against the onslaught of French imperialism under Napoleon."

"You make it sound like a battle of two ideologies rather than a bloody battle in which the city of Moscow was virtually razed to the ground."

Suslov was greatly impressed by the bold outspokenness of this young woman. She was not at all overawed in his presence. "Go on," he said.

Dina cleared her throat and continued, "While it is true that the Grande Armée was decimated on its retreat from Moscow, and Soviet troops eventually occupied the French capital two years later, the actual events of 1812 reflect anything but glory on the Soviet Union. At the Battle of Borodino, tens of thousands of Russian soldiers lost their lives, and Field Marshal Kutuzov was forced to withdraw. This left Moscow undefended, allowing Napoleon to enter the capital and establish his headquarters in the Kremlin itself. Now that is what actually happened in 1812, isn't it?"

Suslov pondered an instant. That wasn't exactly the version given in Soviet history textbooks, but it was actually nearer the truth. "Well, yes, I suppose so," he conceded.

"Good," said Dina. "I'm glad we agree. Now, let me bring you forward a hundred and fifty years or so. What happened in Czechoslovakia in 1968?"

"The Communist Party of that country invited the Soviet Union in to quell the dissident riots."

"You mean the same as happened in Hungary in 1956. You were there when Andropov was the Soviet Ambassador to Budapest."

Mikhail Suslov knew exactly what Dina was driving at. "Are you sure you aren't wired for sound?" he asked, knowing full well that his replies, if truthful, could be highly damaging and compromising if produced as recorded evidence.

"Would you like to search me?" offered Dina, opening her arms wide so that her breasts pressed hard against her silken blouse.

"I should very much like that," said Suslov, relishing the stimulating intellectual argument tempered by sexual undertones, "but please conclude your discourse first."

Dina relaxed her arms and folded them across her lap. "Let me return then to Czechoslovakia in 1968. A progressive faction of the Soviet-dominated Czechoslovak Communist leadership under First Secretary Alexander Dubcek initiated a wide-ranging programme of liberalisation and democratisation in order to gain greater independence from Moscow." She knew that she could talk like this to Mikhail Suslov, who, although the pillar of Soviet Marxist Communist dogma, was not a prisoner of his own dogma and had a greater awareness of world politics than probably anyone else in the Politburo, with the possible exception of Gromyko. "The Soviet Union saw this as a threat to the solidarity of the Warsaw Pact and an invitation to other satellite states to defy the Moscow line. Consequently, on August 21st, half a million Soviet allied troops invaded and occupied Czechoslovakia, under the pretext of preventing a counter-revolution backed by the Western imperialist powers.

"In the face of adverse reaction, Dubcek was allowed to resume office, but in 1969, when the heat had died down, he was replaced by the Soviet puppet Gustav Husak. Nationalist outbursts were suppressed, and censorships of all kinds were reintroduced. All the political, economic, and social reforms were put in reverse. Czechoslovakia was shackled to the Soviet Union, whether it liked it or not. It was no longer a free, independent state. It was no longer free." She stopped momentarily to allow her words to sink in.

Suslov cupped his head in his hands and nodded thoughtfully. He was in the presence of a remarkable young lady.

Dina took this as a general agreement of her statement of the facts. "Now my father..." she began. She felt a lump rise in her throat at the very mention of his name. "Now my father," she gathered herself, "composed a symphonic poem entitled 'Freedom for Czechoslovakia'. And it is this title which has landed him in the Serbsky Institute, accused of anti-Soviet expression, which is regarded as a psychological disorder worthy of treatment."

"You know as well as I do," interrupted Suslov, "that dissent is regarded as a psychological disorder."

"If that is true," retorted Dina, "then ninety-nine per cent of the Soviet population is in need of treatment. It is only the fear of what will happen to them that prevents them from speaking out. If Tchaikovsky were alive today and wrote the 1968 Overture, would he be incarcerated in Lubyanka Prison for the implications implicit in the title? The 1812 Overture marked the inglorious defeat of the Soviet armies at Borodino and the occupation of the Kremlin itself by the invading French. Should we ignore those parts of history we as a country would rather forget, pretend they never happened, rewrite the history books? Or should we face the truth? What is so frightening about the truth? Is it such a corrupting force that it has to be distorted or even suppressed?"

By now, her voice was raised in exultation as much as in anger. In contrast, Suslov said very quietly, "You must love your father very much."

She, in return, responded equally quietly. "I do. I do."

Suslov could not find the words to adequately reply to this impassioned outburst.

Dina herself felt spent. The cathartic effect of unburdening her soul to Mikhail Suslov left her quivering and drained. A meaningful silence descended between them. Dina felt she had put her case. Now it was up to Suslov to respond.

Finally, he said, "I take it you are appealing to me in my capacity as Chief Ideologue to pardon your father and expedite his release."

Realising that she was pushing her luck, Dina replied, "There is no question of pardon, for he has done nothing wrong, committed no crime. He has never appeared before a court of law. Freed yes. Pardoned no."

Mikhail Suslov had to marvel at the total integrity of this young woman. Compromising her principles was anathema to her. She was either a very brave or a very foolish person, for she must have known that he could have her detained and interned merely on his say-so. "You know that strictly speaking, it is the duty of the commission of enquiry to decide the outcome of your father's case."

"But you could point them in the right direction," replied Dina.

"Hm," said Suslov, knowing that he could do precisely that. "Who is the chairman of the commission and when does it next meet?"

"Boris Vladimirovich Shostakovich is in the chair," said Dina, "and they meet again on the fifth of November at the Serbsky Institute."

"I could certainly put pressure on Minister of Health Petrovsky and Chief Psychiatrist Sneshnevsky," conceded Suslov, "and through them influence Professor Morozov, Director of the Institute. But..." he emphasised, staring Dina straight in the eyes, "everything has a price, and what you are asking me to do will not come cheaply."

Dina's heart sank at the realisation of what was about to follow. Suslov continued, "You are a beautiful young woman and I am an old man. I have the power to make you happy and you, well, you..." his voice tailed off as the implication was self-evident.

Dina struggled to find a way out of having to fulfil her side of the unspoken bargain. "I thought that you were not interested in swallows," she said desperately.

"But you are not a swallow, are you, Dina?" replied Suslov, for the first time addressing her by her name. "Have no fear," he said, leaning forward and patting her on the knee. "I am a seventy-three-year-old man. I make an undemanding lover. Too much excitement is bad for my heart, or at least that's what my doctor tells me."

Dina was now being confronted with the inevitable sacrifice she would have to make to secure the release of her father. Unless The Marble Index made a miraculous reappearance in the KGB files in the next few days after forty years, the only bargaining counter she had left was herself. It was all she had to give. It had been too much to expect that Suslov would be moved by her emotional appeal. For too long, he had been used and abused by the Brezhnev mafia, not wanting to gain his embittered revenge on others, no matter who.

Suslov had allowed her time to reflect on his offer. Finally, he said, "Do we have an understanding?"

Slowly, Dina nodded her head as much in an act of submission as by way of agreement.

"Good," said Suslov in a business-like manner. "I'm glad that's settled. Now, how about another cup of tea, Dina?"

He leaned back in his chair. The invitation was for her to serve him. The terms of their bargain were already being brought into play.

Dina poured two fresh cups and handed one to Mikhail Suslov. "Why don't you put a record on the stereo?" he said. "As a matter of fact, I have a copy of your father conducting a performance of his piano concerto in C sharp minor. Or perhaps you would prefer a little Tchaikovsky. Romeo and Juliet, perhaps, or Eugene Onegin or maybe even the 1812 Overture. The choice is entirely yours."

Dina appreciated the nicety of the irony in Suslov's suggested choice of music. A tear rose in the corner of her eye as she turned her head away.

Gleaming on the smoked black glass top of the stereo system was a hypodermic syringe.

Alexei was lying on his bed, waiting for dinnertime to arrive. He could hear Marriott moving about next door and was dreading the moment when they again came face to face. After placing so much confidence in him, Alexei felt betrayed that Marriott should have collaborated with Dr McCabe to trap and ensnare him. To what end, he was not yet sure, but he certainly did not relish the idea of being a guinea pig.

He recalled their excursion to London in covert pursuit of the English tutor. It had all been a put-up job. They had been leading him by the nose.

He felt foolish to have been so easily taken in. He remembered the turning point in West Kensington tube station when they'd had to split up. If he had insisted on going West rather than East on the District Line, that would have spoilt all their well-laid plans. Instead, he had fallen right into their preconceived trap. Whilst he had surreptitiously been overhearing the conversation outside the RFE building between the Russian woman, McCabe, and the computer expert from ICL, they had presumably been putting on a special performance for his benefit, knowing full well that he was hiding in the shadows.

The question was what reaction were they expecting from him? Alexei was now faced with several choices. Should he simply expose their little ploy to test his loyalties or go along with it? After all, if they were working for the British secret intelligence services, he might eventually need their assistance and cooperation if he decided to defect to the West with Dina.

It all hinged on which side they were working for. Alexei thought it ironic that, from their behaviour, they could have been working for either side. As he searched for the tell-tale remark or action which would swing him one way or the other, there was a knock at his door.

Expecting it to be Andrew Marriott, he shouted, "Come in," and was most surprised to see the figure of Dr Fischer framed in the doorway. It suddenly occurred to him that the senior tutor could also be involved in the conspiracy.

"Mr Kunayev," said Fischer gravely, "I'm afraid I have some bad news for you." All his effeminacy was gone, and the man seemed genuinely sincere. This only served to make Alexei twice as suspicious. "It's your father," continued Dr Fischer in the absence of any response from Alexei. "We have received a telephone call from the Soviet Embassy in London. Your mother has contacted them to inform you that your father is seriously ill. I have already been in touch with Professor

Harcourt at the Cavendish to have you released from your duties at the Laboratories, in case you wish to return home. I'm sorry to be the bearer of such tragic news." He turned towards the door. "If there's anything I can do..." his voice trailed away.

Alexei was dumb struck. Was this another ploy to test his reactions?

Surely not. Dr Fischer was not a player in this game. Alexei even suspected his father of becoming deliberately ill to thwart his plans, if indeed the news were true at all. Maybe the KGB had been behind this all the time, had found him wanting, and had contrived to bring him back to the Soviet Union on a family matter. Whatever the case, he would at least be reunited with Dina Russakov, providing she too had not joined her father in the Serbsky Institute. Dina.

For one terrible moment, it crossed Alexei's mind that she had been planted to ensnare him also. After all, her first words to him had been an admission, 'Our meeting was not entirely a coincidence.' Perhaps her father was not in fact a prisoner of the state, and The Marble Index did not exist, except in her imagination. How then could he explain his discoveries in Cambridge? Alexei began to doubt his own sanity.

13

Alexei had plenty of time to reflect on his return journey to Moscow. The tedium of the three-hour Aeroflot flight had only been relieved by the familiarity of Russian voices, but the novelty was short-lived. The strain of having to think and speak in English had become so automatic that he had to override his brain and put it on manual in order to readjust. He felt trapped in a kind of no-man's land between Cambridge and Moscow.

As the flight path took them over Moscow State University and Moscow State Circus with its broad plaza shaped like a large, wide-brimmed hat, Alexei marvelled at the criss-cross sections of the motor-route system, encircled by the hundred kilometres of the Ring Motorway. The MKAD, as it was known, formed a circle around Moscow with an average at any point of twenty kilometres from the Kremlin. This road marked a border beyond which foreign tourists to Moscow were forbidden to pass without a special visa. Thus, such delights as Kolomna with its ruined Kremlin and the ancient town of Zvenigorod with its monastery and Cathedral of the Assumption were beyond the reach of foreigners. Alexei reflected that neither had he visited these places, and yet ironically, he was familiar with the history and architecture of the city of

Cambridge.

The Ilyushin passenger jet began to descend over the suburbs of Odintsovo and Solntsevo on its inevitable approach to Vnukovo airport. The approach was smooth and measured. Before he knew it, Alexei had disembarked and was making his way through customs with his hand luggage. He was travelling light. There was no sign of a KGB reception committee, and yet he wondered whether he would ever set foot in England again.

His mind went back to Dr McCabe's story about the disappearance of Piotr Kapitsa, Lord Rutherford's assistant at the Cavendish, who had supposedly gone to Moscow on holiday in 1934 and never returned. Had Kapitsa really been a willing agent planted by the KGB from the very beginning, or had he been coerced into submission? The annual photographs of the research students told their own story. The absence of Kapitsa from the 1935 photograph provided a graphic illustration of his demotion or detention. Alexei wondered in the years to come whether generations of foreign research students would make similar deductions about him.

He boarded the airport bus and settled into the journey to the Moscow Air Terminal. It had been mid-afternoon when they had left Gatwick. From a mild English Autumn day, Alexei was now forced to readjust to sub-zero Moscow temperatures. He shivered uneasily inside his overcoat. This was not the kind of homecoming he had envisaged. Meanwhile, the bus skirted the North-West section of the Ring Motorway and turned up Ulitsa Gorkogo into Leningradsky Prospekt, where it pulled into the Air Terminal. There, passengers from all the outlying Moscow airports were deposited. Situated between the twin towers of the Ministry of Civil Aviation and the five-hundred-bed Aeroflot Hotel, the massive glass structure of the Aerovokzal was a blaze of light amid the twilight gloom.

As Alexei alighted from the bus, he had to shield his eyes

from the reflected glare. Having readjusted, his eyes were drawn automatically to the rank reserved for official Party cars. A solitary black Chaika with its distinctive radio aerial was standing with its engine running. The exhaust fumes hung like clouds of human breath on the chill air. Suddenly, the rear door opened and out stepped Alexei's mother, Irena Kunayev. She looked like a total stranger to him. He had been away for less than a month, and yet even from this distance, she appeared to have aged several years. Alexei speculated whether it was the strain of his father's illness that had told on her. She appeared to be anxiously scanning the crowd of faces in an attempt to pick out her son. Alexei proceeded to walk slowly towards her. Several times, she seemed to look straight at him without recognition. It was as if she were looking right through him. It was only when he was a matter of paces away that an expression midway between delight and anguish lit up her features. She held out her arms as if to a young child who was learning to walk for the first time. She opened her mouth as if to speak, but no sound was uttered. Alexei found himself speechless, too.

They embraced a silent embrace before the impassive KGB driver got out and held the back door of the Chaika open for them. Alexei steadied his mother's trembling body and held her arm as she got into the car. He then followed in behind her, and the Chaika pulled away. It headed back along the MIO Motor Route in the direction of the centre of Moscow, past the Dinamo Stadium. At the corner by the Young Pioneers Sports Complex, the Chaika turned right into Begovaya Ulitsa and then right again into Botkinsky Proezd. Here was situated the Botkin Hospital, one of the largest in Moscow.

It was there in 1922 that Lenin had undergone an operation to remove a bullet that had remained in his body after the assassination attempt of 1918. Alexei wondered what exactly was wrong with his father. It was obviously something serious in view of his mother's state. It crossed his mind that maybe Boris Kunayev had also been the subject of an assassination attempt, but he immediately dismissed this as a foolish thought. He and his mother had still not spoken, and Alexei did not want to be the one to break the ice.

The car drew to a halt outside the Botkin Hospital. The driver got out and opened the door for them. Alexei helped his mother out, and together they mounted the steps and reported to reception. Irena Kunayev seemed to want her son to take the initiative. Sensing this, Alexei said, "Boris Kunayev. Where do we find him?"

The receptionist consulted her patient register and replied, "On the private ward. Intensive care on the third floor."

Alexei was going to ask her what he was in for, but decided to wait and find out for himself. He was trying to work up an appropriate sense of filial compassion for his father, even though deep down he could just as easily have been visiting a stranger in the hospital. He had no feeling whatsoever.

He was totally numb. For the sake of his mother, he would have to put on a show and be suitably upset. The lift doors reopened, and Alexei found himself in clinical white surroundings dominated by a hushed, almost monastic silence. He approached the ward sister, afraid to raise his voice above a whisper. "Boris Grigoriyevich Kunayev," he intoned. "I'm his son."

The sister nodded and led them off to a separate wing down a corridor to the left. There were white plaster busts on pedestals of the pillars of Soviet medicine and science. Alexei was reminded of the marble busts lining both sides of the Wren Library and also those in the antechapel of Trinity College. His thoughts returned to The Marble Index and thence to Dina Russakov. Now, both of them were in a similar position. Their fathers were interned in medical institutions. The only difference was that his father was there by choice. The ward sister stopped outside room seventeen, where an armed guard in a KGB uniform was posted. He obviously took his protection detail very seriously as he challenged them. "Who are you? Comrade Kunayev is not to be disturbed."

"I am his son, and this is comrade Kunayev's wife," replied Alexei.

"Wait there," said the guard, disappearing inside the room.

As Head of the First Department of the First Chief Directorate, Boris Kunayev was a very important patient and warranted the best medical attention as well as the closest military protection.

Almost immediately, the door reopened, and a middle-aged man with bushy silver hair in a white coat emerged. "I am Dr Kornilin," he introduced himself. "And you must be Alexei," he said, "Mrs Kunayev," he added formally, nodding his head in her direction. "I'm sure your mother has already explained your father's problem to you."

Alexei nodded in agreement, although he was still totally in the dark, and his mother said nothing to contradict the doctor's remark.

"The words 'coronary thrombosis' strike fear into people's hearts," continued the doctor. He coughed nervously at the realisation of his unintentional pun. Now Alexei understood. His father had suffered a heart attack.

The doctor pressed on hurriedly. "A coronary covers a multiplicity of ills. It is generally caused by muscle damage, which weakens the pumping power of the heart. This may be severe enough to cause shock if the output of blood falls drastically and the blood pressure drops sharply. In very severe cases, the circulation to the brain and to the heart itself will suffer and may even fail completely. The patient then loses consciousness and dies." The doctor stopped, sensing Alexei's reaction of alarm. "This is all hypothetical, of course, and not directly related to your father's case. We are now past the critical twenty-four-hour period, and the slow road to recovery has begun. Under normal circumstances, one could expect the muscle damage to heal within three months. However, initial exploratory electrocardiography has revealed a ventricular septal defect. In other words, a hole has appeared between the chambers of the heart, caused by rupture of the muscle, as well as the usual damage to the coronary arteries..."

Alexei had been listening to this medical discourse completely dispassionately. He felt as if he were being given an anatomical lecture rather than an update on the state of his father's health. And what was even more disconcerting was the fact that his mother still had not uttered a single word. She was obviously still suffering from shock, and the doctor, for all his diagnosis of a heart complaint, did not seem to recognise the symptoms of a person in shock standing right next to him.

The doctor continued, "It has therefore been deemed advisable, not to say necessary, to recommend open heart surgery for your father, both to perform a coronary artery bypass grafting and also insert a patch over the ventricular defect."

Alexei found himself involuntarily expressing concern. "Is he going to die, doctor?" he said, uttering the cliché which was the staple of every fictional medical series he had seen both in the Soviet Union and particularly in the United States.

Dr Kornilin put on his most reassuring bedside manner. "The risks associated with the operation are remarkably small. The mortality rate is as low as one or two per cent. Your father is a low-risk patient. He is under seventy years of age and has an otherwise sturdy constitution. Besides, he will have the benefit of the most skilled Soviet surgeons and post-operative nursing care. Would you like to go in? I'm sure you'd like to see your father now," he said, placing his hand on the door handle.

Nothing could have been further from the truth. Alexei

was dreading this moment.

The doctor opened the door and ushered Alexei and his mother into the private room. As he passed, Dr Kornilin grabbed Alexei's arm and whispered, "Your father has only recently come out of shock. He has been given injections of morphine to relieve the pain. He is in a stable condition. Neither say nor do anything that is likely to upset him."

Alexei wondered whether the doctor had been briefed by the KGB about the poor relationship between father and son. After all, they seemed to know everything else about everyone. Alexei nodded as he broke away from the doctor's grasp. The parallel between Dina and her father and him and his father became even more sharply defined as he saw Boris Grigoriyevich Kunayev lying almost naked on the bed. There were electrodes attached to both his arms and legs, as well as to his chest. The dozen or so leads were connected to an electrocardiograph machine, which produced a continuous monitoring of the heart's action. It could just as easily have been a dissident in Lubyanka Prison being subjected to electric shock treatment in order to restore his socialist consciousness. Alexei took a quick look at the series of peaks and troughs on the screen of the oscilloscope. The impulses looked stable and regular to his untrained eye.

Suddenly, his mother spoke for the first time. "It's your father," she said, as if introducing Alexei to a total stranger. "I told him he'd been working too hard. All that stress. It's not good for him. I kept telling him not to smoke so heavily. To take more exercise. Lose a few kilos. Eat less fatty foods. But he wouldn't listen. He wouldn't listen." Irena Kunayev seemed to be running the whole gamut of symptoms and causes of heart disease.

"It's all my fault," she sobbed. "I should have been firmer with him. I should have insisted we spend more time relaxing at the dacha in Pirogovo."

Alexei put his arm tenderly around his mother's shoulders. "You mustn't blame yourself," he said. "Father was only happy when he was driving himself into the ground. Living life to the full. Besides, after the operation has been successful, he will be forced to take it easy. The doctors will see to that."

At this moment, Boris Kunayev opened his eyes and said, "Leave us, Irena. I wish to speak to Alexei alone."

Without a protest, Alexei's mother allowed herself to be steered by Dr Kornilin out of the room, and the door closed softly behind them. For a long moment, the only sound audible was the regular bleep emanating from the electrocardiograph. Alexei noted that his father was struggling to keep his eyes open, presumably against the depressant effect of the morphine injections. With seemingly great effort, he beckoned Alexei to come and sit on a chair next to his bed. Dutifully, Alexei obliged and was struck by the pale skin quality of his father, similar to the plaster busts in the corridor outside and the marble statues in Trinity College Chapel, which was presumably caused by the loss of blood and the impaired circulation.

"I've got something to tell you, Alexei," said his father, "something you should know before I go."

The implication of imminent death was not lost on Alexei. "You're not going anywhere, Father. The doctors expect you to make a full recovery."

Boris Kunayev gave a wan smile and shook his head. "No, I believe my time has come, and I want us to part if not as friends then at least not as enemies."

Alexei made as if to interrupt his father, but Boris Kunayev held up his hand as if to halt his son. "No, let me finish. There is something I have wanted to tell you for many years, ever since our time in the United States. You remember when I worked as Director of the External Relations Unit of the United Nations Information Department?"

Alexei nodded.

Boris Kunayev continued. "Whilst at the same time I was holding down the post of Colonel in the KGB and working closely with the Soviet Foreign Minister, Andrei Gromyko. It is mainly for this duplicity that you have despised me, accused me of a lack of integrity, of being a betrayer of principles, a willing pawn in the hands of a corrupt state in order to further my own career at the expense of others."

Alexei had to admit inwardly that this had in fact been the case.

"Did it never cross your mind that things might not have been exactly as they seemed?"

Alexei gave his father a puzzled look. He wondered whether the effects of the morphine were having a delirious result. "I see that it didn't," concluded Boris Kunayev. "Well, as you probably know, the United Nations was then and still is the most important base of all Soviet Intelligence operations in the world. It offers legitimate access for our officers to information about foreign administrations and their personnel. Soviet intelligence agents are concealed as in a Trojan horse behind the walls of the UN. The infiltration even went as high as the Secretary General himself. His special assistant, Viktor Lessiovski, was also a Colonel in the KGB. Believe it or not, I was appalled by the corruption. Upon becoming a diplomat at the United Nations, one has to take an oath renouncing one's national interests and so becoming an international civil servant, responsible and answerable only to the United Nations itself. However, soon after my appointment, I was instructed to begin using my position as editor of the literature produced by the UN to promote a pro-Soviet bias. For a while, I obliged until my conscience, yes, I do have one," he emphasized, staring hard at Alexei, "could take it no longer. Strangely enough, I had already met my FBI contact socially at one of the many functions I was expected to attend. We had many clandestine ideological discussions, and in the end, I was turned, as they call it, to work for the other side. The KGB still thought I was working for them, whilst in fact I was a paid agent of the FBI. I didn't want to take money from both sides and indeed found that hard to reconcile with my principles."

Alexei couldn't believe what he was hearing. This confessional outpouring left him mesmerised and shattered all his previously held conceptions of his father. "Why didn't you tell me all this before?" he pleaded.

Boris Kunayev answered his question with another question. "Would you have thought more of me if I had?"

Alexei did not know the answer to this. "It would certainly have been different between us," he conceded.

His father smiled faintly.

It suddenly occurred to Alexei that his mother must have played an active role in this conspiracy of silence. "What was mother's part in all this?" he asked.

"She doesn't know," replied Boris Kunayev.

"But she must," retorted Alexei. "How could you keep it from her?"

"I managed to keep it from you all these years, didn't I?" said his father.

"Yes, but..." faltered Alexei, "you must tell her now, before..." he faltered again.

"I thought you said I wasn't going anywhere," interrupted Boris Kunayev, throwing his son's own words back in his face.

"You know very well what I mean," replied Alexei.

"This could be the very first occasion we have actually understood one another," said his father triumphantly.

"You really are infuriating, Father," said Alexei, actually bursting out laughing, as much to relieve the tension as out of a sense of amusement at the irony of the situation.

"No, your mother must never know," said Boris Kunayev gravely, "for the simple reason that she cannot tell what she does not know."

The veiled implication in this statement of the KGB's methods of extracting information from unwilling subjects sent a shiver of horror up Alexei's spine. "Do the KGB suspect you of double-dealing?" he asked.

"Not so far as I know," replied Boris Kunayev.

"Then why are you confiding in me? Are you not afraid that I may turn you over to the authorities?"

"Like Pavlik Morozov?" said his father. "I think not."

Alexei recalled the bi-annual evaluation session of the Komsomol when he had openly cursed the name of Pavlik Morozov, the fourteen-year-old who had informed on his father for giving refuge to some kulaks and had been subsequently held up as a shining example to Soviet youth for his sense of duty to the state above duty to his family. "You know me better than I give you credit for, Father," said Alexei.

"Maybe I do," said Boris Kunayev with a sense of satisfaction. "What is of greater concern to me, however, is that you come to know me even now, at this late stage."

Alexei was disturbed by his father's constant references to his imminent demise, although the doctor had given a reassurance that Boris Kunayev would come through his heart operations safely.

At this moment, there was a knock at the door. Boris Kunayev put his right index finger to his lips and made a gesture to Alexei to keep silent about their conversation.

Dr Kornilin appeared in the doorway. "I think that is enough for one day," he said. "You may visit your father again tomorrow."

Boris Kunayev lay back on the bed, closed his eyes, and allowed himself to be taken over by the effect of the morphine injections.

Irena Kunayev seemed much more composed now. Alexei wondered whether the doctor had seen fit to administer a tranquilizer. She said to him, "Come along, Alexei, let's go home."

Firmly, he resisted his mother's attempt to grab his arm and replied, "No, not yet, Mother. I have something I must do. You take the car. I'll make my own way back home."

She knew better than to argue with him and allowed the doctor to steer her in the direction of the reception, where the KGB chauffeur was in attendance.

Alexei took one last look at his father.

"Remember what I told you," said Boris Kunayev, momentarily reopening his eyes before floating away again into drug-induced oblivion.

Alexei rapidly made his exit from the hospital, just in time to see the red taillights of the black Chaika limousine bearing his mother disappearing into the distance.

Partly retracing his steps, he returned to Leningradsky Prospekt, where he entered the Belorussian Station and made his way to the metro. Changing lines at Ploshchad Revolyutsii, Alexei travelled East for five stops before alighting at Izmaylovskaya. He had not actually been to his destination before, but he knew exactly where he was going. Dina's address of 370, Izmaylovsky Park apartments, was imprinted on his brain.

As he made his way across the green expanse of Izmaylovsky Park in the direction of the Sports Palace, Alexei felt guilt-ridden that he had misjudged his father so badly over the years. It was only now, when it was too late, when he was virtually on his deathbed, that the truth had been revealed.

Alexei had always considered his father a ruthless opportunist, a pragmatist who used circumstances to his own ends. The principled student his mother had first met in Kislovodsk had not succumbed to the double standards of the Soviet Communist Party regime. He had been actively working to redress the balance. He could be proud of his father's achievements just as Dina Russakov was proud of hers.

One thing puzzled Alexei, though. His father had insisted that he was about to die, and yet the physician, Dr Kornilin, had predicted at least a ninety-eight percent chance of full recovery. Who was right and who was wrong? Perhaps Alexei had misinterpreted his father's remarks. Maybe the drug-induced delirium had brought about this pessimism. If that was the case, however, could not Boris Kunayev's confession have been equally a product of the morphine injections? Could the whole story have been a fabrication in order to win back the love of his son at a time when he felt most in need of love and support from his family?

Alexei's pace began to slow. Everything seemed to be happening too quickly. His father had insisted that his mother did not know and should not know anything about his revelations. Could this really be because he knew them to be totally untrue and without foundation? Was it a clever ploy on his father's part to stop him from seeking verification from his mother? Or was the oblique reference to the KGB and its methods of extracting information genuine proof of his desire to safeguard his mother's wellbeing? Maybe Boris Kunayev expected not to die from heart disease but as a victim of the KGB assassination squad. If they had got word of his treachery, they could use the cover of his heart complaint to ensure that by some unfortunate accident, he died on the operating table. The permutations seemed endless. Alexei hoped that Dina would help him to straighten out his confused state of mind.

He arrived at the Izmaylovsky Park apartment block and went up to the third floor. At number 370, he knocked and waited. The hollow sound reverberated down the long corridor. He knocked again, sure that she would be in at that time of the evening. After all, where could she go? Perhaps she was frightened to open the door in case it was the KGB come to seize her as they had her father in the middle of the night. An unexpected knock at the door was one of the most frightening sounds in the Soviet Union.

He called out. "Dina, it's me, Alexei."

There was still no response. Then he remembered that the Russakovs' best family friends, the Slobodas, lived in the same block. Rather than spend the evenings on her own, Dina would probably seek their company and support. He went down the stairs again and consulted the residents' list in the entrance hall. There it was –Dr and Mrs G. Sloboda, apartment 14A. Alexei returned to the first floor and knocked at number 14A. Almost immediately, the door opened, and Dr Sloboda appeared. "Yes, young man, can I help you?" he said.

"My name is Alexei Kunayev," he introduced himself.

"Ah, yes," said Sloboda. "Dina has talked of you."

"Is she with you?" asked Alexei.

"I'm afraid not," apologised Sloboda.

"Do you know where I can find her? She doesn't seem to be in her apartment. I thought..."

"Well, yes," replied Sloboda noncommittally. "Why don't you come in?"

"Yes, alright," said Alexei, "but I can't stop long. If you'd just tell me where she is..."

"Come in, come in," pressed Sloboda, anxious not to continue the conversation in the corridor. "This is my wife, Larissa," Sloboda introduced the woman sitting on the couch. "And this is Alexei Kunayev."

Mrs Sloboda rose and shook his hand. "I'm terribly sorry to hear about your father," she said. "I hope he will make a full recovery."

"Thank you," said Alexei. "I'm sure he will." Although in view of his recent reflections, he was far from sure about this. "And Dina, how is she?" asked Alexei, launching immediately into his real subject of concern.

Sloboda and his wife looked anxiously at one another.

"What's the matter?" asked Alexei, conscious of their

unease. "Has something happened to her?"

"No, no," Sloboda reassured him. "It's just that..."

"Well?" coaxed Alexei.

"The fact is that she's gone," said Sloboda bluntly.

"Gone," echoed Alexei incredulously.

"Moved, that is," explained Sloboda, "to an apartment on Kutuzovsky Prospekt."

"Kutuzovsky Prospekt?" echoed Alexei once more. "How on earth can she afford to live down there?"

"It's not exactly her apartment," explained Larissa Sloboda.

"Then whose is it?" asked the baffled Alexei.

"It belongs to Konstantin Boychenko, Director of the computer data centre where she works."

"What?" exclaimed Alexei. "Are you trying to tell me that she's living with another man?"

"I can't believe it either," said Sloboda, shaking his head. "It all happened so quickly. One minute she was here. The next minute, she had gone. And she never even told us. I found out through a third party. It's so unlike Dina. I can only think that it's been brought about by the stress of her father's internment. That's the only way I can explain it. She went out to dinner with this Boychenko one night. The next thing I know, she's moved into his apartment."

As if the blow of his father's heart attack had not caused him sufficient distress, this blow of Dina's was too much for him to bear. He turned on Sloboda and said accusingly, "Are you sure you're telling me the truth?" His recent experiences had led him not to trust or believe anything anymore.

"I can assure you, young man, that I am not in the habit of lying," replied Sloboda.

Realising his mistake, Alexei apologised. "I'm sorry, but I just can't believe it. Dina wasn't expecting me back. There must be some good reason behind all this. Is her father still in Lubyanka?"

"Why no, he's been moved to the Serbsky Institute," replied Sloboda. "His case comes up for reassessment next month."

"I see," said Alexei. "As soon as I am out of the way, everything changes. Tell me this address on Kutuzovsky Prospekt. I'd like to talk to Dina."

Sloboda looked at his wife, who nodded in return. "It's number 23/49," said the doctor, "but please be careful. I feel that there is something terribly wrong here, but I don't know what. I sense danger. For your sake and for Dina's sake, please be careful."

"I will," said Alexei. The advice was sound. Something did not ring true. Dina could be acting under duress. He had to proceed with extreme caution.

As he left the Izmaylovsky Park apartments and made his way back in the direction of the Izmaylovskaya metro station, Alexei was tempted to go straight to the address on Kutuzovsky Prospekt and have it out with Dina.

What on earth was she playing at? There he was toiling away in Cambridge on the verge of discovering the significance and whereabouts of The Marble Index, which could be used to bargain for the release of her father, and all the time she was two-timing him with her boss from work. No, it just wasn't credible. There had to be more to the situation than met the eye. He decided instead to return to his mother at home. After all, she needed his moral support right now. If there were time later that evening, he could pursue his investigation into Dina's behaviour. Or maybe it would be better still to sleep on it until the next morning.

As he travelled along on the metro train, his route took him through Baumanskaya, the location of the Bauman Institute, where he was registered as a student. His research into radio astronomy seemed light-years away. However, as he passed, he was reminded that he would have to convey Professor

Harcourt's respects to Director Kuznetzov. Perhaps he could ask him where the two had met. He was curious to know what Kuznetzov made of Harcourt and whether he knew of his real identity as an exiled Polish Jew.

The two cultures of Cambridge and Moscow began to converge in Alexei's mind as he changed onto the Circle Line at Kursk Station and continued his journey South. At Taganskaya, he got out and emerged into the Square. Having crossed the Bolshoi Krasnokholmskiy Bridge, Alexei made his way up the embankment to the apartment block on Maksima Gorkogo overlooking the Moskva River. Arriving at the third floor, he used his own key to unlock the door to the family apartment.

His mother did not hear him enter and seemed surprised by his arrival as she was in the middle of an animated telephone conversation. On seeing her son, she put the receiver down immediately, although it was obvious that the call was not at an end.

"Who was that?" he asked.

"The doctor from the hospital," replied Irena Kunayev.

"There's nothing wrong, is there?" asked Alexei.

"No, no, he's just fine. As well as can be expected," replied his mother. Alexei decided not to press her and assumed she was merely anxious to make regular check-ups on Boris Kunayev's state of health.

"Where have you been that was so important?" she quizzed him.

"Oh, nowhere in particular. I just needed time on my own to think, to readjust."

She made a visible effort to enliven her own mood. "You never told me at the airport how you are enjoying your time in Cambridge."

"Oh, fine, just fine," replied Alexei noncommittally.

"When are they expecting you back? I'm sure you have

plenty of work to be getting on with," continued his mother.

"Just as soon as father is off the danger list after his operation, and I've satisfied myself that you can cope with the situation. By the way, when is the operation scheduled to take place?"

"Anytime in the next few days. They promised to keep me informed," replied Irena Kunayev. "I believe Dr Bykov will be leading the team of surgeons. He is one of the most highly regarded heart specialists by the Academy of Medical Science."

Alexei joined his mother on the sofa and took her hands between his. Squeezing them gently, he said, "Then we have nothing to worry about. Father will make a full recovery, then you can take him off to Pirogovo for as long as you like to recuperate. I shall back you up on that."

Irena Kunayev smiled at her son and said, "Thank you. I'm glad you came home."

They embraced warmly, and immediately Alexei began to feel better. He had always been very close to his mother, much closer than to his father, although the revelations of the day had gone a long way to changing all that.

He still found it hard to believe that his father had been leading a double existence all those years. And he found it even harder to believe that his mother knew nothing about it. He smelt treachery in his father's story. It reeked of a man who was trying to buy sympathy at a critical time in his life. And yet, he had seemed totally convincing.

Alexei was torn between keeping his word to his father and confiding in his mother. He was sure she could either verify or disclaim Boris Kunayev's claims of being an FBI agent. She must know. On the other hand, if she didn't know, and Alexei broke his father's secret to her, he could be endangering his mother's life by making her a knowing accomplice in the eyes of the KGB – if they ever found out. It was an agonising decision to have to make, but Alexei just had to know one way or the other.

"You remember when Father asked you to leave us alone in his hospital room." Alexei began to broach the subject.

"I remember," she said. "What of it?"

"What did you think he wanted to talk to me about?" continued Alexei, hedgingly.

"I don't know. I suppose he wanted to talk to you man to man, without me acting as a peacemaker for once. You've given him a hard time recently, you know. And he's more sensitive than you give him credit for."

"I know," agreed Alexei. "In fact, I think I've misjudged him all along the line. That's what I wanted to talk to you about. Did father tell you much about his work in New York?"

"If you mean his working undercover for the KGB at the United Nations, yes, I knew all about that," replied his mother.

"But did he actually tell you what he was doing, discuss the ethics of it with you, his political stance, his social conscience if you like?"

"I don't know what you're driving at, Alexei. We've tried to explain to you before that your father was manipulated by the Party as far back as his time at the Marx-Engels School in Gorky. He wanted to forge a career with the Party Executive but ended up graduating from the Lenin Technical School as a fledgling spy. He had no choice. That was the career laid down for him. Just as you will eventually join the Moscow State Institute of International Relations and from there, follow in your father's footsteps."

"Over my dead body," exclaimed Alexei.

"How can you say a thing like that?" A look of horror crossed Irena Kunayev's face.

Alexei wasn't sure whether it was caused by his blasphemy, in view of his father being virtually on his deathbed himself, or genuine shock at his attitude. He had always felt that his mother held a fairly sympathetic view of his liberal politics and revulsion at the Soviet regime.

Sensing his surprise at her reaction, she re-joined quickly, "Of course, we all want to revolt against the system when we are young and idealistic, but you'll grow out of it."

"Like father, you mean," said Alexei.

"That's right," said Irena Kunayev.

"The only thing is," countered Alexei, "I don't think father has grown out of it."

"Whatever do you mean?" said his mother with a puzzled look.

"Just what I said," he re-emphasised. Now he was getting down to the heart of the matter. "That is what our frank discussion at the hospital was all about."

"I don't understand what you are trying to say," said Irena Kunayev.

Alexei now had a critical decision to make. Even though his father had sworn him to secrecy and confidentiality, he had to find out whether Boris Kunayev was lying. "To put it bluntly," he said, "father has been spying over the years, but for the American FBI and not the KGB."

His mother burst out laughing. "Why, that's ridiculous. Is that what he told you?"

Alexei nodded.

"And you believed him?"

Alexei nodded again, but with less conviction. His worst suspicions about his father's sincerity were being confirmed. He tried one last line of justification. "But he told me you knew nothing about his secret work and that it might be dangerous for you if you did know."

"How can you live with a man for thirty-odd years and not know something like that? I ask you, Alexei. Can you really see your father as a double agent?"

"Well..." he began.

His mother cut him off. "Of course not. What did he say

anyway?"

"He told me he had a crisis of conscience about the abuse of his privileged position at the UN, and allowed himself to be recruited by the FBI."

"And did he tell you whether he was still actively working for the Americans here in Moscow?"

"He never mentioned it. And I forgot to ask him."

"Now, how can you believe that, Alexei? You know very well from your own discussions with him that your father's conscience is now tied wholly to the Communist Party line. Look at that argument you had with him about your girlfriend, Dina Russakov and her father. We both know what his public opinion must be on such matters – predictable Party rhetoric. But in the privacy of our own home, he still justified Vladimir Russakov's internment in terms of anti-Soviet activity. Is that the voice of a man with pro-Western sympathies?"

"I suppose not," agreed Alexei reluctantly, wanting desperately to believe that his father had told the truth. "Then why did he say such a thing?" he argued.

His mother shook her head. "Bravado. To raise your estimation of him in your eyes. Sheer mischievousness. How should I know?" She shrugged her shoulders.

Alexei was crestfallen. His father was as hollow a vessel as he had always suspected; brainwashed by Party doctrine and dogma. How could he have been so easily taken in? His mother had seen straight through the facade. Irena Kunayev was right. She would have known if her husband had been 'turned', such was the transparency of his character.

"Oh, I'm sorry, Alexei," said his mother comfortingly. "I know you so desperately want to believe in your father's integrity, but believe me, he lost that a long time ago."

Alexei was rather puzzled by his mother's attitude. She was the one who usually sprang to the defence of Boris Kunayev and acted as mediator in their family arguments.

Now she actively seemed to be taking sides and denigrating her husband in Alexei's eyes. Perhaps she had endured the role of peacemaker for too long and had decided now to speak her mind. Alexei's shoulders began to droop.

"You must be tired," said his mother, "what with the long flight and this business of your father's illness. Why don't you go to bed? Have an early night."

Alexei nodded in agreement. A good night's sleep could only help to sort out the confusion that was reigning in his troubled mind. He kissed his mother on the cheek and went into his bedroom. As he was getting undressed, he could hear the distant, muffled sound of his mother lifting the telephone receiver and dialling a call.

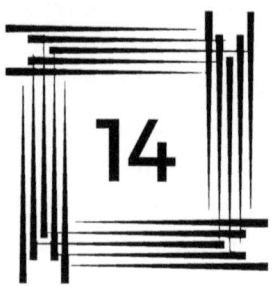

14

Alexei awoke early and drew back his bedroom curtains. He had to make an early start. He wanted to catch Dina before she went to work and confront her with his worst suspicions.

Having dressed, he padded stealthily across the lounge in the direction of the front door. At the telephone table, he stopped and looked down. There were two numbers scribbled on the pad. One was the Botkin Hospital, presumably for his mother to contact Dr Kornilin for an update on Boris Kunayev's state of health. The other was also a local Moscow number, but there was no name with it. Alexie copied down the hospital number into his diary in case he needed to get in touch with them. He was about to close his diary and put it back inside his wallet when, for no particular reason, he also wrote down the other number as well.

Quickly, he made his way out of the apartment block and down onto the embankment. It was still dark at that time of the morning. Wearily, he tramped up Maksima Gorkogo. Later that day, he would have to pay a second visit to his father in the hospital. It was not an encounter he was looking forward to. He was tempted to call him an outright liar and have done with it, but after all, the man was still his father and was about to undergo a serious heart operation. Maybe silence was the best policy.

He pushed this dilemma to the back of his mind as his thoughts turned to Dina Russakov. How could she be living with another man, only a matter of weeks after they had pledged one another their love? Ever since he had departed for Cambridge, his whole world had been turned upside down. He no longer knew whom he could trust, his father or his mother, or even his girlfriend. He no longer knew where he was going with his life.

Having crossed Serafimovicha Road Bridge, he cut the corner of the Alexandrovsky Gardens, where the Tomb of the Unknown Soldier was situated.

It was dedicated on the eighth of May 1967 when the eternal flame was brought from Marsovo Polye in Leningrad. The Battle of Moscow was fought in December 1941, and twenty-five years later, the remains of an unknown soldier who fell on the Leningradskoye Shosse were re-interred there.

Alexei looked down at the tomb and read 'To those who fell for the Motherland 1941-45. Your name is unknown. Your deed is immortal.' And to the right were the names of the 'Hero-Cities' Leningrad, Odessa, Sevastopol, Kiev, Volgograd, Minsk, Novorossiysk, and Kerch. The ever-present guard of honour stood impassively to attention in the cold early morning drizzle. Commemorative wreaths and small posies of flowers gathered the droplets of rain. Alexei was sharply reminded of the antechapel of Trinity College. Beyond the gaze of the silent statue of Sir Isaac Newton stood a commemorative wall bearing the names of former students of the college who had fallen in battle during the Second World War. Reminders of the act of dying for one's country were not a uniquely or wholly Soviet phenomenon. And yet, it was only the victors who glorified death. Defeat brought only ignominy and disgrace, and worst of all, oblivion.

Alexei entered the Kalininskaya metro station on the corner of Prospekt Karla Marksa and Prospekt Kalinina and travelled West.

The train rumbled on via Kiev Station and Studencheskaya until it reached Kutuzovskaya. Alexei emerged onto Kutuzovsky Prospekt, turned right, and began to walk along the avenue which overlooked Tarasa Shevchenko embankment and the Moskva River.

He had never met Konstantin Boychenko, although Dina had mentioned her superior's name. If his memory served him rightly, she did not have a very high opinion of comrade Boychenko, and Alexei could not imagine her forming an amorous attachment with him, let alone moving into his apartment.

Kutuzovsky Prospekt was the home of many Party luminaries such as Leonid Brezhnev himself, Mikhail Suslov, and Yuri Andropov. Boychenko may have been a high-flyer, but Alexei thought that he was hardly in the big league.

In that case, what was he doing living in an apartment on the most exclusive and fashionable avenue in Moscow?

Alexei looked at his watch. It was still only seven-thirty, and Dina didn't start work until eight. Besides, she was now only three metro stops away from the KGB Data Centre on the Sadovaya Ring Road, instead of having to travel right across town from Izmaylovskaya. He was confident she would still be at home. At number 49, Alexei mounted the steps to the apartment block and took the lift to the second floor. The second door on the left was marked 23. He walked right up to it and was about to knock when he heard a man's voice. Instinctively, he stopped and listened.

The voice sounded older than he had expected. Boychenko was only supposed to be in his forties, but this man was definitely much older than that. The voice said, "Come along now, young lady. You know as well as I do that you're a KGB swallow." The tone sounded quite threatening in a high-class sort of way, although he did not understand the content of the speech.

Without further time for reflection, Alexei knocked on the door.

Immediately, the voice stopped, and there was a long pause before Dina's voice asked, "Who is it?"

Alexei replied, "Come along now, Dina. There are a few things I want to talk to you about."

"Alexei," said Dina's disbelieving voice from the other side of the door. "Is that you, Alexei?"

"Open this door, Dina. I know he's in there with you."

"Be quiet," hissed Dina as she unlocked the door.

Straightaway, Alexei burst in and, brushing his way past Dina in the hallway, stormed into the lounge. When he found no one there, he went into the kitchen, then the bathroom, and the bedroom. There was still no one.

Returning to the lounge, he stood in the centre of the room, turning first this way and then that. In the silence he had created, Alexei heard the front door snap shut.

Dina reappeared. He hadn't noticed it before, but she was still dressed in her nightgown. As she made her way to the sideboard, she said, "Is this what you're looking for?" She depressed a button on a portable tape recorder, and her voice said, "A swallow, what on earth is a swallow?" The man's voice followed. "It's no use playing the innocent with me. Your masters have tried every conceivable trick to compromise me sexually." She pressed another button, and the sound stopped.

Alexei answered her question with another question. "Why are you still in your nightgown? Isn't it time you were at work? Where is Boychenko, and whose is that voice on the tape?"

"I thought you were still in Cambridge," Dina replied flatly.

"That is obvious," replied Alexei venomously. "I thought we were going to say what we meant in the morning," he added, remembering that first weekend they had slept together in his parents' apartment.

"That was that morning," she replied, fixing onto his line of thought.

"This is a completely different morning altogether. Where do you want to start? And will you go first or shall I?"

"You obviously haven't heard about my father," said Alexei.

"What about your father?" retorted Dina.

"He had a heart attack and is in the hospital for an operation."

"So that's why you're back in Moscow."

"That's right," agreed Alexei. "And that's my story. Now, how about yours?"

Not altogether satisfied, Dina pursued the subject further. "But I thought you hated your father. So why come all this way to see him? Isn't the real reason that you wanted to spy on me?"

"Spying certainly has a lot to do with it,' conceded Alexei cryptically, "but not on my part."

"What do you mean by that?" said Dina indignantly.

"Just how many men are you sleeping with?" asked Alexei. "One, two, three, or more. I'm coming to the conclusion that you're not really interested in securing the release of your father. You'd much rather spend your time screwing around. You're just like all the other KGB groupies. My father was right about you."

"Why this hero worship for your father all of a sudden? Don't tell me you're a born-again Communist. And as for me, I'm not screwing anyone right now. You were the last person I made love with."

Alexei scoffed, "You don't really expect me to believe that, do you? How can you be cohabiting with your boss and not screwing him at the same time?"

"Do you see Boychenko here?" she retorted. "You've looked in all the rooms. Why don't you take all the bedsheets away for forensic examination to test for semen stains? Boychenko doesn't live here. The apartment belongs to him, but he lives in a beach-house in Strogino."

"Even if I accept that," said Alexei, "which I'm not sure that I do, why should you leave your family apartment in Izmaylovsky Park in order to move in here? And don't tell me to be closer to work. Besides, I'm not the only one worried about you. Dr Sloboda and his wife are very concerned and upset."

Dina felt a pang of conscience at this latter remark. It was the source of a great deal of personal heartache, what they must be thinking about her behaviour right now, but it would be too dangerous for them to be let in on her plans. The less they knew, the better. If the KGB ever uncovered her conspiracy, they could genuinely plead ignorance. What worried her even more, however, was the news of her behaviour getting back to her father via the Slobodas. On her next visit to the Serbsky Institute, she would have to reassure him; that is, if he were in a lucid mental state at the time. An even bigger if was whether she would be allowed to visit her father again at all before the reconvening of the commission of enquiry. The nurse had warned her that she had put her visiting rights in jeopardy by the hysterical scene she had created the previous Thursday.

"Are you listening to me, Dina? Are you listening to me?" repeated Alexei, trying to gain her attention.

"What. Yes, of course I am," replied Dina indignantly. "Did they tell you where to find me?"

"Who?" asked Alexei.

"Dr Sloboda and his wife."

"Yes, that's right. Don't worry, I haven't been spying on you. I came around here straightaway, as soon as I found out.

I flew in last night. What's happened to you, Dina? To us? I don't understand what's happening to us," he pleaded with her. "You still haven't told me why you're living here."

"I just needed time," she replied.

"Time. Time for what?" asked Alexei.

"Time to try and find The Marble Index in the KGB Archives. Boychenko allowed me to go on secondment for as long as I wanted to the Central Index building on Prospekt Marksa. He thinks my motive is to ease the pressure on my work comrades. He also allowed me time off during office hours to go and visit my father. And in return for these concessions, I agreed to move into his apartment." From her point of view, it all sounded perfectly plausible.

"But don't you realise what he expects in return?" argued Alexei.

"Oh, I know what he wants," replied Dina, "but don't worry, he hasn't got it yet, and I intend to ensure that it stays that way."

"How do you propose to achieve that?" marvelled Alexei at her naïve stubbornness.

"The man on the tape," she nodded in the direction of the tape recorder. "Do you know whose voice that is?"

"No," said Alexei.

"It's Mikhail Suslov. You know, Second Secretary and Chief Ideologue of the Communist Party of the Soviet Union." She said this with some pride.

"I know who Mikhail Suslov is," replied Alexei. "Is he your lover?" he said, recalling the recorded snippet of conversation about being sexually compromised.

"Yes, he is," admitted Dina, much to Alexei's horror. "In name only, though."

She added, "He thinks he is, but he hasn't consummated it yet. Don't forget that he's a seventy-three-year-old man and not exactly in the peak of good health. He hasn't felt up to it yet. He regards it as more of a status symbol in name only to have a young, attractive mistress."

"What do you want with Suslov?" pleaded Alexei. "You're getting yourself into really deep water with him."

"His signature could get my father released from the Serbsky Institute at a moment's notice without another question being asked," she replied bluntly but frankly, according to her own terms of logic.

"So you're playing Suslov and Boychenko off against one another," said Alexei.

"No," replied Dina, "I've got them both working for me."

"And the tape-recording?" asked Alexei.

"Oh, just a little insurance in case all else fails. Suslov mistook me for a KGB prostitute sent to contrive a blackmail plot against him. It struck me as a good idea that I could use in my own right. Although I have an even better scheme up my sleeve." She pointed at a hypodermic syringe on the sideboard.

"What's that?" asked Alexei with some alarm.

"Insulin," replied Dina. "Suslov is a diabetic. I persuaded him to put me in charge of providing his twice-daily injections. Says he has a tendency to forget about them and wouldn't like to succumb to hyperglycaemia, you know, high blood sugar levels. And you know what happens if he doesn't get his regular shots of insulin. First of all, he begins to breathe more rapidly, to feel nauseous; he has an insatiable thirst. He begins to feel listless and drowsy, and finally, he falls unconscious. If he does not receive the proper medical attention, he lapses into a coma. And it's goodbye and farewell to Comrade Suslov."

"How can you be so callous and calculating?" said Alexei.

"You remember that my father's life is at stake," replied Dina. "If I can't find The Marble Index, I'm willing to trade Suslov his own life in return for that of my father. I'll get him to sign the release form in one hand with the hypodermic in the other if necessary."

"You can't possibly hope to get away with a strategy like that," said Alexei.

"It's my only hope," replied Dina, "unless you can come up with something better."

Alexei was impressed with her tenacity and resourcefulness, but also shocked by the outrageous audacity of her plans. "Maybe I can," he said. "The Marble Index."

"What about it?" asked Dina.

"I think you may be right. I believe that it's in Cambridge. With a little more time, I believe that I could unearth it. The only trouble is, I may not be the only one who is aware of its existence. It's just a feeling, but I want you to run some names through the KGB Central Index computer. Do you think you can do that?"

"I can certainly access the computer files, but I may not be able to get you printouts of the actual details." She stopped and reflected. "On the other hand, maybe I can. I have a friend who works in the tape and disc store." She remembered the young, fresh-faced technician, Nikolai Koroteyev, who had covered for her with Boychenko when she was late for work. He obviously had a crush on her. She could use his puppy-like affection to gain unlimited access to the files and printout facilities without having to log her requests in the Data Centre register. A few extra pages of computer printout could be covered under the pretext of maintenance or end-of-roll wastage. She was sure he would do it for her.

"Yes, I'm sure I can arrange it," she replied confidently. "You mean you've actually tracked down The Marble Index from the information I gave you to go on. That's fantastic. My suspicions were right. Burgess did take the list back with him to Cambridge after his visit to Moscow with Blunt in 1934. What are the names you are interested in? Write them down for me." She took a pad and a pencil from a drawer.

Alexei thought a moment and then said out loud as he

wrote, "Professor Sir James Harcourt, Director of the Cavendish Laboratories; Martin Harvey, Director of the Mullard Observatory; Dr Anthony McCabe, an English tutor; Andrew Marriott, a postgraduate student in English; Dr Gerald Fischer, senior tutor and lecturer in philosophy. All three are members of Trinity College. Oh, and while you're at it, can you find out about a Russian student who was at Cambridge in the 1930s? His name seems to crop up at every turn, and he was also in Moscow in 1934. I'm convinced he's involved in The Marble Index in some way."

"What's his name?" asked Dina.

"Piotr Kapitsa," replied Alexei.

"Kapitsa," echoed Dina. "I'm sure I've already come across him in the Archives. Yes, I'm positive. Burgess and Blunt compiled The Marble Index for the personal attention of Nikolai Bukharin, Chief of the Comintern. And Burgess's approach to Bukharin in order to gain acceptance into the Comintern was cross-referenced with an item under Kapitsa's personal file. I can look that up myself in the Archives. Marvellous. The pieces are beginning to fit together. I now feel we're getting somewhere. Maybe I won't need Boychenko or Suslov after all. When are you going back to Cambridge?"

Alexei thought Dina was being a little over-optimistic about their chances of success, but was pleased nonetheless to have given her morale a lift. "As soon as my father's operation has been completed and he's on the road to recovery."

"How long will that take?" asked Dina, disappointedly.

"I suppose it could be some time," admitted Alexei realistically.

"But we can't wait that long," pleaded Dina. "You must return to Cambridge right away."

"I can't," repeated Alexei apologetically.

"Why this sudden concern for your father?" exclaimed Dina. "I don't understand it. Before, you couldn't care less if he lived or died. I'm supposed to be the one battling for my father's existence, not you."

"Something's changed," he admitted. "Something's happened to make me think differently about him."

"Well, what is it?" she asked.

"I don't know if I should tell you," said Alexei.

"Why ever not?"

"It could be dangerous. The knowledge could be dangerous."

"I think I'm entitled to know," Dina pressed him.

Alexei paused for a long moment of reflection. "Very well," he said finally. "My father, Boris Grigoriyevich Kunayev, a Major-General in the KGB, ex-diplomat at the United Nations, and currently Departmental Head in the First Chief Directorate of the KGB, is also a counter-intelligence agent for the American FBI."

"Never," scoffed Dina.

"That's exactly what I said at first," Alexei admitted, "but he convinced me." His mother's denial had curiously drifted into the background. Perhaps Alexei wanted to believe what his father had told him at the hospital. The pendulum of his credibility was swinging violently this way and that. Maybe he was being unduly swayed by a feeling of compassion for a man about to undertake a serious heart operation.

"So you're willing to sacrifice my father's life to save yours," argued Dina bitterly.

Alexei found himself acting as the unwilling defender of his father's principles. "Why should a man who is critically ill lie to his son? No, I believe he was and still is a double agent. Don't ask me why he did it. All I know is that I've got to stand by him now." Alexei's original intention of going to the hospital and throwing Boris Kunayev's pack of lies back in his face had evaporated.

"Has he given you any concrete evidence of his work?"

asked Dina sceptically.

"No," admitted Alexei, "but I'll get him to give me some when I visit him for the second time later this morning. That should prove it one way or the other."

"If he comes up empty," said Dina, "then will you denounce him and go back to Cambridge?"

"Yes," agreed Alexei.

"Just so long as we know where we stand," said Dina.

Alexei was beginning to understand Dina's motivations, mainly because he now found himself in a similar situation. Both were fighting for their fathers. His initial disgust at her seeming involvement with Boychenko and Suslov had subsided. He now appreciated just how much she was willing to sacrifice in personal terms in order to restore Vladimir Russakov to his rightful position in society. And he admired her for that. In that instant, he realised that here was the woman he wanted to spend the rest of his life with. The question was, did she feel the same way about him? Or was he merely another tool, such as Boychenko and Suslov, to be manipulated in order to obtain her ultimate goal – the release of her father? Since her mother had died of cancer, Dina had assumed the role of wife as well as daughter in the Russakov family. She was everything to her father, and he was everything to her. The question was, where did Alexei figure in this scheme of things?

"Do you love me?" he asked. "Or will I always come second in your affections to your father?"

"It is possible to love more than one person," she replied. "Of course I love you."

"When this is all over, will you marry me?" asked Alexei.

"If we are alive, free, and sane, I shall."

In view of the dangers inherent in their schemes, it was by no means certain that all of these conditions could be fulfilled. He put his arms around her waist. She reciprocated by wrapping her arms around his neck.

"I'll hold you to that," said Alexei.

"You can hold me now," she said.

He embraced her tightly. They did not kiss. They simply pressed their bodies hard against one another. It was not a sensual embrace. It was more a matter of needing to be very close. They pressed so hard that it hurt, but there was pleasure in the pain. Slowly but gradually, they released their grip on one another. All the anxiety and tension were gone. It was as if they had never been apart. All the problems that beset them drifted away. It was just the two of them.

"We're not going to make love, are we?" said Alexei.

"No," she affirmed. "Not until this is all over. Until we are free." Alexei smiled and brushed her forehead lightly with the back of his hand. "I hate to break this up," he said, "but we have work to do. I must pay a visit to Director Kuznetzov at the Bauman Institute and then visit my father at the hospital. And you must go to the Data Centre and obtain those computer printouts I asked for."

"And don't forget Piotr Kapitsa," Dina added. "I'll call at the Archive building and check on that cross-reference."

"Is it safe for me to return here at lunchtime?" asked Alexei.

She nodded.

"Then I'll see you back here at twelve." He headed for the door. "Be careful," he said. "I love you," and closed the apartment door behind him.

It was in a more optimistic mood that he emerged into Kutuzovsky Prospekt than when he had first arrived. As he headed for the Kutuzovskaya metro station, it occurred to him that he should have added the name of Dinmukhamed Kunayev to the list he had given Dina. He still had not found out the identity of the man mentioned by Dr McCabe, who bore the same surname as him. It was only of minor importance, however, and could wait till later.

As he boarded the metro train, he wondered what story he could tell the Director of his Institute about his research thus far. Still, as he had been recalled unexpectedly early to Moscow due to his father's illness, Kuznetzov would not be too hard on him. Uppermost in Alexei's mind was the need to establish what the Director could tell him about Professor Harcourt and Dr Harvey of the Cavendish Laboratories. Could he corroborate or disclaim what McCabe and Marriott had told him about their backgrounds?

He changed at Kiev station onto the Shcholyovskaya Line and continued his journey as far as Baumanskaya. In the early morning rush hours, progress was slow with many people getting on and alighting at every station. Gradually, however, the crowds began to thin out. And after crossing the intersection with the Circle Line at Kursk Station, the flow had returned to normal.

He emerged from the Baumanskaya metro station and walked along Baumanskaya Ulitsa past the Lefortovsky Palace. The buildings of the Higher Technical Academy loomed up ahead of him. Behind the high iron railings, he could make out the early original nineteenth-century facade designed by Domenico Gilardi. A more recent twentieth-century facade on the bank of the Tauza overlooking Lefortovsky embankment had been added, but this was less in keeping with the general military character of the district. The open-sided galleries supported by columns reminded Alexei of the Great Court and cloisters of Trinity College. He appreciated that he had merely traded one academic environment for another.

Up the stone steps between the central portico, Alexei passed into the main body of the Academy. He stopped outside the Director's door and knocked.

A deep, gruff voice from within exclaimed, "Enter."

Doing as he was bidden, Alexei found himself face to face

with Director Kuznetzov, Head of the Institute. Unlike his relatively youthful, even boyish counterpart in Cambridge, Kuznetzov was, like the principals of all Soviet institutions, well into his seventies. His rather decrepit, wizened exterior belied an inner warmth and affection for his students. He made a point of knowing them all by their first names.

"Ah, Alexei," he said from behind his gigantic desk, "I was expecting you. Come and sit down."

Alexei suspected that news of his return to Moscow might have filtered through.

"I'm truly sorry that it is such unfortunate circumstances that have necessitated your presence. How is your father?"

"Fine, just fine," confirmed Alexei. "He's due to undergo open-heart surgery at any time now."

Kuznetzov nodded approvingly. "Good. Good."

Alexei stepped in again. "I'm afraid I have very little news, if any, to bring you on the academic front. I have barely had time to settle down at the Cavendish yet."

"Don't worry, Alexei," Kuznetzov reassured him. "I fully appreciate that. As a matter of courtesy, however, I am pleased that you have called in to see me."

"Professor Harcourt sends his respects," said Alexei.

"Ah, my good friend, Sir James," said the Director. "He's a very clever man. What did you make of him?"

Returning to his earlier observation, Alexei replied, "He's very young."

Kuznetzov laughed out loud. "In comparison to myself, you mean. Rutherford was only forty-eight when he became Director of the Cavendish, so he is certainly not the youngest."

"I didn't mean to offend you," said Alexei with embarrassment.

"That's quite alright, Alexei. It is only in the Soviet Union that old age is the primary qualification for senior appointments. The Cavendish Professors have always been appointed on the basis of ability. Maybe you can aspire to a professorship one day. No one can ignore genius."

Alexei felt flattered, but the idea was not beyond the scope of his ambition.

Kuznetzov continued, "I think of myself as more of a journeyman academic. My inspiration springs from dedication to my scientific discipline and loyalty to the State rather than from a fountain of original thought."

"Have you ever met Professor Harcourt?" Alexei asked. "He certainly seemed to know a lot about the history of the Bauman Institute."

"Yes. He came over on an exchange visit five years ago, and we also met at an international symposium at the Kalinin Polytechnical Institute in Leningrad."

So that explained the relationship between the two men, thought Alexei to himself. He now began to broach Dr McCabe's allegations about Harcourt's background. "I understand Sir James was originally a Polish Jew exiled by the Germans," he said.

"Where on earth did you get such a story?" said Kuznetzov.

"From a work colleague," replied Alexei vaguely. "He told me Harcourt changed his name and became a naturalised Englishman."

"To my knowledge," said the Director, "James Harcourt is his real name. His family is descended from the Huguenots, but he is decidedly English from many generations back."

"I must have been mistaken," said Alexei, wondering whether McCabe had been lying or whether the truth had simply been concealed from Kuznetzov. He would like to have pursued the questioning concerning Martin Harvey, Director of the Mullard Observatory, and his Russian and chess connections, but decided against it, at least for the moment. "At any rate, Sir James is a brilliant scientist. Indeed, he must be to have won the Nobel Prize in 1972."

"Without a doubt," Kuznetzov echoed Alexei's praises. "Indeed, he follows in the long tradition of physics research established by Lord Rutherford. But whereas Rutherford was concerned with nuclear physics and radiation, Harcourt's main field of research is in high-energy physics."

"He didn't show much interest in radio astronomy," said Alexei, remembering how the Director had dismissed him rather brusquely from his office.

"Well, it is hardly his field, is it?" replied Kuznetzov. "We are all far happier on home ground. Besides, he has a very capable deputy and astronomy expert in Martin Harvey. I expect you will be working more directly with him."

"That's right," agreed Alexei, happy that it was Kuznetzov who had introduced the name into the conversation. "Yes, he is based at the Mullard Observatory at Lord's Bridge, some five miles outside Cambridge. I understand he is a fluent Russian speaker and translates chess books into English." Alexei slipped the latter sentence into the conversation.

Kuznetzov looked puzzled. "To my knowledge, Harvey doesn't speak a word of Russian. Who told you he did? Ah, don't tell me, a work colleague."

Alexei hurried on without answering. "I share my time between Lord's Bridge and the New Cavendish Site on Madingley Road. In fact, the new complex has only recently been completed."

"It is several years since I was last in Cambridge," reflected Kuznetzov. "Ten years or so now. At that time, the Cavendish Laboratories were crammed into what was called the New Museums Site in the centre of Cambridge."

Alexei saw his chance to pursue yet another line of enquiry. "Was the Mond Laboratory there then?" he asked as innocently as he could.

"Yes, it was," replied Kuznetzov. "Why, isn't it there now?"

"The Mond is still there," confirmed Alexei, "but it's no

longer used for the purpose for which it was originally built. It now houses the Department for Aerial Photography. The low-temperature physics group now works from the New Site. Are you familiar with Piotr Kapitsa's work, Professor?"

"Why yes, yes of course," Kuznetzov stuttered.

Alexei was amazed that the mere mention of Kapitsa's name could cause such distress, not only in Professor Sir James Harcourt but also in Professor Kuznetzov. This was in addition to Kapitsa's name frequently turning up in the Central Index of the KGB Archives. "You might say that I was following in his footsteps," said Alexei.

"What do you mean?" said Kuznetzov anxiously.

"I'm in a long line of research students to benefit from the hospitality of the Cavendish Laboratories," replied Alexei. Piotr Kapitsa seemed to be an equal source of embarrassment to the Russian academic world as to the current guardians of the Cavendish research projects. It begged the question whether he was, in fact, recruited by the Cheka to obtain Western scientific secrets as McCabe had maintained or whether his masters had decided that he was contributing too much of his knowledge to his adopted scientific home and needed to be whisked away back to the Soviet Union to be taught a lesson. Whatever the reason for his "holiday" in 1934, Kapitsa had never returned to Cambridge. Alexei remembered that McCabe had told him Kapitsa was appointed Director of the Academy of Sciences, the premier accolade in the Soviet Union. Was this in genuine appreciation of his contribution to Soviet science or as a sinecure to lure him home? And what had happened to him since then?

"Where is Kapitsa now, Professor?" asked Alexei.

"The last I heard, he was a consultant at the Kharkov Institute in the Ukraine, but that was a long time ago." Kuznetzov sat up straight in his chair and adopted a business-like attitude. "Anyway, enough of these reminiscences. I have a very busy day ahead of me, and I'm sure you would much rather be at your father's bedside. It was very good of you to call." He stood up and extended his right hand.

This was obviously the signal for Alexei to take his leave. The dismissal was much the same as he had received from Professor Harcourt's office.

They shook hands. Kuznetzov shuffled some papers on his desk, and Alexei closed the door behind him. He decided to take up the Director's suggestion and pay a second visit to his father in the hospital. He had to get to the truth from someone. Everyone around him seemed to be lying or at least had something to hide.

Alexei felt he was spending all his time on a merry-go-round of underground metro trips as he re-entered the Baumanskaya station. He travelled as far as Dzerzhinskaya before changing lines. He walked the short distance underground to the interconnecting Kuznetsky Most station and took a northbound train on the Planyornaya Line.

Alighting at Begovaya, Alexei walked the short distance up Begovaya Ulitsa before turning left into Botkinsky Proyezd. It was with mixed feelings and divided loyalties that he mounted the steps of the Botkin Hospital. He did not bother reporting to reception as he already knew which room his father was in. He took the lift to Intensive Care on the third floor and set off down the corridor of private rooms past the ward sister's office. Counting the numbers as he went, Alexei looked ahead for the landmark of the KGB guard outside his father's room. There was none in sight. He began to wonder whether he was on the right floor. Having reached room seventeen, he began to have serious doubts about whether he was in the right place. One corridor of rooms looked very much like any other. He put his ear to the door and could hear no sound. Quietly, he opened the door and peered inside. The room was empty. The bed looked freshly made. Alexei shrugged his shoulders and was about to the door when he spied the electrocardiograph machine in the corner. Whilst the hospital would have more than one of these pieces of equipment, Alexei was now sure that his father had been in this room. Maybe he had been moved for security reasons, or maybe he had been taken away for further tests.

Alexei retraced his steps down the corridor and knocked on the ward sister's office door. "You may remember me, sister. My name is Alexei Kunayev. I've come to visit my father, but he doesn't seem to be in his room. Can you tell me where they've moved him?"

The sister looked rather agitated. "Didn't you know? Didn't they tell you that he went into the operating theatre over an hour ago?"

"No," replied Alexei in a state of shock. He had been away from the family apartment for over three hours now, having first of all visited Dina Russakov and then Professor Kuznetzov at the Bauman Institute.

"It all happened so quickly," she continued. "The surgeon arrived, and the order was given to operate on comrade Kunayev."

"Is he still in the operating theatre now?" asked Alexei.

"No, no, he isn't," the sister faltered.

It struck Alexei that it must not have been as complicated an operation as he had expected in order to be completed so quickly. "I'd like to see him if that's possible," he said.

"I think you had better see Dr Kornilin. I'll page him for you." To her obvious relief, the ward sister disappeared back into her office and dialled an internal call on the telephone. She re-emerged and said, "Dr Kornilin is on his way. Won't you please take a seat?"

Alexei was about to ask her some further questions when she turned on her heels and walked off down the corridor. Curious, thought Alexei to himself as he sat and waited.

After what seemed like a very long time, Dr Kornilin emerged from the lift and began to approach. Alexei got to his feet.

The doctor's demeanour was grave. "My condolences, Alexei," were his first words.

They didn't seem to register. These were the words people used when someone had passed away. "I'm not with you," said Alexei.

"Didn't the sister tell you?" said Kornilin.

"Tell me what?" said Alexei.

"Your father, he's dead," said Kornilin with an air of finality.

"Dead," echoed Alexei, "but I only saw him yesterday," he added in the illogical vocabulary of the bereaved.

"He died on the operating table less than half an hour ago. There was nothing we could do."

Alexei uttered a sound halfway between strangled laughter and a cry of despair. "But how could it be?" He turned his frustration, sorrow, and anger on Kornilin. "You told me only yesterday that the mortality rate associated with his operation was only one or two per cent. In other words, he had a ninety-eight percent chance of recovery."

"That still leaves two per cent unaccounted for, I'm afraid," apologised Kornilin.

"You called him a low-risk patient," continued Alexei.

"That is correct," affirmed the doctor, "but low risk does not imply no risk."

"I can't believe it," exclaimed Alexei, clenching his fists and throwing back his head. "What happened?" he asked.

"Machine failure," replied Kornilin.

"Machine failure?" screamed Alexei.

"Let me explain," said the doctor, placing his hand on Alexei's shoulder, causing him to sit down again. "During the open-heart operation, the patient is connected to what is known as a heart-lung machine, which takes over these same bodily functions. The tubes which connect the patient to the heart-lung machine are placed in the great veins so that all the blue blood usually entering the heart will flow into the machine instead." The doctor looked down at the seated figure of Alexei Kunayev to see if he was taking in the explanation.

Alexei was staring straight ahead with glazed eyes at the wall.

Dr Kornilin continued regardless. "Another tube is placed in the aorta so that the oxygenated blood from the machine can be returned to the body, having bypassed the heart. Once the patient is connected to the machine, no blood enters the heart. With the dry heart conditions provided, the surgeon can safely open the heart and make the necessary repairs without danger of losing blood."

Alexei came around momentarily from his traumatised state. "But you still haven't told me how he died," he said in a rather subdued, resigned voice, in sharp contrast to his initial anger.

"The blood is oxygenated in the machine by an artificial lung or oxygenator," said Kornilin. "It is this oxygenator that failed. The blood continued to circulate but was not being resupplied with oxygen. This blue blood caused the brain to be starved of oxygen, and comrade Kunayev died not of heart failure but of brain death."

Kornilin's explanation all seemed so rational to Alexei's untrained ear, but he still found it hard to believe. "I want to see the surgeon in charge," he demanded, determined to take it right to the top.

"I'm afraid Dr Choglokov is no longer here," replied Kornilin.

"Choglokov," said Alexei. "I thought the surgeon in charge was Dr Bykov."

"He was..." faltered Kornilin, "but there was a change."

"Alright then, I wish to see Dr Choglokov," pressed Alexei

again.

"I'm afraid you can't."

"Why not?" asked Alexei.

"Because he has already left Moscow. He is based at the Kirov Military Medical Academy in Leningrad."

Now Alexei really began to smell a conspiracy. "Is this Dr Choglokov a heart specialist?" he asked.

"I really don't know. I've never met the man," replied Kornilin lamely.

"I entrusted you with my father's life!" retorted Alexei, "And all you can offer me now is incompetence and ignorance. I don't believe a word of your story. In fact, I'm not even sure that my father is dead. Where is his body? I want to see it." Alexei held out his hand before Kornilin could reply. "Don't tell me. You don't know. I'm going to get to the bottom of this either with or without your help." He headed for the lift and pressed the call button. "I shall take this matter to the Academy of Medical Science and to the Minister of Health Petrovsky if I have to," came Alexei's parting shot.

Kornilin's face turned pale, but he made no reply as the lift doors closed.

Alexei was seething with rage as he emerged into Botkinskiy Proyezd.

He wanted to hit something or somebody–– anybody in order to relieve his pent-up anger. Now he would never know whether his father had been telling the truth. Perhaps someone had wanted to prevent him from finding out. But who? It smelt of the KGB. If Boris Kunayev had really been an agent for the FBI, the KGB, or the GRU would want to snuff him out as quickly as possible.

Under the cover of a serious heart operation, they could easily arrange for the patient not to survive. It bore all the hallmarks of a KGB assassination. His father had been called into the operating theatre at very short notice.

The next of kin had not been informed. The original surgeon had been replaced with an unknown, out-of-town doctor who had since conveniently disappeared.

But the ward sister and Dr. Kornilin were obviously frightened—a sure sign that they had been got at by the KGB and sworn to silence, or something unspeakable would happen to them or their families. If this were the case, however, how had the KGB found out about Boris Kunayev's revelations? It must have been a recent occurrence.

Then it struck Alexei. The only person he had told was Dina, apart from his mother, that is, who had dismissed the story as fantasy. It had been four hours since he had told Dina. The wheels of state had obviously been turning mighty quickly in the meantime. Alexei shook his head in disbelief.

How could Dina betray his trust? But it had to be her. She was the only person he had told. Then he remembered the deal he had struck with Dina.

As soon as his father had been operated on or he had discovered that his father was not telling the truth, Alexei had agreed to return to Cambridge to conclude the search for The Marble Index and assist in Dina's single-minded quest to have her father released. She had obviously resented his divided loyalties over their two fathers and had shown herself to be totally ruthless in her willingness to trade Mikhail Suslov's life for her father's, such was his importance to her. She would evidently stop at nothing to achieve her own ends. She would even sacrifice his father in order to save her own.

Alexei reflected ironically that the only positive thing to come out of this was the fact that Boris Kunayev must have been telling the truth; otherwise, he would still be alive. That was the only consolation left to him. He had lost his father and the woman he thought he loved in one fell swoop. There was now nothing left. He was filled with self-righteous indignation. He had to go and confront Dina with her treachery.

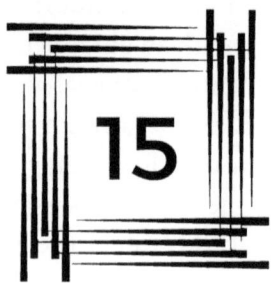

15

Alexei entered the Begovaya metro station. It was fast approaching noon. By the time he got back to Boychenko's apartment on Kutuzovsky Prospekt, Dina would have returned.

Changing onto the Circle Line at Krasnopresnenskaya, he travelled one stop as far as Kiev Station before changing again onto the Molodyozhnaya Line. He emerged from Kutulovskaya metro station in the same mood of anger and despair as when he had left the Botkin Hospital.

Alexei entered apartment block number forty-nine, Kutuzovsky Prospekt, and went up to the second floor. He knocked at room number twenty-three and prepared himself to face Dina.

"Who is it?" came her voice from inside.

"It's Alexei," he replied.

Quickly, the door opened, and she flung her arms around his shoulders.

He just stood there impassively before reaching up and loosening her grasp.

He then pushed past her into the apartment. She closed the door and followed behind.

"What's the matter?" she asked him. "I have so much to

show you – details of the files from the Central Index and those computer printouts you wanted. I've got them all. You should be pleased, Alexei. Tell me what the matter is."

"The matter is," he spat, "my father is dead and you killed him."

"What?" exclaimed Dina.

"It's no use," said Alexei. "Don't try feigning ignorance or remorse. Remember that I've seen the virtue of your acting talents at work on Boychenko and Suslov. They even worked on me. But no longer. I should have known your fanatical plans to have your father released at any cost would eventually involve me in paying the price, but I did not realise it would be paid in my father's blood." He shook Dina by the shoulders, slapped her across the face, and threw her down on the couch.

"What are you talking about, Alexei?" she pleaded with him.

"I'm talking about the confidence you betrayed. As soon as I was out of the way this morning, you contacted the KGB and told them about my father being an agent for the FBI. If they were able to corroborate this, you knew they would arrange to have him killed. His heart operation would provide the ideal cover. Then you could sweet-talk me into going back to Cambridge to pursue The Marble Index and so ensure that your father stayed alive."

Dina began to understand the drift of what Alexei was saying to her.

"Even if what you say has happened, why do you suspect me of turning informant?"

"You were the only person I told, and besides, your motives are so apparent."

"Where did Boris Kunayev reveal his secret to you?" she asked.

"In his private hospital room," replied Alexei.

"And were you alone together?"

"Yes," he affirmed. "There was a doctor, a ward sister and a KGB guard in attendance, but they all waited outside together with my mother. Father insisted on speaking to me alone."

"The room had a KGB guard," reflected Dina, "then you can be sure it had first of all been bugged."

It had never crossed Alexei's mind that a listening device might have been planted in his father's hospital room.

"No," he said, "it's not possible."

"Well, of course it is," she replied emphatically. "That is how they found out. But your father is dead. I just can't believe it." She shook her head.

The realisation that Dina could be right caused him to rethink. "I..." he began. He leant over and caressed Dina's reddened cheek with his hand.

"I'm sorry. I shouldn't have hit you. It's just that I thought..."

Showing remarkable resilience, Dina replied, "We must trust one another, Alexei. That's all we have left. Otherwise, there is nothing." A look of horror suddenly crossed her face. "The KGB knows that you know about your father's betrayal. Your life could also be in danger now. Were you followed here?"

"I don't know," replied Alexei. "I didn't see anyone."

"We have to get out of here," she reflected. "Somewhere safe. If you have been followed here, the KGB only knows that the apartment belongs to Boychenko. They can't connect him with me. That's good. So far, there is nothing to link us." She had a sudden brainwave. "Dr Sloboda and his wife. They'll take care of us. We must go to their apartment."

She picked up the files and the computer printout. "There's just one thing I don't understand," she said, stopping at the door. "As a high-ranking KGB officer, your father must have been well aware of state security procedures and must have realised that his room would be bugged. By speaking out to you as he did, he was virtually signing his own death warrant. Why should he do that? I hate to say this, Alexei, but it's almost as if your father committed suicide."

These were harsh words, but Alexei understood their reasoning. He was reminded of the conversation in that hospital room when Boris Kunayev had made several references to his imminent demise. Alexei had dismissed them at the time. Now, everything that Dina said made sense. It was as if his father had made one last defiant gesture in his life by revealing his secret to his son, whilst at the same time, he knew that the KGB assassination squad would consequently descend on him like a host of avenging angels.

"You leave by the front entrance," said Dina. "I'll go out the back. Walk around a while, and when you're satisfied you're not being followed, or have lost your tail, meet me in the forecourt of the Ukraina Hotel. We can get a taxi from there. I suggest we go and see Dr Sloboda at work. He will know what to do about your father's death, getting in touch with the coroner, initiating an enquiry, obtaining a post-mortem, ascertaining the real cause of death and so on."

"I'm sorry I misjudged you earlier," admitted Alexei. "I promise that from this moment on, I'll never doubt you again." He kissed her deeply on the lips before hurrying off down the corridor and descending the staircase into the entrance hall. There was no one about. Alexei doubted that he had been followed in the first place, but decided to take no chances. He went down the steps into the Kutuzovskaya metro station, bought a newspaper, and stood reading it for several minutes whilst surreptitiously looking around for any suspicious characters. He then purchased a ticket and passed through the turnstile. Immediately, he ran down the escalator two steps at a time and entered the southbound passage. Once on the platform, he was lucky enough to mingle with a crowd just alighting from a train. In their midst, he headed up the exit passage and found himself back in the street. From there, he retraced his steps back up Kutuzovsky Prospekt to the Ukraina Hotel. A taxi was idling in the forecourt with its back door open. He recognised the back of Dina's head through the rear window. He jumped in quickly, slammed the door, and immediately the taxi took off.

"Any problem?" asked Dina, turning to him.

"None at all," replied Alexei as they shot over Kalininsky Bridge. "Where are we going?" he asked.

"The First Municipal Hospital," replied Dina. "Dr Sloboda is head of neurology. He is also Secretary of the Moscow branch of the Soviet Society of Neurologists. Maybe he can bring his influence to bear in this case."

The taxi turned right down Smolensky Boulevard and into Zubovsky Boulevard. It crossed the Moskva River on Krymsky Bridge and turned right again along Leninsky Prospekt. On the right-hand side of the road stood the First Municipal Hospital, which also incorporated Golitsyn Hospital, making it the largest in Moscow. The taxi dropped them off outside, and they walked up the steps between the early nineteenth-century portico.

At the reception desk, Dina asked for Dr Sloboda. The nurse told them to take a seat whilst she paged him. It was not long before the white-coated figure of Dr Sloboda appeared.

"Dina!" he exclaimed, embracing her, "Larissa and I have been so worried about you. What are you doing here? Why didn't you come to see us at the apartment? Is there something wrong?" He then caught sight of Alexei standing a few paces behind Dina.

"Can we go to your office, where it's private?" she said. "I think you've already met Alexei Kunayev."

"Why yes," replied Dr Sloboda. He was still rather bemused but said, "Come along, follow me." This was the first time he had seen Dina since she had cancelled their dinner date in order to go out with Konstantin Boychenko. The next thing he knew, she had moved into his apartment. They went past his secretary and consulting rooms into the inner office.

"Is your office bugged, doctor?" asked Alexei as they sat down.

"Why, no, of course not," replied Sloboda.

"Forgive me for asking," added Alexei, "but the reason will become clear, I assure you."

"We need your help, Uncle Georgi," began Dina, "both professionally and as a friend."

"Is it to do with your father?" asked Sloboda.

"No, it's Alexei's father. He's dead. We have reason to believe that he's been killed–– assassinated by the KGB."

"No!" exclaimed Dr Sloboda with disbelief.

"Let me explain," offered Alexei. "My father was admitted to the Botkin Hospital for open heart surgery this morning. He died on the operating table. According to one of the doctors, death was attributed to the machine failure of something called an oxygenator. The surgeon in charge was changed at the last moment, and the actual surgeon who carried out the operation has mysteriously disappeared. Not only that, the staff at the hospital are scared to death and won't even tell me where my father is now."

"This all sounds highly irregular," admitted Sloboda, "but where do your suspicions of a KGB assassination plot spring from?"

"It's probably better that you don't know the full details," replied Alexei. "All I can safely say is that it concerned some damaging political revelations by my father from his hospital bed, which we, that is Dina and I, believe may have been picked up on listening devices hidden in his room. That is why I asked you whether your room was bugged or not."

"I see," reflected Sloboda. "Well, it has been known for the

KGB to place listening devices on hospital premises, and there are certainly a number of stukachi among the hospital administration staff, but are you sure they didn't find out another way?"

"The only person Alexei told was me," interrupted Dina, "and I certainly didn't betray his trust."

Alexei leaned over and squeezed her hand.

"I see," reflected Sloboda. "And now you want me to find the people responsible for your father's death or at least prove there are grounds for believing his death was suspicious."

"Can you do that?" asked Alexei.

"In my professional capacity, I can challenge the medical aspects of the case, but the rest is out of my depth. Who was the original surgeon in charge, and what was the name of his replacement? Can you also remember what the doctor told you about the cause of death? And then I want you to tell me, Dina, what has been happening to you over the past few days. I think you owe us an explanation."

"I will," said Dina contritely.

Alexei began, "The original surgeon's name was Bykov."

"Ah, yes, I know him," said Sloboda. "He is one of the finest heart specialists in the Soviet Union. His professional integrity is beyond reproach."

"Go on."

Alexei continued. "Bykov's replacement was a man called Choglokov, supposedly from the Kirov Military Medical Academy in Leningrad."

"Hm," pondered Sloboda. "That name doesn't ring any bells with me. One moment." He picked up the telephone and buzzed his secretary. "Would you please connect me with the Registrar of the Kirov Academy in Leningrad?" He held the telephone receiver in one hand and tapped his writing pad with a ballpoint pen in the other. Alexei and Dina heard a click on the line as the connection was made. "Good day," said

Sloboda. "PPS to Minister of Health Petrovsky here. I require some information concerning your Dr Choglokov." There was a response at the other end of the line.

"Never mind that, my good man. If you want your current application to the Department of Special Medical Aid to be tied up in red tape in the Minister's office, go ahead and make your enquiries. I need the information now." Dr Sloboda's tone was extremely authoritative and convincing.

Alexei and Dina smiled at one another, revelling in the doctor's little deception.

"That's better," said Sloboda. "I see. I see. Thank you. Goodbye." The doctor replaced the receiver and said, "Choglokov was only on loan to them; he was called away unexpectedly to Moscow and is now believed to have returned to his home base."

"Where is that?" asked Alexei.

"According to the Registrar, he's a consultant at the Municipal Hospital in Alma-Ata in Kazakhstan."

"Kazakhstan," exclaimed Dina. "Why, that must be twenty thousand kilometres from Moscow."

"And a good deal more from Leningrad," added Alexei. "It's almost on the Chinese border."

"In other words," said Sloboda, "it's about as far away from the scene of the crime as possible. How very convenient. It's so remote that the only thing I know about the Republic of Kazakhstan is that it is the launching site for our Soviet cosmonauts. Do you want me to telephone through to the hospital in Alma-Ata?"

"No," replied Alexei. "It would be pointless. I think we get the idea. Make those responsible as inaccessible as possible."

Sloboda nodded in agreement. "After my initial scepticism about the circumstances surrounding your father's death, I'm beginning to think you are right, Alexei. Allow me to make another phone call." He again lifted the receiver and buzzed his secretary. "Get me the coroner's office of the Moscow Regional Health Department." The connection was made. This time, he used his real identity. "Dr Georgi Sloboda here. I have been instructed by the relatives of the deceased comrade Boris Grigoriyevich Kunayev, who died at the Botkin Hospital this morning, to authorise an autopsy."

There was a response from the other end of the line.

"What?" exclaimed Sloboda. "On whose authority?" He listened intently to the reply. "And where is the body now? Thank you. Goodbye." He replaced the receiver and faced the expectant Alexei and Dina. "A post-mortem has already been carried out, and he was buried in Novodevichy Cemetery less than an hour ago. Irena Kunayev gave her consent and was present at the interment."

"Mother!" exclaimed Alexei. "She couldn't have. I doubt if she even knows Father is dead yet. I wanted to be the one to break the news to her. No, it just cannot be," he sobbed. "Give me the telephone. I must speak to her."

Solemnly, Sloboda handed over the phone whilst Dina looked on, unsure of what to say in the circumstances.

Alexei dialled his home number directly. "Mother," he said. "Tell me it isn't true. Father..." he faltered.

A tearful stream of words emanated from the other end of the line.

Dina and Dr Sloboda shot a glance at one another.

Alexei listened to his mother, swearing to himself under his breath from time to time. "Those bastards. I'll kill them," he exclaimed. "Will you be alright? Stay where you are. Don't answer the door until I get back." He slammed down the receiver and said, "She had a little visit from two people purporting to be doctors and two militiamen. They told her Father was dead, bundled her into a car, took her to the cemetery, forced her to sign some forms, and even took photographs of her watching the coffin being lowered into the grave. Bastards."

"It sounds like the tactics of the arrest party who came to seize my father in the middle of the night," said Dina, as if this shared experience were some kind of consolation. "I know how your mother must feel. Oh, Alexei, what are we going to do?"

"I know what I'd like to do," retorted Alexei with some venom, "but no doubt the people concerned will also be on their way back to Kazakhstan by now, just like Dr Choglokov."

"Hm," agreed Dr Sloboda reflectively. "Both you and Dina, as well as your mother, could be in grave danger now. On the other hand, they may let the matter rest with the elimination of your father. I think it's best if you can find out all you can from your mother, Alexei, and then you and Dina return to my apartment. You'll be safer there."

"No, I must return to Kutuzovsky Prospekt," insisted Dina.

"Why?" asked Alexei. "You were the one who thought it would be dangerous to stay there in the first place."

"You've forgotten about Boychenko and Suslov," argued Dina. "If I suddenly disappear, that will only put extra pressure on me. I must keep up appearances. Besides, I need to keep on Boychenko's good side in order to guarantee my continued freedom of movement. And Suslov will at least expect me at regular intervals to administer his insulin injections. I'll come back to Dr Sloboda's apartment later this evening when we can look over the computer files and those extracts from the KGB Archives."

"Alright," agreed Alexei, "but you must be careful. We still don't know whether the KGB has us both under surveillance. I'm going home to see my mother."

"Take care, both of you," said Dr Sloboda.

Alexei and Dina walked together along Leninsky Prospekt in complete silence. They both had a great deal on their mind. They travelled on the metro together as far as Oktyabrskaya before changing onto the Circle Line.

It was there that their ways parted. Dina headed westbound towards Kiev Station and Kutuzovsky Prospekt. Alexei headed eastbound in the direction of Taganskaya. As he held onto the strap, he was reminded of his adventures on the London underground when he and Marriott had followed Dr McCabe and his Russian lady friend. They too had parted company in the West Kensington tube station, with Marriott taking the westbound and he the eastbound train. These two parallel incidents threw into sharp relief the fact that his whole life was becoming a choice between East and West in more ways than one.

Alexei turned the key slowly in the lock of the family apartment on Maksima Gorkovo embankment. He had tried rehearsing on the train exactly what he was going to say to his mother, but now that the time had come, he was totally lost for words. They seemed inadequate to express his feelings anymore.

His mother had blamed herself at the hospital for Boris Kunayev's original heart attack. He was fearful that she would now be even more guilt-ridden, shouldering the blame entirely for his father's death. Alexei was caught in an unenviable dilemma of choosing to allow her to continue under her burden of guilt, or causing even more pain by telling her that Boris Kunayev had been a murder victim of the KGB.

His father had even foreseen his own death. That was why he had sworn Alexei to secrecy—— a pledge he had in fact broken by divulging his father's secret to his mother. If only the hospital room had not been bugged, Boris Kunayev would still be alive.

As the door to the apartment swung open, he was haunted by his father's words: "No, your mother must never know, for the simple reason that she cannot tell what she does not know."

At the time, he had taken this to mean that Irena Kunayev could not be tortured by the KGB to divulge information about his work as a double agent if she did not know in the first place. But his father's words had been highly ambiguous. They could equally have meant that he feared that she, being of good socialist consciousness, might have turned him over to the authorities on account of his treachery.

Hypothetically, if the hospital room had not been bugged, and if Dina were not responsible for betraying the confidence, that only left Irena Kunayev.

She was the only other person who knew. He had initially suspected Dina because the rushed heart operation had taken place only hours after he had left Dina in the apartment on Kutuzovsky Prospekt. But surely even the efficiency of the KGB machine could not have lumbered into motion so quickly. The additional twelve hours would have allowed the KGB time to lay their plans. Her reaction had also given him cause for concern. But what about her story of being dragged to the cemetery to witness Boris Kunayev's burial? It could have all been part of a cosmetic cover-up. Alexei no longer knew what to think. He had always been very close to his mother, much closer than to his father. By questioning her, he was also questioning himself. The mental agony he was now suffering was even leading him to doubt his own sanity.

"Alexei, is that you?" came a weak and tearful voice from the sitting room.

"Mother!" exclaimed Alexei, all his doubts and fears suddenly evaporating.

He opened the door and found his mother sitting in a chair by the window, still wearing her coat and headscarf. Her cheeks were red and streaked with tears. If she had been a willing accomplice to the KGB assassination plot, Alexei speculated that her acting talents would be more at home on the stage of the Bolshoi Theatre.

The suggestion put forward by Dina that Boris Kunayev had, in fact, courted his own death by speaking out so openly in his hospital room began to appeal to him more and more as the most likely explanation.

As he walked past the telephone table, Alexei remembered the numbers written down on the pad. The top sheet had now gone. "When did you find out?" he asked.

"They told me when they knocked on the door," sobbed Irena Kunayev.

"You mean they didn't tell you when you rang the hospital?" said Alexei.

"I didn't ring the hospital," she replied.

"I thought you might have rung this morning like you rang last night," said Alexei.

"No, no," wept his mother. "They told me not to bother them... that they would tell me if and whether there were any developments... a change in his state of health... the time of his operation. If only that heart-lung machine hadn't failed..." her voice tailed away.

"You knew about the operation then," suggested Alexei.

"No. They told me what the cause of death was on the way to the cemetery."

"I see," reflected Alexei. He realised he was being rather harsh on his mother. He couldn't bring himself to tell her that the circumstances made it look like a quiet assassination job. She would probably not question the speed and efficiency with which Boris Kunayev had been dispatched. But surely, she must suspect foul play. "You remember what I told you last night about what father told me in confidence in his hospital room," began Alexei.

His mother nodded.

"Well, do you think that could have had anything to do with his death?"

Irena Kunayev looked puzzled. "How do you mean?" she questioned.

"Well, if the KCB had found out that he had really been a

double-agent all these years, they would have wanted immediate revenge."

"I told you your father's claims were a lot of nonsense. And besides, Boris Grigoriyevich wasn't killed; he died during the course of an operation." She swallowed hard. It was obvious that it was distressing her to talk about it.

Alexei decided he had to persist in his quest for the truth. "Doesn't it strike you as a coincidence that he was rushed into an operation only hours after his revelations, and that the surgeon was changed at the last moment for someone who cannot now be traced?"

"Ah, yes, that man from Kazakhstan. I thought that Dr Bykov was going to undertake the operation," protested Irena Kunayev.

"He was," agreed Alexei. "And what about the haste of Father's burial? The authorities obviously don't want the exposure of a thorough autopsy."

"You know what the health authorities are like," said his mother. "They don't have time for compassion or sentimentality."

Alexei was struck by how reasonable his mother was reacting under the circumstances. Outwardly and emotionally, she was displaying all the normal signs of a bereaved widow, but her words were cold and unfeeling.

"Well, I have no intention of leaving the matter there," said Alexei indignantly. "I've already sought the help of Dr Sloboda, a family friend of Dina Russakov and her father. He's going to take it up with the Academy of Medical Science and the Moscow Regional Health Department."

"Oh, don't, Alexei," pleaded his mother. "If you do, they'll only make life more difficult for us. I wouldn't want anything to happen to you. You're all I have left now." She took his head and embraced it on her breast. "Promise me you won't do anything foolish."

Alexei wondered whether they'd issued any veiled threats about his own or his mother's safety in the future. "Don't worry, mother. They wouldn't dare harm us. One suspicious death in the family is one thing, but not all three. Besides, I may have something that the KGB wants."

"What's that?" asked Irena Kunayev.

Thinking of The Marble Index, he replied, "I can't tell even you yet, Mother. Let's just say that I have discovered something in Cambridge which could make father's supposed indiscretions pale into insignificance."

She was about to question him further when Alexei pulled himself away.

"Will you be alright here on your own for a while?" he asked.

"One of the doctors gave me some sleeping pills," she replied. "I think I'll take a couple."

"I want to visit Father's grave," said Alexei. "Did they leave you the car?"

"Yes, the driver's gone, but I have a spare set of keys. They're on the sideboard. Please be careful, Alexei."

He kissed his mother on the forehead, took the keys, and put them in his coat pocket. There was a photograph on the sideboard of his mother and father taken when they had first met in the Caucasian mountain spa of Kislovodsk. They looked young and happy. Alexei thought about how much he looked like his father, and for the first time, it struck him that Dina bore a striking resemblance to his mother. Maybe that was why he was so immediately attracted to her.

Reflecting on this thought, he ran down the stairs and went out through the rear entrance into the courtyard where the residents' cars were parked. The black Chaika stood in its reserved place. Gunning the limousine into life, he drove off along the embankment before joining the Ring Road at the Bolshoy Krasnokholmsky Bridge. He followed the Sadovoye as far as Zubovskaya Ploshchad, where he turned left down Kropotkinskaya Ulitsa. This merged into Bolshoy Pirogovskaya Ulitsa, to the right of which a high brick wall protected the grounds of the Novodevichy Convent, also known as the New Convent of the Virgin.

Alexei swung the car right and turned left through the main entrance past the Gate Church of the Transfiguration. Bringing the Chaika to a halt on the gravel drive outside the Cathedral of the Virgin of Smolensk, Alexei went the rest of the way on foot. Beyond the South wall of the Convent, through the Gate Church of the Intercession, lay the Novodevichy Cemetery itself.

This was a very exclusive resting place and one of the most famous burial grounds in the whole of Russia. Writers such as Gogol and Chekhov, the composer Prokofiev and politicians such as Mikoyan and Khrushchev had been laid to rest here. Alexei's father was in very good company. In fact, the KGB had been extremely clever in laying him to rest in the Novodevichy. They knew perfectly well that it would be regarded as a great honour for Boris Kunayev, and no authority would dare give permission for the body to be exhumed and another autopsy carried out. There would have been a public outcry if it had been suggested that a burial plot in the Novodevichy should be dug up. Alexei knew in his heart of hearts that his father had been laid to rest for good. Whatever secrets he had carried, either in his mind or in the circumstances surrounding his death, he had carried to the grave.

In the failing light, Alexei walked about among the immaculately kept graves with their imposing headstones. In the southeast corner, he finally came across the most recent plots. The last headstone bore the legend – Boris Grigoriyevich Kunayev 1917–1975. The earth was still soft underfoot. The ground was barely compacted. Alexei felt he could have used his bare hands to claw away the earth and uncover his father's coffin.

He didn't really know why he had come – maybe just to be close to his father one last time. He realised he had never really known the man. And in view of recent events, Alexei felt that he had known him even less than he had realised. Boris Kunayev was a stranger to him in death as much as he had been a stranger in life.

He bent down and took a handful of moist earth. He then began to squeeze it with all his might. The tears welled up in his eyes and rolled uncontrollably down his cheeks. The butcher responsible for his father's death was now twenty thousand kilometres away in the remote Republic of Kazakhstan. He paused as he remembered his mother's comment about the change to the surgeon in charge of the heart operation. It was she who had mentioned that Choglokov was from Kazakhstan. How had she known that? Dr Kornilin at the hospital had only told them that the replacement doctor was from the Kirov Academy in Leningrad. It had taken a high-level telephone call from Dr Sloboda posing as a representative of the Minister of Health's Office to establish that Choglokov was in fact based in the Municipal Hospital of Alma-Ata, the capital city of the Republic of Kazakhstan. It was, of course, possible that the KGB visiting party had told Irena Kunayev, but they were hardly likely to volunteer such damaging information.

Alexei felt in his wallet and pulled out the piece of paper on which he had copied the two telephone numbers taken from the pad in the family apartment. Late last night, his mother had made a phone call. She had only just denied phoning the hospital, so who had she been phoning? What was the second number on the piece of paper? He had to find out.

He let the crumbling pieces of earth in his hand fall on the white gravestone, smeared the back of his dirty hand across his cheek and walked slowly back through the now darkened and eerie grounds of the Novodevichy Cemetery.

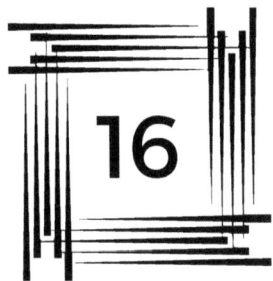

16

Dina laid out the files on the bed. Dr Sloboda had offered them the spare bedroom belonging to their son, who was working at the Military Institute of Physical Culture in Leningrad. The room had two single beds, which gave Dina and Alexei the option of sleeping separately or together.

"Which do you want to see first?" she asked. "Your Cambridge comrades or Piotr Kapitsa?"

"Let's start with Cambridge," replied Alexei, taking a sip from a large tumbler of vodka. "I take it you didn't have any trouble at the Data Centre."

"No, my good friend Nikolai Koroteyev, the technician in the tape-storeroom, was able to obtain hard copies of extracts from the personnel files for me. He even smuggled them past security and out of the building."

"Good," said Alexei. "Just so long as the requested files can't be traced back to you or me. Let's see what we have here."

"There was nothing on the first one–– Andrew Marriott," said Dina. "Now then, Professor Sir James Harcourt!" she continued, picking up another file.

"Here, let me see," interrupted Alexei, eager to discover

the contents.

He read extracts out loud. "Born 4th August 1921, son of the late Professor E.H.S. (Stefan) Sierpinski. Name at birth – Kazimierz Sierpinsky. So, McCabe was right," exclaimed Alexei. "Harcourt is an exiled Pole, and he has changed his name." He continued to read. "Father was a distinguished Professor of Physics at the Polish Academy of Sciences in Warsaw. He was a medical student at the Branicki Medical Academy in Bialystok, the administrative, cultural and industrial centre of north-east Poland. Between 1941 and 1944, the Nazis in occupation murdered fifty-five per cent of the Bialystok population, including almost the entirety of its Jewish contingent. Both his mother and father, and his elder brother, were killed because of their Jewish roots. After the Jewish ghetto revolt of 16 August 1943, Kazimierz Sierpinski joined the Polish underground, which was partly sponsored by the Soviet Secret Intelligence Service. After the war, he was the sole remaining member of his family and moved to Manchester in the North-West of England, where he took out British nationality. He changed his academic discipline from medicine to physics, probably in deference to his dead father's wishes and married a French student, Michele Harcourt, adopting her maiden name as his naturalised British surname, then changing his Christian names to James Steven. Graduating from Manchester University with a BA in 1948, he moved to Trinity College, Cambridge, where he took an MA in 1950 and a PhD in 1954. He was named the Isaac Newton Student in 1954. Appointments included Lecturer in Physics, Reader in Physics, Visiting Professor of Physics at Massachusetts Institute of Technology, and Visiting Professor at the Polish Academy of Sciences in Warsaw. Attended the International Symposium at the Kalinin Polytechnical Institute in Leningrad. Contacted by Director Kuznetzov with a view to recruitment by the KGB. Turned down."

"Well, well, well," said Alexei. "So my own Professor made an approach to Harcourt. Still, they appear to be on quite friendly terms, so their contact cannot have been that unamicable." He continued to read. "Chairman of Nuffield Foundation's Committee on Physics Education, President of the Institute of Physics. Appointed Cavendish Professor of Physics in 1970. Shared the Nobel Prize for Physics in 1972. Knighted 1973."

"How about Martin Harvey?" said Alexei, picking up the next file.

"Professor Martin Harvey, MA, PhD, FRS. Professor of Radio Astronomy, University of Cambridge, since 1967. Fellow of Trinity College, Research Fellow of Gonville and Caius. Assistant Director of Research 1958–1962. Lecturer in Physics, University of Cambridge, 1962-1967. Visiting Professor in Astronomy at Yale in 1965. Foreign Honorary Member of Moscow Higher Technical Academy." This took Alexei by surprise. Harvey had not mentioned that he had once been associated with the Bauman Institute. "Approach made by Professor Kuznetzov. Rejected. Made Honorary Member of Moscow Chess Congress. Swallow Katrina Goncharova planted, but no response. Suspected homosexual tendencies. Further approach pending." Alexei had to laugh to himself about this. If a target did not rise to the sexual bait, he was dismissed as a pervert by the KGB. So Harvey did have a chess connection, and it looked as if he did speak Russian after all. No wonder Director Kuznetzov had denied the allegations made by McCabe about Harcourt and Harvey. He was the one responsible for trying to recruit them as agents of the KGB.

He picked up McCabe's file. "Anthony McCabe, born in Glasgow in 1940. Son of Alistair McCabe, active member of the Communist Party of Great Britain and the Scottish Nationalist Party. Educated at Heriot-Watt College in Edinburgh. No political activity. MA in English at Trinity College, Cambridge,

1963. PhD in 1967. Chairman of the Literature Panel of the Arts Council in Cambridgeshire. Broadcaster on the Eastern Division of Radio Free Europe. Appears to have revolted against Communist Party roots."

Disappointedly, Alexei put down the file. There was virtually nothing there he did not know already. It did not contain the startling revelations he had expected. He picked up the last Cambridge file, that of Dr Gerald Fischer, the Senior Tutor of Trinity. "Born in Krakow, Poland, in 1932 as Jerzy Kozlowski. Son of a clothier, Juliusz Kozlowski. Father collaborated with the Nazis and was killed by the Polish Free Army. Mother and son fled first to London, then settled in Manchester. Mother worked in a cotton mill – killed in an industrial accident when Jerzy was eighteen. He worked as a laboratory assistant in the Department of Mechanical Engineering whilst studying in the evenings. Entered Manchester University as a full-time student in 1952. BA in philosophy, 1955. Moved to Trinity College, Cambridge. Changed name by deed poll in 1956 to Gerald Fischer, but maintained Polish nationality. PhD 1959. Fellow of Trinity College. University Lecturer in Moral Science, 1960–1966. Sidgwick Lecturer in Moral Science 1966–1968. Knightsbridge Professor of Moral Philosophy, 1969–1975. Member of the Mind Association. Vice-President of the Aristotelian Society. Annual Philosophical Lecture to the British Academy in 1973. Writings on Wittgenstein's Tractatus Logico-Philosophicus. Blatant homosexual. Recruited as a talent spotter by the Polish Secret Intelligence Service. Passed to KGB for further exploitation. Possible use as bait for other homosexuals in sexual entrapment and blackmail."

"So," declared Alexei, "it is Dr Fischer who is the spymaster and not McCabe as I suspected." He thought it an interesting background fact that both Harcourt and Fischer were exiled Poles. Both had changed their names, and both had obviously been deeply affected by the deaths of their fathers.

Harcourt had dedicated his life to the pursuit of the subject pioneered by his professor father. Fischer had possibly attempted to atone for the guilt of his father's treachery in embracing Nazism. By now espousing the cause of Communism, Alexei speculated that Fischer was now repaying a family debt.

"Right, let's see what you have on Piotr Kapitsa," he said as Dina handed him a copy of the file from the Archives of the KGB Central Index.

"On the other hand, you know more about this," he said. "Why don't you give me a breakdown on what you've found out?"

"Well," said Dina, "as you already pointed out, Piotr Kapitsa was back in Moscow from Cambridge in 1934 at the same time as Burgess and Blunt. They were there to try and impress Nikolai Bukharin, Head of the Comintern, to have themselves recruited. The names on The Marble Index were supposed to act as an incentive to sway Bukharin in their favour and show their good faith and ability to promote the Communist cause. They also had an audience with Vyacheslav Menzhinsky, Head of the OGPU State Security Services. As an upper-class homosexual with refined tastes in art, music and literature, Menzhinsky was the ideal contact for the young Englishmen. And as a matter of interest, he too was a Pole like his predecessor Dzerzhinsky."

Alexei took the point and nodded with interest.

Dina continued, "Menzhinsky, for all his artistic background, recognised that the only worthwhile intelligence to be gained abroad was in the field of science. Burgess and Blunt were men of letters, English and fine art. The university contacts they had were with like-minded people. On the other hand, Kapitsa had access to the scientific circles. And as Rutherford's assistant at the Cavendish, his integrity was beyond reproach. Let me put this hypothesis to you. Kapitsa could pick out the vulnerable targets, and Burgess and Blunt were the ones who could do the recruiting."

"So you think that the names on The Marble Index are those of science students," interjected Alexei.

"That's right," agreed Dina. "The Soviet Secret Service realised that Cambridge as a whole was a much more Marxist-oriented university than Oxford. Cambridge was preoccupied with science to a greater extent than Oxford, and those on the science side were more in tune with Communist materialism than those absorbed purely in classics and the humanities. Kapitsa had already given Menzhinsky detailed reports of the trend of university thought and how Marxist dialecticism among the scientists had already begun to affect students. Trinity College in particular became a focal point for pro-Communist sympathisers. Burgess, Blunt and Philby were members. Piotr Kapitsa was a Fellow of the College."

"You've forgotten someone else," interrupted Alexei.

"Who's that?" asked Dina.

"Me," he replied. "I'm a Fellow of Trinity as well."

Dina smiled at the nicety of the irony.

"Do you think that Kapitsa was instrumental in selecting the targets for recruitment?" he asked.

"I do," she replied, "and Burgess and Blunt compiled The Marble Index on the recommendation of Piotr Kapitza."

It suddenly dawned on Alexei where Kapitsa would have targeted his recruits amongst the research students of the Cavendish Laboratories. Apart from accepting graduates from many countries in the world, the Cavendish also welcomed the cream of young British scientists, particularly in the field of physics. Alexei had assumed that as Blunt and Burgess were the compilers of The Marble Index, those on the left would have been students from their specialised fields of English, literature, fine art, philosophy and so on.

These were the kind of people who would go on to make

a career in the civil service, commerce, the Foreign Office, and even MI5 and MI6. Dina had highlighted the fact that Menzhinsky considered espionage in the field of science to be the most profitable area for the Soviet Union to exploit. Trinity was also a College renowned for its science intake. Look at Rutherford himself, Harcourt, Harvey and the rest. The spectre of the gallery of annual photographs at the Cavendish rose before Alexei's eyes. He saw the year 1933–1934 and now came to the firm belief that the names on The Marble Index would also figure on the subtitles to that photograph. But which names? And where was The Marble Index hidden now?

"Well?" asked Dina, probing Alexei's silence.

"Did you know that The Marble Index was a quotation from the poet, William Wordsworth?" he replied.

"No, but I often wondered about its origin."

Alexei quoted from memory: "And from my pillow, looking forth by light of moon or favouring stars, I could behold the antechapel where the statue stood of Newton with his prism and silent face, the marble index of a mind for ever voyaging through strange seas of thought alone."

The foreign verse meant little to Dina.

Alexei explained. "The Marble Index refers to a statue of Sir Isaac Newton in the antechapel of Trinity College. That marble statue is The Marble Index."

"What does index mean in that context?" asked Dina.

"Well," replied Alexei, "an index is a place where information is stored.

"Presumably, in this case, the information is the list of seven names. An index is also an indicator of pointing, as in one's index finger." As he uttered these words, Alexei suddenly visualised the statue of Newton. Unlike the busts in the Wren Library, this depiction of the great scientist by the sculptor Roubiliac had arms. In his left hand, he held the prism through which he had discovered the composition of white light. His right hand was outstretched, the index finger pointing towards infinity. Maybe this had literally been pointing him in the right direction all along. The Marble Index was hidden in the statue. Could it be that it was concealed either in the prism or in the index finger of the statue itself? "I think I know where to find The Marble Index," he declared, much to Dina's surprise.

"Well, where? Tell me where," she urged.

"No, not until I'm sure," he replied. "How big would it have been when it was filed in the Central Index?"

"It looked as if it had originally been stuck to the back of a card, say six inches by four inches," recalled Dina.

"So the names were written on a smaller card, say four by three."

Dina nodded.

"Could it have been a photograph?" speculated Alexei.

"Yes, I suppose so," agreed Dina.

The framed group photographs hanging in the gallery of the Cavendish Laboratories were several feet across, but presumably each individual would have ordered a smaller print to keep as a memento. Rather than write down the seven names, Kapitsa could have simply ringed their faces on the group photograph. Their names were imprinted below like the members of a sports team. He could even have obtained the negative, which could easily have been rolled up and concealed.

"There was something very peculiar on the card on file in the Central Index," recalled Dina.

"Oh yes," said Alexei with interest. "What was that?"

"On one corner, there was a coloured drawing. It looked like a rainbow. What do you suppose that could mean?"

Alexei knew right away. Burgess was reputed to be a practical joker with a love of intrigue. Newton's prism had revealed to him the composition of white light and the spectrum of colours in the rainbow. Burgess's little drawing was designed to be a further clue to the whereabouts of The Marble Index. The clue meant Isaac Newton and Alexei thought that he had worked out the rest. "It means that I'm now more sure than ever that I know the hiding place of The Marble Index. I must return to Cambridge as soon as possible."

"Do you think that we could use it to bargain for my father's release?" asked Dina.

"If it's as important as we think, it could even buy a passage for all three of us to the West."

"What about your mother?" asked Dina.

"I don't think she'll be going anywhere," he replied.

Dina looked puzzled.

"I think she may be the one who turned Father in to the KGB."

"No," she exclaimed. "What makes you think that?"

"I have my reasons," he replied. He produced the piece of paper with the two telephone numbers from his pocket. "Do you recognise that second number?" he asked.

Dina looked and shook her head.

"Dial it for me," he said bluntly.

Without questioning, Dina picked up the extension receiver and dialled.

She listened to the voice at the other end and, without saying a word in response, replaced the receiver. She turned to Alexei and said, "It was an answering machine for the office of Comrade D.A. Kunayev, First Secretary of the Communist Party of Kazakhstan."

Alexei burst into the family apartment on Maksima Gorkovo embankment. His father's parting words – 'your mother must never know, for the simple reason that she cannot tell what she does not know'–– echoed in his ears.

If Alexei had taken heed and kept the vow of silence he had sworn, his father would still be alive. Instead, he had chosen to place his trust in his mother and reveal to her his father's act of national treachery in pursuance of his own principles. The truth was she had been a stukach or informant all along. She had let slip a couple of things that afternoon, which now helped him to confirm her conspiratorial role. Although she hadn't been to the hospital, she knew about the heart-lung machine. And even more damning was her reference to 'that man from Kazakhstan', when to all intents and purposes the surgeon, Dr Choglokov, was from the Kirov Academy in Leningrad. And last of all, the telephone number.

He shouted, "Mother," as he put the lights on in the entrance hall. There was no reply. He went into the lounge and then remembered that Irena Kunayev had said she would be taking some sleeping pills given to her by one of the doctors. If her grief were genuine, she would by now be heavily sedated.

Alexei went into his parents' bedroom and switched on the light. His mother was lying fully clothed on the bed with her eyes open. They stared at one another for a long moment.

"You know, don't you?" she said finally.

"Yes, I know," spat Alexei.

"Have you come here to kill me?" she asked coldly.

Alexei didn't know what he was going to do. Premeditation didn't enter into it. All he knew was that at that moment in time, he needed to be in his mother's company. "Why, why did you do it?" he asked.

"It was what I was trained to do. I couldn't help myself."

"I don't understand," said Alexei, slumping down on the bed.

"It doesn't matter now anyway. I have nothing left. I'm of no further use. I loved your father. Not in the beginning. But I loved him and now there's nothing left." At the side of the bed, she grasped a photograph of her and Boris Grigoriyevich Kunayev, identical to the one on the sideboard in the lounge. Alexei saw that she had been crying. She pointed at their happy, smiling faces. "That was taken when we first met," she said, "at the spa town of Kyslovodsk in the Caucasus. Your father had just graduated from the Marx Engels School in Gorky. The authorities had sent them all away to the resort as a reward. Although they didn't know it at the time, they were taking their first step on the ladder of the Moscow Secret Service. And I... I was also sent there. The Komsomol recruited me as a 'swallow', you know what that is?"

Alexei nodded.

"To seduce and marry your father. He was my appointed target. I was to reinforce and sustain his belief that what he was doing was for the good of the Soviet Union. I had to maintain his socialist consciousness at a high level so that he wouldn't question his destiny as an eventual spy. Even though at first it was a pretence, I came to enjoy our walks on the banks of the Olkhovka and the Beryozovka. Kyslovodsk is an idyllic setting, conducive to young people in love. The beautiful Sosnovaya Gorka Park on the banks of the Olkhovka has many waterfalls. We used to strip off and bathe naked in the secluded pools and make love behind the cover of the falls, with the crash of water ringing in our ears. We explored the cataracts of the Honeyed River and climbed to the top of the Great Dzina Peak. Those were wonderful days when we didn't have a care in the world." She clutched the photograph tightly to her breast.

Alexei didn't know whether to feel compassion or revulsion. His mother had betrayed his father because he had turned against the hypocrisies of Communism. And he had paid the price with his life. Irena Kunayev had been true to her training. She had acted instinctively, almost against her own judgment. Could Alexei find it in his heart now to forgive her?

He thought not.

"What are you going to do now?" she asked.

"I'm going back to England," he replied. Then he remembered he had told his mother that he had made a discovery in Cambridge which the KGB would be interested in. "Are you going to inform on me as well?" he asked.

Irena Kunayev realised what he was referring to. "No, it is not my place. My job is done. Maybe I will take the sleeping pills after all." The full bottle stood on the bedside table.

The implication of intended suicide was obvious to Alexei. He couldn't bring himself to plead with her to spare her own life. After all, she would make her peace with herself in the way she thought best. It was out of Alexei's hands. He turned and went towards the door.

"Put the light out, please, Alexei," said his mother softly.

He pressed the switch, casting the bedroom into total darkness.

When Alexei returned to the Slobodas' apartment, everyone had already gone to bed. He let himself in with the spare key and stealthily padded down the hall towards the second bedroom.

When he opened the door, he found Dina lying on one of the single beds in the same position as he had left his mother. She was fast asleep.

Alexei was struck again by the resemblance between Dina and Irena Kunayev as a young woman. The reading lamp was on at the side of the bed, casting a warm red glow over her whole body. He had been touched by his mother's description of how she and Boris Kunayev had made love behind the waterfalls on the Olkhovka River. He ached for the time when he and Dina would again make love, perhaps on the banks of the River Cam in Cambridge or the seclusion of Byron's Pool at Grantchester. He wanted to make love to her there and then, but remembered their pact not to do so until they were both free. He undressed and got into the other bed with its cool white sheets.

He reached over and switched off the bedside lamp.

Through the open curtains, he could see the navigation lights of an airliner flashing on and off in the distance and gradually disappearing altogether.

As Alexei drove the Chaika down Kropotkinskaya Ulitsa past the Pushkin Museum on the right, Dina began to be filled with trepidation. She was still unsure whether she would be allowed access to the Serbsky Institute in view of the circumstances surrounding her last visit. The nurse had warned her that she might have jeopardised her visiting rights. She had asked Alexei to accompany her, knowing full well that only immediate family and representatives of the medical profession were permitted to visit. She had, however, prevailed on the better judgment of Dr Sloboda to allow Alexei to accompany her.

If possible, Dina wanted Alexei to meet Vladimir Maksimovich Russakov whilst his faculties were at least still partially intact. She consoled herself with the belief that after the reconvening of the commission of enquiry the next month, her father was bound to be exonerated and released.

This moment could arrive even more quickly if Alexei could unearth The Marble Index and use it as a bargaining counter. However, between now and then, the likes of the dreaded Dr Daniel Luntz, who was also a KGB Colonel, could subject him to whatever drug and psychological treatment took their sadistic fancies.

Alexei swung the Chaika left and came face to face with the high steel gates barring the entrance to the Serbsky Institute of Forensic Psychiatry.

The two armed KGB guards took one look at the official limousine with its distinctive KGB parking permit and waved it through without further ceremony.

Alexei parked immediately outside the front entrance and killed the engine. He helped Dina up the steps and through the main doors.

As soon as the nurse in reception saw Dina, she rang the bell in front of her.

"I'd like to see my father, Vladimir Russakov," said Dina.

The nurse looked from Dina to Alexei and said, "I'm afraid you can't."

"These are statutory visiting hours laid down by the commission of enquiry," insisted Dina. "You cannot stop me."

Alexei interrupted her. "I think it may be my presence," he said. "You go in alone, and I'll wait for you out here."

"That wouldn't make any difference," said the nurse coldly, looking anxiously down the corridor and ringing the bell again to call attention.

"Have you suspended my visiting rights?" asked Dina, fearing that her worst expectations had been fulfilled.

"No, it's not that," said the nurse. "Ah, here comes Dr Shostakovich."

Dina recognised the man approaching as the Serbsky Institute's resident forensic psychiatrist, who had chaired the commission of enquiry.

"How did you get in here?" he demanded. Turning to Alexei, he said, "And who are you?"

"My name is Alexei Kunayev," he replied. "You may have heard of my father, Boris Grigoriyevich Kunayev, recently deceased."

"No, I most certainly have not," replied Shostakovich,

although from the look on his face, he obviously had. Turning back to Dina, he said, "Miss Russakov, since you are here, you had better join me in Director Morozov's office."

"Not without Alexei," she insisted. "Whatever you have to say to me, whatever excuse you have for not allowing me to see my father, I want Alexei to witness it."

Dr Shostakovich looked from one to the other before finally saying, "Follow me both of you, but the first verbal interference from you," he pointed at Alexei, "and you will be evicted from the premises. Is that clear?" Alexei nodded his assent as he and Dina followed Shostakovich down one of the main corridors. They arrived at a door marked 'Director'.

Shostakovich knocked and went straight inside. Behind the desk facing them, Dina not only recognised Dr Georgi Morozov, Director of the Serbsky Institute, but also the man sitting next to him, Dr Daniel Luntz, the forensic scientist directly responsible for the treatment of her father.

Shostakovich introduced them. "Miss Russakov is here to see you, Director. And this is Alexei Kunayev, a friend of the family."

"I see," said Morozov. "I believe you know Dr Luntz," he pointed at his companion.

Dina had painful memories of Luntz's clashes with Dr Sloboda at the commission of enquiry. She took a seat next to Alexei as Shostakovich withdrew to the back of the room and stood by the door.

There was a moment of silence before Director Morozov coughed and cupped his hands in front of him on the desk. Finally, he said, "Your father has not been responding to treatment."

"What do you mean?" asked Dina fearfully.

"Dr Luntz, Head of our Special Examination Department, has been treating Comrade Russakov for his severe psychological disorder and aggressive behaviour."

"You mean with drugs," said Dina, remembering Dr Sloboda's diagnosis that her father had been subjected to aminazin.

"Partly," conceded Morozov, although Dina knew this to mean wholly.

Dr Luntz smiled wickedly and said, "If only you could have persuaded him to change the title of his musical piece, it would never have come to this." He shook his head and looked accusingly at Dina.

"Come to what?" she asked.

Dr Morozov was obviously embarrassed by his colleague's frankness. "I regret to inform you, Miss Russakov, that there has been a marked deterioration in your father's health."

"Can I see him?" asked Dina anxiously.

"I'm afraid not," said Morozov.

"You have a statutory obligation to allow her access to her father," interrupted Alexei. Shostakovich stepped forward from the back of the room.

Remembering Alexei's pledge to remain silent, Dina put her hand on his arm. "No, no, it's alright, Alexei. I'll handle this." She looked over her shoulder at Shostakovich, who returned to his original post.

"I have a prepared statement I'd like you to sign," said Morozov, addressing her. He passed a typewritten sheet across the desk.

Dina picked it up and read: "At the time of his emergency hospitalisation on the twentieth of September 1975, my father, Vladimir Maksimovich Russakov, was suffering from acute paranoid schizophrenia. Rather than subject him to forcible treatment, I willingly gave my authority for his evident ideological transgressions and dissident way of thinking to receive suitable treatment under the auspices of the Serbsky Institute. I fully appreciate the risks of such treatment and am satisfied that the authorities did all in their power to restore his socialist consciousness to its former level."

"Why should I sign this?" asked Dina.

"Because if you do not," interrupted Dr Luntz, "you will never see your father again."

"This is blackmail," snorted Alexei, unable to restrain his anger, and you have the temerity to call yourselves members of the medical profession. You are nothing more than inhuman torturers."

"I warned you, Comrade Kunayev," said Shostakovich. "I think you'd better leave."

Alexei got up from his chair.

"Go on," urged Dina. "Wait for me outside in the car."

Not wishing to cause her any more distress, Alexei begrudgingly obliged, but not before giving the entire assembly of doctors his blackest looks. Two orderlies escorted him back to reception and saw him off the premises. He got into the Chaika and slammed the door.

It wasn't many minutes before Dina appeared in the doorway, ran down the steps and tearfully got into the passenger seat beside him. He put his arm around her, and she buried her face deeply in his chest.

"Did you sign?" he asked eventually.

Dina shook her head. "It wouldn't make any difference anyway," she said through her tears.

"Except to save their public face," added Alexei. "Did they tell you how your father really was?" he asked.

She nodded. "They said... they said he'd been treated with aminazin... that his memory had gone... that he had become violent... had assaulted two nurses... and finally developed a brain tumour, before... before lapsing into a coma."

"A coma," exclaimed Alexei.

"He'll never come around again," sobbed Dina. "I'll never see him alive again."

"Where is he now?" asked Alexei. "Is he still in the Serbsky Institute?"

"No, he's been moved to an asylum, but they wouldn't tell me where. Not unless I signed. What are we going to do?" She broke down.

"Bastards," cried Alexei, hitting the steering wheel hard with his fist.

He looked over to the entrance to the Institute, where all three doctors were standing silently on the steps. He rammed the Chaika into gear. The back wheels spun fiercely, sending hails of gravel into the air. Pounding the horn with one hand, he shot out through the iron gates, much to the surprise of the two armed KGB guards who jumped back to safety. As he looked into his rear-view mirror, Alexei saw the doctors turn their backs and return to the sanctuary of the building.

17

As the train approached Cambridge railway station, Alexei found it hard to believe that he had actually been allowed to leave the Soviet Union at all.

Even as he had checked through passport control at Vnukovo Airport, he was expecting the hand on his shoulder, but it never came. The KGB must have satisfied itself with the elimination of his father. After all, the Politburo was terribly image-conscious. They could justifiably cover up the death of Boris Kunayev in the context of a serious heart operation, but for the son to die or disappear under mysterious circumstances would have been stretching credulity to its limits and would have allowed the Western press to have a field day.

However, it was with some relief that Alexei had stepped off the Ilyushin passenger jet at Gatwick. It was not unknown for a whole planeload of people to be sabotaged for the sake of eliminating one individual on board. The fact that Alexei knew about his father being an agent for the American FBI could not in itself be damaging to the Soviet Union. Whatever damage Boris Kunayev's revelations had wrought was in the past, and retribution had been swift and merciless. It would certainly act as an example and deterrent to others.

Alexei's conscience was troubling him about what he was

about to do next. If his deductions about the significance and location of The Marble Index were correct, it would provide a great deal of ammunition for the Soviet Secret Intelligence Services to discredit the integrity of top-level British scientific circles and call into question the effectiveness of MI6 to prevent such infiltrations in the first place. He found it hard to reconcile the fact that he was going to hand over a document which could be highly damaging to Britain, the very country in which he was about to seek political asylum. If the British authorities discovered he was responsible for unearthing The Marble Index and turning it over to the KGB, they were hardly likely to look favourably on his application. It was a chance he would have to take. He hoped that turning over The Marble Index would ensure that Dina and her father would be allowed to leave the Soviet Union. After that, it was up to the three of them to fight for the right to remain on British soil. A campaign had already been mounted by civil rights activists to liberate Vladimir Russakov. After all, he was the premier conductor and composer in the Soviet Union. Had he been a peasant or a car worker, maybe the international outcry would not have been so vociferous. So, the groundswell for allowing Vladimir Russakov to remain in Britain was already there. And by association, his daughter Dina would also be welcome. The fact that Alexei was to be married to Dina and was already engaged in useful research work at the Cavendish Laboratories in Cambridge would also clearly work in their favour. The outlook was hopeful.

There were several things, however, that preyed on his mind. It worried him that his own professor, Director Kuznetzov of the Bauman Institute, had attempted to recruit both Professor Harcourt and Martin Harvey to the Soviet cause. What was even more worrying was the fact that Kuznetzov had not once inferred that he himself should carry out spying activities whilst at the Cavendish Laboratories. He was reminded of his father's protest that during his training as a student at the Marx-Engels Institute, he did not know that it was being run by the Recruiting Division of the Moscow Secret Service Headquarters. Maybe he, too, was now being trained up as a spy without really knowing it. The indoctrination in Soviet educational institutions was so subversive and deeply entrenched that no individual could rely on the independent judgment of his motives and actions.

Alexei knew that his judgment had at least been wrong on two counts. Dr Fischer was, in fact, the recruiter for the Communist agencies of the Soviet Union and Poland, and not Dr McCabe as he had originally thought. That still left unexplained how McCabe knew about Dinmukhamed Kunayev. Was it simply a coincidence that he was the First Secretary of the Communist Party of Kazakhstan, the Republic from which the doctor assigned to dispose of Boris Kunayov's life originated? As a broadcaster on Radio Free Europe, McCabe would be conversant with every member of the Politburo, however obscure, including Dinmukhamed Kunayev. Very soon, Alexei would have the opportunity to pose these very questions to the people themselves.

As he got off the train, Alexei's thoughts were far removed from contrasting the architecture of Cambridge railway station with King's College, as had been his original preoccupation on his first visit. Neither did the black Camtax taxis in the station forecourt hold any fears for him by association with the Soviet KGB Chaikas. He jumped into the back seat of the first cab on the rank and said simply to the driver, "Trinity College."

The short journey down Hills Road, into Lensfield Road and along Trumpington Street into King's Parade passed quickly. It had just turned seven o'clock. The members of the college would already be assembled in the Great Hall for dinner. Alexei didn't feel hungry. He passed through the porter's lodge unnoticed and crossed Great Court. In the far corner, he mounted the stairs to the first floor.

His room, Sir Isaac Newton's old room, on E4 Stairs, had the 'oak up'. Alexei opened the outer door, took out the key from his pocket and unlocked the inner door. The room felt cold and unlived-in. The windows were wide open, and an icy blast of air welcomed him home. Alexei closed the windows and turned on the radiators. He shivered as much out of trepidation at the prospect of what lay ahead of him in his chosen new life. Having re-accustomed himself to his old surroundings, Alexei took off his coat and draped it over the back of a chair.

His time of arrival back in college presented the ideal opportunity to explore the antechapel. Between seven and seven-thirty, everyone would be sitting down to a formal dinner in their gowns. Excitedly, he descended the stairs, listening intently all the way in case there were any stragglers about, but Great Court was deserted.

Staying in the shadows of the screened passage around the quadrangle, Alexei arrived at the entrance to the antechapel. He grasped the large iron ring and pushed open the heavy oak door. This time, he knew exactly where to look for the statue of Sir Isaac Newton. Casting his eyes left, he saw the white marble figure sculpted by Francois Roubiliac. It was just as he had remembered it. The great scientist with his 'prism and silent face' and 'mind forever voyaging through strange seas of thought alone'. The lines of Wordsworth captured exactly the mood of the creation.

Standing larger than life-size, some ten or twelve feet tall on a solid three-foot pedestal, Newton looked in command of all he surveyed. He was also unknowingly (if Alexei's suppositions were correct) the guardian of a list of English scientists who had betrayed their country. Alexei was now faced with the problem of reaching his prize.

He remembered that the porters had been working on the light fittings at the foot of E4 Stairs. Quickly, he retraced his steps and found what he was looking for: a step ladder and a bag of tools. He picked the ladder up and swung it onto his shoulder before bending down and grabbing the bag in his free hand. He only hoped the workmen didn't return from their dinner before he had accomplished his task.

Without being seen or heard, he returned to his post beneath the statue. There, he opened up the step ladder and, once satisfied that it was secure, Alexei gingerly went up the steps until his chest was level with that of Sir Isaac Newton. In close-up, the personage was even more intimidating. He felt as if he were about to rob a grave or desecrate the sanctity of the statue. Alexei reached out his hand towards the glass prism in Newton's left hand. It felt solid enough to the touch. The device was actually slotted into a metal groove inserted in the palm of Newton's hand. Taking a large screwdriver from the bag, Alexei attempted to prise the prism from the statue's grasp. If this did in fact conceal the hiding place of The Marble Index, it would have been well sealed up in case of its being accidentally discovered.

Alexei took a pair of pliers from the bag and prised back the lip of the groove. This time it did move. The prism slowly but surely became disengaged, and he was able to pull it entirely free from its fitting. Carefully, he placed it on the top step of the ladder and put his free hand into the hole left in Newton's open palm. Feeling around in the hollow interior, his fingers explored every nook and cranny. There was nothing.

Alexei's disappointment was intense. He was not sure exactly what he hoped to find, but he expected it to yield the secret to The Marble Index in one form or another. He replaced the prism securely in Newton's grasp and, with the pliers, turned down the lip on the groove. Everything was back as it had been before.

Alexei just stood there at the top of the steps. Thinking. Suddenly, he heard the sound of metal and wood engaging. He thought someone must be entering the antechapel. Frozen with fear, Alexei became rooted to the spot.

He had no proper excuse for his being there and could think of nothing to say in his defence. There was a distant sound. Alexei turned his head in the direction of the door. He homed in on the metal ring on the inside, expecting it to turn at any moment. Then he realised that the sound was actually coming from above. With a deafening clang, the bells in the clock tower began to chime. It was a quarter past seven. The danger was a false alarm.

Alexei breathed a sigh of relief. Even so, in another quarter of an hour, those who had been served first would be making their way out of Great Hall and pass directly in front of the chapel. With little time to waste, Alexei went down the step ladder and moved it around to the other side of the statue. Nimbly, he reached the top step and examined Newton's outstretched right hand. It looked solid enough. The index finger was about one inch in diameter and some five or six inches long. Using the screwdriver, he scratched the surface of the marble, which was slightly discoloured with age. There was a definite crack running around the circumference of the finger where it joined the knuckle of the hand. Could this be it?

Alexei applied the slightest pressure. Nothing happened. He applied greater and greater force until the finger gave with an almighty crack like the report of a gun, which echoed round the bare walls of the chapel. It seemed to evoke a sensation of silent disapproval from the other marble statues, though Newton himself remained unmoved, keeping his white pupilless eyes fixed straight ahead. The release of the pressure caused the step ladder to rock alarmingly. Alexei thought he was going to topple completely over, but somehow, equilibrium was restored. Alexei held onto the ladder with one hand whilst he clutched the detached finger with the other.

It was hollow. Stuffed inside was a lump of cotton wool. Carefully between his thumb and forefinger, Alexei pulled out the wadding and then tipped the contents of the hollow finger into his hand. Rolled up tight and secured with a rubber band was a faded black and white photograph, and also a small metal canister. Gingerly, Alexei unscrewed the lid. Inside was the negative of one frame of film. He held it up to the light. It was a group photograph, alright, and probably the negative of the rolled-up print from what he could make out. He undid the rubber band and uncurled the photograph.

It was unmistakable as a smaller version of the group portraits hung in the gallery of the Cavendish Laboratories. Underneath it bore the legend 1933–1934 and the names of all the subjects row by row. A shiver of triumph ran through Alexei as, sitting on the front row three from the right, was a figure he recognised. The subtitles confirmed this. It was Piotr Kapitsa.

What was more, seven of the names inscribed were underlined in red crayon. And on the reverse side, there was a statement signed by the seven dedicating themselves to the Communist cause. Alexei was sure. This was indeed The Marble Index.

He looked at his watch. It was now twenty-five past seven. He would have to hurry, and he had a choice to make. Either take The Marble Index with him or put it back in its original place. Alexei thought that, as only he and Dina knew the exact whereabouts of The Marble Index, it would be better off in Newton's safekeeping rather than in his college room. As a precaution, he reached into his inside pocket and brought out his wallet, from which he took a pencil and a scrap of paper. He then made a rapid note of the seven underlined names. Finally, he replaced the elastic band around the photograph and the canister and put them back inside the hollow index finger, sealing the end with the wad of cotton wool. Fortunately, the finger had broken cleanly along its original line. The problem was how to reattach it to Newton's hand securely and so that no one would notice the join.

He felt around inside the workman's bag. In the bottom corner, there was a dirty ball of putty. It was still soft. Alexei moulded it in his hand, placed the index finger in position and smeared the off-white putty all around the join. It was a good match for colour and held the finger securely in place. By the time it dried in the morning, and from ground level, it would blend in perfectly. Quickly, Alexei put all the odds and ends back in the bag, went down the steps, took a sharp look at his handiwork, and with an air of satisfaction closed the ante-chapel door behind him, as the clock tower bells began to chime half past seven.

Rather than return to his own room, Alexei turned right and went through the archway into Nevile's Court. The sooner he set his deal in motion, the sooner Dina and her father would be able to join him in Cambridge. He ducked under a low portal and came face to face with a door bearing a brass plaque announcing 'Dr Fischer'. Alexei knocked. There was no reply. The senior tutor had obviously not yet finished his dinner. As he waited, Alexei could hear footsteps approaching. He braced himself.

Wearing his formal gown, Dr Gerald Fischer turned the corner and came to an abrupt halt. "Alex!" he exclaimed, "Mr Kunayev, I wasn't expecting you back so soon. How is your father?"

"He's dead, as you probably already know, Gerry, or can I call you Jerzy?"

Fischer smiled nervously. "I'm not with you."

"Come along, Dr Kozlowsky. No need to be so modest. I know all about you."

"I can see your time in Moscow hasn't been wasted," said

Fischer. "You'd better come inside." He unlocked the door, took off his gown and poured himself a large whisky. "What did you want to see me for?" he asked.

"Well, it wasn't to discuss Wittgenstein," replied Alexei.

"Am I to take it that you know all about me and my activities?" asked Fischer.

Alexei nodded.

"I gather from your tone that you don't exactly approve. Am I to take it that by way of revenge for your father's death, you wish to unmask me? If you were to cooperate, I'm sure we could work in harness together for the mutual benefit of Poland and the Soviet Union."

"No, thank you," said Alexei, pouring himself a drink without waiting to be invited. "After all, our fathers died in rather different circumstances."

This was obviously a very touchy subject with Fischer. "Leave my father out of it," he snapped. "I've paid many times over for his treachery. You are the one who should be concerned about restoring the good name of your family."

"My father's only crime," retorted Alexei, "was to stick to his principles. My guilt lies in not realising this fact until he was on his deathbed. My only concern now is to save the life of another's father-- Vladimir Russakov."

"The dissident composer," said Fischer.

"Yes, and his daughter Dina."

"Ah," said Fischer. "The love of a woman is a powerful driving force."

"That is something you would know nothing about," said Alexei with a snide reference to Fischer's homosexuality.

"If you've just come here to insult me," retorted Dr Fischer, "I have been the butt of experts. If you've decided to reveal my activities as a Communist agent in this college, I can only tell you that there are many others who can immediately take my place. Trinity has several Communist sympathisers comprehensively trained and capable of acting as full-time recruiters."

Alexei hadn't thought beforehand whether he intended to unmask Dr Fischer as a spymaster and recruiter for the Communist Secret Services.

"No," he said finally. "All I want is to do a deal, and I want you to act as a go-between. I have some very valuable information, and I want to exchange it for the safe passage of Dina Russakov and her father to the West."

"If you mean your work at the Cavendish Laboratories," said Fischer, "you can forget it. We already have inside sources there."

Alexei remembered the references in the KGB Central Index files of the approaches made to Professor Harcourt himself and to Martin Harvey. Although they had refused, presumably other members of staff had been targeted and asked. Some must have agreed for whatever reasons principles, money, sex.

"No, it's nothing to do with the Cavendish," replied Alexei. "Or rather it is, but not as it is today. It concerns a secret KGB file called The Marble Index, which contains the seven names of prominent English Cavendish scholars in the 1930s who were turned to the path of Communism and have remained under deep cover even to this day."

"You're making it up," scoffed Dr Fischer.

"There's one easy way to check. If I give you the exact reference of the file in the KGB Central Index Archives, you can communicate to your masters where to find it."

"If it's in the KGB files, why can't our researchers find it themselves?" said Fischer.

"Because the files only prove the existence of The Marble Index and not its whereabouts."

"I see. And you are the only one who knows where it is."

"Right," confirmed Alexei. "And I can tell you that it is

here in this very college. Trinity. Before you get any ideas, I don't have it on me, and it's not in my room. It's still in its original hiding place from forty years ago. I've satisfied myself that it's still there."

"I see," repeated Fischer. "And in return, you want Vladimir and Dina Russakov delivered into your hands in this country, where you intend to seek political asylum. Is that right?"

Alexei nodded.

"Hm," pondered Fischer. "What if the British authorities turn you down? Is the deal off?"

"No, that's our responsibility," replied Alexei. He took a piece of paper from his pocket on which Dina had written down exactly where to find the reference to The Marble Index in the KGB Central Index Archives. He handed it to Dr Fischer. "Is it a deal?"

"I'll pass it on to my contact at the Soviet Embassy in London," replied Fischer. "If it's what you say it is, this Marble Index, as you call it, our people will be very interested."

"And tell your people," interrupted Alexei, "if they get any ideas about harming Dina or her father in order to get The Marble Index for nothing, I'll kill them all, starting with you."

The two men stared at one another.

"I'll be sure to convey your warmest greetings to the KGB," said Fischer drily as he knocked back the remains of his whisky.

Things were beginning to move more quickly now, Alexei thought to himself as he made his way back to his room in Great Court.

He was just turning his key in the door when Andrew Marriott emerged from his room next door. "Hello," he said flatly.

"Hello," replied Alexei.

They looked at one another suspiciously, each trying to

read the other's mind.

"I'm just going to see Dr McCabe," said Marriott. "Do you want to come?"

"That depends," said Alexei cagily.

"On what?" asked Marriott.

"On whether you're going to give me the truth."

"I think that can be arranged," agreed Marriott.

"Then I'll come," said Alexei, falling into step with his companion.

Neither spoke further as they made their way to the English tutor's room in New Court. Marriott knocked on the door, and they went inside. McCabe was working on some papers at his desk with his back to the door. When he turned around to face his visitors, even his normal composure was obviously disturbed. Finally, he said, "We were hoping to see you before you left for Moscow."

"I had to leave in rather a hurry," replied Alexei. He noted the use of the word 'we', confirming his suspicion that McCabe and Marriott had been working in collaboration.

"Yes, we heard about your father," continued the English tutor.

Alexei wasn't sure whether he meant that they had heard about his heart coronary or the fact that the KGB had him eliminated. Both sides were playing their cards very close to their chests.

McCabe spun round on his swivel chair and gestured for them to sit down whilst he poured some drinks. "I know you're not keen on it, but will vodka do? It's all I have left," said McCabe, handing round the glasses.

"Why not," replied Alexei. "After all, it will remind me of home." There was a long silence whilst all three sipped their drinks.

Eventually, Alexei decided to break the deadlock. "I suppose you'd like to know which side of the fence I'm on, so to speak. After all, that's what your little charade set out to prove, isn't it?"

"I'm not with you," replied McCabe.

Alexei looked at Marriott. "I thought you said you were going to come clean."

Marriott, in turn, gave McCabe a knowing look and said, "I think it's alright. In the circumstances."

"If it's of any help to you in making up your minds, I shan't be returning to the Soviet Union. I've decided to seek political asylum in England."

McCabe raised his eyebrows.

He looked even more surprised when Alexei asked bluntly, "Do you work for the British Secret Intelligence Service?" When there was no immediate response, Alexei continued, "If so, I want you to promote my case to MI6, the Foreign Office, the Home Secretary, or whoever else is responsible for making these decisions. Hopefully, in the next day or two, I shall be joined by Vladimir and Dina Russakov. You may have heard of the former. He's a celebrated Soviet composer and conductor, and his daughter is my fiancée."

"Well," said McCabe, "in view of such frankness, I suppose we should come clean as well. You are correct in surmising that I am a recruiter within Trinity College for suitable candidates to both MI5 and MI6. Marriott here has been accepted and will enter the service at the end of this academic year. It is true that together we have been sounding you out. By making you suspect that I was a spymaster for the Communist agencies, we were able to gauge your reactions and discover where your ideological sympathies lay. We not only recruit British students but also foreign nationals from Communist countries who can continue to work for us once they return to their native countries. In this respect, we are in fierce competition with Communist infiltrators amongst the academic staff who seek to reinforce the Marxist principles of visiting students from behind the Iron Curtain as well as promoting their ideologies among our own British students."

This made Alexei think about Dr Gerald Fischer, who was directly competing with McCabe for the hearts and minds of Trinity College undergraduates.

His initial reaction had been to keep quiet on this front, but his dislike for the man caused him to speak out. "What would you say if I told you that Dr Fischer, the senior tutor, was working for the other side?"

"Oh, we know all about him," replied Marriott.

"You do?" said Alexei, surprised. "Then why don't you reveal his activities to the university authorities and have him dismissed?"

"He would only be replaced by someone else," said McCabe. "Better the devil you know than the one you do not."

This roughly tied in with what Fischer had told Alexei himself. The two opposing sides were living quite happily alongside one another, fighting over the spoils of battle in the cold ideological war. It struck him that they were both playing the same game - a dirty game in which those in the middle sometimes came to grief, like his father and Dina's father. Neither had the right entirely on their side, and the truth was a very rare commodity indeed.

"One last question I'd like to ask you," said Alexei.

"Go ahead," replied McCabe.

"When we first met, you asked me if I was related to a Dinmukhamed Kunayev."

"I remember," said McCabe.

"At the time, I'd never heard of him, but he has since made a rather dramatic entrance into my life. Will you tell me what your interest in him is? I also overheard you talking outside the offices of Radio Free Europe in London when you and Marriott here took me on that wild espionage goose chase. There again, the topic of conversation was Kunayev. At the time I assumed you were talking about me, but I now realise it could have been this other man with the same surname."

"I take it that you now know the identity of Dinmukhamed Kunayev," said McCabe.

"Yes," replied Alexei. "He's First Secretary of the Communist Party of Kazakhstan and a member of the Politburo."

"Correct," replied McCabe. "And he's also a close associate of Leonid Brezhnev–– a member of the 'Brezhnev Mafia' as it is called. The Republic of Kazakhstan holds a particular significance. It contains the training grounds for Soviet cosmonauts and the launching sites for manned and unmanned satellites."

Alexei remembered Dr Sloboda mentioning this fact to him.

"It is therefore a very significant area of intelligence gathering for our agencies. If you had been a close relative of comrade Kunayev, you could have provided us with a very useful line of access to the man."

"I'm sorry to disappoint you, but I'm not," replied Alexei. "Hopefully, I can still be of some worth to your government. After all, my field of specialisation is radio astronomy. And I could be a vital member of the Cavendish Laboratories research team for many years to come. My compatriot, Piotr Kapitza, attained the position of Assistant Director to Rutherford. I should strive to emulate him and one day maybe even become Director."

"It's up to you to sell yourself to the British authorities," agreed McCabe. "I can, of course, put in a good word for you on your application for asylum. What about your relations remaining in the Soviet Union? Your father is dead, as we know, but what about your mother? How do you feel about leaving her behind, and could the Soviet authorities put pressure on her to induce you to return to Russia?"

Alexei did not know whether his mother was alive or dead, and he did not care. "There is no problem there," he said flatly.

"My mother and I did not see eye to eye. Now, if you'll excuse me, I'd like to go to bed. I've had a long journey and I'm very tired. Besides, there are a lot of things I have to do tomorrow." Without another word, he made for the door.

The break with the Soviet Union seemed complete.

The strain of the past few days and the rigours of the journey from Moscow had taken more out of Alexei than he had anticipated. When he was rudely awoken by a loud knocking at his door and looked at the clock on his bedside table, he wasn't sure whether it was twelve o'clock midday or twelve midnight. He remembered going to bed around nine and assumed at first that he must only have been asleep for three hours.

He rolled over and groaned, "Go away." He began to drift away again into semi-consciousness, but the knocking persisted. This time, he opened his eyes and was surprised to see light streaming into his room around the side of the thick velvet curtains. He concluded, after all, that it must be daytime.

For a moment, he couldn't remember where he was, such was the extent of his disorientation. Then it all came flooding back to him like the events of a recurring nightmare. As he was gathering his thoughts, the door opened, and Dr Fischer appeared.

"I was beginning to think you were dead," began his visitor, which seemed a highly inappropriate gambit in view of Alexei's recent bereavement with his father.

"Sorry to disappoint you," he said, sitting up in bed.

"I thought you'd want to know as soon as possible that the KGB has sanctioned your deal. In fact, I was on the telephone straight after you left last night, and I understand that the Soviet Embassy cleared it with Moscow Centre within an hour. They certainly must think that your Marble Index is intelligence of the highest order."

"Hm," said Alexei half-heartedly.

"I thought you'd be pleased," said Fischer. "After all, you've got what you wanted."

This was true, but Alexei couldn't help feeling a sense of betrayal as The Marble Index would do untold damage to his adopted country. He could only hope that they never found out the source of the information. On the personal level, however, it would allow Dina and her father to join him in the West. Alexei continued to lie there contemplating his mixed emotions.

"Well, aren't you going to get up?" said Fischer. "She'll be here any time now."

"She," echoed Alexei. "Who?"

"Why, Dina Russakov, of course," replied the senior tutor.

"Already?" exclaimed Alexei. "I expected it to take a week or at least a few days."

"When the KGB decides to move, it moves with alacrity," said Fischer.

Alexei should have realised this from personal experience, given the speed with which his father had been dispatched. "Yes, I know," he said poignantly. "You mean they're already on their way then," he continued.

"Not they," replied Fischer. "Just Dina Russakov."

"What about her father?" asked Alexei.

"I couldn't tell you anything about that. I was informed that Dina Russakov left on the seven forty-five plane from Moscow this morning. That's all I know. Now, are you going to tell me the location of The Marble Index?"

"Oh, I see," said Alexei contemptuously. "They've decided to hang onto Vladimir Russakov until I hand over The Marble Index. I thought the KGB would be more devious than to arrange a straight swap. Any undertaking they engage in must always be biased in their favour. Well, you can tell them that the deal is off until both Vladimir and Dina Russakov are delivered safely into my hands."

"Before you come to any hasty conclusions," said Fischer, "I think you'd better talk to your fiancée first."

As Alexei was about to embark on a further tirade about the trustworthiness of the KGB, there came another knock at the door. It was Dr McCabe. When he caught sight of Dr Fischer, his hackles were visibly raised. Almost ignoring the presence of his counterpart, he addressed Alexei. "You have company. There's a young lady at the porter's lodge. She'd like to see you." He permitted himself the luxury of a smile.

"You mean..." began Alexei.

McCabe nodded.

Alexei jumped out of bed and began to dress quickly. "Could you bring her up here?" he asked.

"Of course," replied McCabe as he disappeared again.

"What about our deal?" asked Dr Fischer.

"I'll tell you after I've spoken to Dina. Wait for me outside the door to the college chapel." He didn't think he was giving too much away, as even the KGB could not get away with demolishing whole eighteenth-century chapels in search of hidden files.

Begrudgingly, Dr Fischer did as he was asked. He was passed in the hall by Dina, coming the other way. She stood an instant framed in the doorway. Instead of running towards one another, as if their moment of meeting could not come quickly enough, their reunion was a strangely subdued affair.

"It looks like we made it," Alexei said.

"Yes," she replied, holding out her hand.

He took it between both his hands and pressed it tenderly to his cheek, then kissed every finger one by one. He looked into her eyes and said, "I love you."

"I love you, Alexei," replied Dina. "Now nothing can keep us apart."

"What about your father?" asked Alexei, anxious for news of Vladimir Russakov.

A look of anguish crossed her face. "He's dead."

"Dead," echoed Alexei, horrified.

"Yes, he never recovered from the coma. They switched off the life support machine."

"Did you see him before he died?" asked Alexei.

Dina made a motion with her head, which he didn't know meant either yes or no. He didn't press the point. He couldn't help feeling that the KGB had exacted one last painful act of revenge on the couple before finally releasing them. He now wanted to get the deal finished and over with, to wash his hands of the affair once and for all. "Oh, I'm so sorry, Dina," he said. "All we have left is one another. Let's hope that will be enough. Come on, let me show you where The Marble Index has remained hidden for the past forty years."

Hand in hand, they went down the steps into Great Court. At the foot of the stairs, Alexei grabbed the stepladder he had used the previous evening. It was still there, leaning up against the wall. Dina didn't ask any questions. She didn't speak at all as they joined Dr Fischer outside the college chapel. Alexei pushed open the door. The antechapel was deserted.

Dr Fischer looked around. "Here?" he asked.

Alexei nodded as he set the stepladder up against the marble statue of Sir Isaac Newton. Unlike the previous evening, he did not feel inhibited by caution or trepidation. He knew now exactly what he was looking for and where to find it. As he stood on the top step, he could hear Dina say quietly below, "The Marble Index." Alexei reached out and unceremoniously snapped off the index finger along the false joint. He descended the stepladder and placed the hollow finger in Dr Fischer's hand. "I think you'll find what you're looking for inside. It is up to you what you do with the information."

At that moment, Alexei did not feel at all proud of himself. Meanwhile, Dr Fischer had emptied the contents of the finger and had briefly examined them. Once satisfied as to their authenticity, he turned away and, without another word, closed the antechapel door behind him.

Alexei gave a huge sigh made up of relief and resignation, relief that he and Dina had been reunited in the West, but resigned to the fact that he had surrendered to the Soviet Secret Intelligence agencies information which could be damaging to Britain.

He looked up at the silent figure of Sir Isaac Newton, whose face appeared to bear a disapproving expression. His disfigured right hand drew even more attention to itself now. Alexei looked along the extended line of the great scientist's arm and hand towards the object of his permanent gaze. He was struck again by the Latin inscription on the far wall – 'Pro muro erant nobis tam in nocte quam in die' (They were a wall unto us both by night and day) MCMXXXIX – MCMXLV, and below were column after column of names of Trinity College students who had been killed in the Second World War.

His thoughts turned to the similar number of young Russian soldiers who had died on the Eastern Front, and he was reminded of his early morning walk in the Alexandrovsky Gardens in Moscow, where the Tomb of the Unknown Soldier was situated. The inscription read – 'To those who fell for the Motherland 1941-45. Your name is unknown. Your deed is immortal.' Both he and Dina had lost their fathers, and for all he knew, his mother was dead too. Each, in their own way, had died for their Motherland.

Alexei and Dina stood in deep silence. Suddenly, Alexei's attention was taken by one of the names on the far wall. It seemed familiar to him. Loosening his grip on Dina's hand, he walked forward for a closer look. Then it struck him where he had seen that name before. He took out his wallet and produced a small scrap of paper. He checked off the names one by one. They were all there. Alexei didn't know whether to laugh or cry.

This was the piece of paper on which he had written down the names on The Marble Index, the young science research students from Trinity College who were now supposed to be under deep cover, occupying exalted positions in the British scientific world. They were all dead. Cut down in the prime of their youth, before they could become effective, and in a conflict in which, ironically, Britain and the Soviet Union had fought on the same side.

It was worthless. The Marble Index was worthless. His conscience was instantly cleared. He couldn't help himself. He had to laugh. Out loud.

Dina stepped up beside him and gave him a bemused look. She didn't understand. "What are you laughing at, Alexei? Are you alright?"

He laughed until the tears rolled down his cheeks. He laughed and he cried. "The Marble Index," he said.

"What about it?" asked Dina.

"Names. Empty, dead names and nothing more."

The last laugh was on the KGB. They had nothing in return for Dina's freedom, except for a piece of useless paper. And Sir Isaac Newton had the last laugh on them all. He had finally yielded up his well-kept secret, and in so doing, had contemptuously pointed the finger at the futility of the revelation.

Alexei screwed up the piece of paper and flung it on the floor. He turned to Dina and said, "Come on, let's go. The KGB can't touch us now. We're free. Let's start the way we mean to carry on." He opened the external door and was greeted by a gust of wind which whipped around the antechapel, lifting the paper into the air and sending it spinning away.

As Alexei closed the door behind him, he was sure he saw Sir Isaac Newton's eyes turn in his direction. The statue looked as if it wanted to speak, but there was no sound.

Irena Kunayev had spent all morning cleaning the dacha at Pirogovo.

It had been a long while since she had spent so much time at the beach house away from the pressures of Moscow city life. The domestic chores no longer troubled her. In fact, she enjoyed them. They helped keep her mind off other things. It was getting near lunchtime.

She took off her apron and walked out onto the veranda overlooking Pirogovo Reservoir. She took off her slippers and eased on a pair of good, strong shoes. She walked down to the shoreline and listened to the water lapping peacefully over the golden pebbles. A few boats were sailing out in the middle of the expanse of water, taking advantage of the bracing breeze that had blown up in the last few days.

A hundred yards further along the shore, a wooden jetty jutted out into the heart of the reservoir. Irena Kunayev reached it and mounted some rickety wooden steps. She pulled herself up onto the top and stopped an instant to take in the view afforded by this vantage point. She breathed in deeply several times. The air smelled fresh and good.

Idly, she began to walk along the jetty. The reservoir was well-stocked with freshwater fish. At the very end of the jetty, a lone figure sat, dangling his feet over the side, his line spinning out into the waters below.

Irena Kunayev approached him. "Have you caught anything?" she asked.

"No," he replied, "Not yet, but I don't mind."

Irena Kunayev turned and began to walk away. "Don't be long," she said.

"No, I won't," he replied.

THE END

About Atmosphere Press

Founded in 2015, Atmosphere Press was built on the principles of Honesty, Transparency, Professionalism, Kindness, and Making Your Book Awesome. As an ethical and author-friendly hybrid press, we stay true to that founding mission today.

If you're a reader, enter our giveaway for a free book here:

SCAN TO ENTER
BOOK GIVEAWAY

If you're a writer, submit your manuscript for consideration here:

SCAN TO SUBMIT
MANUSCRIPT

And always feel free to visit Atmosphere Press and our authors online at atmospherepress.com. See you there soon!

About the Author

HOWARD'S love of writing began at university, where he wrote and directed plays, one produced on BBC national radio and another performed on the Fringe of the Edinburgh Festival. During the 1980s, he wrote three novels which remained unpublished until now, The Marble Index being one of them. Two of his other books have been successfully published, one entitled 'Tai Chi Training in China' about his experiences of living, working, and studying in China. Subsequently, he became the British, Hong Kong, and double world champion in tai chi. He lived in mainland China for five years and Hong Kong for seven years, teaching English at various colleges and universities. He also wrote the English language handbook for all the sports at the Beijing Olympics in 2008. He is currently the Chairman of the north-west London branch of The English Poetry Society.

When he was 13, he achieved national fame by making front-page headline news in all the British national newspapers. He saved himself and the lives of his parents when they were held up by a gang at gunpoint while on a family camping holiday in France, by using his schoolboy French to negotiate with the gunmen. He went on to take a BA Honours degree in French at university.

Background relevant to 'The Marble Index'

After graduating from university, his first job was teaching at Cambridge Sixth Form College. He went on to work for the Cambridge Evening News and later became the administrator of The Cambridge Society for the Blind.

He worked in the national headquarters of a government department in the 1970's where he rose to head of the correspondence branch. He went on to work in the IT department as a systems analyst.

www.ingramcontent.com/pod-product-compliance
Ingram Content Group UK Ltd.
Pitfield, Milton Keynes, MK11 3LW, UK
UKHW042005120126
10061UKWH00004B/234